CELILO'S SHADOW

VALERIE WILCOX

BLACK ROSE
writing™

ISBN: 978-1-61296-880-3
PUBLISHED BY BLACK ROSE WRITING
www.blackrosewriting.com

Printed in the United States of America
Suggested retail price $20.95

Celilo's Shadow is printed in Book Antiqua

In Memory of James W. Worthington

ACKNOWLEDGEMENTS

Writing a novel is a unique experience. It's a solitary activity aided by the contribution of numerous others. I am grateful for the time and expertise of all those who contributed to the writing of Celilo's Shadow. Specifically, Rita Gardner, who patiently and expertly edited a multitude of manuscript revisions; fellow writers Irene Fernandez, Joyce O'Keefe, Roger Schwarz, and Rev. Fred Jessett for their insightful critiques; Julia Stroud of ShrinkWrite for sharing her knowledge of the writing craft; Beth Schliehert for her artistic talents; the staff at The Dalles-Wasco County Library and the Columbia Gorge Discovery Center and Museum for answering my many questions while researching historical material; Mary and Dennis Davis for generously opening their home when I needed a place to stay; Joseph Lawrence for reading the novel in weekly installments, which motivated me to finally get to "The End." A special thank-you to the friends and relatives who have supported my writing career over the years. You've kept me going whenever self-doubt rears its ugly head. And, as always, David Wilcox for his unwavering love and belief in me.

Author's Note

As a youngster, I lived in the Oregon town where the novel takes place. My father was one of the skilled workers employed by the U.S. Army Corps of Engineers to build The Dalles Dam. I have many fond memories of living in The Dalles and especially cherish my friends in the Class of 1963. Although historical figures and real places appear in the novel and the destruction of Celilo Falls, Native American burial sites, and village did occur, the story, characters, and some locations are entirely fictitious.

CELILO'S SHADOW

The truth is rarely pure and never simple.
    ~Oscar Wilde, *The Importance of Being Earnest*

A lie told often enough becomes the truth.
    ~Lenin

You made your nets and tested the knots seeing that they held. Little did you know what was to hold you after the sound of water falling over what used to be.
    ~Ed Edmo, Celilo poet

Prologue

Present Day

The storm was just a local story at first. Despite nearly a week of fierce winds and record-breaking rainfall for the Pacific Northwest, property damage was minimal and there'd been no injuries or loss of life reported. With no drama to cover, media interest in the storm faded fast. Nothing to see here, folks. Move along. Then a ten-year-old boy and his dog went exploring along the muddy banks of the rain-swollen Columbia River. The skeletal remains they stumbled upon were, according to the boy, "scattered across the shoreline like pickup sticks." Their discovery grabbed national headlines after authorities speculated that the storm had dislodged an ancient burial ground, possibly Native American. Archaeologists and tribal activists flocked to the site until it was determined that the bones belonged to a single individual who had been buried for only sixty years or so. Further forensic examination confirmed that the individual had been a victim of foul play.

Sensational murder cases—even those sixty years old—tend to bring out the tinfoil hat crazies, the "Jesus told me who did it" nutters, and other assorted fruit loops with no credibility. I'd moved 3,000 miles and a lifetime away from the Oregon town I once called home, but I knew all about the circumstances surrounding the murder that had just been uncovered. I'd left town the day I turned eighteen and vowed never to come back or tell anyone what I'd witnessed— and I'd done just that until the past's hidden remnants were finally exposed. The telling was overdue and I could no longer keep silent. As far as my credibility was concerned, the only thing I had to offer was the truth. If, as the saying goes, "the truth shall set you free," I was more than ready to lay my silent burden down. For that to happen, I would have to relive the long hot summer of 1956 and, in so doing, betray the best friend I'd ever had.

Her name was Ellie Matthews and the first time I saw her was the day she moved into the new house across the street from mine. The last time was the day she disappeared. We were both fourteen-year-old girls living in a small but rapidly growing town called The Dalles. That's where the similarity between us began and ended. All these years later, I still cringe when I think about the striking contrast between Ellie's mature beauty and my unpolished, juvenile appearance. She was a tall willowy blonde while I was short and skinny with unruly red hair that only my Irish grandmother found attractive. The sun loved her and, despite a fair complexion, she tanned easily. All I had to show for a summer in the sun was a mass of freckles dotting my cheeks like a bad case of measles. I insisted on wearing a bra which, even with a ton of toilet tissue stuffed inside, didn't do much to enhance my flat, boyish chest. Ellie's breasts were undeniably movie-star perfect with or without padding. I hated her instantly.

As soon as she saw me standing on the sidewalk coldly assessing her enviable features, she flashed a cheerful, dimpled grin and waved. Her teeth were so white and straight that there was no way I'd expose my mouth full of braces by smiling back at her. Whenever I felt uncomfortable or inadequate—which happened frequently during my teens—I'd compensate with a cocky attitude. And standing in Ellie's beautiful shadow that day was enough to provoke me. I gave her outfit—shorts, sleeveless blouse, and sandals—a disapproving once-over and quipped, "Hot enough for you?"

Ellie shrugged off my inane comment and invited me into her house. By the time the movers had finished unloading her family's belongings out of the Mayflower van, she'd begun to win me over. It was clear to me that this friendly, pony-tailed new girl on the block would be a hit. Ellie Matthews' good looks wowed the boys, of course, but there was also a gentle sweetness about her that quickly endeared her to everyone in our Hillcrest neighborhood. As I got to know her better, I came to believe that she wasn't as guileless or as

10

naïve as she first seemed. Whatever doubts I had about Ellie's true character, I would never have predicted the pivotal role she would play in the tragic events of that summer.

I'd volunteered to tell the homicide detective in charge of the case everything I knew about what had happened back then and the persons involved, but before we could schedule a date for my interview he cancelled it. He said there was no longer any need to meet with me since the murder victim had now been identified and their suspect in custody had confessed. The district attorney predicted a slam-dunk conviction. That sounded like a reasonable explanation for my dismissal, but I couldn't accept it—not when I knew they were wrong about everything. So, I pushed back. Repeatedly.

I've been retired for some time, but I worked as a freelance investigative journalist for over thirty years and am proud to say that I earned several awards for reporting excellence throughout my career. I had a reputation for not giving up when following an elusive story or a hard-to-get interview. No obstacle was too great to deter me from chasing down a major scoop. My colleagues called me P.B. (Pit Bull), which I took as a compliment even though I suspected the nickname wasn't meant to be particularly flattering. Given my history, I wasn't used to walking away from something important. Despite being told the case was solved, I continued to pepper the police with requests to meet with me. I don't know whether I convinced Detective Don Templeton that I had information critical to the case or whether he just wanted to get rid of a persistent pest, but he finally agreed to a meeting. He said he'd take my formal statement as soon as I could come into the station.

I made the necessary travel arrangements and two days later, I flew from New York to Oregon. I drove a rental car some eighty miles east of Portland on Interstate 84 before pulling off the highway to stretch my legs. The rocky bluff where I stopped was a popular tourist spot due to its panoramic view of the scenic Columbia River Gorge. It should have been an ideal place to take a break, but as I climbed out of the car I experienced such a dark, uneasy feeling that I had second thoughts about the wisdom of contacting the police. I considered whether to cancel my hard-won appointment and drive straight back to the airport or disregard my eerie misgivings and carry through with what I'd started. The decision was made for me when a busload of tourists arrived and I was swept along with the sightseers as they surged toward the edge of the bluff for a better view.

I was so distracted by the spectacular scenery that the anxiety I'd felt earlier didn't seem quite as troubling—until I spotted Celilo Falls and the Indians fishing along its banks. It didn't make sense. The falls weren't located here. The sight caused a furious pounding in my chest almost as loud as the thunderous roar of the rapids below. Suddenly nauseous, I might have fainted had it not been for the cool mist drifting from the river up to the bluff where I stood. The vapor embraced me like a thoughtful lover and calmed the fears that threatened to overtake me. Still, it was several moments before my brain registered what my eyes were telling it.

I watched as the Indians, perched on wooden platforms suspended precariously over Celilo Fall's turbulent waters, dipped their pole nets into the foam. The fish they sought—Chinook, bluebacks, steelhead, and Coho—leapt to impossible heights over the sharp rocks, driven by the primal need to reproduce at all costs. In the nearby village, smoke from several small fires of willow and maple branches spiraled upward. A light breeze carried the tantalizing scent of root soup as it cooked. Women with long braids stirred the broth while others readied drying racks for the day's catch.

I stood transfixed by the scene until the haunting echoes from the past collided with the intrusive present—the images evaporating along with the mist. The thunderous roar was not the rushing waters of Celilo Falls, but semi-trucks rumbling across a modern bridge; not fish drying or soup cooking, but diesel fumes biting the nose; not fishermen salmon-dipping, but wind surfers riding the waves; not free-flowing rapids, but a massive concrete dam; not the continuation of an ancient way of life, but change and loss.

The disconnect between my memories and present-day reality was so jarring that I began to shiver despite the oppressive heat. After what seemed like an eternity, my legs ceased trembling and I could walk back to the car. Stopping at the bluff had been a mistake; another painful reminder of why I'd left home so many years ago. Despite my discomfort, I drove the final stretch of highway to The

Dalles while rehearsing aloud the story I planned to tell the police.

Any doubts Detective Don Templeton may have had about me were not evident by the courteous way he greeted me upon my arrival. I'd only spoken to him previously by telephone, but I recognized his throaty, hoarse voice immediately. A smoker's voice. For some reason, I'd pictured him as short and balding but he was at least six feet tall with a full head of steel-gray hair. Although stoop-shouldered, Templeton had a commanding presence that was lacking in the younger man he introduced as his partner, Detective Steve Burroughs.

"I'm sorry, but I can't stay," Templeton said, his words tumbling out in an excited rush. "There's been a new development." As he shrugged on his suit jacket, he nodded toward his partner. "Steve here will be happy to take your statement."

Steve Burroughs shot him a look that conveyed exactly what he thought of the task he'd been saddled with. The look was mostly for my benefit since Templeton had already hustled out the door. The last-minute change didn't bother me, but I figured it had to be frustrating for the detective left behind. Who'd want to listen to the ramblings of an old woman when all the action took place somewhere else? Burroughs stared at the door Templeton had exited and heaved a deep sigh. Apparently resigned to his fate, he offered to fetch me a cup of coffee. I declined, but he said he needed the caffeine, whether I did or not.

While he was gone I took stock of my surroundings. There was a large mirror on one of the dingy walls in the small interview room. Anyone who has ever watched a TV cop show would know the mirror was also an observation window. I could feel eyes staring at me through the glass, studying me like a specimen under a microscope. Given the status of the case, I didn't expect such intense scrutiny. Maybe this so-called new development that had Templeton racing out of the station had poked some holes in their supposedly air-tight case.

Now that I sat in the hot and stuffy room by myself, I wondered if I'd misjudged my ability to convince the police that what they believed had happened so many summers ago was all wrong, that their prime suspect was innocent, that what I was about to confess was the truth. Detective Burroughs had probably used the coffee as an excuse to let me stew awhile. I figured he was assessing my motives this very moment. God only knew what judgments he'd already made about me.

I'd been waiting for half an hour when the door opened and Burroughs returned with two mugs of steaming coffee. "In case you change your mind," he said, setting the mugs on the table that separated us. As soon as he sat down, he gestured to the recording equipment in the room. A video camera mounted atop a tripod stood in the corner and a large, commercial grade tape recorder sat on the table. "Our conversation will be recorded and video-taped," he said officiously.

There was nothing wrong with my eyes. Someone as young as Detective Burroughs probably thought a person my age was too doddering to understand the setup. He couldn't have been much more than thirty and still had problem acne, which he tried to cover up with a closely cropped beard. His gel-spiked hair, designer glasses, and charcoal power suit projected a "man on the way up" image, but came off like a kid trying too hard. I was neither impressed nor intimidated, but he did worry me. Ambition could be problematic when so much was at stake. Biting back a sarcastic retort, I said, "Of course. I understand the need for documentation."

He activated the video with a remote and then punched one of the buttons on the tape recorder. After an introductory statement giving the date, time, and our names, he said, "How much do you remember about the summer of 1956?"

The way Burroughs asked the question made it seem like 1956 was ancient history. At his age, it probably felt that way. To me, it felt like yesterday. Even so, I qualified what I was about to reveal. "You know," I said, "memory is a tricky ghost. Images from past events may have faded or disappeared while others may have become larger and more significant. What seems so memorable when it happens is inevitably altered with the passage of time."

"So, you're having difficulty recalling what happened?" Burroughs asked. He was clearly hopeful that he could justify cutting our session short.

"No," I assured him. "Anyone who lived in the area during that tension-filled summer would swear that what they remember is crystal-clear. Despite such dogged certainty, their recollection of events wouldn't be the same. Not even close."

"Yeah," he agreed. "That's the problem with eye-witness accounts. Take any ten people and they'll see the exact same event ten different ways from Sunday."

I nodded. "And, in this case, some would claim the trouble all started when the schemes of a greedy salesman and his mistress spun out of control. Others would blame it on the government, the FBI, or even the Communists. More than a few would insist it was because of a beautiful teenage girl. Then there are those who would tell you they are convinced it was the fault of a hot-headed young Indian hell-bent on revenge."

The detective eyed me carefully. We both knew which scenario the police favored. "And you?" he asked. "What would you say?"

"I'd say it was just an ordinary encounter on an ordinary street corner that set everything in motion . . ."

CHAPTER ONE

Summer 1956

Antonio Rossi stood at the office window facing Front Street and lit a Camel. What he really wanted was two aspirins and a beer chaser. He felt like he'd been kicked in the head by a pissed off mule and his gut didn't feel much better. He was used to winning at poker, and losing last night's game stung like hell, but losing to that dumb shit sheriff was even worse. Tony was twenty-four years old. He was convinced that if he didn't make a change soon, he was no better off than the sheriff and all the other losers in this two-bit town. He glanced at his wristwatch. Nine o'clock in the morning and it was already sizzling hot.

As he loosened his tie, a battered, smoke-belching pickup loaded with stacks of empty cherry boxes crossed the intersection. A page from a discarded newspaper swirled out of the gutter when the truck rattled past the office. Flung upward, the dirty scrap hovered in the dusty air briefly and then floated to the sidewalk. It landed in front of a mangy dog sleeping in the slim shade of a potted maple. The dog lifted one droopy eyelid and yawned as an elderly Indian in tattered jeans and a plaid, long-sleeved wool shirt stumbled into the street. "Where the hell is everyone?" Tony grumbled. "Alls we got this morning are cherry pickers, ugly mutts, and old Injuns."

The Indian weaved slowly from left to right down the middle of the street. Long gray braids swung in tandem against his backside. With his head lowered, he looked like a novice dancer watching his feet for fear he'd miss-step.

Tony smirked as he watched the Indian's dance-walk. *Another loser on display.* Glancing at his Timex again, he said, "Sixty seconds.

I'll give him a full minute. If he takes less than that to get to the curb, I'll put out this smoke and start making calls." He grinned at Mildred hunched over her typewriter. "If the redskin doesn't make it in time, then you and me are going to head over to Dizzy's and order us a couple of cold ones."

"Sure thing, boss." Her adoring gaze was borderline worshipful which Tony took as his due. She was middle-aged and not much to look at with her frizzy gray hair and bulging hips, but she could be counted on. "Old Millie," Tony was fond of saying, "is the perfect secretary — discreet, loyal and madly in love with me."

His seventeen-year-old cousin, Nick, lowered his newspaper and stole a look at the clock on the wall above Mildred's head. She caught his eye and shrugged. "It's gotta be five o' clock somewhere, kiddo."

Another produce truck, newer and faster than the last one, took advantage of the light traffic and picked up speed as it turned onto Front Street. The signal at the intersection was yellow, but the driver barreled on through, passing Woolworth's and Dizzy's at a rapid, hair-raising clip. He arrived in front of Rossi's Realty about thirty seconds into the Indian's trek across the street. Suddenly catching sight of the unexpected pedestrian, the driver braked hard. His rig's super-tread tires grabbed the pavement with a deep rubber-burning growl and lurched to a stop just inches short of the old man's knees.

The Indian spun around in a tight circle and stopped with his back to the truck.

The truck driver sat motionless inside his cab, eyes bulging as he stared at the backside of the man he'd just missed killing.

Meanwhile, his would-be victim didn't seem to register the near-miss. He swayed a little, then grabbed his gut and bent over at the waist.

"What the hell?" mouthed the truck driver, irritation overcoming shock. He slammed his fist on the horn. The booming blast caused the old man to jolt upright, wheel around and stare at the truck with a dazed expression on his wrinkled face.

The driver poked his head out the window. "Hey, Tonto! Get the fuck outta my way!"

Tony snorted and checked his watch. "Forty-five seconds."

Somehow the Indian got himself going again and stumbled over to the curb where he plopped down. Fifty-five seconds.

The truck roared to life and sped down the street. "Damn," Tony said, taking a last drag on his cigarette. As he crushed the butt in a nearby ashtray, he looked out the window again. It was just a reflex thing, a final glance outside before returning to work. And that's when he saw the girl.

She walked hand in hand with a tall, older man. If Tony had to bet on it, he'd say he was her father. Dad and his princess out for an early morning stroll through town. Tony leaned into the window to get a better look. *Damn, she's just a schoolgirl.* Tony shook his head and smiled. *But those tits of hers are all woman.* Her skimpy white blouse left no room for doubt on that score. And then there were her short shorts. They held slender tanned legs, reminding Tony of that movie star — the one in all those Hollywood movies in the thirties. The starlet's name escaped him, but this girl had the same kind of walk, sensual and captivating. Tony couldn't take his eyes off her.

The girl and her father stopped in front of a display in Goldman's Jewelry and, after a moment, turned to cross the street. The couple both had blond hair, but his crew cut was dull and lifeless compared to the way her flowing tresses shimmered and danced in the bright sunlight. She wore her shoulder-length hair in a ponytail, tied back with a pink ribbon. As she strolled across the street, the ponytail swayed from side to side like a hypnotist's trick watch — back and forth, back and forth, back and forth.

"Jesus," Tony murmured, struggling to catch his breath.

Mildred stopped typing and watched Tony watch the girl. Nick tossed his newspaper aside and took in the scene, too. The father and daughter — concern written on both their faces — stopped next to the Indian who was still slumped on the curb clutching his gut.

"Gotcha!" shouted Tony. Grabbing his Stetson from the coat rack, he bolted for the door and called over his shoulder to Nick. "Hold down the fort, kid. I've got a live one on the line."

Mildred laughed and waved a hand at Nick. "Go on," she said. "You won't want to miss this. I'll cover for you."

Nick caught up with Tony and the couple just as the old Indian, his face the color of muddy water, started moaning and rocking back and forth. The man had squatted on his haunches alongside the

Indian as the girl looked on. "What's wrong, fella?" he asked. "Can we help you?"

"He's just had a little too much to drink, that's all," Tony said.

The girl shaded her dark blue eyes from the sun with a cupped hand and looked at Tony. *Hah, she's sizing me up, taking my measure. Give it your best shot, Missy.* He was used to having women look him over once or twice and it never failed to please him. He grinned as he shot his cuffs. *Haven't lost the old touch yet.*

Tony felt the familiar burst of energy that always kicked in when he worked his sales magic. His light-blue summer suit and white shirt set off his dark good looks perfectly. Tony knew he'd already hooked the girl; now all he had to do was get her father on his side. Thankfully, he'd remembered to straighten his new polka dot tie as he'd dashed out the office door. Things like that counted when it came to selling yourself. He never left anything to chance, even the dab of Brylcreem he'd applied earlier that morning. The potion had transformed his thick black hair into a neat, slicked-back pompadour. All part of his sales prep.

With his headache but a distant memory, he tipped his Stetson at the girl. Addressing her companion, Tony said, "I think I know what to do."

"What's that?" the man asked, standing upright. He towered over all of them in an easy, non-threatening way. He appeared to be in his forties, but held his age well. He was muscular and fit as if he'd been an athlete in his younger days and hadn't yet told his body that he'd given up on sports.

"All he needs is some food in his stomach and he'll be okay." Tony stuffed a wad of bills into the Indian's hand. "Here, chief. Take this and go get yourself some breakfast." The Indian looked at the money and groaned.

"Are you sure that's what he needs?"

"Of course," Tony said, striking a reassuring tone. He pointed to the sign above the office door across the street. "I'm Tony Rossi of Rossi Realty and I like helping Injuns almost as much as I like helping folks like you."

The man cocked an eyebrow. "Like us?"

"Yes, indeedy," Tony replied. "When I saw you and the young

lady here stopping to see what you could do for this poor old man, I knew you were good folk. Just the kind of folk we like to have in this nice little town of ours. You are new to The Dalles, aren't you?"

"Matter of fact we are." The man extended his hand to Tony. "Name's Matthews. Sam Matthews." He gestured to the girl. "And this is my daughter, Ellie."

Could he read people or what? Tony shook hands with Matthews and then his daughter. Matthews had a firm grip, but Ellie's was more like a caress. *Damn if she wasn't caressing his hand! And right in front of her father, too.* Tony gave her a knowing wink and squeezed her palm. *This sale was in the bag.*

Selling was like a choreographed dance. It had a definite rhythm and pattern that when performed well, smoothly guided the client from point A to point B. The dance was purposefully timed so that when the music ended, there'd be a signature on the dotted line. Tony called it his applause line. He was well on his way to an applause-worthy performance when Nick cut in.

"I'm Nick Rossi," he said. "Tony's cousin."

Ellie withdrew her hand from Tony's and looked at Nick. She couldn't have been impressed. As far as Tony was concerned, the teen was a Rossi in name only. His scrawny build, dirty blond hair and pasty complexion had to have come from his mother's side of the family. He even had her mousy personality and limited smarts. Worse, Nick's ill-timed introduction was a miss-step that could ruin the entire dance if not corrected.

Tony scowled at Nick, but resisted the urge to cuff him for butting in where he wasn't invited. "My cousin just started working for me," he said. "The kid's green as grass, so pay him no never mind."

A red flush spread across Nick's thin neck and face. There was a moment of awkward silence until Matthews politely intervened. "Ellie and I are very glad to meet you, Nick."

Tony cleared his throat. "Anyways, as I was saying, I like to help newcomers get started in The Dalles. How 'bout we all go for a little ride in my car? Be my pleasure to show you around town."

Sam Matthews ran a hand over the top of his crew cut and frowned.

Tony figured him for the cautious type. *Probably protective as hell of*

20

his little girl.

"I don't know," Matthews said. "Ellie and I have a lot to do and-"

"She's right over there." Tony pointed to a shiny red Cadillac convertible parked at the curb across the street. "It's a limited edition, 1953 Eldorado. Only fifty-three were built in the entire country that year and I was lucky enough to get me one." *Me and my Caddy. Best sales tools in the business.*

"Nice looking automobile, Mr. Rossi, but the old guy—"

"Listen, call me Tony. And don't you worry none about the chief here. I'll get Mildred—she's my secretary—and tell her to make sure he gets something to eat."

"She'd do that?"

"Absolutely. We do it all the time for these fellas."

Ellie had her eye on the convertible, a wistful look on her face, but she didn't say a word. Her father put an arm around her shoulder. "Well," he said, "maybe it'd be all right. We haven't had time to see much of the town yet."

Just what Tony thought. Sam Matthews was a protective *and* indulgent father. "Great!" Tony said, giving a celebratory handclap. "Follow me!"

Nick trailed after them as Tony hustled Ellie and her father across the street. As soon as he'd helped them into the car—Matthews riding shotgun and Ellie in the back—he pulled Nick aside. When they were out of earshot, he said, "I thought I told you to stay in the goddamn office."

Nick's still-flushed face crumpled. "I'm sorry, Tony. I just wanted to watch you in action, that's all."

"Witness the master reel one in, is that it?"

Nick bobbed his head with renewed enthusiasm. "You betcha."

"Fine," Tony said. "Just see that you keep your trap shut from now on. I'm on a roll here and I don't need you messing things up."

Nick ran his thumb and forefinger across his lips in a zipping gesture. "Don't worry. My lips are sealed."

His cousin was a pest but he did come in handy from time to time. "Then make yourself useful. Run on back to the office and pick up my keys and briefcase. And while you're at it, tell Mildred to ring up Sheriff Pritchard." He pointed to the Indian. "I want that stinkin' bum off my street. You got that?"

"I'm on it."

Tony grabbed his arm. "One more thing. Have Mildred tell Pritchard to get the money that thieving Injun stole from me."

Tony stood outside the vehicle and shot the breeze with Sam Matthews while waiting for Nick. He focused on Matthews, but managed to sneak a look or two at Ellie nestled on the seat in the back. She'd slipped off her sandals, curled her slender legs underneath her and closed her eyes. Tony figured she'd probably never been in a car like his—a flashy spit-and-polish rag top with a wrap-around windshield, whitewall tires, tail fins, and sparkling chrome. Then the new car smell. Three years old and his pride and joy still smelled like he'd just driven it off the lot. The Caddy was a real beauty, no doubt about it. But this girl . . . well, this girl cuddled up on the soft leather seat made it a show stopper. The image had him so distracted that he missed Matthews's question.

"Huh? What was that?"

"I just asked you if—"

Tony's attention shifted abruptly when he spotted his cousin. "About time you got here," he snapped. "Toss me the keys and hop in."

As soon as Nick was aboard, Tony put the Cadillac in gear and pulled away from the curb, tires squealing. The sights he pointed out to Matthews and his daughter passed by in a blur: St. Peters Catholic Church, Granada Theater, Masonic Lodge, Recreation Bowl, the junior and senior high schools. The stated purpose of their little jaunt through town was to familiarize them with the area. At this speed, The Dalles wouldn't be anything more than a vague notion, but Tony didn't give it a thought. The tour was just an intro—a mere warm-up act for the main event.

As Tony drove, his eyes drifted to the rear-view mirror. Sometime during the tour, Ellie had plucked the ribbon from her ponytail, abandoning her hair-do to the whims of the wind as it rushed past her in the open convertible. Her full lips were touched with a hint of red lipstick, but it was a little black mole at the corner of her mouth that gave her face a sexy look. Paired with her youthful-appearing dimples, the effect was mesmerizing. Ellie had that rare combination of womanly beauty and childlike innocence that stirred Tony unlike anything he'd ever experienced. When she caught him ogling her, she smiled playfully and then quickly turned her head away. *You little vixen!*

A honking horn jolted Tony's attention back to the road. Somehow, he'd managed to pass through an intersection on a red light, narrowly missing a station wagon. He exhaled sharply and glanced at the grimace etched on Matthews's face. "Whew! That was close," Tony said. Chuckling, he added, "But no harm, no foul."

Tony turned right at the grain elevator near the city limits and shifted into second gear to climb a short hill. As soon as they'd reached the crest, he shook out a Camel from a pack in his suit pocket and offered it to Matthews. "No? Well, it's my last one anyway," he said, steering with one hand while retrieving the dashboard lighter with the other. The cigarette clung to his lower lip as he talked. "You know, Sam, you couldn't have picked a better time to move to Oregon. To The Dalles. Yessiree, The Dalles is the best place in the whole state to raise a family."

Matthews shifted in his seat but didn't respond. Undeterred, Tony continued, "I bet you're thinking 'Why's that?'" He brought the Cadillac to a stop at a viewpoint near the entrance to Sorosis Park and gestured in a broad sweeping arc toward the gorge. "We call this God's country," he said. "Just look down there. It doesn't get any better than that, my friend."

A red-tailed hawk circled overhead, swooped low, then dive-bombed to the wide expanse of the river below. To the north were the dry mountains of Washington. The smooth, rounded topside of the Klickitat Hills was a watercolor wash of browns, golds, copper, and amber that came undone at the shoreline with the jarring violence of its jagged cliffs. Two tall, snow-capped peaks, Mt. Hood and Mt. Adams, overlooked the vast gorge like watchful sentries.

"Tell me something, Sam. What line of work are you in?"

"I'm with the Corps. Construction foreman."

By Corps, Tony assumed he meant the U. S. Army Corps of Engineers charged with building the dam on the Columbia River but he didn't give Matthews time to elaborate. He slapped his hand on the steering wheel and said, "I knew it! When I spotted you on the street today, I said to myself, 'Tony', I said, 'there goes a government man. A man of decision.' And I was right. You're not a man to pussyfoot around. You're the kind of man who knows what he wants and goes after it."

Tony knew he'd laid it on a bit thick, but he never argued with success. In his experience, guys like Matthews ate flattery for breakfast, lunch, and dinner. Satisfied that his spiel had hit the right note, Tony continued. "Being newcomers and all, you might not know this, but . . ." He leaned in closer to Matthews as if to share a secret. "Homes in The Dalles are selling like hotcakes." He pointed to a nearby billboard advertising a housing development called Hillcrest Addition. "And Hillcrest is selling even faster."

The billboard pictured a beaming family in front of a house with a SOLD sign on the front door. As Matthews gazed at the billboard, Tony delivered the punch line. "You can have a dream home just like that family there. But time is of the essence."

They'd been in the convertible less than ten minutes. The sale, like the travelogue, was on the fast track. Pitch ended for now, Tony tossed his cigarette butt out the window and shifted into gear. Spitting gravel, the Caddy lurched forward and onto the main highway again. He drove a few hundred yards further and then turned left onto a dirt road, which had a single cherry tree growing in the center like a traffic divider. As they passed the tree, Tony assured them it would be cut down and the road paved soon. "This whole development used to be a big cherry orchard, but your wife's gonna love this place. I've sold to lots of government families and the wives all say—"

"It's just me and my daughter."

Tony dared a glance at Ellie. "Divorced?"

"No. My wife died ten years ago."

"Oh." Tony bit his lower lip and frowned. "I'm truly sorry about that. Truly."

Matthews shrugged off the sentiment. "Ellie and I have done pretty well, considering."

Tony shut up for a couple of heartbeats before pulling the car to a stop in front of a white house with a large bay window. It was the only house on Cherry Blossom Lane that still had a bright red FOR

SALE banner strung across the front window. "Well," said Tony, rubbing his hands together. "What do you say we take a looksee at this house?"

"Mr. Rossi, we—"

"Please. Call me Tony."

"Right. Tony, we didn't plan to buy a house today."

"I know. I know. I just thought we could look around a little bit. No harm in that, is there?"

Matthews appeared to be thinking it over, but Tony was confident that the hook was set.

Sam half-turned in his seat to face his daughter. "What do you think, Ellie? Would you like to go inside?"

"That'd be great!" she said.

"Tell you what," said Tony, suppressing a grin as he handed Matthews a key on a small chain. "Why don't you two go on ahead? Nick and I will join you in a minute."

Ellie hopped out of the car and darted up the sidewalk but her father took his time, easing his long legs out of the convertible and then stopping to survey the neighborhood in all directions—east . . . west . . . south . . .

"Dad! Hurry up!"

Matthews waved a hand in surrender. "Okay, okay. Hold your horses, I'm coming." At the doorstep, he fumbled with the key while Ellie waited behind him.

Tony climbed out of the car. When he slammed the door shut, Ellie spun around. The loud noise got her attention, but Tony was convinced *he* was what *kept* her attention. Never taking his eyes off hers, he casually leaned against the car, crossed his legs at the ankles and folded his arms loosely across his chest. *Dare you to turn away from me this time, Missy.*

"There," huffed Matthews. "I got the damn thing open."

As her father trudged into the house, Ellie turned around to follow him. But then, pausing mid-stride, she looked back at Tony. A dazzling dimpled grin lit up her face.

Tony tipped his Stetson and laughed. "Hand me my briefcase, Nick. This house is a done deal."

25

CHAPTER TWO

The dam was visible from the highway but Danny Longstreet willed himself to ignore it. A mile and a half of concrete stretching across the Columbia from Oregon to Washington was like trying not to look at a train wreck. The dam's massive size still stunned him even though he'd seen it hundreds of times before. The eighteen-year-old had watched the construction from the very beginning — when it was just a mound of dirt pushed around by bulldozers — to its imposing, yet still unfinished state. He shrugged off the despair he felt whenever he drove past the dam and pressed down hard on the gas pedal. Gunning the old truck past 72 mph was dicey, but speed was exactly what he needed right now. Predictably, the beater shimmied like a bar room floozy, rattling all the way to the Celilo exit.

Once off the main highway, Danny had to slow down when he got stuck behind a lengthy line of vehicles heading toward the village. Hundreds of brethren from the foothills of Mt. Hood, Klickitat, and White Salmon to Rattlesnake Ridge on the slopes of Mt. Adams had been streaming into Celilo since early spring. Word that the salmon were running had swept up the river like the west wind and the comers had packed their belongings and headed out. They came every year, but the spring and summer of 1956 had brought more than usual, some from as far away as Canada. Everyone knew it would be the last time they'd gather by the falls and no one wanted to miss it. The whites had come, too. They took pictures, bought souvenir beads, baskets and salmon, but the big tourist draw was watching the Wy-ams and others fish.

Danny followed the slow-moving procession until his three minutes of patience ran out. Pulling off the dirt road, he drove alongside it, dodging potholes and rocks. The other drivers were forced to slow down even further as great billows of dust churned and swirled as he passed by. Danny tuned the radio to a rock n' roll station and cranked the volume as loud as it would go. Then he stuck his head out the window and hooted, "Shake, rattle, and roll, baby!" With his long dark hair whipping in the wind, he kept time with the music's raucous beat by slapping his hand against the door panel. Some of the drivers pointed and laughed while others honked and shook their fists. If they were Indians, Danny gave them a friendly wave. If they were whites in wood-paneled station wagons or big Buicks, he yelled, "Get a horse!"

When Danny arrived at the village, parking was in short supply. Cars and pickups were wedged together like buzzards around a carcass. Two little boys from the village darted between the parked vehicles as they played tag. Danny tooted his horn and waved at the kids before pulling into the first somewhat open space he could find. When he turned off the ignition, the diesel engine continued to chug-a-lug, almost drowning out an angry shout that came from behind. "Hey, you're blocking my car!"

The fuss-budget was a white guy. Figured. Whites were always fussing about one thing or another. Danny waited a moment to see if the fellow would press the issue. Known around the village as a scrapper, Danny was ready and willing to take on anyone who looked at him crosswise. Despite a hair-trigger temper that often got him in trouble with the village elders and others in authority, Danny was well-liked at Celilo. It was a different matter with outsiders, especially white outsiders like the visitor he'd just encountered. Danny leaned out of the cab to get a better look at the jerk. He was more muscled than Danny would've liked but he had to be forty if he was a day. Easy take down.

The boys stopped their game to watch Danny. He was all set to give them a good show but when he'd climbed halfway out of the cab, he noticed that the guy had a wife and kid in tow. The white man's disapproving scowl was infuriating, but Danny unclenched his fists and let him pass without incident.

"Come on, Sara," the man said, wrapping a protective arm around his wife's waist. "Let's buy some fish and get out of here."

Danny called after them, "No need to hurry! I'll save you a 30 pounder!"

"Hey, man, ain't you gonna fight?" asked one of the boys.

"Nah," said Danny. "Fightin' a chicken ain't my style." He tucked both hands under his armpits and flapped his arms up and down while dancing in a tight circle. "Squawk! Squawk! Squawk!"

The boys giggled and squawked and flapped their arms along with him. After a minute Danny said, "Fun's over, boys. Gotta go." He reached into the truck and grabbed a grocery bag containing the Lucky Lager he'd bought earlier at Johnny's Market.

The sun — directly overhead, bright and bare chest hot — hit Danny full force. As he shaded his eyes from the glare, he remembered the old pair of sunglasses he'd found in the men's room at the Pit Stop the night before. He hoisted himself back inside the cab, reached across to the door-less glove box and fumbled around until he found them. They were cracked in one lens, but workable. After he put on the glasses, he pulled a dirty painter's hat out of his jeans' pocket and slapped the hat against his pant leg. He creased the bill a couple of times, smoothed back his hair, and donned the hat. Ready to fish, he walked toward the falls.

Fishing at Celilo was not easy. The nature of the falls made any convenient access nearly impossible. The sides of the knife-edged cliffs fell twenty feet into the fast-moving water. To get at the salmon, some fishermen fashioned wooden platforms on which they stood, suspended over the turbulence, and lowered their pole nets. Others hitched makeshift scaffolding to long ropes and hoisted themselves down the sides of the cliffs to get closer to the water. Called Tumwater or "great chute" by early explorers, the strong currents of the Columbia River merged upon this one small crack in the basalt cliffs — a crack only 150 feet wide — to churn and stir the water like a witch's brew. The lip of the falls formed an almost perfect horseshoe divided by two large rocks. It was at this juncture that the waters surged forth and the river dropped eighty feet in the span of a few miles.

Chief's Island was in the middle of the Columbia and the hardest place of all to reach. In the old days, the Wy-ams had to row a boat through the swift currents to get to the island. But in the late 1930's when the huge fishwheels were operating, a cableway had been installed across Downes Channel to Chief's Island by the Seufert Cannery Company. Not that the company was doing the Indians any favors — the cableway just made it easier for the fishermen to get out to where the salmon could be caught and delivered more promptly to Seufert's buying station.

Although Seufert's fishwheels had long since been abandoned, the cableway to Chief's Island was still operational. Danny pulled on the retrieval line and hauled the large transport box affixed to the main cable back across the channel to the shore. As soon as the box was ashore, he heaved the grocery bag and himself inside. Pulling on the cable hand over hand, he passed above the raging waters to the island.

As Danny came closer, he saw his grandfather sitting alone on his platform. Few such sites dotted the small island's rocky landscape. Only chiefs or descendants of chiefs were allowed to fish there. Oscar Longstreet had inherited the station from his uncle who had once been a Wy-am chief. As Oscar's only grandchild and heir, Danny would someday own the fishing spot. It was a false inheritance; when the dam was completed, there'd be nothing left to inherit.

Although he'd been fishing since dawn, Oscar sat ramrod straight on an upturned apple crate, patiently awaiting a strike. Danny had seen his grandfather sit like that for hours at a time, ignoring the arthritis that plagued his lower back until he had his catch. Danny winced at the thought of his grandfather in pain. Oscar would never complain but Danny should've gotten here when he'd promised. He could've at least done that for him.

Oscar's voice rose above the roar of the falls, "Huk-toocht! Huk-toocht!" Give me luck. Give me luck.

Danny shook his head. The old man didn't get it. None of the elders did. Luck wasn't what they needed. Only action would save them. It was an old argument. One that'd have to keep for another day. Danny swung his legs out of the carrier, grabbed his grocery bag, and headed to the site.

Before joining Oscar, Danny located an extra safety rope, tied a couple of knots in it, wrapped one end around his waist and secured the other end to the platform. Weather-worn and rickety, the platform's gray boards still had traces of blood and slime from yesterday's salmon catch. His grandfather was getting forgetful. Danny picked up a sand-filled coffee can that was stowed nearby and grabbed a handful of granules. As he scattered the sand over the slippery boards, he could see the churning waters through several wide spots in the platform planks.

When he was a little kid Danny was afraid of these cracks and he still remembered the terror he felt. *No, Grandpa, please.* Peering between the boards at the boiling cauldron, he was sure the river gods wanted his young bones. He could see them reaching out for him, spitting and hissing. *Da-an-ny. Da-an-ny.* Their icy wet tongues licked his face and body, freezing him to the boards. Fingers plucked at his hair, his ears, his mouth. Unable to resist, the gods pulled him closer and closer. And then, just before they wrestled him through the cracks, he was in the air, flying like an eagle. Oscar's strong arms carried his bones up and away from the watery grave.

Stepping confidently over the cracks now, Danny picked up a dipnet pole and thought not of river gods, but of white men and what they wanted. He cast his pole into the water and sat down on his own upturned apple crate. The roar from the raging falls usually made conversation difficult, but the location of their fishing site was positioned on a small basalt outcropping that was acoustically unique. As a result, Danny and his grandfather could communicate without resorting to shouting or hand signals like so many of their brethren were forced to do.

"Who caught the first fish?" Danny asked by way of greeting.

"Wauna Joe."

"Figures." Wauna Joe's people had the best fishing spots on both sides of the Columbia. Wauna Joe had crossed the river between Oregon and Washington so many times that he was given the name Wauna which meant great river.

"Wauna Joe's doin' all right today," Oscar said. "The rest of us, we's still waiting."

Danny looked out over the falls at the fishermen. The closest were Willie Two Bears and Frank Yallum on Standing Island. Across Downes Channel and along the shore were Wauna Joe and his family, then Johnny George and Red Shirt, and finally, Walking Tall. They were all Wy-ams but the Yakamas, Umatillas, Warm Springs and Nez

Perce tribes were also fishing Celilo Falls.

"Did you see the mud swallows?" asked Danny. The birds were a sure sign that a good catch was imminent.

"Yep. They's been here and gone. Still nothin'."

Danny retrieved two Lucky Lager bottles from his bag. He popped the caps with a church key and offered a bottle to his grandfather. The two men drank together for a while, the muted rumbling of the falls the only sound between them. The sun's fierce rays blasted down on them despite their protective hats. Oscar's was a black, wide-brimmed affair with a blue beaded band and a single white feather at the back. Danny couldn't remember him ever wearing anything different. Doffing his painter's hat, Danny wiped the sweat from his forehead with the back of his bare arm.

As he replaced the hat, he looked at Oscar and decided that his grandfather was getting old. He was sixty-three and had aged rapidly in the last few years. His braids were streaked with gray and his broad hat couldn't hide the deep lines on his face or the weary sadness in his dark eyes. There was no mistaking their genetic relationship. They both had tall, sinewy builds, deep-set brown eyes, and angular facial features. For Danny, it was how they differed that was most significant. Oscar was old, he was young; Oscar was passive, he was active; Oscar was reserved, he was bold. As much as he loved his grandfather, Danny would never be like him.

Gulping down the last of his beer, he reached for another bottle and said, "Sorry I was late. Had some business to take care of in town." It was best not to say much more than that. Neither man wanted to talk about Danny's activities away from Celilo; too many harsh words had already been exchanged.

Danny searched for a neutral topic. "You should've seen all the cars headed into the village today. Lots of whites, too."

"Did they have their cameras?"

"I guess so. Why?"

"Whites, they like to take pictures. One summer, when I was about your age, me and some of the guys was picking cherries for the Seufert's and this skinny white man came up and hired us right out of the orchard for picture taking."

"He paid to take your picture?"

"Yeah. He was some big shot photographer from New York City. Took me and Sammy Williams and a couple of others up to Fivemile Rapids. Told us to take off all our clothes. Then he gave us some long sharp sticks and had us get out on the rocks to pretend like we was spearing for salmon."

"Naked?"

Oscar laughed. "Like bare-assed newborns. That man didn't know nothin', but he had plenty of dough. Charlie Slim Jim wouldn't get undressed till the guy gave him a pint of whiskey. Then Sammy asked for two pints. And he got them. Pretty soon we all had a pint and was laughing pretty good. Made more money prancing around in the water for an hour than pickin' for Seufert's all day."

"What do you think he did with the pictures?"

Oscar shrugged and adjusted his dipnet. "Hell, if I know. Whites, they's hard to figure."

"Oh, I've got them figured, Grandpa. And, what's more, I'm going to do something about it."

Oscar shifted his weight on the crate and looked out at the falls. "Should be getting a strike soon."

Danny's tightened his grip on the pole and fought back the urge to have it out with his grandfather. As much as he wanted to, he'd never argue here. Not while fishing sacred grounds. Instead, he laid down his pole, stood and stretched. Across the channel, Danny saw a commotion at a platform on Standing Island. "Can you see what's going on over there?" he asked.

Oscar turned to look where Danny pointed. The distance was too great to hear Frank Yallum but both men could see that he was shouting and gesturing toward the water.

Then Danny got it. "It's Willie Two Bears!" he yelled. "He's fallen in!" Willie never wore his safety rope even though the Bureau of Indian Affairs had threatened many times over the years to make him stop fishing unless he did. Willie was as stubborn as he was fat and wrapping a rope around his wide girth wasn't something he chose to do. As Danny and his grandfather watched in horror, the rapids tossed Willie's big body around like it was a little rag doll.

Danny kicked the apple crate aside and, yanking off his hat and sunglasses, flattened himself belly-side down at the edge of the platform. Clutching his pole with both hands, he thrust it toward the water as far as it would go. If he was lucky, Willie would pass by close enough to grab hold of it. After a moment, Danny decided he was too far away from the water for that to happen.

"How's my rope?" he called to Oscar.

Oscar checked the knots Danny had tied when he'd fastened the rope to the platform on his arrival. "You're good."

Relying on the strength of his safety rope to keep him from harm's way, Danny scooted forward and slid down one of the platform posts until he dangled just above the water's surface. Planting his feet against the post for support, he could lean out over the water to where he thought Willie might have a chance of grabbing his dipnet pole. The rope cut into his waist but he ignored the pain. Thirty seconds flashed by without any sight of him until he suddenly popped out of the churning foam.

Oscar spotted his old friend first. Floating upright at the tip of Chief's Island, he appeared to be heading straight for Danny's net. "He's coming!" Oscar shouted.

"I see him," Danny said, bracing for the impact. When he hit, Danny thought the jolt would surely break the pole. But it held fast and Willie's big frame wedged tentatively against the net. Flailing his arms in the tangled netting, Willie tried for several seconds to grab the pole.

"Come on, man, you can make it," pleaded Danny.

Willie made a desperate last ditch effort to grab the pole but missed and was sucked underneath the water. Just when Danny thought he was a goner, Willie popped out of the foam for a second time. His gray hair, usually worn in a ponytail, had come loose and completely covered his face.

Danny shouted to his grandfather. "Is he still conscious?"

"Can't tell. His face is—"

"I've got him!"

The current had pushed Willie directly into the large dipnet once again, tangling him firmly this time. Danny strained to hold the pole steady and keep him trapped until they could hoist him onto the platform. Willie was motionless, no flailing or grabbing for the pole this time around. His long hair fanned about his head and shoulders like a shroud. "Help me bring him up!"

Grandfather and grandson struggled, fighting the current, Willie's bulk and their own physical limitations. If only there'd been more men to help them, they'd say later. If only they'd been stronger. If only . . .

After several long, frustrating minutes, Oscar said, "He's with the spirits now. It's time to stop."

Danny hung on as Oscar withdrew. "NO! We can't let him go." But his bone-weary arms finally gave way and the pole slipped from his hands. The river gods had won.

Pushed under again but still tangled in Danny's net, Willie Two Bears tumbled downriver. He bounded above the foam once or twice more until he vanished out of sight.

Gasping for breath and shivering, Danny didn't think he had any energy left to climb up the post to the platform.

"Take my hand," Oscar said. "I'll support you."

Once he'd clambered to safety with his grandfather's help, Danny rolled onto his back and closed his eyes.

The nearby fishermen, who'd watched in silence during the rescue attempt, cried out now, loud and strong for Willie Two Bears. "Yi-eeee. Yi-eeee." Their lament, deadened by the falls' ceaseless thunder, lasted several minutes. Then, one by one, they laid down their poles and headed back to the village. No more fishing would take place this day.

Chapter Three

Day shift had been underway for half an hour when Sam Matthews pulled his pickup into the parking lot. His office at the dam was a thirteen-foot trailer atop a hill overlooking the busy construction site. A warm breeze laden with dust and noise from bulldozers, trucks, and other heavy-duty equipment swirled through the cab's open window. Begun in 1952 with a handful of workers, the dam now employed hundreds of skilled men working three shifts a day to complete the project on schedule.

Transforming the untamed Columbia River into a major source of hydroelectric power represented more than just a job. The electricity produced when the transformation was complete would benefit hundreds of thousands in the Pacific Northwest. When water finally tumbled over the nearly 1,400-foot-long spillway for the first time, Celilo Falls would be flooded and silenced forever. The Indians who'd fished the falls for centuries would have their lives profoundly changed. Sam considered their loss regrettable but that was just the way things worked in life. It was a lesson he'd learned the hard way, starting with the loss of his wife.

Ellie was only four years old when her mother died of ovarian cancer and Sam took on the role of single parent. If it was difficult when Ellie was younger, it was doubly difficult now that she was a teenager. She seemed to change from little girl to young woman almost overnight. Her beauty both awed and alarmed him. Sam didn't think she had a sense of just how appealing she'd become. But it didn't escape her father's notice — or that of every male over the age of twelve. The two rules Sam had established years ago were now more important than ever: 1. Trust no one. 2. Suspect everyone. He knew it was a cynical way to live but so far it had kept him alive and

Ellie well protected.

Grabbing his lunch bucket and a set of blueprints, he hoisted himself out of the truck and went inside the trailer. Two battered gunmetal gray desks facing each other dominated the small office space. Metal filing cabinets lined one wall underneath dirt-smudged windows. Graveyard foreman, Ralph Chambers, sat at one of the desks and looked up as Sam entered.

Sam checked the wall clock and winced. "Sorry I'm late," Getting to work at the start of his shift seemed to be a daily struggle these days.

"Everything okay at home?" asked Chambers. It wasn't a rebuke. The white-haired foreman never complained about Sam's tardiness.

Sam eyed the framed photo of Ellie on his desk and sighed. "Okay, I guess — if you can call a motel home."

"Motel living's gotta be tough. When're you moving into your new house?"

"We're just waiting on the bank. There's a paperwork backlog." Tony Rossi had been right about the fast-selling housing market. The sheer number of sales had the bank scrambling to keep up. Sam's pre-assignment briefing had included a detailed description of the Hillcrest Development and its residents before he'd ever met the pushy realtor. According to his bureau chief, "The ranch-style homes are affordable, but more important, you and Ellie will fit in easily with the Hillcrest lifestyle." Meaning a widowed construction foreman and his lovely teenage daughter would be welcomed and accepted by his neighbors without suspicion. As difficult as single parenthood had become, it served his undercover role very well. If Sam had had a choice, he would have preferred a home on an acre or two well outside the town limits. He'd been running his family's farm in Idaho before the war and, although farming was not without its hardships, Sam missed the rural lifestyle. Hillcrest's cookie cutter houses with their neatly manicured lawns inhabited by people of the same social class, watching *I Love Lucy* while eating the same tasteless TV dinners, conforming in every outward respect to a common mold, held no appeal for him whatsoever. But buying a home in the Hillcrest neighborhood served his current mission. So that was that. His only consolation was how happy it had made Ellie.

If Tony Rossi had known about Sam's house buying plans, he wouldn't have bothered with his so-called tour of The Dalles. Ellie had spotted the shiny red convertible long before Rossi dashed out of his office to introduce himself and invite them for a ride. "Look, Dad," she'd said, pointing to the car. "Wouldn't it be fun to have a car like that?" Sam had promised her that The Dalles would be a fresh start for both of them, but he'd made promises before that he couldn't keep. If riding in a convertible somehow helped Ellie believe things truly would be different this time around, Sam had been willing to put up with Rossi's annoying chatter. Even though Sam had downplayed his interest in buying a house, the realtor's timing couldn't have been better for his purposes.

Chambers tucked a number two pencil behind his ear and slid a clipboard across the desk to Sam. "Speaking of paperwork, here's the turnover report."

Sam started to apologize again but Chambers cut him off. "Don't worry about it," he said. "I just now got the damn thing finished anyway."

"Still, I should've been here sooner."

"It's okay I tell ya," Chambers said, lighting a cigarette. "Once you get the house situation settled, you'll be fine."

Sam hoped the man was right, but Chambers didn't have any kids. He couldn't begin to understand what life was like with a teenage girl. Ellie's emotions went up and down faster than a roller coaster these days and Sam didn't always make things easier for her. She'd started her period this morning, but he'd forgotten to buy the supplies she'd requested and had to make a quick trip to the corner grocery before heading to work.

"Maybe you're right," Sam said, retrieving the clipboard. "Living at Hillcrest should be better. There's gotta be a helpful mother around to bail me out from time to time."

Chambers smiled through yellow-stained teeth. "Yeah, the ladies will be falling all over their selves to help a good-lookin' widow man like you. Especially the single ladies."

There was something about a man raising a daughter on his own that tugged at the heartstrings of most women. While Sam welcomed their willingness to step in when he needed them, it often had unintended consequences. No matter how much he insisted that he wasn't looking for a wife, no one seemed to believe he really meant it. Sam couldn't begin to count the number of women he'd been told would be "perfect" for him or how many times there'd "just happen" to be a single woman at whatever dinner or activity he was invited to. Not that he was opposed to dating, but his work was complicated enough without adding romance to the mix. He had a lot of secrets to keep and ensuring his daughter's safety and happiness had to be his paramount concern. Sam had made some serious mistakes lately which had damaged his relationship with Ellie. The last thing he needed was to hurt someone else he loved.

Chambers watched as Sam skimmed through the report. "Can you read my hen-scratchings?" he asked.

Sam nodded. He suspected Chamber's hard-to-decipher scribbles had more to do with the arthritis plaguing his rough, liver-spotted hands than bad penmanship. He wondered if the guy would last long enough to retire when he turned sixty-five next month. Besides swollen, painful fingers, Chambers' résumé included a heart attack and a bum knee. Sam admired the man's grit but when he expressed concern about his ailments, Chambers quickly downplayed the seriousness. "I'm like one of them Timex watches. I take a lickin' and keep on tickin'."

Sam's undercover assignments had often involved construction work. He hadn't known Chambers before coming to The Dalles, but he'd worked alongside quite a few of the other men when he was stationed at Bonneville and Chief Joseph dams. His skills were notable so his background as a former Seabee who'd served with the Department of Navy during the war was never questioned. There was some overt resentment when he made foreman, however. Sam didn't know whether it was sour grapes or rumors about his past that had caused the trouble. Like all rumors, there was just enough truth mixed with the nonsense to raise a few eyebrows. Whatever the reason, he'd had some difficult days at the dam in the beginning.

"Your crew will come around in time," Chambers had assured him. "Who you need to watch out for is Phillip Beckstrom. That college boy don't know shit from shinola, but he's in charge, so try not to cross him." Sam had managed to win over his crew as

Chambers predicted, but lead engineer Beckstrom was still a work in progress.

The two men discussed the shift report and then chatted for a few minutes about Chambers' favorite topic — fly fishing. Sam had learned early on that establishing a connection with key people was a valuable practice. He never knew when things might turn dicey and having a friend or two in his corner had saved his butt on more than one occasion. A few tall tales later, Chambers stubbed out his second cigarette and pushed away from the desk. "Well, I better get out of here and let you get some work done."

Sam unrolled the blueprints he'd carried into the office as Ralph Chambers shuffled to the door. As much as the old man claimed he was looking forward to retirement, he seemed like the kind of guy who would miss the job no matter how good full-time fishing proved to be. Even without the report as an excuse, Chambers could always find a reason to linger at the office a bit longer than necessary.

"Oh!" Chambers said, halting at the door. "I almost forgot. Beckstrom was here earlier looking for you."

"What'd he want?"

"Hell, if I know. I buried my nose in the report until he finally scurried off to make trouble for someone else."

"Why don't you admit it?" said Sam, grinning. "You're going to miss Beckstrom's ugly mug when you retire."

Chambers hooted and wagged his backside. "Kiss my ass, Matthews."

Finally, alone, Sam unscrewed his thermos and using the lid as a cup, poured his first coffee of the day. Shuddering at the bitter taste, he opened his desk drawer and stared at the half-empty Jim Beam bottle inside. "Damn," he muttered, slamming the drawer shut. Some promises were much harder to keep than others.

A second cup of the unspiked brew later, he heard shouting outside the trailer. The office window was too dirt-encrusted to see anything so he stepped outside and spotted Phillip Beckstrom striding briskly up the hill. The skinny twenty-five-year-old had a master's degree in engineering from MIT and was on the management fast track with the Corps. Beckstrom had an officious, know-it-all attitude which, coupled with his limited on-the-job experience, made dealing with the man an ongoing challenge.

Trailing closely behind Beckstrom were Brad Dutton and Johnny Patterson, two of Sam's best crew members. They were both big men with well-developed muscles honed from long days of physical labor at the dam. They looked mad enough to chew the engineer into tiny pieces and spit him out with no apologies for bad table manners. Dutton and Patterson weren't choir boys but Beckstrom had a way of goading even a saint to fury. Sam tried to insulate his crew from the man as much as possible.

The engineer clutched a clipboard tightly against his spindly chest and ignored the waving and shouting coming from Dutton and Patterson. Once they crested the hill, Dutton managed to overtake Beckstrom and blocked his path. As soon as Beckstrom stopped, Patterson planted himself alongside his coworker. The men dwarfed Beckstrom's slight, five-foot-seven frame.

A red-faced Dutton glared at Beckstrom, "That order is nuts!" he barked.

"And you're even nuttier to suggest it," Patterson added.

"It's not a suggestion," Beckstrom said. He scuttled around the two men and resumed his trek to the office. When he saw Sam standing by the trailer door, he pointed at Dutton and Patterson. "You need to get these guys back to work."

"What's going on?" asked Sam.

"The problem is—"

"The problem is College Boy here," Dutton blurted before Beckstrom could finish. "He wants us to take out the diversionary dike. But everyone knows that concrete's still green."

"No, it's not," Beckstrom said. "It's just—"

"Weaker than a limp dick," quipped Patterson.

Beckstrom snatched a pencil from his shirt pocket and jotted something on the pad attached to his clipboard. Despite his impressive educational credentials, Beckstrom didn't have a good handle on air entrainment, which was the new process they were now using for mixing concrete. Either that, Sam thought, or he was acting deliberately obtuse. Beckstrom's blustery posturing was even worse than usual and did nothing to allay Sam's growing suspicions about the man. When the engineer looked up from his clipboard, his eyes were cold and unflinching, his diminutive physique rigid with military-like bearing.

Here it comes. When all else fails, assert your authority. If nothing else, the man was predictable. Understanding that characteristic was useful information. Sam didn't consider Phillip Beckstrom his enemy but he believed the admonition to "know thy enemy" applied anyway.

"I'm the lead engineer on this project," Beckstrom said firmly. "If I decide it's time, it's time."

Dutton and Patterson eyed Sam, silently pleading for backup. "You know, Phillip," he replied, "they're right about the wall. Like Dutton said, the concrete is still green. We've got to let it set another week before we remove the dike or we'll have hell to pay later."

"What I know is that if you'd get here on time I wouldn't have to do your job for you." He tucked the pencil back in his pocket. "I've made my decision and it stands. All you have to do now is get your crew to stop their belly-aching and carry out my order."

"Damn it!" yelled Patterson. "He's telling us to fuck up. And we'll be the ones to take the heat when the wall breaks, not him."

"That's enough!" ordered Beckstrom. "Get your men out of here right now, Matthews, or I'll write up all of you for insubordination."

Dutton and Patterson, like most of Sam's crew, were skilled and experienced workers. They could be rough talking at times, but Sam didn't consider them hotheads. He didn't blame them for getting riled at Beckstrom's foolish order. Before things escalated any further, however, Sam nodded in the direction of the work site and his men got the message.

Beckstrom watched the men stomp back down the hill and said, "We need to have a serious talk." Once inside the trailer, he tossed his clipboard onto Sam's desk where it upended the thermos and splattered coffee onto the blueprints. Sam righted the thermos while Beckstrom rescued the blueprints, knocking two other rolls onto the floor in the process. "Shit!" Beckstrom screeched. Plucking a monogrammed handkerchief from his trousers' back pocket, he dabbed at the coffee-stained drawings. "I could use some help here," he said, glaring at Sam.

Sam grabbed a wad of paper towels to soak up the coffee that had pooled on his desk and then draped the wet blueprints over the back of a chair to dry. When the mess had been dealt with, Beckstrom repeated his previous demand that they have a talk. He then spent the next ten minutes delivering a spirited, one-sided dialogue about Sam's frequent tardiness and lack of respect for Beckstrom's authority.

"Listen," Sam said when Beckstrom finally paused to take a breath, "I know you're under a lot of pressure to make the gate closure on time, but removing the dike before the concrete's ready isn't a good idea. If anything, it'll cause us more delay because we'll just have to redo it when the wall breaks. And, trust me, it *will* break."

Beckstrom took off his hard hat and ran slender fingers through his reddish-blond crew cut. "In case you've forgotten, I have the engineering degree, not you. And that means you shouldn't even think about questioning my decisions. The order stands."

Sam sighed and poured what remained of his morning coffee into the cup.

Beckstrom's eyes lingered on the thermos. "I hope there isn't anything stronger than coffee in there."

Sam ignored the dig but Beckstrom carried it a notch further. "I know you think I'm still wet behind the ears, but from what I've heard, you're a drunken screw-up."

It wasn't possible that Beckstrom knew the full story behind Sam's fall from grace, but the rumors were out there. As much as Sam wanted to forget the past, there was always going to be someone around to remind him of how much he'd lost. It was his life now and he couldn't afford to be needled into doing something that would jeopardize his current assignment. With men like Phillip Beckstrom it was best to let them think they had the upper hand. It had proven to be a useful tactic over the years. "You've made your point," Sam said, donning a hard hat and retrieving the still-damp blueprints as he left.

When Sam arrived at the job site, he gathered Dutton, Patterson, and the rest of his crew together for a tailgate meeting. He told them to remove the dike as the lead engineer had ordered. After a moment or two of inevitable groaning and grousing, he added, "But I have a feeling that the removal's going to take a while. Probably another week or so."

He shrugged off the questioning looks from his men. "You know how it goes, fellas. Bulldozers break down, people get sick, parts go missing, and important things just have to be delayed." His meaning quickly sank in. He acknowledged the grins on the faces of his crew with a grin of his own. "Building a dam is like that sometimes."

CHAPTER FOUR

Reba watched the shuyapu stand in front of the Long House and stare at the faded yellow flag atop the structure. Most whites were unaware that the flag — hanging limp and flat in the windless afternoon — signaled a village in mourning and the temporary suspension of fishing at the falls for three days. This time it was in memory of Willie Two Bears but there'd been others in the past. Whites would be disappointed and sometimes angry when they realized that they'd come all the way to the village for nothing.

The sweet smell of arrow-wood and young salmon cooking over open fires hung in the smoky air and Reba was sure that the mouth-watering Noo-sak soup she tended was what turned the man's attention in her direction. She poked at the smoldering fire with her stick as she kept a careful eye on him. After a moment's hesitation, he began to lumber across the wide expanse of the village's communal area toward her fire.

He was the biggest white man she'd ever seen. Even from a distance she could see sweat dripping off the fleshy folds that framed his round, ruddy face. Willie Two Bears was fat, but he'd been comfortable in his skin. This man looked betrayed by his body. His gray business suit was thin and shiny in spots; not from overuse but by the extra effort it took to contain his heavy frame. His watermelon-gone-soft belly hung over his belt and jiggled with each labored step he took. Pausing midway in his trek, he loosened his tie and pulled a handkerchief from his jacket pocket. As he mopped the sweat from his brow, Reba studied his face for telling details. What she saw in the determined set of his jaw convinced her that this white man was neither angry nor disappointed. No, he was not pushing his bulk through the dusty heat of the village to watch men fish; he was here

44

for some other purpose.

Her experience with white men was limited but whatever reason had brought the big shuyapu here couldn't be good. She remembered with distaste the last time a man with the same determined look on his face came to their village. He called himself sheriff and spoke with a harsh tongue about her son. He accused Danny of doing bad things, destructive things, things that could get him locked up if he didn't stop.

She tightened the grip on her stick as the man reached her fire. "How do, ma'am," he said, wiping his blotchy red face and neck with the handkerchief again. He wasn't wearing a hat and his bald head was shiny and wet. She wondered what he would've done if he'd had a hat. She'd seen white men tip or remove their hats in the presence of a lady and believed the gesture was a form of respect.

Reba's guess was that this shuyapu didn't consider her a lady deserving of respect. At least not like any white lady. Did he even notice her clean denim blouse and skirt, the coin and feather earrings dangling from her pierced ears, or the double strand of beads around her neck? Was he aware of her tall, slender figure? Did he consider her young-looking for her thirty-eight years? Or did he see just another "old squaw" as the sheriff had called her? At least his eyes didn't linger on her breasts. Remembering how the sheriff's cold stare had made her feel, she pushed back a strand of her waist-length black hair and straightened her shoulders. She would not let herself be intimidated again. She raised her eyes to meet the shuyapu's and waited for him to state his business.

"Uh . . . my name's Hiram Potter, reporter for *The Dalles Chronicle*, and I'm looking for a Dan or uh . . ." He withdrew a small spiral notebook from his back pocket and thumbed through a couple of pages. "Let's see here . . . Danny. That's it. Danny Longstrand." He consulted his notebook again. "Or maybe it's Longstreet. Whatever," he said, flipping the notebook shut. "Do you know where I can find this boy?"

Reba knew Danny wouldn't have business with a white man but she was curious. What was a reporter for the town's only newspaper doing at Celilo? Why would he want to find her son? Had something happened? Was Danny in trouble again? Forcing herself to remain calm, she asked, "Why do you seek Danny?"

"These shoes are killing me," the man said, grimacing and shifting his weight from one foot to the other. "I missed the turnoff and then backtracked for several miles. I was running low on gas so I just decided to leave the car where it was and walk the rest of the way. Big mistake. I must've walked a hundred miles to get here."

It was a frequent problem for visitors. Celilo Village was not well marked with directional signs and it was easy to miss the turnoff. At forty-one acres, the village was larger than most people realized.

"I gotta sit down," he said, looking around for a place to perch. After settling on a nearby log, he removed his dust-covered shoes and rubbed his hand over the instep of each foot. "Ah, that's much better," he said. "Now, where were we?"

"You were about to tell me why you are looking for my son."

Potter stopped rubbing his feet. "Your son? The Longstreet kid is your son?"

Reba nodded. "But he won't talk to you."

"Maybe yes and maybe no." He gazed at her thoughtfully, tapping a pudgy finger against his ample chin. "You're here, though. I could talk to you."

Potter's reply confused her. Why would he want to talk to her? The reporter retrieved the notebook and pencil that he'd laid down by the log. Flipping to a blank page, he smiled through crooked teeth and said, "How'd you like a voice in the newspaper?"

"What do you mean?"

"It's called *quid pro quo*. I happen to know that the Wy-ams, and your Danny in particular, have been quite vocal in their opposition to the dam. You get your son to tell me about what happened at the falls yesterday and I'll include a blurb on the Wy-ams. He noted her confused stare. "You know, a write-up about why they won't agree to a monetary settlement with the government like the other tribes have. Or something along those lines." He consulted his notebook. "Do you know the Injun . . . uh, that is, the fellow who was killed?"

"Willie Two Bears."

"Yeah, that's the one. We heard the kid tried to rescue him from drowning."

"He failed."

Potter nodded. "Right. My editor thinks the rescue attempt would make for a good human interest story. Especially, he says, since Danny Longstreet is a known trouble maker."

His characterization of her son stung. It was true that Danny was impulsive and sometimes reckless, but wasn't that often the way of young people? He was a good boy with strong beliefs, especially about the dam, and wasn't shy about expressing himself. She realized that his actions could be interpreted differently by others, especially the whites, but that didn't make her any more receptive to hearing about it from this stranger. She was usually slow to anger but the shuyapu caused her to speak sharply. "What possible interest would that be to your readers?" Frowning, she added, "Your white readers."

Potter either missed the fire in her voice or was amused by it, for he laughingly said, "You know, I asked my editor that very question. He said our readers are interested in what happens to you folks out here at Celilo." He waved his hand toward the river. "Because of the falls being destroyed and all." His eyes took in the pot of soup brewing on the open fire as if seeing it for the first time. "I guess it's because your way of life is ending. Just like the South during the Civil War."

"I see," Reba said. Although she didn't know what he meant about the South, the war reference was clear enough. War changes everything. And so will the dam. She poked at the embers with her stick. Unlike her son, she accepted the dam as their new reality. No warrior could change that, not even Danny.

A fly buzzed around Potter's head. He swatted it away and said, "So we're agreed? If you or your son tells me what happened to this Willie Bears fellow, I'll write about your side of what building the dam means to your people."

"It's Willie Two Bears." Except for a couple of dogs and some children playing ball, the area was almost deserted. While Reba finished cooking soup for her family's evening meal, the other women who'd been tending salmon on drying racks had already left for home. Later they would slice and pulverize the dried salmon to be placed in large circular baskets lined with steelhead skins to keep for their sustenance during the long winter months. The reporter seemed to be waiting for her to say more. "I already said Danny won't talk to you."

"Yes, you did. But perhaps he'll change his mind when you explain to him how important a big article in *The Dalles Chronicle* would be to your cause. People ought to hear the Indians' side of things first hand, don't you think? Talking to me about how he tried to rescue his buddy could make that come about."

Reba weighed her options. She didn't trust the shuyapu but what he said made some sense. Maybe Danny could be persuaded to talk. His tactics so far hadn't converted any whites to their side. If anything, the stunts he'd pulled had done just the opposite. The sheriff made that point perfectly clear the last time he'd accused Danny of some foolish prank. She tried to think whether that was before or after he'd pulled up the government's survey sticks at the dam site and replanted them at a new housing development in town. "You think an article in your newspaper would really make a difference?" she asked.

Another fly landed on the reporter's bald head. He swatted the fly and said, "Absolutely, ma'am. People respect the written word."

Reba knew that was a lie and called him on it. "Like they respected the written treaty that gave us fishing rights at Celilo Falls for all time?"

Potter raised one eyebrow as if surprised by her frank response. "That was the government's doing," he said with a dismissive shrug. He wet the tip of his pencil with his tongue. "Now, let's get started. I'll need some background. Your name, how long you've lived here, stuff like that."

She shook her head, unwilling to tell this white man about herself. How long had she lived at Celilo? The years had passed so quickly; it was hard to believe she hadn't always lived in Oregon. She was a member of the Lakota tribe and had come west with her parents when she was still a young girl. How different life was then. The rivers and coastal streams abounded with salmon; fish weighing fifty and sixty pounds were common. Nowadays when one is caught that weighs thirty pounds, it's cause to celebrate. She didn't like to think about what would happen to the salmon runs when the dam was completed.

The reporter tried a different approach. "Okay, then. Could you tell me something about the Wy-ams?"

"We're called Wy-am-pums. It means people who have always heard the echoing waters of the Great Falls." Reba didn't explain further, but water was their life and their name reflected that. Like the Wascos or Was-co-pums, the last part of their name meant people. The Was-co-pums also fished at the falls and their name signified the people and their bowl. It referred to the place where they drew their water.

"That's good," Potter said. "Very good. Now we're getting somewhere. What about your husband? Was he fishing at the falls when that old guy fell in?"

Reba tugged on one of her earrings. Jimmy had given the jewelry to her the first year they were together as husband and wife. She remembered how they'd argued at first. They were both very young and headstrong. She'd been angry, accusing him of caring more about fish than her. He'd responded by telling her about the creation. "First," he said, "deep, thundering waters covered the earth. Then the Creator spoke. He brought huge rocks up out of the deep, raised high mountains between which cascading waters poured in a turbulent river—the Columbia. On the spray-drenched rocks the Creator placed his chosen people, the Wy-am-pums. To us he sent the Great Food— salmon—so we would never suffer hunger." Then Jimmy had cradled her in his arms and whispered, "The Creator gave me fish to fill my belly and you to fill my heart."

"My husband was killed many years ago."

"What was it? The falls again?"

Reba turned away from the reporter and gazed at the fire's dying embers. His presumptuous questions offended her. She wished he'd just leave.

"What's going on here?"

Reba whirled around at the sound of her son's voice. Danny stood with his arms folded across his chest. How handsome he looked, even in his wrathful pose. The reporter ignored Danny's hostile stance and stood upright, extending his hand in greeting. "Hello. I'm Hiram Potter, reporter for *The Dalles Chronicle*." Danny kept his arms folded.

Undeterred, Potter withdrew his hand and asked, "And you are?"

When several seconds passed and it became obvious Danny

wouldn't respond, Reba said, "My son."

Potter eyed Danny with new enthusiasm. "So, you're Danny. Just the person I wanted to talk to."

"I have nothing to say to you—or any reporter."

"Now, son, as I explained to your mother here, I'm prepared to write up your side of the dam issue for publication in our newspaper." He offered one of his crooked-tooth smiles. "Be mighty good publicity for you folks. And I must say, you're in need of some good publicity right about now."

Danny's dark eyes narrowed to mere slits. "First of all, I'm not your son. And second, there's no way your newspaper is going to publish anything about our cause. Except to discredit us."

Potter held his right palm in the air as if taking an oath. "I swear to you. If you let me interview you, I'll print every word you say about why your people are opposed to the dam. Trust me."

Danny snorted. "Trust!" Here's what I know about trust: a hundred years ago, your government signed a treaty giving us fishing rights here. Forever. But they conveniently ignored that pledge and began building a dam across the river. It will flood the falls out of existence when it's completed and then it's good-by fishing rights."

Potter shrugged. "We need the water for power. Electricity, you know. It's called progress."

"It's called betrayal."

"That's a harsh word."

"But accurate. Maybe you're right, though. Do you like inconsistent better?"

Potter jotted some notes on his pad and then said, "You're losing me, pal."

"For the record, I'm not your pal, buddy, or friend. You claim you want to report why our people are opposed to the dam. Fine. Let me spell out the facts so even you can understand: your country, the good ol' U. S. of A., sets itself up as a model of democracy. It spends billions of dollars to help other nations, nations they owe no obligation to, while a people—whose country they seized by force of arms, incidentally—are not only refused help but have the very treaty obligating the help overturned."

Danny's speech brought an approving smile to Reba's lips, but

50

Potter was not impressed. "Wait a minute, here!" he said, waving his notebook. "Wait just a doggone minute. The government has offered help to your people, and your chief refused. The Warm Springs are going to get over four thousand dollars, the Umatillas a like amount. Why, I happen to know for a fact that the Nez Perce tribe will get almost three million dollars. That sounds like mighty good help to me."

"Chief Thompson refuses to sign our salmon away for money."

"Well, there you go," Potter said. "Let's talk about the rescue attempt for a moment. I understand you were on Chief's Island when the accident happened."

"Mother, I believe that fire is out now. Let's take our supper and go home." To Potter he said, "Don't forget your shoes when you leave. Our people could make effective use of fine leather like that."

"Huh?"

Danny smiled without warmth. "You know, to craft a pouch to hold all that money the government has promised us."

"Damn savages," Potter muttered as Reba and Danny left. "I knew this stupid assignment wasn't going to work." Bending over with some difficulty, he picked up his shoes and rubbed the dust off with his sweat-stained handkerchief, "Hold their money, indeed!"

CHAPTER FIVE

"I'm telling you, kid, selling houses is as easy as farting. Alls you gotta do is point the client in the right direction and let 'er rip."

Nick laughed before he realized Tony wasn't cracking a joke.

"I'm serious as a heart attack," Tony said, elbowing his cousin. "Pay attention to what I say and do and you'll learn a lesson you can take straight to the bank every time."

"Got it," Nick said quickly. "Watch and learn."

When Uncle Sol sent Nick to The Dalles he'd ordered Tony to show his cousin the ropes. "Learn him something useful," their uncle had said, "something that counts." At Nick's age, Tony had already figured out what it took to succeed and went after it. Claiming this gangly no-nothing as kin was an embarrassment. But he had to give the guy credit. Nick was eager—and if anyone could teach him a thing or two about sales, it was Tony Rossi. He'd been a top used car salesman in Portland when Uncle Sol tapped him to run the branch office of his realty business. He could sell warts off a bullfrog and the two years that he'd been selling homes in The Dalles proved it.

Rossi Realty had originally housed a one-man law firm specializing in estate planning before Tony's uncle leased the space. The facility came furnished with desks, office equipment, fully stocked supply room, and a spacious reception area for clients. All items of significant value—oil paintings, Persian rugs, leather furniture, and Tiffany chandelier and lamps—had been confiscated when the lawyer was arrested for bilking several of his elderly clients out of their life savings. The scandalous circumstances surrounding the lawyer's downfall had adversely affected the owner's ability to attract a new tenant. The property had been languishing on the market for several months when Uncle Sol—always one to spot an opportunity—approached the owner. Despite negotiating a drastic below market rate for the lease, Uncle Sol refused Tony's pleas to duplicate the lawyer's opulent décor. "You're supposed to sell houses," he snapped, "not impress people with a goddamn fancy office." As a result, Rossi Realty had a strictly utilitarian look.

The temperature had reached 98 degrees earlier in the day and the office still felt like a pressure cooker when Tony and Nick walked in at five o'clock. The realty's part-time salesmen—Hoffman and Jensen—were nowhere in sight but Mildred was still on duty. She wasn't much of a secretary. Her typing was of the hunt and peck variety and her shorthand was even worse. She never talked about her personal life, but it was common knowledge that her former husband was a mean drunk who'd used her as a punching bag for years. Tony figured there was more to her story but he wasn't interested in her dirty linen and never asked. "I gave her more than a job," Tony had told Nick when he asked why he'd hired her. When her husband's booze-damaged liver finally did him in, Mildred's self-esteem was as non-existent as her bank account. "I gave her a second chance at life and, believe me, that kind of gratitude is worth ten times more than what crackerjack typing and shorthand will ever get you."

Mildred had dimmed the overhead lights and drawn the shades in a futile attempt to cool things off. Tony paused at the door to loosen his tie and starched collar. He'd already shed his suit jacket and would've done the same with his sweat-drenched shirt if he had another shirt handy. The summer was just beginning and it was already too hot for comfort. Tony decided it was time he stashed a change of clothes at the office. Despite the stifling heat, he whistled a cheerful tune, doffed his Stetson and sent it sailing across the room where it made a perfect landing on the top peg of the coat rack. "Tony scores again," he said. "How're you doin' Miss Millie?"

She looked like a wilted dandelion but Mildred never complained. She slipped a protective cover on her Remington typewriter and beamed at Tony. "Good, boss. Really good."

"You're a trooper," he said. "Where're Hoffman and Jensen?" The two part-time salesmen were hardly ever around. They took the term *part-time* to mean *as little work as possible*.

"Knocked off early. Too hot, they said."

"Ha! When it's hot, I get hotter. Ain't that right, cousin?"

"Absolutely," said Nick.

Tony took a folder from his briefcase and slid it across Mildred's desk. "Here, Millie, take a gander at this."

She opened the folder and scanned the sales agreement tucked inside. "No wonder you're in such a great mood. That wraps up the Dry Hollow sub-division, doesn't it?"

Tony sat down in his desk chair, leaned back and stretched. "Yep," he said. "It's all sold out."

"Who's the buyer?"

"Same as Hillcrest. A government man like Sam Matthews. Typical dam workers, the both of 'em. All muscles and no brains."

"Well," said Mildred, "this calls for a celebration." She opened her desk drawer and retrieved a bottle of Jack Daniels and two whiskey glasses. She poured healthy shots into both glasses. When Nick reached for a glass, she snatched it away. "Hold it, buster. You're a little young for the hard stuff."

"Aw, Millie," Tony said. "Give the guy a break. It's been a long and stinkin' hot day."

She rummaged around in her desk and found another glass which she filled for Nick. "To Dry Hollow and Hillcrest," she said.

Tony lifted his glass. "To the U. S. Government. My favorite cash cow."

"Hear, hear," Mildred said.

Nick saluted Tony. "To the master salesman."

A moment or two of silent drinking passed until Tony rubbed his finger along the rim of his glass. "I've been thinking . . ."

"Uh, oh, Nick," Mildred teased. "Sounds like trouble's coming our way."

"Can it, will ya?" Tony said, tossing her a sharp look. "I'm thinking we should get a little gift for Matthews and his daughter. You know, sort of a thank-you for buying the Cherry Blossom house. For wrapping up Hillcrest."

Mildred's frizzy eyebrows shot up. "That'd be a first."

"So, what? I'm not talking big bucks here. Besides, we can put it on the expense account."

"What about Dry Hollow? You want a gift for that buyer, too?"

"Naw," he said. "Just Matthews and his daughter."

Mildred looked a little befuddled but, as Tony expected, she said that whatever he wanted was fine by her. The surprisingly perceptive smirk on Nick's face, though, gave him pause. "On second thought," Tony said, backtracking quickly, "let's get something for both families."

"Your uncle is going to love that."

"Who the hell cares?" Tony growled. He gulped down his drink and then wiped his mouth with the back of his hand.

"Speaking of Uncle Sol, he called while you were out. Twice."

"Like I said, who cares?"

"Okay, but he wants you to call him." She dipped a shoulder at Nick who had finished his drink and was idly flipping through the pages of a magazine. "Maybe he wants to check up on young cousin here."

"Then let him call young cousin," Tony said. "Any other calls?"

Mildred handed him a thick stack of pink message slips and a sealed envelope. "The envelope is from Sheriff Pritchard. The money he got back from the Indian the other day is inside. The messages you can see for yourself."

"It's about time Pritchard returned my dough," Tony said. He tossed the envelope to Nick and told him to count the cash. Noting his cousin's questioning look, he added, "I don't care if he *is* sheriff. I don't trust that loser." Tony quickly thumbed through a few of the messages before pushing the stack aside, scattering the notes across his desk and onto the floor. "Anything in all this mess that's important?"

"Your sweetie, Clarice, called four times. Says if you don't call her back she's going to parade down Front Street in the nude until you do."

"Ha! That'd be a sight. Better not call her."

"You'll have to deal with her sooner or later, boss. Her hubby's been sniffing around the office quite a bit lately." It was no secret that Mildred didn't like Clarice, but Tony dismissed her concerns as simple jealousy. He knew she was right, though, about Clarice's husband.

"Yeah, I hear ya," Tony said, eying his empty shot glass. "He's one man I need on my side right now." Noticing that Nick had finished counting the cash, he reached across the desk and grabbed the envelope from him. "All there?"

"Yep."

Tony tucked the envelope in his back pocket. "Here's another lesson for you, kid: don't be screwing your banker's wife when you've got an important deal cooking."

Nick sat upright in his chair. "I understand," he said, assuming a sober and attentive look. "No screwing."

"Jesus, lighten up. I was only joking." He turned to Mildred. "Forget Uncle Sol and Clarice. Did I get any calls of import?"

"Just Stan Feldman. He wants to meet with you later today about the bluff property."

Tony slammed his fist onto the desk. "Damn it all, woman! Why'd you wait so long to tell me?"

Mildred flinched as if he'd struck her. "Sorry, boss," she said, hanging her head. "It won't happen again."

"See that it don't," Tony said. He believed her apology was genuine. After all, she lived to please him and the fact that she'd upset him couldn't help but distress her greatly. He reined in his anger and spoke in a gentler, conciliatory tone, "Why don't you head on out now," he said. "Nick and I will lock up."

"Thanks," she said, offering him a grateful smile. She pointed to the half empty whiskey bottle. "Do you want me to leave this out for you?"

"Yeah. Probably be here a while." He paused with his hand on the telephone receiver. "Millie?"

"Yes, boss."

"Be sure and get those welcome gifts that we talked about."

"What did you have in mind?"

Tony rubbed his chin a moment. "Hell, I don't know. Something nice. He shot a quick glance at Nick. "Something nice for both families. You can start with the Matthews girl."

"O-kaa-y" Mildred drawled. "What can you tell me about her? How old is she? Any hobbies or special interests?"

"Come on," he snapped. "It's not all that complicated. She's just a teenage girl."

Mildred looked at Nick. "Then maybe you should pick out a gift for her."

"M-m-me?" he stuttered.

"Why not? You're a teenager. You'd know what the kids like these days better than I would."

"Look," Tony said. "Forget I even mentioned it. Just forget the whole damned thing."

***

The meeting with Stan Feldman was set for eight o'clock that evening at the Carlton Hotel. Built in 1921 as a get-away spot for Portland's country club set, the hotel was located twenty-five miles west of The Dalles on a high cliff overlooking the Columbia River. The hotel offered luxurious accommodations, exquisite dining, and a spectacular setting, but it was the Carlton's reputation for privacy that made it a favorite spot for sensitive business dealings. Tony had reluctantly agreed to let Nick sit in on the meeting. "You'll need to keep your trap shut. Feldman's a real prick but I know exactly how to handle him and I don't want you getting in my way."

"Sure thing, Tony."

"Tonight, you'll see what the art of finessing a deal is all about."

The ornate décor inside the hotel lobby oozed money—from the fine leather furniture and black marble flooring to the brilliant crystal chandelier overhead. When Nick paused to look around, Tony cuffed him on the shoulder. "Stop gawking like a damn rube, will ya? You're embarrassing me."

Since they had time before Feldman showed up, Tony decided they should get some dinner. "Try to act like you belong here," he cautioned before entering the dining room. A tall, elegant blonde hostess ushered them to a corner booth. When she leaned over to hand them the menus, her ample breasts strained the flimsy fabric of her low-cut gown. Nick averted his eyes but Tony leered openly. "Dining at the Carlton is a true feast," he said, winking.

"Bon appetite," she purred.

Tony sighed as he watched her walk away, hips swaying

suggestively. But the woman's overt sexuality didn't stir him half as much as Ellie Matthews' coltish come-ons. He couldn't stop thinking about her, even when he was with Clarice.

"What're you going to order?" asked Nick, scanning the menu.

His cousin had barely registered the hostess. What seventeen-year-old guy doesn't notice tits and an ass like hers? Their uncle had it all wrong. Tony should be teaching Nick how to seduce a woman. Now that's salesmanship the kid could really use. "Jesus, who cares what we eat? It's all good."

Later, after their drinks had been ordered, Nick asked whether Stan Feldman was a client of Tony's.

Tony snorted. "More the other way around."

"You're buying property from him?"

Tony nodded. "The Baker Bluff deal's been cooking for months and I think it's finally going to go through." He shifted in the booth to cross his legs. "But we still have a few kinks to work out."

"So that's why he wanted the meeting tonight? To work out the kinks?"

Tony eyed Nick over the menu. "What's with all the questions?"

Nick shrugged his bony shoulders. "I'm interested, that's all."

Tony tossed the menu aside as their drinks arrived. "Fine, but don't go asking a lot of questions when Feldman gets here. Him and me still have some talking to do. The deal ain't over yet."

Tony sipped his martini quietly for a few moments. "You know," he said, "two years ago, I'd never even heard of The Dalles. When Uncle Sol told me he wanted to open a branch office here, I said to him, 'The Dalles? What kind of name is that?' The old fart snapped back, 'A name that's going to make us very rich, that's what kind.'"

"And has it? Made you rich, I mean?"

Tony popped an olive in his mouth. "Listen," he said as he munched, "when I got to town I couldn't believe how bad it was. Nothing but cherry pickers and fish flingers everywhere I looked. And the wind! It came howling through the gorge, whirling dust from the orchards until everything you owned was covered with it. Unbelievably cold in the winter—and as you've seen so far—hot as Hades in the summer. If that didn't get you there was always the stench from Seufert's fish cannery. It clung to your clothes like a whore's cheap perfume and no amount of soap could wash it out."

Tony signaled their waiter for another round. "By nine o'clock at night the town might as well have rolled up the streets because nobody—I'm talking not even an Injun or Chink—was out and about."

"Considering everything, though, you've done pretty well here. Haven't you?"

"I have to say one thing about our uncle. He was on the mark about The Dalles becoming a boom town. When I opened the doors of Rossi Realty, the influx of government workers arriving to work on the dam had already begun. I sold two houses the first day and it's been smooth sailing ever since."

"Then Uncle Sol's prediction has come true. You're very rich now."

"You believe that, kid, and you're as stupid as Sam Matthews and all the rest of them government types."

When the waiter brought his second martini, Tony took a couple of sips before continuing. "Let's get something straight right now. There ain't nobody getting rich here except Uncle Sol. I do all the work and he gets all the dough. He's never even set foot in this God-forsaken town. Leased the office space sight unseen. I mail the checks to him at the first of every month and if I'm so much as a day late, our greedy old uncle is on the phone to complain."

"Is that why he's always calling?"

Tony's fingers tightened around the glass stem. "Hell, yes! And to tell me how to run things like I'm his stupid little puppet." He shook his head. "But all that's about to change."

"Oh? How's that?"

"Baker Bluff."

"What do you mean?"

"Later," Tony said, "Here comes the waiter with our dinner."

When they'd finished eating and were drinking after-dinner coffees, Nick steered the conversation back to Tony's deal with Feldman. "This property that you're buying, does Uncle Sol know about it?"

Tony choked, spraying coffee onto the white linen tablecloth. "Of course, he doesn't know about—"

"Hey, Antonio, my man!"

Tony groaned as he spotted the person who'd hailed him.

"Who's that?" asked Nick tracking his cousin's gaze.

"A certified idiot I used to work with in Portland." Tony threw his linen napkin onto the table. "Shit! Harvey Greenberg is the last person I need to run into right now."

Greenberg strode purposefully to their table and, without waiting for an invite, slid his wiry frame into their booth. He ignored Nick as he greeted Tony, "What the hell are you doing at the Carlton, old boy? Last I heard, your uncle got a bug up his ass and shipped you off to the boonies. How're you doing?"

"Fine, fine," Tony said, making a show of consulting his watch. "Say, Harv, I'd like to chat about old times, but I've got an important meeting in a few minutes."

Greenberg waved to a waiter hovering nearby and ordered a gin and tonic. "Why do you think I'm here? Got an important meeting of my own," he said, launching into a story about the deal he had in the works.

Tony's attention wandered until he spotted Feldman standing next to the hostess station, scanning the room. "You're gonna have to stop jaw-boning now," Tony said. "My appointment has just arrived."

Greenberg half-twisted in his seat to look at the man signaling Tony. "You're meeting with Stan Feldman?"

"Yeah, so what?"

"You better watch that guy, Tony. I heard he was trying to dump some property the government has been looking at."

Tony searched Greenberg's narrow face. "*What* property?"

"Not sure," he said, taking a quick sip of his drink. "Something to do with the Indians and a cemetery."

"*Cemetery?*"

"I'm a little fuzzy on the particulars. Hell, I could be all wrong, but I'd watch my backside just the same." He took his drink and slid out of the booth. "Nice seeing you again, Rossi. And good luck with Feldman." A snide smile played at the corner of his mouth. "You're gonna need it."

CHAPTER SIX

"Hello?" Clarice's voice sounded raspy when she answered the phone.

"I need to see you," pleaded Tony.

"Who is this?"

"Don't tease. I'm not in the mood."

"Where are you?"

"Where do you think? Monty's."

"Goddamn it, Tony. I've called you half a dozen times lately and I've never heard back."

"You're hearing from me now."

"It's after midnight! You're lucky Warren's a sound sleeper."

"Are you coming or not?"

"You don't sound so good. What's wrong?"

Tony snickered. "Nothing that a little pussy couldn't cure."

"Is that any way to sweet talk a girl"

"I thought you liked it rude and crude."

Her laugh was soft and low. "And rough. Don't forget rough."

"Oh, baby, you're killing me."

"Good. You deserve to suffer a little."

"Clarice?"

"What?"

"Please."

"Give me fifteen minutes."

Monty's Motel was a run-down excuse for lodging on the outskirts of town. Tony and Clarice found the raunchy atmosphere titillating; but most important, the location afforded their clandestine coupling a modicum of secrecy. The owner was an out-of-town slumlord who didn't care about the property's upkeep or what went on in its rooms. The on-site manager didn't care either, so long as he got paid "a little something" for looking the other way about what happened on the premises.

After he hung up the phone, Tony lit a cigarette with trembling hands. He had a headache and his gut felt like he'd been sucker punched. All thanks to Harvey Greenberg. With his so-called warning about Stan Feldman, the meeting had been jinxed before it even got started. *Injuns and cemeteries! Who knew what the hell Greenberg meant by that? He probably didn't even know himself. Nothing had changed since they worked together in Portland. Greenberg would cheat his grandmother out of her last dime if he thought he could get away with it. It would be just like him to start a rumor for his own benefit. Still . . .*

Tony eyed the nearly empty Jack Daniels bottle on the battered nightstand. He'd felt so lousy after the meeting ended at the Carlton that he'd dumped Nick at his apartment, rescued the bottle from Mildred's desk, and headed for Baker Bluff. The sun had set by the time he'd arrived, but there was a full moon and enough light to appreciate the view of the river. Tony had thought the sight would calm his jangled nerves, but it had the opposite effect. All he could think about was how his dream was starting to look more like a nightmare. He'd stayed at the bluff for a couple of hours, drinking and trying to talk himself out of his dark mood. When it finally became apparent that he was feeling worse, not better, his thoughts turned to Clarice and he drove straight to Monty's.

Tony and Clarice had a standing reservation for Room Six and met there at least once a week or oftener if Clarice could get away without her husband knowing. Warren was a sharp banker but without a clue when it came to his wife's sexual needs, which were considerable. He was on the downhill side of fifty with a gaunt and sickly look that caused small children to stare and old ladies to offer him a good home-cooked meal. He'd lost the ability to do much more than a little cuddling and groping every Saturday night. Clarice found it frustrating but tolerable—so long as he continued to lavish her with jewelry and kept her checking account substantially funded. Her appetite for shopping was as insatiable as her sex drive.

Tony had never given Warren much thought until the banker had become vital to the plans involving Baker Bluff. Fooling around with

Clarice had been all fun and games until then. Money had upped the risk considerably and Tony wondered, not for the first time, if old Warren had finally gotten the picture. Hadn't Mildred said he'd been popping by the office a lot lately? Not that Tony was worried. *If I can't deal with someone like Warren, I might as well cash in my chips and call it a day.*

He gazed hungrily at the nearly empty whiskey bottle and lit another cigarette. He'd already had far too much booze but the urge for more was as strong as his need for Clarice. At thirty-six, Clarice Nestor was the oldest woman Tony had ever bedded but she was also the hottest. And the only female he didn't have to slap around from time to time. He'd met her at a fancy charity event at the local country club soon after he'd hit town. Ordinarily, he would've avoided such a function like the plague, but he was trying to establish himself back then and needed to be seen out and about in all the right places. He was bored out of his skull and itching to leave, which he planned to do as soon as he'd shaken enough hands and distributed enough business cards.

A beautiful woman hardly ever escaped Tony's radar, but he hadn't noticed Clarice until he approached her table to introduce himself. She was with a group of the town's most prominent leaders and looked as bored as Tony felt. She was fashionably dressed in sparkling diamonds at her neck and wrists but seemed out of place among the other women at the table. While nicely attired themselves, they were the type of matrons you'd expect to see married to a bunch of mucky-mucks. In contrast, the bottle-blonde Clarice Nestor was a dressed-up tart with luscious tits who'd apparently landed herself a sugar daddy.

Tony got the impression from the way Clarice smiled at him that his arrival had caught her interest. She'd certainly caught his. After he'd introduced himself to everyone, the orchestra struck up "The Autumn Waltz" by Tony Bennett, and Clarice started swaying to the beat. Tony took the hint. "May I have the honor of dancing with your lovely wife?" he asked Warren Nestor. Warren was deep in conversation with the editor of the local newspaper and oblivious to the spark that had just ignited between Tony and his wife. He waved them off without a word. Tony led Clarice to the dance floor and forgot all about leaving early.

Tony soon realized that his affair with Clarice was more than just sexual. She was a lot smarter than she appeared. He'd come to depend on her for advice and while he appreciated her insights and contacts, he sometimes felt that she had too much control in their relationship. He had to give her credit, though. She'd managed to set herself up as an independent real estate appraiser and had hatched a sure-fire money-making scam for them. A little control wasn't always a bad thing.

It'd been her idea to buy the Baker Bluff property. Tony had long dreamed of opening a big-time luxury resort complex that would rival the Carlton Hotel in amenities, prestige, and popularity. Clarice had dreams of her own. An able singer, she'd always wanted to pursue a musical career. They'd been just dreams until the bluff property came on the market. Its location overlooking the Columbia River was perfect for what they envisioned for themselves. Yes, Baker Bluff was perfect. The perfect ticket out of Uncle Sol's greedy grasp.

Clarice introduced Tony to Stan Feldman and the negotiations began in earnest. The asking price was an outrageous sum but doable with Clarice's help. She'd arranged for the loan that was needed to finalize the sale by convincing Warren that it was a good deal for the bank. Tony had set aside several thousand for the down payment which came by way of skimming Uncle Sol's share of the realty business.

Convincing Mildred to "cook the books" in his favor had been easy enough, but keeping his uncle in the dark took some fancy footwork. Uncle Sol had a good nose for business and it was especially good at sniffing out monkey business. Tony had to get this deal finalized before Uncle Sol figured out what was really going on with his cash flow. When construction of the resort began, the sums needed could escalate into the six-figure range. As usual, Clarice assured him that that was doable as well. After all, she reminded him often enough, she'd set up the profitable Destiny Group scam for them. Tony had no doubt she was capable of just about anything when it came to money. That was before Greenberg showed up. Now everything suddenly seemed in jeopardy.

Man, oh man, what a mess. The whole enterprise was fast becoming

64

a disaster and he didn't know what to do about it. What he did know was that he needed another drink. He finished his cigarette and reached for the Jack Daniels. His hands were still trembling as he unscrewed the cap and sucked the last drops of liquor from the bottle. With a belch, he fell backwards onto the bed and passed out.

****

When Clarice opened the motel room door, she surveyed the scene and shook her head. Tony had shed everything except his boxer shorts and lay sprawled on his back, legs and arms akimbo, snoring loudly. His clothes were scattered about the room like toys carelessly left behind for mommy to pick up. Clarice was no mommy and Tony was a big boy who could pick up after himself. The cramped room and its shabby furnishings reeked of alcohol and cigarettes. The stale air was oppressive, as if broken promises and despair had used up all the oxygen in the room. Clarice quickly opened a window and inhaled deeply. Although it was after midnight, the temperature hadn't dropped below 80 degrees. Still, the fresh air had a cleansing effect on their love nest.

After chucking the empty liquor bottle in the wastebasket, she slipped out of her sandals and sundress. She sat down on the lumpy bed next to Tony and removed her lacy lingerie. Leaning close to his ear she whispered, "Wake up, Romeo. It's pussy time." When Tony didn't stir, she gently pulled his shorts down to his knees and stroked his flaccid penis. Tony moaned and shifted slightly, but despite her efforts, failed to awaken. "Okay, Rip Van Winkle," she said, re-positioning herself, "it's on to Plan B." This time she took him in her mouth.

"Oh, baby, Tony murmured. "That feels so-o-o good."

Clarice stopped and said, "It might feel good, but nothing much is happening."

Tony propped himself on his elbows, looked at her a moment, and then fell back onto the bed. "I'm drunk."

"No foolin'," she said, sitting upright. "What happened today? I haven't seen you this bad in a long time."

Tony moaned and covered his eyes with a forearm. "Turn out the light, will ya? I've got a raging headache."

"You need some coffee."

"No, I need you." He patted the bed. "Lay down with me."

Clarice frowned. "What for? You're too drunk to get it up and it's late." She snatched her bra off the nightstand. "I didn't come all the way over here for the same useless dangle I get with Warren."

Tony struggled to a sitting position again, made a grab for her bra and missed. "Leave it off," he slurred as he encircled her in a clumsy embrace and tried to fondle her exposed breasts.

Clarice twisted away from him. "Don't."

"Listen, baby, I need you. I met with Feldman at the Carlton tonight and the deal ain't looking so good."

Her brown eyes narrowed. "I thought the negotiations were almost over."

"Yeah, I did, too. So far, the give and take has been predictable: he jacks up the asking price, we counter, and then he's back with another offer, and on it goes."

"Right," she said, "but I told you he was manageable if given enough time."

"The thing is, he's suddenly anxious to sell at our original, low-ball offer. In fact, he had the papers all prepared and ready for our signature. He hinted that he'd lower the price even further, if necessary."

"That sounds terrific. So, what's the problem?"

Tony rubbed his aching temples and told her about his chance encounter with Harvey Greenberg. "He ruined the meeting with a mysterious rumor about the Injuns and some property that Feldman owns. Every time I looked up, there was Greenberg smiling at me from across the room like the smug-faced Mona Lisa. He got me so rattled that I stalled Feldman and said I'd have to think about his new offer."

"How'd he take that?"

"He said I was putting him in a tight spot and that he couldn't hold the property for us much longer—especially at that price. Supposedly he has other buyers waiting."

"I doubt that."

Tony thought a moment and then asked, "You know why the government is gonna move the Injuns' burial grounds, don't you?"

"Of course. They're located on those islands right in the middle of the river. As soon as the dam is finished and the flood gates are opened, goodbye bones." She shrugged. "What has that got to do with the Baker deal?"

"I may be drunk, but it's obvious even to me. I think the real reason Feldman is so all-fired anxious to meet our offer now is that he's got wind of where the government plans to relocate the Injuns' cemetery."

"Baker Bluff?"

"Bingo. And if the government exercises their right of imminent domain, he won't get as much money as we're offering."

Clarice said, "I can find out if that's really what the government has in mind for the property. But even if it's true, that shouldn't be a problem."

Tony threw both hands in the air. "No problem? There go all our plans. No big resort, no lounge act, no life of luxury, no nothing. Just a bunch of old bones."

Clarice gently cuffed his bare shoulder. "Stop with the gloom and doom. You sound like a nervous old lady."

"Why the hell shouldn't I be nervous? I've worked my butt off for over two years now, squirreling away whatever cash I could get my hands on, and for what? Just when I think financial freedom is within my grasp the damn Injuns spoil it for me."

"No, Tony. We'll spoil it for them."

"I'm dead serious and you're talking nonsense," he said, rolling to the edge of the bed. He stumbled to his feet, pulled up his shorts and scanned the room. "Goddamn it, where'd my pants go?"

Before he had a chance to begin hunting and gathering, Clarice scooted off the bed and grabbed him by the arm. Tony started to resist until she pressed her naked body against him in a tight embrace. "I'm serious, too," she said, releasing him slightly and slowly walking her fingers up his chest. When she reached his neck, she wrapped her arms about him and thrust her hips forward in a grinding motion against his crotch.

"Jesus," he murmured. As she nestled her head on his shoulder, he closed his eyes and held onto her ass with both hands. Thus embraced, they began a slow and undulating dance in place. Tony may have been drunk and angry but her naked body pressed against him had a calming effect. Calmness quickly turned to arousal. When her ministrations had accomplished the desired result, she led him back to the bed and they lay down together.

Their lovemaking, while brief, was uncharacteristically tender. Clarice kissed him repeatedly and even caressed his still aching head. It was a comforting gesture that surprised and pleased Tony. For the first time, he considered whether he might be falling in love with this woman. But it was just a fleeting thought, easily dismissed. *What do I know about love? It was a Jack Daniels fuck and nothing more.*

As they shared a post-coital cigarette, Clarice asked, "Tell me, Tony, what do Indians fear as much as the dam destroying their fishing grounds?"

"I don't know. Running out of beer?"

She laughed. "No, silly, they fear the desecration of their ancestral burial grounds."

"Dese-what? Speak English, woman."

"Desecration. Mutilation. Making their cemetery unusable."

"You've lost me, babe."

"That's okay. Just follow my lead and the Baker Bluff deal will go through without a hitch."

Tony had no idea what Clarice had in mind, but it didn't matter. He could always depend on her to fix things. Nude or fully dressed, he'd follow this woman anywhere. But nude was always better. As he snuggled against her, he congratulated himself once again for having had the smarts to hook up with such a clever dame.

CHAPTER SEVEN

The Mayflower van had been parked across the street for a couple of hours but Dessa still hadn't caught sight of the new neighbors. Thanks to her mother, almost everyone living in Hillcrest had heard about Mr. Sam Matthews and his teenage daughter long before their arrival. Maureen Feldman worked part-time at Pacific Savings and Loan and had met Mr. Matthews when he came in to sign the loan papers for his house. The day after his appearance at the bank, Maureen hosted the monthly meeting of Petal Pushers—a neighborhood gardening club—and let it intentionally slip that she had first-hand information about their newest residents-to-be. Although dedicated to learning about native flowering plants, the ladies-only members were quite willing (eager, in fact) to table the scheduled discussion about cultivating roses to hear what Maureen knew, especially when she said there was no Mrs. Matthews. Delighted to take center stage, Maureen drew out the suspense by serving coffee and cake before launching into a description of the handsome widower who'd soon be living amongst them.

Dessa made it a practice to hang around the house whenever her mother hosted the garden club. Most of the time the topic of conversation was beyond boring—she couldn't care less about growing dahlias, rhododendrons, azaleas or any other flower-related discussion. But sometimes the ladies proved to be a valuable source of items that she could publish in *Heard on the Hill*, a neighborhood newsletter that Dessa had started last spring.

Originally, the one-page newsletter was a school project, but demand had proven so great that she upped the price from a nickel a copy to a dime and continued publishing it during the summer. It was a laborious process since she had no printing press and had to rely on an old Smith-Corona that she'd rescued from the trash bin. It came equipped with sticky keys and even worse, required a ton of carbon paper and retyping to duplicate each issue. Consequently, her "print run" was limited and usually ended when she got tired of typing. She figured she spent more of her allowance on paper than she made selling the newsletter, but that wasn't the point; Dessa loved being in the know.

She had discovered that people liked to see their names in print and it wasn't too difficult to get them to talk about themselves. The fun part for Dessa was when they dropped interesting tidbits about others in the neighborhood. Then Dessa had to use her editorial judgment as to just how much she could publish without getting into trouble. The best stuff, unfortunately, never made the cut, but she had noticed that sales doubled whenever she included anything even remotely bordering on gossip. It was a fine line she walked as editor and sales manager.

She had listened intently as her mother described Mr. Matthews in gushing terms but she'd said little about his daughter other than mentioning in passing that she was fourteen. Now that father and daughter were finally moving in, Dessa was eager to get a look at them for herself. Just not for the reason her mother had hoped. Dessa didn't have many friends, which bothered Maureen Feldman more than it did her. Her mother was an unabashed social climber and Dessa's lack of interest in bolstering her own popularity was a constant source of friction between them. Dessa shared her mother's fiery red hair and green eyes, but resembled her short, bony father in every other physical attribute that counted. And as her mother frequently pointed out, she had inherited her father's stubborn, opinionated personality.

It was bad enough that Dessa didn't try to make friends with kids who lived at Hillcrest, but her refusal to swim or play tennis at the country club where she could meet the "right" kind of girls—meaning the daughters of the town's most influential and wealthiest families—was particularly vexing to Maureen. "Wasting time writing a silly gossip sheet is never going to help you socially, Odessa." She had no desire to imitate her mother's embarrassing efforts to win approval from the country club set, especially since the Feldmans weren't even full-fledged members due to the "No Jews Allowed" clause in the club's by-laws.

Although neither parent would admit it, Dessa believed that their family's provisional membership was granted solely because the board members counted on Stanley Feldman's extensive and lucrative business dealings to fund their own projects. His substantial donation to the construction of a lavish new clubhouse next to the golf course was an additional inducement. Dessa considered herself more aligned with her mother's Irish Catholic roots than her father's Jewish heritage but it didn't matter. The family didn't attend church or synagogue or observe any religious traditions or practices unless going to Bingo night with her grandmother at St. Peter's counted. In any case, Dessa was sensitive to discrimination and her parent's so-called country club membership bugged the heck out of her. "I'd rather die than suck up to those snobby, anti-Semitic hypocrites like you do," she told her mother. Maureen's response was always the same, "Your looks aren't going to get you anywhere in life, young lady, so you had better stop being such a stubborn smart-ass and figure out how to fit in." So far, the only thing Dessa had figured out was that writing was what she wanted to do in life—and it didn't require either good looks or the ability to fit in. In fact, she told herself, a smart-ass attitude might even help. It certainly hadn't hindered sales for *Heard on the Hill* whenever she slipped in a snide remark or two in an article.

As she peeked out her bedroom window for the hundredth time, she saw that the Mayflower movers had stopped their labors to take a smoke break. They'd had several other breaks since their arrival, which was mostly due to the interruptions caused by a steady stream of neighbor ladies dropping off "welcome to the neighborhood" goodies. Now that the dust had settled a bit, Dessa decided to use the lull in activity to meet the newcomers. Since Mr. Matthews was old news by now, she hoped to learn something about his daughter that she could include in the next edition of the newsletter. Dessa had no illusions about developing any kind of friendship with her, especially since her mother had pushed the idea. "This is the perfect time to make friends with her, Odessa." The unstated sentiment was that Ellie was too new to know about Dessa's unpopular reputation with the teenage crowd.

As she crossed the street, she overheard the movers talking. When it became apparent the three men were talking about Ellie, she stopped alongside the truck's rear wheel well to listen.

"How old do you think she is?"

"Ha! You're talking serious jailbait, my friend. Serious."

"Man, oh man, ain't that the truth? She's a looker, though."

"Shit. If I had some of that tail, I'd be a non-stop pokin' machine."

A burst of laughter followed the coarse remark. Wow, thought Dessa. That's the kind of exchange she wished she could print. The quote would sell out the newsletter in a flash. One of the men shushed the others. "Hey, cool it," he said. "Dollface just came outside." They ground out their cigarettes and resumed working. As they began to wrestle a large couch out of the truck, Dessa walked onto the sidewalk. When Ellie spotted her, she grinned and waved.

Although crudely put, the movers' assessment of Ellie's beauty was, if anything, understated. She wasn't merely good looking; she was the prettiest teenage girl Dessa had ever seen. She had long blonde hair, dark blue eyes, perfect white teeth and a killer body. If she hadn't known better, she would've guessed that Ellie was at least sixteen. No fourteen-year-old that Dessa knew had boobs that impressive. Simply put, the new girl was stunning. Embarrassed by her own shortcomings and the absolute certainty that she'd never ever look half as good as Ellie, Dessa was momentarily speechless. She had always believed that brains were a better attribute for success than beauty, but in reality, girls like Ellie had it made. Dessa hated her instantly. Eying her barely-there shorts and low-cut blouse, Dessa wondered if Ellie realized just how provocative she appeared. Could she be that unaware of her own natural beauty? Or, was her suggestive attire a calculated attention-getting ploy? Whichever the case, Ellie Matthews could be dressed in a flour sack and still look good. Feeling suddenly mean-spirited, Dessa blurted out the first snarky comment that came to mind. "Hot enough for you?"

She didn't expect an answer and Ellie didn't offer one. "Hi," she said cheerfully, "I'm Ellie. What's your name?"

"Dessa."

"I've never known anyone named Dessa before. Is it a nickname?"

She nodded. "It's short for Odessa. But only my parents call me that. To everyone else I'm just Dessa."

"Well, just Dessa, would you like to come inside my house and cool off with a Coke?"

Much to Dessa's surprise, she found herself intrigued by Ellie. She seemed friendly and nice, but that was to be expected when you were new to a neighborhood. Once she settled in and met some more kids, she could change quickly. In Dessa's experience, the good looking, popular girls at school couldn't be bothered with her—until they needed her to bail them out of an academic jam. If Ellie were just putting on an act, Dessa would find out soon enough. She had a knack for detecting bullshit when she heard it. "Okay," Dessa said. "A Coke sounds good."

As is usually the case on move-in day, the Matthews' house was a chaotic mess. Packing boxes—some partially opened, others still sealed and stacked one atop the other like building blocks—competed for space with an assortment of chairs, end tables, lamps, and other furniture. Dessa passed on Ellie's offer to give her a tour since the layout of the 1,000-square foot house was the same as every other house in Hillcrest. It had a living room, dining room, kitchen, one bathroom, and two bedrooms on the main floor with laundry and storage space in the unfinished basement. Dessa's mother wanted to live in Fremont Heights, a prestigious enclave of larger homes with more amenities, but Stan Feldman had a major financial stake in the construction company that developed Hillcrest. He refused to live anywhere else, no matter how supposedly rich they were or how often his wife called him a stingy, stubborn bastard.

Ellie cleared a pathway that led to the kitchen and opened the fridge. "Here," she said, grabbing two Cokes and handing one to Dessa. "There should be a bottle opener around her somewhere." She rummaged through a couple of drawers with no success. "Probably still packed," Ellie said, irritably.

Just then Mr. Matthews entered the kitchen with a cardboard box labeled *Dishes*. He looked the way Maureen Feldman had described him to the garden club ladies, although she'd failed to mention that his ears stuck out a little too much and his nose was crooked like it'd been broken at one time. Maureen had said he "radiated sex appeal" but Dessa thought that was ridiculous. Mr. Matthews was at least forty or maybe even forty-five. Sex passed him by a long time ago.

He set the box on a Formica dining table and asked Ellie, "What are you trying to find?"

"Bottle opener," Ellie said, slamming the drawer shut. "Can't find anything in this stupid mess!"

So, thought Dessa, the girl has some fire in her. Surprisingly, his daughter's outburst didn't seem to faze Mr. Matthews. If Dessa had acted the same way, her mother would've been all over her. "Hand your bottles to me," Mr. Matthews said, patiently. After setting their bottles on the table, he reached into his back pocket and pulled out a knife. Dessa had never seen a knife with so many strange looking blades. "It's called a Swiss Army knife," he said, catching her fascinated expression. "This little gem can do just about anything."

"Thanks, Mr. Matthews," Dessa said when he'd opened her Coke.

Ellie downed half her Coke in one noisy gulp followed by a deep, rolling belch.

"Nice one," Dessa said, giggling.

"S'cuse me," Ellie said between another loud belch and giggle.

"When you can compose yourself, Ellie, perhaps you could introduce me to your friend. She already seems to know who I am."

"Her name is Odessa. She lives across the street."

"Glad to meet you, Odessa."

"She wants to be called Dessa."

"Okay. Dessa it is," Mr. Matthews said, smiling warmly. "Why don't you girls get yourselves a snack?" He gestured to an assortment of cakes, pies, brownies, and numerous other desserts lining the kitchen counter. "We've got plenty of goodies to choose from." Dessa spotted the chocolate chip cookies that her mother had baked that morning. From the looks of things, the entire garden club had followed suit with their own special treats.

The girls grabbed a brownie and took their Cokes into Ellie's bedroom while Mr. Matthews went back outside. "Dad let me choose which bedroom I wanted," said Ellie. "I chose this one because it overlooks our backyard."

"Cool." As Dessa sipped her Coke, she noted that Ellie's choice was also the largest bedroom in the house. Odessa's parents had claimed the same room in their house for themselves. Maureen called it the master suite which she said meant "For Adults Only."

Ellie's room had a bed with several boxes stacked atop a bare mattress. Ellie shoved the boxes aside to make room for Dessa and her to sit. "It looks kind of empty in here right now," she said after they'd settled themselves. "My study desk, chair, dressing table, and chest of drawers are still in the truck. They're all brand-new."

Ellie didn't seem to be bragging, but the inventory-like listing of her new possessions hit Dessa wrong and, without even thinking, she responded in exactly the way her mother said was why she never had friends. "Oh, that's too bad," Dessa said, sadly shaking her head.

"What's wrong?"

"Well, it's just . . . forget it, it's nothing,"

"No, really. Tell me."

"Since you insist. It's just that with all that stuff crammed in here it's going to be much too crowded for slumber parties." Dessa had never been to a slumber party in her life but she knew the popular girls all favored such things. And she had no doubt that Ellie would run with the popular crowd as soon as school started.

Ellie studied her bedroom as if seeing it for the first time. "You really think so?"

The room was practically made for slumber parties. "Maybe. Maybe not," Dessa said, shrugging.

Ellie's shoulders sagged. "You're probably right," she sighed. She paused a moment as if to mull over the problem. "I know what!" she said excitedly, "You could help me arrange the furniture so that it *does* work for sleep-overs."

Dessa stuffed a chunk of brownie in her mouth and washed it down with the last of her Coke while she thought of an excuse.

"Pretty please," Ellie begged. "I bet you know exactly what to do."

"I don't think I—"

"Let me show you something first," she said, plucking a folder from the box atop her bed.

Whatever Dessa's shortcomings, a lack of curiosity was not one of them. There wasn't much that went on in Hillcrest that Dessa didn't manage to learn one way or another. She never knew when something she uncovered might be publishable in her newsletter. Not that she expected the folder in Ellie's hands to contain anything useful for her purposes, but she took the bait Ellie waved in front of her. "What is it?"

"My artwork," Ellie said. She removed several pages of pencil sketches from the folder and fanned them across the bed. "Let's decide which ones to put on the walls while we wait for my furniture."

Dessa picked up a few of the sketches without enthusiasm. She had as much interest in decorating Ellie's room as she did in arranging furniture. The sketches were mostly different views of horses—horses galloping; horses trotting; horses grazing. The subject matter was dull but remarkably well done. She was particularly struck by how realistic the horses looked. Almost like photographs. "Hey," she said. "These are really good."

"Thanks," Ellie said, clearly pleased with the compliment.

"Have you ever sketched people?"

"You mean like a portrait?"

"Yeah, portraits."

"No, only horses. I *love* horses."

Girls and their love affairs with horses made Dessa want to puke. Stifling a negative quip, she focused on Ellie's artistry. "I bet you could sketch a face so that the person would be instantly recognizable."

Ellie pooh-poohed the idea but Dessa was convinced that she had the ability. One of the problems she had with publishing her newsletter—besides no printing press—was not being able to include photographs. If Ellie could draw other things as well as she drew horses, Dessa had found the answer to at least one of her problems.

"Furniture's here," Mr. Matthews said, opening the bedroom door. After a quick consultation with Dessa, Ellie told the movers where to place the furniture in the room. Dessa noted with amusement how careful the movers were to keep their eyes focused strictly on their work while Mr. Matthews was present. Once they'd finished unloading the van and had left, Mr. Matthews said he had an errand to run downtown. "You girls will be all right here by yourselves, won't you?" he asked.

"Honestly, Dad," Ellie shot back. "We're not babies, you know. We can take care of ourselves just fine."

He raised both hands as if to ward off an attack. "You're right, you're right. I'm sorry if I sounded like I doubted you." He gazed affectionately at his daughter and added softly, "But you'll always be my little girl, Ellie, no matter how old you are."

Dessa couldn't picture her own father ever apologizing after she'd called him out for something he'd said.

When Mr. Matthews left the room, Ellie complained, "He drives me crazy! Don't do this, don't do that. My father is the biggest worry wart ever. I hate it!"

"Jeez, don't have a cow about it. Your father's no different from any other parent around here." Dessa thought it best not to mention that a young girl in town had been attacked recently as she slept outside in her own backyard. She didn't know if Mr. Matthews had heard about the incident, but every other parent in The Dalles had been on edge ever since. "Let's get back to your art," Dessa said. "Why don't you try sketching me?"

Ellie's interest in drawing had passed. "Not now," she said scooping up the sketches. As she tucked them back inside the folder, the doorbell rang. "Oh, no," she said. "Not someone else with more food."

Dessa looked out the bedroom window and spotted a red convertible parked at the curb. "Yuk! It's Tony Rossi. He has some kind of package with him, but I doubt it's food."

"Mr. Rossi? Really?" She jostled Dessa aside. "Let me see!"

"Don't worry. I'll get rid of him for you."

"NO!" Ellie shrieked. "Why would you do that?"

She had to be kidding. Anyone with eyes and ears could tell the realtor was a fast-talking greaser who would say or do anything to get what he wanted. As newcomer, Ellie probably hadn't heard the gossip about him. Mainly that Tony had a wandering eye and had seduced more than one housewife in Hillcrest. The liaisons usually ended when the bruises from Tony's fists became too difficult to explain. No names had ever been mentioned but Dessa had her suspicions. Just another juicy tidbit that she dared not print. "Everybody says Tony Rossi is nothing but trouble."

"I don't believe that. Mr. Rossi is the reason we're living here. Dad wasn't interested in buying a house but Mr. Rossi could tell how much I wanted this place—and made it happen." She snapped her fingers. "Just like that." When the doorbell rang, she hurried to her dressing table. "I think he's wonderful," she said, checking herself in the mirror.

When the doorbell rang a second time, Ellie was still at the dressing table, running a brush through her ponytail. "Better hurry," Dessa chided. "Sounds like Mr. Wonderful is getting impatient."

Ellie tightened the rubber band holding her ponytail together and, discovering a few loose strands, tucked them behind her ears. After telling Dessa to wait in the bedroom, she dashed off to answer the door.

Dessa didn't know what to make of Ellie Matthews' favorable impression of Tony Rossi. Had he already set his sights on the new girl? Or did Ellie have her sights set on him? Whatever the case, Dessa didn't intend to wait in the bedroom and wonder about it. Tiptoeing down the hallway, she stopped just short of the entry where she couldn't be seen but could still hear everything that happened.

CHAPTER EIGHT

It was ten o'clock in the morning when Danny arrived at the Pit Stop Bar & Grill. Most of the regulars started drifting in around noon but Danny's friends were already there. The Pit Stop was their favorite hangout. When the beer-fueled squabbling got too spirited, a rip-roaring fistfight inevitably followed. The food and music were good, too.

How a red-haired, one-eyed Irishman named Mike Fitzgerald wound up running a booze joint that catered to Indians was the subject of much speculation. The story that Danny liked best was that Fitz was hiding out from the law. He'd been a pit crew boss on the race car circuit back east somewhere until a freak accident blinded him in his right eye. When he took blood revenge on the idiot who caused the loss of his sight and job, Fitz fled west before the authorities had a chance to come after him. With his money quickly running out and a mistaken notion of how to get to the California coast, The Dalles was where he landed. He bought the long-abandoned tavern dirt cheap, slapped on some new paint and called it good.

Although Danny would never admit it, he liked Fitz. The guy literally turned a blind eye to a lot of what went on at the Pit. He had a baseball bat behind the counter and always made a big show of taking it out when the brawls got too wild. As far as Danny knew, he'd never clubbed anyone. What really sealed his approval in Danny's eyes was Fitz's disregard for the law. He made it his practice to be as uncooperative as possible anytime the local authorities came snooping around his place of business, which meant he wasn't above lying if necessary to protect himself or his patrons. It also meant that it was a good place for Danny and his pals to make their plans.

Danny noted that Ernie, Henry and Walter were already at the tavern. Ernie and Henry were playing pool while Walter sat at the counter eating fry bread, hash browns, and eggs with a cinnamon roll on the side. Although he had plenty of young women eager to cook for him, Walter preferred to take his breakfast at the Pit, which he did almost every day. Of all his friends, only nineteen-year-old Walter was as tough as Danny. His strong, rock-hard body gave enemies pause and girls the shivers. Walter had a reputation as a good man to have on your side when a fight broke out, but unlike Danny, he had an easy-going manner and it took a lot to get him fired up. His winning grin endeared him to almost everyone in the village, especially the girls.

Walter read a newspaper while he ate. His eyes were so bad that he hardly ever read anything more complex than a comic book. He had glasses, but thought the sissy-looking things were too embarrassing to wear in public. The Pit Stop wasn't technically a public place, but it was still surprising that Walter wore his glasses today. Danny straddled the stool alongside his friend and snatched the cinnamon roll—a Fitz breakfast specialty—off his plate. "Hey, man," Danny said, taking a big bite, "what's with the specs?" He pointed to the newspaper. "Something in that scandal sheet I should know about?"

Walter removed his glasses and pushed the paper toward Danny. "Read it for yourself," he said, grabbing what was left of his cinnamon roll out of Danny's hand. "It's mostly about you anyway."

Local Indian Drowns at Falls

Celilo Falls claimed the life of Wy-am Indian Willie Bears on Saturday, June 5. According to witnesses, Bears fell from a fishing platform on Standing Island. He was not wearing a safety rope. Sheriff Leonard Pritchard said, "That's not unusual for these fellas. We've warned them time and time again about the necessity for using proper safety gear, but many Indians stubbornly refuse and wind up paying with their lives."

Despite the danger involved, an attempt was made to

80

save the man's life. Danny Longstreet, a well-known outspoken opponent of The Dalles Dam, risked his own life trying to save Willie Bears. Officials close to the incident were surprised that he made such an effort. They describe Danny as a hot-headed troublemaker not given to heroics. Longstreet declined to comment. Sheriff Pritchard said, "Danny Longstreet is the leader of a gang that is actively engaged in disrupting and delaying progress on the construction of the dam. As sheriff, I'm charged with protecting the welfare of the good people of this community and I vow to put a stop to the actions of Longstreet and his band of hooligans before someone gets hurt or killed." Funeral arrangements for Willie Bears were unknown at press time.

    -Reported by Hiram Potter

As Danny finished the article, Fitz came by to warm Walter's coffee. He flashed a lop-sided grin. "Cheers, Danny. I see you've made the paper."

Danny tossed the newspaper aside. "Just the back of page six. Been aiming for the front page."

Fitz leaned his forearms on the counter and frowned. "Don't take this wrong, lad, but you keep messing up and that's exactly where you're headed. And it won't be no hero article."

Danny shrugged. "That so-called reporter couldn't get the story straight if it was dictated to him word for word." He tapped the paper with his forefinger. "He never even got Willie's name right. And he promised me he'd report our side of the dam issue. You see how that made the news."

Walter set his coffee mug on the counter and stared at Danny wide-eyed. "You talked to a reporter?"

"Don't look so shocked. He came to the village and gave my mother a hard time, so I set him straight."

"I guess that explains the printed attack on you," Fitz said, shaking his head. "But the Wy-ams did make the front page."

"Yeah, right," scoffed Danny. "It's a sacred journalistic rule: No Indians on the front page. We'd have to massacre half the town's population first."

Fitz picked up the newspaper and began to read. "Looks like they've made an exception to the rule. This here's a report on the government's plan to relocate your burial sites. According to the article, they've finally located a property for the new cemetery."

Danny and Walter exchanged concerned looks. Danny's father was buried on Memaloose Island, as were both of Walter's parents. Never mind that the dam would flood the island. Just the thought of disturbing—let alone moving—their gravesites, especially by white men, struck Danny as obscene. He couldn't gauge Walter's reaction but Danny struggled to contain his anger as he asked, "Does it say who's in charge?"

Fitz folded the newspaper and set it on the counter. "Naw, just that it's some guy from the government."

"You know who he is?' Danny asked.

The barkeep erupted in hearty laughter. "Hey, now, lad," he said when he'd caught his breath. "I may be a white man but that doesn't mean I know all the white eejits in town." He winked at Walter as he picked up his dirty dishes and then carried them through the swinging doors to the kitchen.

Danny helped himself to a bottle of beer from behind the counter, popped the cap and headed for the jukebox. He inserted a dime and the raucous beat of "Blue Suede Shoes" exploded from the speakers. It was his favorite song when he was angry and right now he was so enraged that he wanted to hit someone. Swing a punch so hard it'd send the bum flying through the bar's front window. He surveyed the room for a likely candidate, but, except for his friends, the place was empty.

He gave the jukebox a swift kick. Not good enough. He needed to destroy something. His eyes settled on a small round oak table. Imagining it as somebody's head, he smashed his beer bottle against its scarred surface. The shattering glass caused Fitz to peer out of the kitchen's open pass-through just as Danny grabbed the table and flipped it over. The table landed on the hardwood floor with an unsatisfying thud. A metal chair was the next to go. When Danny threw it on top of the table, Fitz stepped outside the kitchen with the baseball bat. "Enough, lad! That wee table didn't do nothin' to you."

Danny spotted the bat in Fitz's hand and clenched his fists. The two men glared at each other for a few uneasy seconds until Danny gave in with a shrug. "Shit," he said, slumping into a second, still upright chair.

As Fitz passed Walter, he chuckled and said, "War dance seems to be over."

Walter grinned. "Got a peace pipe?"

"No, but there's a mighty nice broom and mop out back."

Walter retrieved the cleaning supplies and joined Danny. After he'd righted the table and wiped it down, swept up the broken glass, and mopped the beer-soaked floor, he brought two fresh beers from the bar. Setting the bottles atop the newly cleaned table, he grabbed a chair and sat down. "Furniture's good to go for another round."

Danny glared at his friend a moment and then got up to feed the jukebox. When he returned, he took a quick swig of beer and belched. "I don't get you, man."

"Huh? Why's that?"

Danny shouted over the music. "Memaloose! Your parents!"

Walter set his bottle on the table. "So?"

"Aw, Walter," Danny said, shaking his head. "Don't anything bother you? You're just like my grandfather and the rest of the old men in the village. All talk and no action."

Walter reached into his shirt pocket. Leaning forward, he placed a faded and creased black and white photograph on the table. "This was taken right before my parents died."

Danny stared at the couple in the old photo. They were standing by the falls. Walter's father was holding up a large Steelhead, maybe a 40-pounder by the looks of it. Walter's mother, her hand resting on her rounded belly, gazed up at her husband with the same wide grin as her son's. "You mother was pregnant?"

Walter nodded. "Nine months."

Everyone in the village had heard the basic story—his parents' car had broken down on the railroad tracks and Walter was the sole survivor when the train struck. His mother's pregnancy was something new. Walter never talked about the accident. He just went to live with his uncle afterward and that was that. Danny hesitated a moment. He wanted to ask more about the accident, but was reluctant to bring up bad memories. It was unusual that Walter had revealed as much as he had. Restraint was the Wy-am way.

Walter must have sensed Danny's reluctance to pry. "Want to know how it happened?" he asked.

Danny nodded.

"Remember Dry Hollow Motors?"

Danny remembered it well. The car dealership had burned down a few years ago and was never rebuilt. Arson was suspected but never proven.

"That's where my parents bought the used car they were driving when they were killed. My mother had her heart set on a wood-paneled wagon she'd seen on the lot. My father thought the car was silly but he'd do just about anything for her. Saved up his fish money until he had enough to buy it. They were driving back to the village — just a couple of miles from the dealership — when it broke down on the railroad tracks."

Walter took a drink before continuing. "Anyway, Dad lifted the hood and tinkered with the engine. I was only three at the time and they say a little kid can't remember that far back." He ran his fingers across the photo. There was a hard edge to his usually mellow voice when he added, "But I remember *everything*."

Danny suddenly regretted the way he'd attacked him earlier.

"Every time I hear a train I'm right back in that car. As soon as he realized what was happening, Dad rushed to get me out. He pulled me from the back seat and told me to run. A fellow from the car behind us scooped me up in his arms, but I turned my head just in time to see the train hit. The last thing I heard was my mother's scream." Walter paused. "It was probably just the train's whistle."

"I'm so sorry, man. I didn't know."

"Yeah, well. As soon as I was old enough, I burned Dry Hollow Motors to the ground."

"Damn, Walter! "You're a bad ass after all."

"Don't go all mushy on me now," Walter said, shaking his head. "The fire was a failure."

"What're you talking about? It was the biggest blaze they've ever had around here. The whole place was toast in a matter of minutes."

"But the good-for-nothing salesman who sold us that lemon made it out alive!"

Danny had never seen such a fierce expression on Walter's usually amiable face. It occurred to Danny then that he really didn't know his friend as well as he'd thought. He wondered how many others he'd misjudged. If easygoing Walter was capable of such rage, what did it say about himself? After getting more beer from the bar, the two friends sat and drank silently for several minutes. The music had ended but neither man fed the jukebox again. The bar had gotten noisier; banter from the regulars who'd begun to straggle in and the click-clack of cue sticks from the billiard games in progress made conversation difficult even without the added blare from the jukebox. Danny raised his voice to be heard above the din. "I wasn't there when my father was killed and mother never talks about it, but I pestered Oscar until he told me what happened."

Walter put a hand up. "It's okay, Danny. You don't have to tell me."

"No, I want to." Danny figured he'd heard some of the story anyway. "Dad had just bought me a puppy for my sixth birthday. You know, old Tio. He's awfully lame now, but he was a lively pup." He skipped over the part about how he'd begged his parents for weeks to buy the little black Labrador he'd seen in the window of a pet store in town. It made him feel guilty to even think about it. His parents had balked at the notion of buying a dog when he could have had one for free. There was always a stray running around the village, but Danny held fast and his parents finally relented. "My new puppy jumped right out of Dad's arms and ran under a truck parked in front of Dizzy's. Dad got down on his knees and was trying to reach Tio when the guy who owned the truck stumbled out of the bar."

Walter said, "I heard about that. The drunk pulled a knife."

"He thought Dad was stealing his truck." Danny swallowed to keep from choking up. He felt he owed it to Walter to tell the rest of the story, but the emotion that had surfaced was unexpected. Anger he was used to; it was even comforting in a strange sort of way. Anger gave him the edge he needed to keep going. The feeling he was experiencing now was different. Raw. Messy. Childish. Danny looked down at the table, willing himself not to tear up. The quiver in his voice betrayed him. "Oscar said Dad would've had a chance if the guy's buddy hadn't held him down. He was stabbed twenty-two times."

Walter winced. "Naturally both guys walked."

Danny wiped his eyes with the back of his hand. "The sheriff launched a so-called investigation, but it was just a show. No one in town cared. What's one more dead red man? Afterward, Mother trudged all the way into town and found Tio. She hasn't gone back to The Dalles since."

Walter lowered his voice and spoke with steel-like conviction. "I promise you, Danny, Memaloose and Grave Islands will not give up our dead without a fight."

Danny reached across the table for Walter's hand. "Damn straight, man. I'm all for that." After they'd shook on their resolve, Danny said, "Too bad we can't dig up the white man's ancestors. Give them a taste of their own medicine."

"That's not a bad idea," Walter said. "I even know where their Pioneer Cemetery is located."

"I wasn't serious. Digging up a bunch of graves would be more than we could handle."

"Right, but we could tip over a few of their tombstones and make a mess of the place."

Danny grinned. "I like the way you think."

"Of course, any damage we caused would just be symbolic."

"That's what pisses me off. Everything we've done so far—the pranks, the petty thefts, the stupid tricks—they're all symbols of our rage, not the real thing. You read that newspaper article. They called us a gang of hooligans. We're warriors, man. We need to quit playing kid games and declare all-out war."

Walter studied Danny a moment. "If you really mean that, I know someone who's willing to help us."

"Who?"

"His name doesn't matter. What's important is that he's got an even bigger beef against the government than we do. He thinks our cause is just but our protest hasn't changed anything."

"He's got that right,"

"The dam is scheduled to be completed within a few months but if we join forces with his people, he claims we can delay and possibly even destroy the whole project."

"Sounds too good to be true," Danny said. "You sure this isn't some kind of trap? How do you know this guy?"

"Not now," Walter said. "Here comes Ernie."

Ernie jabbed his cue stick in the air like a spear as he approached their table. "You guys want to shoot some pool? I'm on fire today. Henry didn't have a chance. Hell, I bet I could even beat you, Danny."

Danny waved him off. "Later. Walter and I have some business to discuss."

"No shit? You guys workin' on a new battle plan?" At sixteen, Ernie was the youngest in their group. He'd been suspended from school so many times that he finally gave up altogether and attached himself to Danny like an itch he couldn't scratch. He was the skinniest Indian Danny knew, but he was a tough scrapper and up for anything. Unfortunately, he had a big mouth. Any scheme had to be kept secret until the last minute or Ernie would blab to anyone and everyone about it. It still rankled Danny that their last escapade was foiled when Ernie shot off his mouth to the wrong people and almost got them arrested.

Walter tossed a dollar on the table and flashed his familiar grin. "We'll let you know what we're going to do just as soon as we've decided something. In the meantime, beer for you and Henry is on me."

Ernie scooped up the bill. "Thanks, man." He tipped the cue stick at Danny. "I'll be waiting for you at table two."

Danny watched Ernie dance his way to the bar. "Okay," he said when Ernie was out of earshot. "Tell me more about this guy you know and what we have to do."

CHAPTER NINE

Tony whistled a lively tune as he waited on the porch for Ellie to answer the doorbell. Catching sight of Matthews as he left the house without Ellie in tow had made Tony's day. He'd gone to Hillcrest that morning to list a house for a couple who was going to retire and move to Portland to be closer to their grandkids. After he'd secured a signed listing agreement, he decided to cruise by the Matthews' house. Moving day was always hectic so he hadn't planned to stop but when he turned the corner, he saw Sam hop in his truck and drive off. Tony couldn't believe his good luck. He'd been carrying around the gift he'd bought for Ellie in his car until the timing was right to give it to her. *What better time than when her father is safely out of the way?*

He parked at the curb and adjusted the Caddy's rearview mirror to check his appearance. Thanks to a generous application of Brylcreem, his hairstyle was still in place. He donned his Stetson and then popped open the glove compartment to get the bottle of Old Spice that he kept on hand for emergencies. He slapped the fragrance on both cheeks and smiled with satisfaction at his reflection in the mirror. With Ellie's gift tucked under his arm, he strode confidently to the Matthews' front porch.

Ellie didn't answer the door until he'd rung the bell a second time. When she finally appeared, Tony was momentarily taken aback by how sexy she looked. The skimpy all-white shorts and blouse she wore were designed to excite, and it worked. The bulge beginning to strain the fabric of his trousers was proof. She caught the way he eyed her up and down, and teased him with a seductive smile at the corner of her luscious red lips. *Lord, have mercy.* He tipped his Stetson and stuttered, "Afternoon, Ellie. I was beginning to think nobody was home."

"Dad, I mean Sam, isn't here," she said. "He had to take care of an errand downtown."

"Yeah? Too bad I missed him," he said without a trace of sincerity. A pause and then a wide grin. "But I'm *very* glad you're here."

"Really?" she said, blushing. "That makes two of us."

Score! Tony ogled every sensuous swing of her hips as she led him into the cluttered living room. "You suppose there might be a spot where a fellow could sit down?" he asked, looking around at the stacks of boxes that blocked the furniture from view.

Mumbling an apology, Ellie cleared a packing box off the seat of a wingback chair. Tony sank into the surprisingly soft cushion and stretched out his legs on the matching ottoman. "Ah," he sighed. Very comfy."

Ellie perched on the edge of a couch across the room.

"Whatcha doing all the way over there, darlin'?" Tony shifted his feet to the floor and patted the top of the ottoman. "Sit right here," he said. "I won't bite." As she sauntered across the room, he boldly ogled the skimpy blouse. *Damn. This schoolgirl really knows how to strut her stuff.*

Ellie sat down in front of him and asked, "Do you want something to drink? Or eat? We have food. Plenty of food."

"Neighbors been calling, have they?"

"Just the ladies."

"Figures," he said. "Your Sam being a widow man and all." Tony struggled to concentrate on their conversation instead of his growing desire. In desperation, he covered his erection with his Stetson and said, "It won't be long until you get your share of callers, too." He leaned forward in the chair. "But before you do, here's a little welcome-to-the-neighborhood gift from me." He offered her the package he'd carefully wrapped and topped with a pink bow. "Don't panic," he said, catching her startled expression. "It's not food." He thought he heard a high-pitched noise in the hall. It sounded curiously like a giggle but could've been a screech from some animal. "Do you have a cat?" he asked.

"What? A cat?"

"Never mind," Tony said, savoring the sweet fragrance of White Shoulders and the way her fingers lingered on his hand as she took the gift from him. She wrapped her hands protectively around the package as if Tony might change his mind and snatch it away from her. He laughed and asked, "Well? Aren't you going to open it?"

Ellie quickly tore off the colorful wrapping but seemed puzzled by the pink and white striped box she uncovered. She undid the clasp on the lid and lifted the plastic handle to peer inside. She smiled slightly and mumbled a quick thank-you.

Tony noted her confusion. "It's for toting your 45s around," he explained.

"Oh, right," she said. "Records."

"You do have a record player, don't you?"

"Sort of."

"Sort of?"

"It's broken."

Tony grinned and said, "I can certainly take care of that problem. No teenage girl should be without a way to play her tunes. How 'bout I take you downtown to The Music Box? They have a real nice selection of players there. You can pick out whichever one you want. Get some new records while we're at it. My treat." When Ellie didn't respond, he waved a hand in front of her face. "Hello? Earth to Ellie. Are you here?"

She blinked once and giggled. "I'm here."

"Not for long," Tony said, standing upright and donning his Stetson. Taking her hands in his, he pulled her to her feet.

"Mr. Rossi, I—"

"Who's Mr. Rossi? I'm Tony." He placed a hand on the middle of her back to gently guide her toward the front door.

"But my dad wouldn't like—"

"Hush, now. It's okay." *Women! They like to make you work for it.*

They were almost to the door when a frowning, red-haired girl popped out of nowhere. "Leaving without me?" she asked.

"What the . . ."

"Dessa!" exclaimed Ellie. 'I'm so sorry. I forgot all about you."

Tony cringed. "Dessa? Dessa Feldman?"

"The one and only," she said, flashing a metal-mouth grin.

Just his luck. *The first time he gets Ellie all to himself the little gossip queen suddenly turns up. If her father didn't hold Tony's* financial future in the balance, he'd tell her to get lost. And that would be just for starters. But Dessa and her smart mouth could ruin a lot more for him than an amorous interlude with Ellie. "Why, Dessa, of course you're welcome to come with us." He made a point of looking at his wristwatch. "Oh, rats," he said. "I had no idea what time it was. I'm afraid we'll have to take a rain check on The Music Box. I'm late for a very important meeting."

***

Tony was on his second beer at Dizzy's when Clarice joined him at a corner table in the back of the tavern. "There you are," she said, scooting a chair close to his and sitting down. "Mildred said she didn't know where you were."

"Like hell she didn't. I dropped off a new listing at the office and told her I was going to cool off with a brewski. Just where did she think I'd go? The country club?"

"Never mind what she thought," Clarice said. "I have some good news and some bad news."

"Am I going to need a fresh pitcher to hear this?"

Clarice signaled the bartender. "Probably wouldn't hurt."

As soon as the pitcher and another glass arrived, Clarice poured them both a round. "So, which do you want first? The good news or the bad?"

"The good news, of course. I haven't had enough to drink yet to handle bad news."

"This should lift your spirits. Warren played eighteen holes with Stan Feldman the other day and got the skinny on what was happening with Baker Bluff."

"And?"

"Baker Bluff is just one of three properties Feldman owns that the government has expressed an interest in purchasing for the new Indian cemetery."

"You call that good news? Baker Bluff could still be snatched out from underneath us. For a damn Indian cemetery, of all things."

"That's true, but the good news is that we still have a chance to buy the property from Feldman before the government makes its decision. It takes forever for big bureaucracies like the government to figure out the most cost-effective place to buy paper clips. Deciding on a big purchase like land takes even longer."

"Yeah, but there's an urgent time factor at play here. The new cemetery needs to be purchased and the old bones moved from the river before the dam is finished, which, as I understand it, ain't much longer now. The government doesn't have time to be dilly-dallying around. The worst part is that even if we could buy the property, the government could take it away from us by exercising their right to eminent domain—at nowhere near the price we paid for it. Tony slurped down the last of his beer and poured a fresh glass. "So, if that's what you consider good news, I don't want to hear what the bad news is."

"Suit yourself," Clarice said, shrugging. She pushed back her chair and stood.

"Damn it," Tony said, grasping her hand. "Just sit down and tell me."

"The government man charged with making the decision on which property to buy is someone named Sam Matthews. He's told Feldman that he favors Baker Bluff. He thinks it's the best value considering the prime location."

"You've got to be kidding! Matthews is just a dumb ass foreman. What does he know about property values?"

"Enough to impact our plans. Anyway, he's close to making a deal according to what Feldman told Warren."

"You believe him?"

"It doesn't matter whether we do or not. Just the fact that Baker Bluff is in the mix means we need to act fast."

Tony folded his arms on the table and laid his head face down on top of them. "Jesus Christ Almighty," he muttered.

Won't do you any good to call on Jesus," chided Clarice. "It's all up to us now. I told you that we could make Baker Bluff unacceptable to the Indians. When we get through, Matthews will have no choice but to select one of the other properties for their cemetery. So, get your butt in gear. We have work to do."

VALERIE WILCOX

CHAPTER TEN

As lead engineer, Phillip Beckstrom had his own office, but ever since he'd tussled with Sam over the dike removal, he'd been showing up at the foreman's trailer more often, usually just minutes before the day shift whistle blew. His transparent excuse was always the same — he needed to discuss something important with Pete Chambers before the foreman left.

"That's a load of B.S.," scoffed Chambers. "The boy could've just picked up the phone if he needed to talk to me so damn bad."

Despite Sam's efforts to develop a good working relationship with the engineer, he'd made an enemy. If Beckstrom could catch him arriving late or violating some other work rule, it would give him further ammunition to issue the reprimand he'd already threatened. With the success of his mission in The Dalles at stake, Sam wasn't taking any chances. He arrived on time — earlier, if possible — followed Beckstrom's orders without complaint, and did his job to the best of his ability.

He'd swallowed his pride before and he'd do it again, even if that meant taking on whatever thankless tasks Beckstrom handed out. The latest project was to locate a new cemetery site for the Indians. Because the removal and reburial of the ancient remains would most likely be opposed by the Indians at Celilo, Beckstrom wanted nothing to do with it. When he tapped Sam for the job, however, he made it sound like a great opportunity. "Handle this job right," he said, "and you could salvage your reputation." Sam's bureau chief had a different take. "Coordinating with the Wy-am tribe to select a cemetery site is a positive development. You can use your interaction with the Indians to determine if there is any truth to the report that an outside group is supporting their efforts to sabotage the dam."

93

Although Chambers routinely groused about Beckstrom and other aspects of their job that he found annoying, Sam had noticed a troubling change in the foreman's behavior lately. He rarely joked around anymore and what little banter he did engage in seemed subdued and somewhat forced. He hardly ever finished a cigarette before crushing it out and lighting another one as he labored over his shift report. Sam didn't know what was bothering Chambers, but hoped the old guy just had a case of pre-retirement jitters and not some new worrisome medical condition. Whatever the problem, it was serious enough that he'd asked Sam to come in an hour early so they could talk without Beckstrom nosing around.

Sam's shared office space with Pete Chambers was no coincidence. After a string of sabotage attacks at the dam, Sam had been sent by the F.B.I. as an undercover agent to investigate. The consensus at the Portland bureau was that the attacks were instigated by a handful of local Indians opposed to the dam. But the worry in Washington—fostered by J. Edgar Hoover's close association with Senator Joseph McCarthy—was that the Communist Party had infiltrated the Corps and organized the attacks as part of a much larger effort to stop construction of the dam. The successful completion of The Dalles Dam represented a multi-million-dollar investment in the future, not only of the Pacific Northwest but of the United States as well. According to Senator McCarthy, it was a future that the Communists would do anything to prevent. Sam doubted that Chambers was a Communist or involved in any way. It wasn't a decision he made lightly, given his "trust no one, suspect everyone" rule, but sometimes he just had to go with his gut.

Chambers' pickup wasn't in its usual spot in the parking lot so Sam figured he'd gotten delayed at the job site and would arrive shortly. That thought died quickly when he spotted Beckstrom's government-issued rig parked in the lot. Sam's gut twitched uneasily as he tested the hood with a flattened hand. Cold. Fearing the worst, Sam strode into the office.

Beckstrom sat at Chambers' desk talking on the telephone. "Yes, sir," he said. "I understand. Yes, sir. Our full cooperation." His youthful face was drawn and haggard; his shirt and trousers rumpled as if he'd slept in them. When he hung up the receiver, his hand shook as he lit a cigarette. "That was the chief engineer on the phone."

"What's up?" asked Sam.

"All hell is about to break loose."

"Care to be more specific?"

"Pete Chambers is dead."

Sam slumped into his chair. "Aw, hell. What was it? His heart again?"

"We should be so lucky," Beckstrom said, eying Sam through a smoky haze.

Building a dam was a dangerous business and accidents sometimes happened. And when they did, schedules got derailed. In Beckstrom's world, a heart attack would cause him fewer problems than a work-related fatality. Chambers was as careful as any, but with a bum knee, he wasn't always steady on his feet. It wasn't improbable that he'd fallen to his death. "How'd it happen?" asked Sam.

"He was murdered."

"What? How do you know that?"

"I got the call last night. He didn't show up for his shift so I told a couple of his men to go to his house and check on him. That's when they discovered the body. Chambers had been stabbed. Quite a violent attack, judging by the amount of blood at the scene. The Feds are already on their way here."

Since Chambers was a federal employee, the FBI would investigate the murder instead of the local police. Sam should've gotten a heads-up call from his bureau chief, but Sam's position at the dam was tentative at best. The murder of one of the Corps' employees he'd been sent to watch was not good news, any way you looked at it. There were bound to be serious repercussions for Sam. He took a deep breath and exhaled slowly. "Who's the special agent-in-charge?"

Beckstrom ground out his cigarette in the ashtray on Chambers' desk. "I must look like shit," he said, straightening his tie. "Been here most of the night."

"The investigation, Phillip. Who's the agent?"

"Don't know his name, but he's from Portland."

A Portland agent was sure to know Sam. Sure to have at least heard about him: Samuel R. Matthews, the special agent-in-charge whose stellar career had taken a nose dive. A screw-up so bad that he got an agent under his command seriously wounded and his own partner nearly killed. Not many in the bureau would have missed hearing about that. Why he hadn't been fired outright was a mystery to Sam. His experience was a textbook case, a cautionary tale for all concerned. He was just grateful that he'd been given a second chance and hadn't risked asking why.

"I've been designated as the FBI's point man at the dam," Beckstrom said proudly. He checked his wristwatch. "In fact, the agent is due here any minute to meet with me."

Sam pitied the agent. If the man was any good at all, he'd quickly take Beckstrom's measure and banish him from the case. Sam donned his hard hat, tucked a set of blueprints under his arm and stood up.

"Where do you think you're going?"

"To work."

"No, you're not."

If Beckstrom thought Sam was going to stick around and watch him ingratiate himself with the FBI, he had another think coming. "Watch me," Sam said. But the trailer door opened before he could make his getaway.

Guilt is a powerful force. You can push it down deep inside, but it's always there, ready to punch you in the chest when you least expect it. All it takes is something ordinary — a brief glance, a certain food, or a melody on the radio — for regret to strike hard and fast. When you come face to face with the flesh and bones reminder of what you've done, the misery you've caused, the blow is almost overwhelming. Your pulse races, your throat tightens, your vision dims, and your body numbs as if paralyzed. For Sam, the debilitating symptoms were triggered the moment Jess Harmon walked into the trailer.

Harmon had been his best friend and partner until the night everything went sideways. Most of his injuries were internal, but the jagged scar running the length of his left jawline was visible proof of the pain Harmon had suffered. Except for the unsightly mark and a slight limp, the forty-five-year-old looked much the same as before. His crew cut was a little grayer at the temples and he'd lost some weight, but his dark eyes still reflected a razor-sharp intelligence. At six-foot-six, he was an imposing figure under most circumstances but in the trailer's tightly confined space, he had a powerful presence.

Harmon surveyed the room and its occupants with a swift once-over and then focused on Sam. Unable to endure the intense scrutiny, Sam stumbled backward a step and the roll of blueprints he held fell onto the floor. Although certain that his rubbery legs wouldn't hold him upright a moment longer, Sam waved off the steadying hand Harmon offered him. "I'm okay," he insisted, walking back to his chair unaided.

Harmon retrieved the blueprints and tossed them onto the desk. "It's good to see you again, old buddy."

Sam had visited his former partner numerous times while he was hospitalized, but Harmon had been in a coma for most of that time. When he did regain consciousness, he was medicated to the hilt and too groggy to register Sam's presence. Despite repeated phone calls and letters later, Sam hadn't seen or heard from him since the incident. Distancing yourself from the man responsible for your pain and suffering was understandable. Jess Harmon had every right to hate Sam—which is why his friendly, "old buddy" greeting didn't ring true. Both men had worked undercover many times and were experts at deception. Whatever motive was behind Harmon's affable manner wasn't clear, but Sam did not believe for a minute that Harmon was glad to see him.

Beckstrom cleared his throat. "Uh, you two know each other?"

Harmon acknowledged Beckstrom with a brief nod. "Ran into Matthews a time or two out at Bonneville Dam." He offered his hand to Beckstrom. "Special Agent Jess Harmon with the FBI," he said.

"I'm Phillip Beckstrom, Lead Engineer and your designated point man here."

Sam collected himself with some deep breaths while point man and agent shook hands. Although Harmon's sudden appearance had been awkward and unnerving, Sam quickly mastered his emotions. He couldn't change his past but he could control his present. Standing, he tucked the blueprints under his arm once again. "Well," he said, "I'll get out of your hair now so you two can get down to business."

"Where're you off to?" asked Harmon.

"Construction site. I need to hold a tailgate meeting with my crew."

"It better be about the dike," Beckstrom said. "I refuse to accept any more of your delaying tactics." That the engineer would try to make himself look good at Sam's expense wasn't surprising. Beckstrom probably took Harmon's cocked eyebrow as disapproval of Sam. Maybe that was his intention now, but when they were partners a brow lift meant something entirely different. It was a signal they'd give one another whenever they'd encounter an ass-kisser or self-important blow-hard.

"Don't want to add to the delay," Harmon told Beckstrom. "But I'd like to speak to your foreman before he goes."

"But . . . but I don't see how Matthews could help. I'm the point man and I know —"

"It's not about the case," Harmon interrupted. "Just some bureaucratic paperwork left over from his time at Bonneville. Shouldn't take long."

Beckstrom seemed relieved. "I understand completely," he said, frowning at Sam. It wasn't much of a stretch for Beckstrom to believe Sam had neglected to do something.

Whatever Harmon wanted to say to Sam, he didn't want an audience. He pointed to the door with his thumb. "We'll just step outside so we won't bother you."

Harmon cupped a hand against the wind and lit a cigarette as soon as they exited the trailer. He smoked Lucky Strikes, which had been Sam's preferred brand, too, when they worked together. The pungent tobacco smell stirred a familiar craving, but he passed on the cigarette Harmon offered. "I've quit," he said.

"And the drinking? Have you quit that, too?"

So that was it. There was no bureaucratic business that needed a private conference. Harmon just wanted to rub Sam's nose in his problems. "Is that why you've been put in charge of Chambers' murder instead of me? Are you here to tell me I'm fired?"

"Easy, Sam. That's not it at all. The chief still wants you to work undercover. Nothing has changed in that regard."

"Then why the dig about my drinking? Why this little *tête a tête*?"

"Forget I mentioned the drinking. I just wanted to let you know up front that I'm sorry."

"Sorry?"

"You know, for not responding when you reached out to me."

He sounded sincere, but Sam had worked with the man long enough to recognize the tension behind the words. "No need to make amends," Sam said. "I screwed up and you paid for it."

"But," Harmon said, eying Sam, closely. "My wounds have healed. I suspect you're still suffering from yours."

Sam opened his pickup door. "I'll survive," he said. "Good luck with the investigation."

"Hold on a minute. What can you tell me about the vic? I understand Chambers was a foreman, too."

"A month away from retirement."

Harmon winced. "Any idea why someone would want him dead?"

His questioning of Sam was standard procedure. As partners, they'd asked the same questions when meeting with the families and friends of other homicide victims. Sam could predict exactly what Harmon would ask next. "Let me save you some time," he said. "Chambers was well-respected and liked by his crew and the others who worked with him. He had a good reputation and was experienced and skilled at what he did. Report writing gave him fits, but he always got it done.

"He had two main interests in life: construction and fishing. He didn't talk about his personal life much, but he did let it slip that his wife had left him many years ago. They had no children and as far as I know, he didn't have any other relatives living in the area. You'd be better off talking to his crew than to waste time tracking down family members. He played poker with the same buddies every week and won as often as he lost. He didn't appear to be having any financial difficulties, but you'd have to confirm that with his bank. Although he tipped back a few now and then, he didn't drink on the job. He was overweight by at least fifty pounds and had several serious medical issues, including a heart attack last year.

"He seemed worried about something, which I attributed at first to health or impending retirement concerns. But he seemed increasingly anxious in the last few days. I never questioned him, figuring that if he wanted me to know what was bothering him he'd tell me. And, in fact, he asked me to come in early today so we could talk but . . . well, we never got the chance."

"What's your gut telling you about his murder?"

"He must have seen or heard something that he wasn't supposed to," Sam said, as he climbed into his truck. "For what it's worth, I never suspected him of having any Communist ties or being behind the sabotage attacks."

"What about my point man?" asked Harmon.

"Jury's still out."

Harmon grabbed the door handle. "Wait. I have a proposition for you."

Sam waited.

"I'd like you to work this case with me." The absurdity of the situation was not lost on Harmon. He smiled sheepishly and added, "I know it sounds crazy after all that's happened, but I need your expertise."

Sam cocked his eyebrow.

"Don't give me the look," Harmon said without rancor. "We made a dynamite team before—"

"Before everything changed." Sam wrenched the door out of Harmon's grip. "You've got your point man waiting inside the trailer."

Harmon shook his head. "You know that hound dog ain't gonna hunt."

"Maybe, but Beckstrom's all puffed up about his new role. He'd never cotton to my involvement, not to mention what our chief would have to say about it."

"No one has to know. You'd still be undercover, just the way we used to do it."

The protection of federal installations from sabotage or other destructive acts was more effective with a man on the inside. Although opposition to The Dalles Dam was more intense than what he'd encountered at other sites, it remained to be seen whether that figured into Chambers' murder. Getting back in the action was tempting, but Sam didn't trust Harmon's motives.

"I'm not being charitable, if that's what you're thinking," said Harmon. "The bureau chief hand-picked me for this assignment. I'm in line to take over his job when he leaves for his new position in D.C." He ran a finger along his scarred jaw. "Almost getting killed in action has its benefits. I'm a bonafide hero around the bureau now. Solving a high-profile murder case would . . . well, let's just say it would push me to the top of the candidate list."

In other words, it was payback time. "I see."

"Do you? Maybe you owe me this one, but I don't think you're seeing the total picture. Helping me helps you, too"

"How's that?"

"For Christ's sake, Sam! The FBI is your life. You can't tell me that you like being stuck out here chasing Indians."

"Don't forget communists."

Harmon tossed his cigarette on the ground and crushed it out with his shoe. "Hell, we both know Hoover and McCarthy are wound too tight about the Communist angle."

"That may be true, but I've still been tasked with finding out if there is a federal employee at the dam aiding and abetting the Communist Party.

"Which you can still do. But I wager that the sabotage has nothing to do with the communists or a mole in the Corps, and everything to do with a bunch of renegade Indians hell-bent on making as much trouble as they can. You need to be back in Portland doing real investigative work. Solving Chambers' murder is the first step."

"Even if all that were true, and I'm not saying it is, how is working off the grid on a murder case going to help me?"

Harmon smiled, "Because when I make bureau chief—and trust me, I will—my priority out of the gate will be to get you promoted and back in Portland where you belong."

Like that was going to happen, thought Sam. Not even the bureau chief had that much pull. As Chambers would've said, Harmon's promise was nothing but "a load of B.S." but it really didn't matter. Helping Harmon solve Chambers' murder couldn't purge the guilt festering in his belly like a tumor, but it might make it tolerable.

"Okay," Sam said. "I'm in."

CHAPTER ELEVEN

Sam found a parking spot in front of the Wasco County Courthouse and walked up the front steps. Built in the 1800's, the courthouse was a solid red brick building on the corner of Front and Main which, like in those early years, also housed the sheriff's department and jail. Once inside the main lobby, Sam paused a moment to locate the nearest water fountain. The ride into town had been hot and uncomfortable and his throat was bone dry. Thirst quenched, he followed the signs to the lower level of the building where the sheriff's office was located.

It was Sam's practice to meet with local law enforcement wherever he was stationed. The reasons why a construction foreman (or whatever other undercover role he'd undertaken) would have need to introduce himself sometimes required a certain amount of creativity. It was worth the effort because Sam needed to know exactly who he'd be dealing with if things got rough later. Sheriff Pritchard's comments in the newspaper about an Indian named Danny Longstreet concerned him. It wasn't the first-time Sam had heard about the kid and the problems he'd caused. Sam had been planning to look into the matter, but Chambers' murder upped the urgency.

Although destruction of Celilo Falls had the Indians extremely agitated, payment for loss of their fishing grounds had been made to most of the tribes and Sam figured it was only a matter of time before Chief Tommy Thompson of the Wy-ams accepted the government's assistance as well. Besides determining if there were an employee or Communist link to sabotage at the dam, it was also Sam's job to make sure that the Indian situation didn't get any uglier. If Danny Longstreet and his gang were somehow connected to the murder of

102

Pete Chambers, then things had already spiraled far beyond the ugly stage.

When Sam had called to make an appointment with Sheriff Pritchard, he hadn't told him the exact reason for his visit, preferring to get a read on the man and situation before divulging too much information. He'd heard rumors that the sheriff was an Indian hater and not averse to stirring up trouble himself. His statements in the newspaper about the Longstreet kid weren't exactly non-confrontational. Sam wasn't inclined to totally discount the scuttlebutt. It was his experience that gossip often contained a grain of truth. On the other hand, it was always possible that the sheriff was misquoted or the article's harsh tone was more a reflection of the reporter's own bias than anything else. Sam was willing to withhold judgment until he'd dealt with the man first-hand.

The courthouse basement was in stark contrast to the polished marble floors and pleasant sage-green walls upstairs. The sheriff's windowless domain was strictly low-rent with peeling paint, dirt-encrusted floors, and an overpowering musty odor. It would've been easy to get a bad impression of the sheriff based solely on his work environment. Since the dingy trailer that served as Sam's office wasn't much better, he dismissed such evidence as apropos of nothing. He found the sheriff's office at the end of the dimly lit hallway and knocked on the door.

"It's open!" came a shout from the other side of the door.

Sam took the declaration as an invitation to enter. Pritchard sat behind a cluttered gunmetal gray desk with his nose buried in a newspaper. He didn't lower the paper until Sam introduced himself. The sheriff was much older than Sam had expected. Either the job was aging him fast or his narrow craggy face had seen sixty years and then some. He'd made a futile attempt to conceal a nearly bald head by combing a few wispy strands of white-streaked hair over the top. A similarly colored thin mustache lined his upper lip. What he lacked in physical presence was offset by a crisp and spotless tan uniform that shouted officialdom. The man's gray eyes homed in on Sam with a wariness that bordered on hostility. Hoping to set the man at ease, Sam extended his hand. The sheriff brushed his offer aside and told him to take a seat.

103

Pritchard picked up a pack of Camel cigarettes on the desktop and shook one out. "What can I do for you?" he asked.

"Like I told you when I phoned, I'm new to the area and work as construction foreman out at the dam." He pointed to the newspaper Pritchard had been reading. "I saw the article about the drowning at the falls. Looks like there's some trouble brewing with the Indians."

The sheriff tore a match from a matchbook emblazoned with Dizzy's Tavern on the cover and struck it. "Trouble's always brewin' when you got a bunch of redskins around." He lit the cigarette, took a deep drag and exhaled. Squinting at Sam through the blue haze he said, "What's it to you?"

The arrogance behind the question irked Sam but he let it pass. "It's called due diligence."

"Huh?"

"Since I'm in charge of resettling the Indians' burial grounds, I want to ward off any potential problems that might arise."

Pritchard leaned back in his chair and laughed until he began to cough. "You poor devil," he said after a round of labored hacking. "How'd you get saddled with that job?"

Sam flashed him a sheepish smile and shrugged. "Just lucky, I guess."

Pritchard crushed out his half-smoked cigarette and straightened his shoulders. "The lucky part as I see it," he said, tapping his thumb against his chest, "is that you've come to the right man for advice."

Sam considered his next words carefully. It might be possible to use the sheriff's self-important air to his advantage. Flattery often worked well with men like Pritchard. However, Sam wasn't in the mood to schmooze. Better to let the man know his intentions up front. "I'm not seeking advice, sheriff."

"Oh, yeah? Then why are you here?" He made a show of checking his wristwatch. "I'm a busy man."

"I appreciate that so I'll get right to the point. I need information about potential problems that we might encounter when relocating the Indian graves. You were quoted in the paper as saying that it was just a matter of time before opposition to the dam got someone hurt."

"Or killed. I heard you lost a man recently."

Sam nodded. "Foreman Pete Chambers."

"Damn shame. I've known Pete for a long time and I've been sheriff here even longer, but the federal boys pulled rank on me. They can't handle a murder investigation any better than local law enforcement, but what the hell? If they have any smarts at all, they'll recognize that they need my help soon enough."

The sheriff's ego was clearly bruised but Sam did not intend to discuss Chambers' murder with him. That was Jess Harmon's call. "What can you tell me about Danny Longstreet?"

Pritchard lit another cigarette. "Ha! How much time you got?" What followed was a spirited diatribe similar to what had been printed in the newspaper article. He said Longstreet was the leader of a gang that would do whatever they could to disrupt the completion of the dam. He told a story about Danny's father and how he'd gotten blind drunk and tried to stab two good citizens for no reason whatsoever. "The apple don't fall too far from the tree, that's for sure. The Longstreet clan has always been bad news, and now they're agitated big time." He wagged his cigarette at Sam. "I can flat out guarantee you that they'll be looking for ways to foul up your operation. But don't you worry none. I've got a handle on the situation. The days are numbered for those red bastards."

Sam sighed wearily. The sheriff's annoying bravado reminded him of Beckstrom's know-it-all attitude. Not a good sign. The self-serving recitation convinced Sam that his visit had been wasted. The cooperative relationship he'd hoped to form with Sheriff Pritchard was going to be difficult at best. He was about to cut short their meeting when the telephone rang.

"Sheriff Leonard Pritchard here," he said with stiff formality. "What? Where'd you say it was? Okay, I'm on it." He ended the call promptly and rose from his chair.

"Trouble?"

"Some kind of disturbance out at Baker Bluff. 'Fraid our little chat is over," he said, checking his gun belt. "Duty calls."

"Mind if I follow you out there? I have my own transportation."

Pritchard's eyebrows shot up. "What the hell for? This is police business. Not the government's."

The territorial jab was not lost on Sam. "No argument there, sheriff," he said, raising his hands palm-side up. "But Baker Bluff is one of several properties that the government is considering as a possible site for the new cemetery. I'm interested in anything that goes on out there that might affect our decision."

Pritchard looked him over and then shrugged. "Suit yourself," he said, donning his hat. "Just make sure you don't get in my way."

Baker Bluff was located on five acres of verdant grassland about ten miles from The Dalles. Sam had toured the property twice and favored its purchase over the other choices under consideration. The Columbia River Gorge view was breathtaking, but the serene grandeur of the property impressed Sam much more. He was struck by the overwhelming peace he felt when walking the grounds. He didn't consider himself a religious man but there was no other way to describe the feeling except that it was spiritual. For that reason alone, Baker Bluff seemed an appropriate setting for a final resting place.

Sam had driven a motor pool pickup into town after advising Phillip Beckstrom that he needed to check out another possible cemetery site. At first, the engineer had balked at Sam's frequent field trips but now that he was Agent Harmon's point man, he no longer kept tabs on Sam's comings and goings. Sam chuckled to himself as he climbed into the pickup. The duties Harmon had given his point man were nothing more than make-work but were presented in a way that appealed to Beckstrom's out-sized ego. The tactic worked perfectly and allowed Sam the freedom to get things done for a change.

Pritchard led the way through town in his patrol car and traveled west for several miles. It was a scenic drive, but Sam didn't have time to sight-see. He had to floorboard the truck just to keep the sheriff's speeding car in sight. When they reached the turnoff to Baker Bluff, Sheriff Pritchard brought his vehicle to an abrupt stop. A huge "*For Sale by Owner*" sign had been yanked from its post and discarded in the dirt. Pritchard got out of the car to examine the damage. "Crazy punks have done it again," he said, when Sam approached. The sign was awash with red paint that obliterated the owner's name and phone number.

There was no mistaking who Pritchard meant by punks, but Sam asked anyway. "You think Longstreet and his gang did this?"

The sheriff pointed to the graffiti scrawled across the sign's surface. "See them arrows dripping red like blood? That's Danny's signature." He spit a blob of yellow mucous onto the ground. "Looks like I better get on down to the bluff and see what else they've been up to."

When they arrived at the bluff, they came upon a Ford truck that had crashed into a sturdy Douglas Fir. The accident had ignited a small fire that was mostly smoke, but if left unchecked, threatened to engulf the entire property. Sam grabbed the fire extinguisher that was required equipment in a government vehicle and scrambled from the cab. The sheriff followed behind him with a second extinguisher from his patrol car. Within seconds, the fire was out and the men got their first look inside the wreck. An old man was slumped over the steering wheel. A nasty gash on his forehead had bled onto his wool-plaid shirt.

"Good Lord," said Sam, prying open the dented and blackened door. "I think I've seen this guy before." He looked exactly like the sick Indian he and Ellie had encountered their first day in town.

Pritchard stuck his head inside the door. "Well, wouldn't ya know. It's Old Injun George. Deader than a doornail in a stolen truck."

"Stolen?" asked Sam while feeling the Indian's neck for a pulse.

"This here is Tony Rossi's truck."

"Let's get him out!" shouted Sam. "He's still alive."

"If he ain't dead, then he's shitfaced. Can't you smell the booze? It's stronger than the smoke." He stepped away from the truck and kicked aside an empty wine bottle that lay on the ground. "Stupid redskins will drink any old cheap sauce they can get their hands on."

The bottle broke at Sam's feet. It wasn't "any old cheap sauce" judging by the label. Wine wasn't Sam's alcohol of choice, but he knew that this brand sold for a lot more than he could afford. It was a curious detail, but the man's drinking habits weren't important. His head wound still bled profusely and needed immediate attention. "There's a first aid kit in my truck," Sam said, easing the injured Indian onto the ground and kneeling beside him. "I'll try to stop the bleeding while you fetch the kit."

Sheriff Pritchard snorted. "Fetch it yourself. I'm nobody's gofer."

Sam was momentarily stunned. Bravado is one thing, but the

sheriff was deliberately uncooperative. He didn't know if it was because Pritchard was an Indian hater or if he just resented Sam's interference in official police business, but he didn't have time to debate the issue. Resisting the urge to fire off an angry retort, Sam spoke as reasonably as he could manage, "This man is hurt bad. If we work together we might be able to save his life."

"Yeah, and then what? He'll just get drunk and steal someone else's truck. Next time it might not be a tree he runs into."

Sam concentrated on helping George instead of engaging the sheriff further. After temporarily staunching the blood flow with his handkerchief, he raced back to his truck for the first aid kit. When he came back, Pritchard was leaning over George. "What're you doing?" Sam asked.

The sheriff waved a pair of handcuffs at him. "I'm arresting this low-life for drunk driving, trespassing, and stealing Rossi's truck."

"The hell you are. I'm going to patch him up and take him into town. He needs to see a doctor. Now get out of my way. I've got work to do," he said, opening the aid kit.

Pritchard started to say something, but lit a cigarette instead and watched Sam apply antiseptic and a bandage. Afterwards, he said, "You're lucky I don't arrest you for obstruction of justice."

Sam stood and faced the sheriff with fists clenched. "Try it."

Pritchard rested a hand on his gun holster. "Back off, mister. You're threatening the wrong man here."

Sam was tempted to flash his FBI badge but relaxed his clenched fists and tried a less confrontational approach. "Look, Sheriff, I don't want any trouble. I just want to help the old guy. He needs to see a doctor."

"Then you better take him out to Celilo Village. There ain't a doctor in town who'll touch the bum."

Sam couldn't believe that was true, but conceded the point. "Fine. Help me get him into my truck and I'll take him to Celilo."

Pritchard ground out his cigarette. "All right," he said. "But I'll be coming down there later. He's under arrest and I'm holding you responsible for him."

CHAPTER TWELVE

The Music Box hosted a sock hop at the store every Friday afternoon during the summer. The weekly dances were a big draw for bored teens in The Dalles. Ellie wanted to go as soon as she heard about them. "I love to dance!" she said. She rattled off a bunch of rock n' roll dances she favored, including the Lindy Hop, Stroll, and the Bossa Nova. "But my absolute all-time favorite," is the West Coast Swing. She was surprised that Dessa didn't know any of the popular dances and wasn't even interested in learning. "Come on, you have to give it a try. Look at all those kids on American Bandstand. They're having a blast!" Dessa liked rock n' roll as much as Ellie but she had no natural rhythm. Just walking across the room without tripping over her own two feet was a major effort. Dancing was out of the question. Why subject herself to unnecessary ridicule?

Mr. Matthews had fixed Ellie's broken record player, but he was opposed to letting her attend dances at The Music Box. His refusal was hard to figure. Yes, he was overly-protective but Ellie could usually talk him into whatever she wanted to do. "Does he know about Tony Rossi's offer to take you to the Music Box?" asked Dessa. Ellie claimed that she hadn't mentioned his visit or gift. "I don't lie to my father and it's not a lie if I don't say anything," she insisted. Dessa assumed Ellie had never heard of the sin of omission. "I'm not worried," Ellie said after another round of fruitless pleading. "I'll get him to change his mind." Dessa got the impression that Mr. Matthews was fully aware of the realtor's interest in his daughter with or without lying. It was entirely possible that someone had seen Tony's flashy car parked outside their house the other day and tattled. Or, maybe he was reacting to the number of boys in the neighborhood who'd been chasing after Ellie ever since they'd moved to Hillcrest. It could be that he just thought his little girl was growing up too fast. Whatever the reason, Ellie wasn't allowed to attend the sock hops. But, as Ellie predicted, Mr. Matthews eventually relented. All it took was a week of teary-eyed entreaties and emotionally charged turmoil to wear him down. Mr. Matthews had only one requirement: Dessa had to go with her.

Maureen Feldman was thrilled with the idea. She saw her daughter's growing friendship with Ellie as a pathway to the social acceptance which had eluded Dessa for so long. Dessa thought her mother was delusional. Ellie's popularity wasn't going to magically raise Dessa's status. It just didn't work that way with the teenage crowd. They might tolerate her as Ellie's sidekick, but that would be all. Yet, despite her aversion to dancing and low expectations for an improved social life, Dessa agreed to accompany Ellie as Mr. Matthews required. The arrangement was simple: In exchange for Dessa's attendance, Ellie would create pencil drawings for the *Heard on the Hill* newsletter.

For Ellie, deciding what to wear to the first dance took almost as long as the dance itself. She changed outfits several times before finally selecting a black felt poodle skirt and sleeveless pink blouse plus small pink neck scarf. Maureen insisted that Dessa wear a similar outfit. "All the girls are wearing those skirts now. It's important that you fit in." She took her to shop at Mrs. Peabody's, which she said was where all the popular girls bought their clothes. It would take more than a full skirt with a poodle appliqué for Dessa to fit in, but it was pointless to argue with her mother. She walked out of the store with an outfit exactly like Ellie's.

Since they had plenty of time before the dance started, the girls stopped at Woolworth's for ice cream. Primarily a pharmacy, Woolworth's also included a variety store and lunch counter with stools and a few upholstered booths. The food was good, the service fast, and the ice cream was the best in town. The drug store was located right down the street from The Music Box and was considered *the spot* for teens to gather when the dances ended. As a result, Woolworth's older customers avoided the place on Friday afternoons, preferring to get their prescriptions filled and have a bite of lunch or cup of coffee earlier in the day. Or, better yet—on another day altogether. It was still an hour before the sock hop started but the teen-averse adults had already completed their errands.

The store was practically empty when the girls arrived. Dessa bypassed the counter's metal stools in favor of a booth by the window with a miniature juke box atop the table. Ellie inserted a dime and selected J14, *Don't Be Cruel*. Dessa frowned, "Not Elvis, please. He's so overrated". She inserted her own dime and flipped through the pages of selections. She chose B2, *The Green Door* by Jim Lowe and then ordered them both a triple scoop banana split with all the trimmings.

"I can't eat all that," laughed Ellie.

"Sure, you can. If not, I'll finish it for you. I'm going to need a boatload of sugar if I have any hope of surviving this afternoon," Dessa quipped. She wasn't entirely joking. Ice cream was her go-to food when stressed and the prospect of standing on the sidelines while everyone else had a good time at the dance bordered on torture. It was a sacrifice she was willing to make for a newsletter with quality photo-like sketches. It's what any good journalist would do.

The girls were enjoying their ice cream when Ellie's eyes focused on a boy who'd just entered the store. "Hey, isn't that Nick Rossi?" she asked.

Dessa licked a dab of chocolate syrup off her spoon. "Yep," she said, turning to look at the entrance. "Tony's gofer."

Nick paused at the entrance as if he needed a moment to get his bearings. It was unusual to see him out and about by himself. He followed Tony around like an eager-to-please puppy. Dessa thought Ellie looked disappointed that Nick was alone for a change. A large overhead fan ruffled his ash blond hair. As he brushed a few strands out of his eyes, he caught the girls staring at him. Ellie smiled and gestured for him to join them. "He doesn't have Mr. Rossi's dark good looks, but he is cute," she said.

Nick looked around to see who Ellie had waved to. Finding nobody standing near him, he pointed his thumb to his chest and mouthed, "Who, me?"

"I guess he's cute," agreed Dessa. "In an awkward sort of way."

Ellie waved again. "Be nice," she said. "He's on his way over." She scooted closer to Dessa to make room for him in the booth. "Sit here," she told him, patting the vacant space next to her.

He hesitated. "Well, uh . . . I just . . ."

Dessa rolled her eyes. "Sit down already," she said. "Your master—excuse me—your cousin will never have to know."

Ellie quickly diffused Dessa's flippant remark with a fetching dimpled grin. "Please, Nick" she purred. "We'd love to have you join us."

"Oh. Okay, then. Sure," he said, sliding into the booth. "Just for a few minutes. I promised Mildred I'd bring back a large iced tea for her. She's not feeling so good."

"What's wrong?" asked Ellie. "Is the heat wave getting to her?" The temperature had hit the stratosphere for over a week now. Although the locals were accustomed to hot weather, the conditions this summer were breaking all records. There'd been a rash of heat related illnesses reported in *The Dalles Chronicle* and Dessa, too, had written an article in her newsletter about the heat wave. An elderly Hillcrest neighbor, Viola Phinney, had been hospitalized due to heat stroke. Ellie visited her in the hospital and even volunteered to help with anything she needed after she went home.

Since Ellie had never even spoken to the woman before visiting her in the hospital, Dessa couldn't understand her concern. "Kindness doesn't require a prior relationship," Ellie said. The phrase sounded like something straight out of Dale Carnegie's book, *How to Win Friends and Influence People*. According to Maureen Feldman, the book was a blueprint for social and business success and an absolute must read. Following Carnegie's principles was an exercise in futility for Dessa but it seemed a natural part of Ellie's personality. She had quickly become known around Hillcrest as "that kindhearted Matthews girl." The label fit, but Ellie didn't care for it. She said kindness is often mistaken for weakness. "And I'm definitely not weak," she insisted.

"I don't think it's the heat," Nick said. "Mildred may have an ulcer or something along those lines. She's never said for sure."

Dessa concentrated on her ice cream while they chatted. The only interesting bit of information she picked up as she half-listened was that Nick planned to attend college in the fall. The gig with Tony was just a favor he'd promised to do for their uncle. "Believe me," he said. "I have no desire to become a salesman of any kind. I'm majoring in economics." His lips parted in a lopsided grin as he hurriedly added, "But don't tell Tony that. He thinks I'm besotted with real estate."

Ellie laughed and assured him that his secret was safe with them.

Dessa laughed, too, but gave him no such promise. She was a reporter, after all. She'd just scooped the last bite of ice cream out of the bowl when she heard Nick mutter, "Uh, oh." When she looked up, Nick had scrambled out of the booth. If he'd been trying to avoid being spotted by Tony as he sat shoulder to shoulder with Ellie, he was too late. Tony had gotten a good look at them as he passed by the drugstore window. He strode through the front door with a scowl as big as Texas plastered across his dark face. "The fit's really going to hit the shan now," Nick said, worriedly.

"What for?" asked Dessa. "It's a free country, isn't it?" Nick had always struck Dessa as something of a wuss but her opinion of him had risen several notches when he said he planned to attend college in the fall. If he wasn't going to pursue a real estate career, Dessa couldn't see what difference it made whether or not Tony was upset with him.

"Mildred's still waiting for that iced tea," Tony said, glaring at Nick. The tone he used made it sound like poor old Mildred had nearly died of thirst while Nick had been frittering away the afternoon.

Nick started to apologize but Ellie cut him off. "It's all my fault, Mr. Rossi. I insisted that Nick hang out with us for a while."

Tony absolved Ellie of any responsibility for his cousin's behavior and quickly dispatched Nick to the office with Mildred's tea. He was all smiles when he turned back to Ellie. "Are you going to the sock hop today?" he asked. A nod from Ellie's beaming face was all the answer he needed. "Let's go, then," he said, offering his hand to help her out of the booth. "I'm a great dancer!" Winking, he added, "Slow dances are my specialty."

Tony ignored Dessa except to hand her the check for their ice cream before he shepherded Ellie out the door. Although Mr. Matthews hadn't said it in so many words, Dessa believed he expected her to watch out for his daughter. Why else would he insist that she accompany Ellie to the dances? Referring to a creep like Tony Rossi as Mr. Wonderful spoke volumes about her lack of discernment

113

when it came to the male species. Dessa paid the check and rushed to catch up with Tony and Ellie.

A blast of hot air hit her like a mugger's fist as soon as she stepped outside the drugstore. The suffocating weather didn't deter Tony from wrapping his arm around Ellie's waist as they strolled down the sidewalk. When a woman across the street shouted, "Tony! Tony, wait up!" he dropped his arm to his side faster than a kid who'd been caught raiding the cookie jar.

Dessa recognized Clarice Nestor as the woman who'd hailed Tony. The ladies in Maureen Feldman's garden club unanimously agreed that Clarice's sexy, low-cut dresses, gaudy jewelry and flirty behavior was highly inappropriate for a banker's wife. "I don't trust her," was Maureen's complaint when her husband said Clarice was interested in buying their Baker Bluff property. Dessa didn't know the details about the property sale, but her father's claim that all the many meetings with the woman was "just business" sounded lame even to her.

Gaudy or not, the gold jewelry at Clarice's neck and wrists sparkled in the bright sunlight as she hobbled across the street in flimsy, mile-high heels. "Thank God I found you!" she said, grabbing hold of Tony's arm. "We've got a problem."

Tony twisted out of her grasp. "It'll have to wait," he said. "I've promised to escort this special young lady to The Music Box."

"Hey," said Dessa, sidling closer to Tony. "He's escorting *two* special young ladies."

Clarice gave Dessa and Ellie a quick once-over. "Babysitting the ankle-biter set today are you, Tony?"

"No need to be rude," he said.

"Maybe not, but we do need to talk." She grabbed his arm again. "And I mean right now." She pulled him a few steps away from the girls.

"Who is that woman?" asked Ellie when they were out of earshot. "She seems awfully possessive."

"Her name's Clarice Nestor and the skinny making the rounds is that she's Tony Rossi's current mistress. I guess she believes that gives her the right to yank him off the street whenever she wants."

"His mistress? But . . . but she's married. I saw the ring on her left

114

hand."

"I hate to break it to you, but marriage vows don't mean a thing to men like Tony Rossi."

Whatever Clarice had to talk to Tony about didn't go over very well. Even from a distance the girls could tell that he was angry. His voice was strained when he trotted back to say, "I'm so sorry, Ellie, but something important has come up and I have to deal with it."

"That's all right," Ellie said, smiling bravely. "We understand." Her smile faded as she watched Tony and Clarice walk across the street and enter Dizzy's. She sighed as if her heart had been broken.

"Oh, for Pete's sake," Dessa chided. "So, you got dumped for the town slut. If you're lucky, she'll keep Tony in her bed until you wise up and dump the dirt bag yourself."

Ellie whirled around to face Dessa. The lovesick schoolgirl look had disappeared. "Not. One. Word. More," Ellie hissed through clenched teeth. Her fury was so intense that Dessa instinctively backed up a step.

"Jeez, I'm sorry," Dessa said. "I didn't mean to rattle your cage." This was how it always seemed to go. Her smart mouth had gotten her in trouble again. Her mother was right. She'd never make friends. Even the so-called "kind-hearted Matthews girl" had limits. Ellie dismissed her apology with a shrug and stomped off. "Hey, where're you going?" Dessa called. The Music Box was in the opposite direction.

"Home!" shouted Ellie over her shoulder.

Dessa's short legs were no match for Ellie's long strides but she caught up with her at the corner. Ellie ignored her as she watched for a break in the traffic. "What about the dance?" Dessa gasped, struggling to get her breathing under control.

"I'm not going."

"What? Why not?"

"Don't feel like it anymore," Ellie said, darting across the street.

"Fine," Dessa said, running after her. She'd never wanted to go to the dance in the first place. "But walking all the way home in this heat is crazy. It feels like 150 degrees out here!" Maureen Feldman had agreed to drive the girls home after the dance. Dessa dreaded the scene her mother would make when she learned how her daughter

115

had messed up another friendship. But it was better than suffering a heat stroke. "Mom can still give us a ride."

"I'd rather walk," snapped Ellie.

Ellie's offended act grated on Dessa's nerves but she was determined to make peace. Loss of a friendship was one thing. That she could deal with. Loss of Ellie's artistic talents for her newsletter was another matter. If keeping her mouth shut about Tony Rossi was what it took for Ellie to continue sketching, then Dessa would never utter another discouraging word about him. "I know a shortcut home," she said, assuming a friendly, let's bury the hatchet tone of voice. "I can show you, if you'd like."

Ellie wasn't impressed with her conciliatory offer. "You mean the Pioneer Cemetery? Don't bother. I know the way."

The rebuff hurt but Dessa shrugged it off. "Okay," she said, "I'll just follow you then."

CHAPTER THIRTEEN

Reba had just filled a big metal pan with water to cook the roots she'd gathered for a village-wide feast when a government pickup followed by a string of barking dogs roared into the village yard. Startled, Reba dropped the pan, splashing water over the front of her dress. The driver swerved to avoid some children at play before he came to an abrupt, dust-swirling stop in front of the Long House. A government vehicle at Celilo always attracted attention and a fair amount of concern. In the villagers' experience, the government's presence at Celilo usually meant something bad had happened or was about to happen. And the way this driver had barreled through the village at top speed intensified their fears. Within minutes, a large crowd of wary villagers had gathered outside the Long House.

A tall, sandy-haired government official jumped from the cab and rushed to the back of the truck. "There was an accident," he said, opening the tailgate. Reba was too far away to see what the man was pointing to. Word passed through the throng of onlookers that it was George Featherstone. "Easy, there," the official said to George when he attempted to sit upright. "He's been hurt," he explained. "Is there anyone here with medical training?"

The anxious villagers who'd been pushing and jostling one another to get a closer view, parted to make way for Chief Tommy Thompson. Reba was relieved to see him, for his presence had a calming effect on the gathering. Despite his advanced years and the need for a walking stick, Chief Thompson had a proud and stately gait. He had been their leader for as long as Reba had lived at Celilo and was widely recognized as a great man even by non-Indians. Their chief would know how to handle the situation.

Reba and the rest of the villagers watched the government man carefully. Much could be learned about the man's character when he met Chief Thompson. He was taller than the chief but he didn't carry himself in an intimidating way. As the chief approached, the stranger straightened his shoulders and dipped his head slightly while casting his eyes downward. His show of respect for Chief Thompson caused a murmur of approval to ripple through the crowd. Danny should be here, thought Reba. He needed to see that some shuyapus—even government shuyapus—can possess some good qualities.

Chief Thompson responded with a welcome nod and then turned his attention to George. "We will care for our brother," he said, directing four young men to carry George into the Long House. They carefully lifted him out of the truck using the gray blanket he laid on as a stretcher. "Where's Reba?" the chief asked. "George needs her healing."

Reba had begun to push past the women and children at the fringe when the need for medical assistance was first raised. "I'm here, Chief Thompson," she said as she reached the front of the onlookers. She told him that she would go straight home and get her medicine bag. The government man slammed the tailgate shut and addressed the chief, "Sir, could I have a moment of your time to speak in private?" Chief Thompson led him into the Long House. Near the door, they passed a little carved bird named Pi-a-koot sitting atop a pole. Chief Thompson carved the bird many years ago to replicate a bird he saw in a vision. He believed that the spirit of Pi-a-koot carried his prayers and messages to the Creator. Reba quickened her pace toward home with myriad questions racing through her mind. *What kind of accident did George have? How did a government man find him? Why did the man need to talk to Chief Thompson? Was his unexpected arrival at the village a blessing or a curse? What message would Pi-a-koot carry for the chief today?*

She returned to the Long House a few minutes later holding a small leather bag in one hand and a couple of clean rags in the other. Oscar followed closely behind her carrying a canvas folding cot. After overseeing George's transfer from the dirt floor where he'd been placed to the cot, Chief Thompson nodded to Reba and said, "George is in good hands now." The men who'd attended George in Reba's absence departed and the chief led the white man to a couple of metal chairs across the room.

Reba noted with relief that George was conscious, although disoriented and complaining of a headache. Someone had already applied a makeshift bandage to his head but it was now blood-soaked. The stench of alcohol on his body was overpowering. His skin felt clammy, and when she checked his pulse it was racing. Alarmed, she quickly removed a short, thin needle from her bag and pulled George's shirt open at the abdomen. Holding the syringe in one hand and, grasping a fold of his skin between her fingers and thumb in the other, she inserted the needle at a 45-degree angle. Once the needle was through the skin, she pushed the plunger on the syringe.

As Reba monitored George's reaction, she told her father-in-law that she would need some water. Oscar went outside and retrieved the metal pan she'd dropped earlier and refilled it with fresh water from the yard pump. Reba dipped one of the rags into the water and washed George's dirt-smeared and bloody face and neck. Soon, George declared that he was healed and tried to sit up. She gave his shoulders a gentle push. "No, George, you need to rest," she said, settling him back onto the cot. Next, she removed the sodden bandage from his head and examined the gash carefully. She took a jar of herbal paste from her bag and applied it to the wound and then wrapped the other rag she'd brought with her around his head. She secured it with a knot tied at the front.

Every now and then Reba stole a glance at the shuyapu while she worked. She decided that he had a kind face for a government man. Although he wasn't smiling as he talked to Chief Thompson, she had seen laugh wrinkles at the corner of his blue eyes. She didn't like his short hair, but knew that was the way of white men. She ran a finger over one of her dark braids and concluded that the ways of her people were much better. Wearing long hair showed the Creator that they had not changed since the beginning of time when He placed them on the rocks to fish. A short-haired man cannot catch big salmon.

Several minutes later, Chief Thompson and the man stood and shook hands. The meeting of hands was a good sign. With their talk concluded, they walked over to George's cot. The chief introduced Reba and, after exchanging a few words with George, left the Long House. The government man—Sam Matthews as the chief had called him — didn't seem in any hurry to leave. He knelt beside George and asked him how he was feeling. George closed his eyes and didn't answer. "He'll be all right, now that he's had his medicine," Reba said.

"I saw you inject him with some kind of needle."

"Insulin."

Sam Matthews' eyes widened. "He's diabetic?"

Reba nodded. "Since he was a youngster. I started administering his insulin after his wife died a few years ago."

"That explains a lot. I thought his shaking and slurred speech was caused by the accident or possibly too much liquor."

Alcoholism was a problem with many villagers, but not George. "White people think all Indians are drunkards," she shot back.

"Whoa, there," Matthews said. "That's not entirely accurate."

Reba considered his reaction. She had offended him. "I'm sorry," she said.

He smiled. "It's okay. I'm sure there's some truth to what you say, but not in my case."

His words sounded sincere. She felt reassured enough to ask him the questions that had been uppermost in her mind since he'd arrived at the village. "Please tell me what happened to George. How did you find him?"

"He stole a truck and drove it into a tree."

She knew that couldn't be true. "Didn't Chief Thompson tell you? George wouldn't steal a truck. His vision is too poor to drive."

"The diabetes?"

"Yes. And he doesn't drink, either. I don't understand why his clothes smell that way."

"We found an empty wine bottle near the truck," he said. "So, we naturally assumed . . ."

"We?"

Sam Matthews didn't answer. Reba decided he was judging whether he'd disclosed too much to her, a mere woman. She felt a surge of anger warm her face. Were his smile and considerate words covering up something? Could she really trust a government man with the truth? But, she reasoned, Chief Thompson had seemed to accept him. "What did you tell our chief?" she asked.

"Look," he said. "Don't be alarmed, but based on what I've learned here, I think the circumstances surrounding George's accident are highly suspicious. I've warned Chief Thompson that Sheriff Pritchard will be coming to the village sometime later today."

Reba's heart sank. If the sheriff were involved, there would be trouble—for George, Danny and possibly the entire village. She glanced at George sleeping unaware on the cot. "Why is the sheriff coming here?" Reba asked.

"He's investigating the accident and theft of the truck. It's his job."

"And you?" she asked. "What's your job?"

He was quiet again. This shuyapu chose his words carefully. "My job is to make sure the sheriff gets his facts straight. To that end, I have a couple of questions for you."

Reba didn't want to answer any questions but he had answered hers so she heard herself say, "Go ahead."

"Do you know of any reason why George might have been on the road to Baker Bluff today?"

"I don't know this place, this bluff you speak of."

"It's a big meadow overlooking the river about ten miles from here."

The white man was mistaken. "George would not have gone such a distance. The only place he goes with any regularity is into town. He cannot fish because of his medical condition, but he likes to feel useful. He takes orders for salmon from the locals."

"I thought you said he didn't drive. How does he get to town and back? It's a long way to walk."

Did he think she was not telling the truth? "He hitches a ride with whoever happens to be going that way. My son takes him a lot."

"I see," Matthews said, stroking his chin. "One more thing. Does George have any enemies?"

Reba considered the question for a moment. Of course, George had enemies. They all had enemies. "You mean enemies besides your government?"

"My government?"

Was he blind to the obvious? "The dam," she said simply.

Reba didn't know how to interpret the nod he gave her. Did he agree with her assessment or was he just placating her? She decided it was probably a little of both when he answered, "You have a point." He said he didn't have any more questions for now. "Chief Thompson is aware that the sheriff intends to come to the village. It's very important that no one disturbs George. No one, including the sheriff, should question him regarding the accident if I'm not present. He's still incoherent and needs rest. Do you understand my meaning?"

"Yes," Reba said. This white man surprised her. He seemed to grasp how risky their situation was with the sheriff. It was an unusual development and she wondered what his intentions really were.

"Good," he said, flashing another engaging smile. "I'll be back in time for the feast this evening."

Chief Thompson had apparently invited him to the Memory Feast. She hoped that he hadn't been misled by the man's kind eyes and reassuring manner. Unlike her people, shuyapus often said one thing and did another. The worst accusation you could make against a Wy-am-pum was to say he lied like a white man. As she smoothed the blanket over George's shoulders, she recalled the warning her husband had given her so many years ago. "You can never really know a shuyapu's true heart."

Chapter Fourteen

Tony and Clarice stayed at Dizzy's long enough to cool off with a pitcher of beer. It looked like half the town had the same idea. Even the teetotalers had ducked in to get out of the heat. Under normal circumstances, the buzz from the elbow-to-elbow, beer swilling crowd would have energized Tony. He'd finalized more than one deal at Dizzy's and considered the tavern a gold mine for referrals, but there'd be no deals made today. From the moment Clarice had dragged him away from Ellie to tell him that her so-called solution for saving the Baker Bluff deal had gone belly-up, he was too angry to even think about working the room. He should've known that any plan involving a drunk like Injun George wouldn't succeed. Clarice believed she could come up with an even better plan but Tony didn't share her confidence. As far as he was concerned, his dream was as wrecked as his truck.

It was still early in the day, but Dizzy's looked and sounded like a rowdy Saturday night. "What did you say?" asked Tony. Clarice downed the last of her beer and slapped a dollar bill on the table. "I said it's too noisy in here! Let's go to the office." Clarice held onto her straw purse with one hand and clung to Tony's arm with the other as they pushed their way through the raucous crowd.

At the realty office, they found the shades drawn, a "CLOSED" sign hanging in the window, and the door locked. "What the hell's going on?" Tony asked, pounding his fist on the door.

"We're closed," came a muffled voice from inside.

"Like hell you are," Tony shouted, pounding on the door again. "Open this door NOW." Tony cursed a steady stream when he didn't get a further response from the person inside.

"Don't you have a key?" asked Clarice.

"Not on me," Tony said, patting his pockets and cursing loudly.

The door opened a crack. "Oh, hi," said Nick, peering through the opening. "It's you."

Tony pushed open the door wide enough to enter and elbowed Nick out of the way. "Damn right, it's me."

"I . . . I was just leaving," Nick said, clutching a folded newspaper to his chest.

Tony snatched the "CLOSED" sign out of the window and tossed it on his desk. "Where's Mildred?" he asked, looking around the darkened office.

Nick stuttered, "Uh . . . well, she . . . Mildred, she got sick and had to go home. Jensen and Hoffman left earlier and since you weren't here, I thought I should close up."

"Since when did I give you permission to run things around here? You leave when I say you can leave."

"For Christ's sake," Clarice said. "Let the kid go. It's better to have the place all to ourselves anyway."

Tony scowled as he nudged his cousin's shoulder. "I should bust your chops but the lady is right. Hit the road."

"Yes, sir," Nick said. He held the newspaper in front of him like a shield as he stepped around Clarice and Tony.

"Is that today's paper you have there?" Clarice asked.

Nick turned to face her. "Uh, maybe. I mean, no. I don't think so."

"Give it to me," she demanded with outstretched fingers. "I need to check something."

Nick stared at her polished red nails as if they were claws and shook his head. "No, I can't."

"What's wrong with you?" snapped Tony. "Hand over the damn paper." When Nick refused a second time, Tony snatched the newspaper out of his grasp. Two bound leather ledgers fell to the floor with a dull thud. Tony broke the shocked silence that followed. "Son of a bitch! What the hell are you doing with our record books?"

"I just—"

"What did you hope to find out, you sneaky prick?"

Nick backed up a few steps. "Nothing. I mean, I can explain."

Tony overtook his cousin's clumsy retreat. "Explain this," he said, punching Nick in the nose. His fist made a hollow sound when it hit followed by the crunch of cartilage breaking. Red mist sprayed from Nick's nose as he fell to his knees.

"I didn't want them! The records were Uncle Thol's idea," Nick frantically lisped, dabbing at his nose with his shirt sleeve. "He thought—"

"You're a lying fuck," Tony growled. Grabbing the front of Nick's shirt, he jerked him to his feet. "You sent Mildred and the others home so you could find those ledgers. And I damn well know why. You were going to blackmail us, you conniving bastard. Always asking questions, wanting to know what the Destiny Group was, watching every move I made. You—"

"No!" You've got it all wrong. Uncle Thol wanted the records, not me. I'm telling the truth!"

"Liar!"

"Back off, Tony," Clarice said. "I want to hear what Nick has to say about your uncle."

"It doesn't matter what he has to say."

"Think about it, Tony. Are you certain your uncle had no other motive in mind for sending Nick here? A more compelling reason than to learn about the wonderful world of real estate? I've never met the man, but I doubt he became as financially successful as he is without some larceny in his soul. Even if that's not the case and he's a straight-arrow, any astute businessman would eventually question whether your sales figures were on the up and up." She pointed to the ledgers lying on the floor. "And those records Nick tried to steal are just the proof he would need."

"Thass right," Nick said, nodding vigorously while pinching his nose to stop the bleeding. "Uncle Thol thpected that you were cheating him and he wanted me to bring him evidence of it. Thass the only reason he thent me here."

"Great," Tony snorted. "Just what I need right now: A snitch." Tony resumed his attack on Nick, pummeling him until his cousin fell to the floor. Then he kicked him in the kidneys for being such a weakling. "Come on, kid," Tony taunted when Nick began dry-heaving. "Don't make this so easy for me." He held out a hand to help Nick stand up. "I'll even give you a moment to catch your breath. Then you can take your best shot."

"No," Clarice said. "That's enough."

"What do you think, cousin?" asked Tony. Had enough?" Nick grimaced and flailed his arms at Tony, but couldn't make contact. "Guess not," Tony said, slamming a fist into Nick's blood-splattered face.

"I said to stop," Clarice said, grabbing Tony's arm.

With Tony temporarily distracted by Clarice, Nick made his move. He rammed a fist into Tony's stomach with such force that Clarice's grip on Tony's arm gave way. She quickly stepped to the side as Nick nailed him in the chin with an uppercut followed by several punches to the side of his head.

When Nick's blows finally ceased, Tony staggered to a chair and sat down. He wiped the blood out of his eyes with the back of his hand. "Too easy for you?" Nick mocked, confidently striding toward Tony's chair. Tony closed his eyes and raised both arms in front of his face to ward off another series of punches. Instead of another round of pounding, there was a curious popping sound. Tony opened his eyes just as Nick fell face down in front of his chair.

Tony scrambled to his feet and stared in wide-eyed disbelief at the silver pistol Clarice held in her right hand. "You shot him!"

"No shit, Sherlock." Clarice dropped the gun into her straw purse and knelt beside an immobile Nick. She felt his neck for a pulse and then shook her head.

Sweat rolled down Tony's face, plastering greasy hair to bloodied forehead. His life had spun so far out of control that he didn't even care that he'd begun to cry in front of Clarice. "Why, Clarice?" he sobbed. "Why'd you have to kill him?"

"Why do you think?" she snarled. "He was going to tell your uncle everything—with or without the ledgers. It seems he's been keeping his eyes and ears open a lot more than we realized. Our plans would've been just a memory when that kid got through spilling his guts. Besides, he was knocking the shit out of you."

"I . . . I can't believe you shot him," Tony said, shaking his throbbing head. "Nick got in a few lucky punches, but I could've taken him down."

"Of course you could, darling, but look at it this way: he definitely won't be squealing to your Uncle Sol."

"But he was family! Oh, man . . . what're we going to do now? The screw-up at Baker Bluff was one thing, but this . . . oh God, oh God."

"Pull yourself together, Tony. It's not the end of the world, but we need to act fast. Lock the door while I call the sheriff."

"The sheriff?" Clarice always seemed to be two steps ahead of him, but she'd completely lost him now.

She exhaled in a forceful rush. "Jesus, do I have to think of everything? Put the "CLOSED" sign back in the window and lock the goddamn door!"

Tony's entire body ached and his face was a bloody mess. He couldn't think straight. Couldn't do anything but follow Clarice's orders. With shaking hands, he did as she had asked and then collapsed in a chair as far away from Nick's body as possible.

Clarice's phone call to the sheriff was brief. When she hung up she said, "I know you're hurting, but we have a lot to do." She went into the restroom and returned with some towels and bandages. Handing them to Tony, she told him to wipe his face and put a bandage on the cuts. "I'll take care of the ledgers and mop the floor," she said, "but when Pritchard gets here, you'll need to quit moaning and groaning and deal with the situation."

"You're one heartless broad," he whined, draping a towel over his wounded head. "I'll be lucky if you don't kill *me* before this is over."

Clarice's take-charge attitude softened and she walked over to where he sat. Pressing his towel-draped head against her chest like a mother comforting a child, she said, "It'll be okay, sweetie." After a moment, she gently applied the bandages for him. "I know things are a little dicey right now, but we have to stick to our plan."

"I know, I know. But Jesus Christ . . . Nick is the one who wound up dead, not some dumb redskin. How in the world are we going to explain this to Uncle Sol?

"Don't worry about your uncle. We can still salvage the bluff deal and cover up Nick's death at the same time—what's more, Pritchard will help us do it. He owes us."

He owed them all right. If Pritchard hadn't let Sam Matthews tag along with him when he went to "investigate" the accident, old George would be dead right now. It was supposed to have been so simple. Get him drunk and set the accident in motion. Clarice had supplied the booze while Tony got George behind the wheel and pointed the truck in the direction of the cliff. He hadn't made it that far, but the tree and fire should've worked just as well. What Pritchard was thinking by dragging a witness-turned-hero out to the scene was beyond belief. "Well," Tony said, "he better come through this time or—" A loud knocking at the door cut him off.

"That's Leonard now," Clarice said. "Sit tight while I let him in."

Judging by the sheriff's startled expression at the sight of Nick's lifeless body sprawled face-down on the office floor, Clarice hadn't mentioned the shooting when she called him. "What in blue blazes have you done now?" he said, eying Tony.

"Ask Clarice. She's running this show."

Clarice filled him in on what had happened. "So, as you can see, Leonard, we need your help."

Pritchard shook his head and folded his ropy arms across his chest. "Not on your life. I went along with your little stunt at the bluff 'cuz you assured me it would be a done deal by the time I got there. Only it didn't quite work out that way, did it? Now I got a do-gooder on my ass." He pointed a thumb at Nick's body. "This here's first-degree murder. And I'm an officer of the law, in case you forgot."

Clarice's brown eyes flashed darker. "You can drop the righteous attitude. In case *you* forgot, we're the reason you have any money to keep feeding your habit."

The sheriff bristled at Clarice's not so subtle reminder of his failings. He was a loser at poker and just about every betting game invented, but he couldn't stop gambling. His losses would've sunk him if Clarice hadn't stepped in with an offer he couldn't refuse.

"How many times are you going to bring that up?"

"As many times as it takes for you to realize that your future solvency depends greatly on my future." She looked over at Tony for the first time since her exchange with Pritchard began. "And his future, too."

Tony grinned at the sheriff and then winced as a sharp pain shot through his jaw. He had to hand it to Clarice. She knew just what to say when it counted the most. Despite Tony's initial misgivings, Clarice had been right to recruit Pritchard in the Destiny Group. They actually made a good team: Tony located the properties to flip,

Clarice did the appraisals for the bank and got Warren to approve the loans for their straw "buyers", and Sheriff Pritchard made sure the courthouse records were doctored to their advantage. It was a nifty setup that did little to cheer Tony now. They were in big trouble and he felt way out of his league. The sheriff might be a loser, but he was no pushover. Clarice had thrown Tony the ball and now he had to run with it. Rubbing his jaw, he said, "There's also another matter to consider. You owe me a thousand big ones." Poker wasn't Tony's best game, but he managed to win more than he lost when playing with Pritchard.

Pritchard looked surprised, then angry. "I owe you squat!"

"Wrong," said Tony.

"That debt was supposed to be settled once I took care of things at the bluff."

Clarice laughed without a trace of mirth. "Ha! You took care of nothing." She joined Tony and rested her hand on his shoulder. "We had a deal and you blew it. Speaking of which, what were you thinking by dragging someone up there with you?"

"It shouldn't have mattered," Pritchard said. "If George had been killed in the wreck like you'd planned, Matthews' presence would've been no big deal. But you failed to get the S.O.B. drunk enough to drive over the cliff." He shook his head disgustedly. "You should've plied him with the rotgut he was used to swigging instead of that high-class shit. No wonder he wouldn't drink any of it." Folding his arms across his chest again, he smirked, "Knocking him out and pouring the booze all over him was really brilliant. No, it seems to me that you two were the ones who blew that little caper."

The man's arrogance was astounding. "Shut up, you stupid prick!" shouted Tony.

"Yeah," Pritchard said, "I've been stupid all right. Doctoring courthouse records made sense, but going along with that so-called accident you rigged up was a mistake. And now you want me to cover your back for a murder? I'm not *that* stupid!"

Clarice eyed Pritchard a moment. "How much?"

"Lucky for you I'm not greedy. A couple of C-notes for my trouble should do just fine." He looked at Tony. "And my debt to you is paid in full—like we already agreed."

Tony sprang to his feet and immediately regretted it. Every muscle in his body ached. "You blackmailing S.O.B.!" he cursed through clenched teeth.

Clarice gently pushed him back into the chair. "There's no need to resort to name calling. We accept your terms, Leonard. Of course, we have just one little stipulation."

He eyed Clarice warily. "What's that?"

"This payment is a one-time only thing. It changes nothing about the Destiny Group split. If you squeeze us for any more dough, then I'll be the one doing some name calling."

Tony groaned. *Did she think a little name calling was going to shut this loser up?"*

"What do you think, Leonard?" Clarice prodded. "You ever wonder what names people might call you? Especially if they knew the real reason why your wife left?"

This line of attack made no sense to Tony. The story he'd heard about Pritchard's wife was that Lydia hated The Dalles and when the sheriff wouldn't move to Portland, she left without him. End of boring marriage. End of boring story. "What do you mean, the *real* story? Tony asked.

"Don't, Clarice," Pritchard whined. "Please."

"Poor Leonard," Clarice said. "It's such a sad, sad tale. Seems our sheriff's little woman had an itch hubby couldn't scratch. So, she ran off with someone who could—a big virile brave from Celilo."

Despite his injuries, Tony clutched his gut and hooted. "Oh, man. No wonder you hate Injuns so much."

Sheriff Pritchard shouted. "Stop it!"

Tony and Clarice exchanged satisfied looks. The ruthless kitten had Pritchard by the balls and he knew it. He owed his re-election success to their flag-waving on his behalf. A little racy gossip about his wife and the Celilo bunch and he wouldn't get elected Dogcatcher. If they didn't need him to help with this new mess or to fix papers at the courthouse a while longer, Sheriff Leonard Pritchard could kiss his job good-bye right now.

Pritchard's shoulders drooped in defeat. "Okay, okay. I give up. But not because I'm afraid of what people will say about me. You have your big plans for blowing this town when you get enough dough together and so do I."

Tony took in this news with a sneer. He could just imagine what big plans the sheriff had in mind: a high stakes poker game seven days a week. His stash would be wiped out faster than he could say "deal 'em."

"So," Sheriff Pritchard said to Clarice, "what exactly do you want me to do this time?"

CHAPTER FIFTEEN

It was Danny's idea to raid the Pioneer Cemetery and the others jumped on it. Walter said it would send a more powerful message than anything else they'd done so far. Danny agreed, but complained that a message wouldn't stop anything. The dam would still be built and their ancestors would still be dug up and tossed into a mass grave without regard for their beliefs or customs. "Look at it this way," Walter said with an impish grin. "Destroying the graves of the white man's ancestors will be a shitload of fun." Danny laughed along with Henry and Ernie but warned that they were more likely to experience a shitload of trouble. Walter assured him that they had nothing to worry about. "We've got some powerful people behind our cause now." Danny had pushed him for more details but Walter was vague about who these supposedly powerful people were or how he knew them. He claimed that the only detail that counted was that they had money and were willing to spend it to destroy the dam. "They've got plans that make our protest look like nothing more than a spoiled kid's tantrum."

How those plans involved Walter and Danny remained unclear. Danny wasn't a worrier by nature, but until he knew more about the plans and who was behind them, he'd remain cautious. The only people with money that he knew about were white people—and that was reason enough to be concerned. "You've gotta let go of that kind of thinking and learn to trust," Walter told him.

"Trusting white people is a big risk for us. Always has been and always will be," Danny countered. Walter knew that as well as he did.

"Big risk brings big reward," Walter said. "But if it makes you feel better, I've set up a meet after the Memory Feast tonight. You can judge for yourself whether they are trustworthy or not."

Since he had some time to kill before the feast, Danny decided to check out the Pioneer Cemetery. The guys wanted to make a midnight raid later in the week and Danny liked to be prepared. Walter didn't think a scouting trip was necessary but told him where the two-acre plot was located. He said there wouldn't be anyone around during the day to bother him and he could look around all he wanted. Nighttime was a different story. "White kids like to hang out at the cemetery to drink and make out. Scaring them off will be a hoot," Walter said.

A small sign at the entrance on East Scenic Drive indicated that the pioneers' graveyard was established in 1860, which was practically yesterday compared to how long the burial grounds on Memaloose and Graves Islands had existed for the tribes who fished along the Columbia River. No sign indicated how many centuries ago his ancestors' final resting place had been established. Everyone knew it was ancient. And, unlike the whites who'd abandoned the pioneers for a newer cemetery in town, the tribes still buried their loved ones alongside their ancestors.

It was just a short trek across the roadway where he'd parked to the wrought-iron entry gate, but the brief exertion in the hot sun left him feeling bone-tired. Sweat quickly pooled between his shoulder blades and dotted his brow. Hot weather was bothersome but it wasn't the root cause of his discomfort. Anger for a constant companion was just as physically draining as it was energizing. Worse, continuing to fight without achieving victory was demoralizing. As strange as the idea seemed, joining forces with Walter's white partners might be what it took to win the fight.

As he paused to wipe the sweat from his forehead, he was struck by how eerily quiet the cemetery seemed. Not even a chirping bird or chattering squirrel broke the silence. It made him feel uneasy. Since he didn't have any respect for white people, he didn't think dead white people would be any different, but he wondered now if the trespass he intended was a good idea. Disturbing the dead had consequences. White or Indian, a graveyard was a sacred, spiritual place. He didn't belong here anymore than the government belonged on Indian grounds. But, as he reminded himself, that was the whole point: Demolish the pioneer cemetery so the whites would see how wrong their government was to do the same to his ancestors' final resting place. The cause was justified and remembering that fact was enough for Danny to shake off any doubts or unease he had about today's scouting trip. With renewed resolve, he opened the unlocked gate and walked onto the grounds.

He estimated that there were about 200 or so graves in the cemetery. Some had large, ornate markers with elaborate inscriptions while others were plain and non-descript. Most were in decent condition but a few tombstones were cracked and barely standing. The grounds seemed well maintained except for a few broken beer bottles and cigarette butts scattered about. Walter said that white kids didn't honor their ancestors and the debris they'd left behind proved that he was right.

Danny hadn't expected that he would recognize any of the pioneer names, but one large monument for Judge Joseph Garner Wilson (1826-1873) caught his attention. Danny had driven by a school called Joseph G. Wilson on the way to the cemetery, which he figured must have been named for the former judge. He'd just stopped to read the inscription on his headstone when some movement in the distance caught his eye.

Danny felt his heart thumping furiously as he tried to make sense of what appeared to be an apparition gliding rapidly across the grounds. Danny's grandfather said he often felt the presence of departed souls when visiting their loved ones' graves. Oscar said the dead would sometimes appear in the form of animals or other images and Danny's initial thought was exactly that—he'd seen a departed soul in the form of an angel.

He would later attribute the vision to a trick played by the blinding sunlight. For as the spirit-angel drew closer, he realized it was just a girl. No, two girls. They were dressed in nearly identical outfits but they didn't resemble each other at all. One was a short and skinny redhead who struggled to keep pace with the determined gait of a long-legged blonde in the lead. Even from a distance, he could tell the tall girl was pretty. Or, what he assumed most guys would call pretty. In Danny's opinion, white girls were too pale, too fragile, and too silly. Not to mention stuck-up and bossy. He figured this girl wouldn't be any different. She certainly wasn't an illusion as he'd first thought. No, she was as real as the redhead who scrambled after her. Still, there was something about her that seemed spectral or other-worldly. To his surprise, Danny hoped that she'd see him and . . . and what? Stop and chat? Absurd as that thought was, it was exactly what he hoped would happen. He wanted more than anything to find out who she was, why she seemed so different, and why she made his heart beat so fast.

Still unaware of his presence, the girls walked single-file along what appeared to be a well-worn path from the back of the graveyard to the entrance gate. As they approached him, Danny was convinced his heart would jump out of his chest. Up close, the blonde was even prettier than he'd first thought. When she spotted him, she stopped so abruptly that the redhead almost ran into her. "Who are you?" she demanded. Her tone was arrogant and as off-putting as the stink-eye look she gave him.

The redhead spoke up before Danny had a chance to respond. "Oh, my gosh! That's Danny Longstreet."

It was clear his name meant nothing to the blonde. Her eyes never left Danny as she asked, "Who?"

"Danny Longstreet," the redhead repeated. She lowered her voice and cupped her hand to partially cover her mouth as she leaned toward her friend's ear. "He's the baddest of the bad Indians!"

Despite her efforts, Danny could hear perfectly well. That was all it took to snap him out of his trance-like state. He was disgusted with himself for getting so worked up, spooked even—over a mere girl, of all things! If Walter knew how he'd reacted, he would never let him live it down. "Yep, that's me," Danny said, staring boldly at the girls. "Big bad Indian boy. Better run for the hills!"

The redhead looked ready to skedaddle as fast as her short little legs could carry her but her friend just giggled. Most girls squealed like baby pigs in trouble when they giggled but she had a delightful, almost melodious laugh. "And just what is a big bad Indian boy doing in a pioneer cemetery?" she asked with an amused grin.

The redhead groaned.

"What's her problem?" asked Danny.

The blonde shrugged, but didn't say anything.

Danny shook his head. "Girls. They're all the same."

"What do you mean?"

"If they aren't mouthin' off at you, they're giving you the silent treatment."

"And I suppose you've had a lot of experience with girls?"

"Enough to know they're trouble."

The redhead had heard enough. "Not us! We're no trouble at all. In fact, we were just leaving." She tugged on her friend's arm. "Let's go!"

As they hurried toward the gate, the blonde looked over her shoulder at him and gave a friendly wave. "Bye, Danny Longstreet."

A wide grin spread across his face. "Hey," he called after her. "What's your name?" When she didn't answer, he shouted, "So it's the silent treatment, huh? I took you for the mouthin' off type."

CHAPTER SIXTEEN

Dessa had never been to Celilo. Her mother said the village was a filthy, stinking, fly-infested dump littered with dilapidated shacks, abandoned junkers, mangy dogs, and grubby little kids running wild. Not a proper place for a young girl. However, when Mr. Matthews asked if Dessa could come with him and Ellie to a special feast at the village, she suddenly had a change of heart. "Why, how thoughtful of you to invite Odessa. She would be delighted to go." Maureen blathered on and on about the cultural opportunity that such an event would provide the girls in a lame attempt to appear unprejudiced. Dessa was relieved when Mr. Matthews stopped the flow of her mother's hollow platitudes by tipping his hat and making a polite, but quick getaway.

It wasn't surprising that her mother agreed to the outing. Maureen had been disappointed (angry) that the girls hadn't gone to the sock hop. She was convinced that any activity in which Ellie was involved would be beneficial to Dessa's popularity. Celilo seemed like a stretch in that regard, but Dessa didn't argue the point. She couldn't wait to see for herself what the village was like and already had a headline in mind for her next newsletter: *Hillcrest Girls Attend Celilo Feast.*

They rode to Celilo crammed together in the cab of Mr. Matthews' pickup. He often let the girls ride in the back but he said the truck bed was too dirty for them today. He didn't want them to get their pretty sundresses ruined, which was a nicer way of saying no. On the way to the village, Ellie was her usual bubbly self. She'd been so mad after Dessa's crack about Tony Rossi and his skanky girlfriend that she wouldn't even talk to her on the walk home from town. Dessa wasn't used to keeping her opinions to herself but it was clear that any disapproval of Tony Rossi, direct or implied, would not be tolerated. As difficult as a zipped lip would be, Dessa was determined to comply. She didn't want to give Ellie a reason to quit illustrating the Hillcrest newsletter, but even more than that, she didn't want to lose her friendship. The latest flare-up notwithstanding, the girls were becoming good friends all on their own. And that *was* a surprise to Dessa.

The encounter with Danny Longstreet in the Pioneer Cemetery snapped Ellie out of her bad mood. Dessa was spooked by his sudden appearance but Ellie giggled like it was a big joke. She even flirted with him, which Ellie adamantly denied. "I was just being friendly," she insisted. Despite his tough-guy reputation, Danny Longstreet didn't seem all that scary. In fact, the more Dessa thought about it later, the more she believed he looked distressed and maybe even a little vulnerable. Could it be that *he was afraid of them*? Ellie said that was ridiculous, but agreed that he seemed to be in a trance initially. Although Dessa didn't bring it up, there was another explanation for his dazed, glassy-eyed look: the so-called bad Indian was just a guy. He acted exactly like every other guy did in Ellie's presence. Her ponytail had come undone and she was sweaty and bedraggled from their walk in the hot sun, but Danny took one look at her and went gaga. In any case, the banter they engaged in *was* flirty. Dessa didn't know which was worse—Tony Rossi, the skirt chaser or Danny Longstreet, the wild Indian.

Once they arrived at Celilo, Mr. Matthews parked alongside the Long House. It was a large wooden structure that was shaped like an elongated teepee with walls. It was situated so that the front door faced east and the sides faced north and south. The pleasant aroma of salmon wafting outside the building made Dessa's stomach growl. Mr. Matthews said the village women had probably been cooking and preparing for the feast since sunrise.

As they joined the assembled crowd outside the Long House, Mr. Matthews explained what would happen. He pointed out Chief Thompson and his wife Flora and said they would enter the Long House first. Mrs. Thompson wore a blue velvet dress trimmed with elk teeth, beads, porcupine quills and buckskin. The chief wore buckskin leggings, a heavy beaded apron around his waist, a fringed buckskin shirt and an elaborate eagle-feather headdress. His long hair was braided with strips of otter fur, which Mr. Matthews said signified his status as chief. The couple was followed by the two young men who were to be honored at the feast, also dressed in their finest. It was called a Memory Feast because the men were enlisting in the army and would need good memories of home while they were gone.

Mr. Matthews and the girls hung back from the crowd as they streamed into the Long House behind the chief's procession. As the last of the celebrants entered the east door, they were greeted by a tall woman dressed in an ankle-length green gown adorned with white shell beads. Dessa had read somewhere that it was customary for Indian women to wear two feathers in their headband if they were married and one feather if unmarried. Since the woman wore no feather, she was most likely a widow.

"Welcome to our Memory Feast," she said. "I'm Reba Longstreet."

If Ellie registered the significance of her last name, she didn't respond to Dessa's elbow nudge. Introductions were made and hands shook but Mr. Matthews and Reba had undoubtedly met before. "It's good to see you again," Reba said. "Your wife, she did not come with you?"

"Ellie's mother died many years ago."

Reba turned to Ellie and said, "I'm so sorry. My son Danny has been without his father and I know how difficult the loss of a parent can be."

Ellie glanced at Dessa before flashing a reassuring smile at Reba. "I'm doing fine. Dad takes good care of me."

"Speaking of care," Mr. Matthews said. "How's George doing?"

"Okay," Reba said. "As you requested, I told him not to speak to anyone about what happened. He said that wasn't a problem since he couldn't remember the accident at all. He doesn't even remember how he came to be in the truck."

Although Ellie didn't say anything, the questioning look she gave her father was clear: *Who was George? What accident? How did you know about it?*" Her father thanked Reba for her help but didn't explain what their exchange was about.

Reba led them into the Long House. Dessa estimated that the

building was at least fifty feet long with a dirt center extending about ten to fifteen feet between the north and south sides. It quickly became evident that the center area was sacrosanct, as everyone carefully avoided walking there. At the west end of the structure were several large drums. The villagers sat on tule mats, men on the north side and women on the south side near the cooking area. Reba explained that because Mr. Matthews and the girls were guests, they would sit with her on a wooden bench.

The feast began when one of the elders asked a blessing on the food and the young men who would be leaving soon. Everyone stood as he rang a bell to begin the prayer. They raised their arms during the blessing and when the elder had finished, they turned to the right and walked in a tight circle. Reba said that was to signify their agreement with his words. The food was served buffet style on long tables set up near the cooking area and included the salmon Dessa had smelled earlier, elk and deer meat, root soup, potatoes, fry bread, and huckleberry and cherry pies for sweets. Mr. Matthews asked for some coffee, but Reba said that the only beverage served at feasts was water, which they considered holy. The atmosphere in the Long House, while festive, did seem holy. Even the children were respectful and well behaved.

After everyone had finished eating, several young men dressed in brightly colored costumes, feathers, and jangly bells on their wrists and ankles entered the sacred center of the gathering. Accompanied by six other young men on drums, they began a lively dance. Dessa recognized Danny right away and poked Ellie in the ribs. She shrugged as if she didn't care, but her eyes were focused on him during the entire dance. The dance steps were intricate and the precise movements that they executed had an artistic flair. "Wow," said Dessa. "They are really good." Ellie didn't comment one way or the other.

When the dancing ended, Chief Thompson addressed the gathering. Reba directed their attention to the peace pipe that he held in his right hand and the beaded bag in his left. She said the bag contained his copy of the Middle Oregon Treaty of 1855. "The treaty was signed by the government and two Wy-am chiefs named Stoecketli and Ice. It gave our people fishing rights here for all time."

Reba glanced at Mr. Matthews before continuing. "But the federal government has broken that treaty and is building a dam to destroy our salmon." Ellie said something to Reba, but Dessa couldn't hear what it was. Did she feel the need to apologize for her father's work on the dam?

Chief Thompson's talk, however, didn't focus on the dam or their problems. He told stories of the battles his people had fought to help their white brothers. "Our people promised Lewis and Clark that they would always be friends to the white men." Dessa caught some of the dancers, including Danny, shake their head and grumble softly. The chief ignored them and directed his attention to Mr. Matthews and the girls. He welcomed them to the feast and introduced them as "our friends," too. Chief Thompson concluded his talk by telling stories that he hoped the young men honored tonight would remember as happy memories of home as they served in the army.

The Memory Feast ended with Chief Thompson and Flora Thompson leading the crowd out of the Long House. As the dancers filed past them, Reba tapped her son on the shoulder. "Danny, wait. I want you to meet our guests."

He sighed as if her simple request had terribly inconvenienced him. This was not the Pioneer Cemetery Danny. This was costumed and face painted Danny with an attitude that lived up to his reputation. One of the dancers lingered nearby, but Danny told him to go on. "I'll catch you later."

After introducing her son, Reba said, "This is Sam Matthews and his daughter Ellie and her good friend Dessa." Danny acknowledged Mr. Matthews and Dessa with a cursory nod but Ellie was rewarded with a sly grin. "Ellie Matthews, huh? Nice name."

Ellie matched Danny's grin and teasing tone. "Nice dancing."

"I'm glad you could see him perform," Reba said. Danny has been dancing ever since he was a toddler."

Danny shrugged. "It's not a big deal. My friends started early, too."

"Nevertheless," Mr. Matthews said, "the dancing was amazing."

Danny brushed the compliment aside. "It's what Indians do. And without our fishing grounds, we'll have plenty of time to dance."

Reba tried to deflect her son's harsh tone. "Danny, Sam Matthews isn't here because of the dam. He saved George's life today."

"So, I heard," replied Danny. "But who's going to save the rest of us?"

"You have reason to be concerned about the dam," Mr. Matthews said. "In fact, I'd like to talk to you about that. Maybe there is some way I can help."

"I've heard that line before," scoffed Danny. 'The government is here to help you.' And how do they help? By destroying our way of life and digging up our ancestors. Thanks, but no thanks." A nearby dog barked once as if to put an exclamation point on Danny's outburst.

A tense silence followed. Reba looked uncomfortable but if she felt differently from her son, she didn't say so. Ellie spoke up first. "Don't judge my father so harshly, Danny." "He's a good man and I know he will do the right thing."

"Well said, young lady." Sheriff Pritchard's sudden arrival in the middle of an already strained moment became even more anxious when the sheriff waved a piece of paper in the air. "This here is a legal warrant for the arrest of George Featherstone."

A vein throbbed in Mr. Matthews' temple as if it were about to burst. "Wait a minute, sheriff," he said. "There is some question as to whether George was under the influence at the time of the accident. I need to talk to you before you arrest him for the DUI."

Sheriff Pritchard handed the warrant to Mr. Matthews. "Read it and you will see this has nothing to do with a DUI. Or theft of the truck, for that matter."

"Then why are you busting him?" demanded Danny. "You have no authority here anyway. Celilo is under the jurisdiction of our tribal police."

"Not in a capital murder case."

A collective gasp. "Murder? What?"

"You heard me right," replied the sheriff smugly. "George is wanted for the murder of Nick Rossi."

The girls looked at each other in disbelief and shock. Both started talking at once. "No! Nick Rossi? We just saw him this afternoon! It can't be true."

"Sorry to say, but it's the God's honest truth. George Featherstone killed Nick Rossi in cold blood. And, as I recall, Mr. Matthews here took personal responsibility for the man. It's time to turn him over."

"Hold on, sheriff," Sam said, handing the warrant back. "When and how did all this supposedly take place?"

Pritchard shook his head. "I'm not under any obligation to tell you."

Danny's dark eyes narrowed and his painted face exploded in a storm of furious colors. Danny couldn't have signaled his feelings about the sheriff's claims more plainly. Anticipating her son's next move, Reba frantically grabbed his arm. "No, Danny," she pleaded. Don't do it!" He easily shook free of her grasp and lurched toward the sheriff with clenched and raised fists.

Pritchard placed a hand on the holster at his hip and glared at Danny, as if daring him to proceed.

Mr. Matthews quickly intervened by stepping between the two men. "Let's not make the situation any more difficult. Danny, you need to back away. I understand your outrage, but it's best if I deal with the sheriff." Proudly defiant, Danny stood his ground until Reba urged him to do what Mr. Matthews said. With a final menacing glance at the sheriff, he turned around and walked back to where his mother stood. "Now," Mr. Matthews told Pritchard, "If you want my cooperation, you better explain what this warrant is all about."

"Are you sure you want the ladies to hear the gruesome details?"

Despite her summer tan, Ellie's face had turned a sickly ashen color. Dessa was sure her face looked much the same. Mr. Matthews regarded them both and then asked Reba, "Could you take care of the girls? I think they both need some water."

"No, Dad," Ellie protested. "I'm fine."

Dessa seconded the notion. "Please, Mr. Matthews. Let us stay." As much as the news about Nick had upset her, she didn't want to miss the story behind the arrest of his killer. Her article for the newsletter had just taken a shocking turn.

"Come with me," Reba said, taking both girls firmly by the hand. "Let's go inside the Long House for some water as Mr. Matthews suggested."

CHAPTER SEVENTEEN

"Okay, sheriff," Matthews said after ensuring the girls were safely out of earshot. "Let's hear it."

Danny didn't know the dead guy — Nick Ross or whatever they called him — but he was certain that George had nothing to do with his death. If Danny's numerous run-ins with Pritchard had taught him anything it was that the sheriff was determined to destroy Celilo Village, one Indian at a time. He'd made no bones about his dislike of "their kind" even before Raymond Sun Dancer ran off with his wife. Since then, the man's mission in life had been to pin whatever misdeed he could on someone at Celilo, which was usually Danny or one of his friends. That Pritchard hadn't accused Danny of the murder was something of a miracle, given his track record.

His first impulse was to attack the sheriff and would've flattened him, gun or no gun, if Matthews hadn't intervened. Danny didn't trust Sam Matthews any more than he trusted the sheriff, but the way he'd confronted Pritchard was interesting. When Matthews demanded an explanation, Danny decided to let things play out a little. He knew whatever the sheriff had to say would be a web of lies, but he was curious as to how his mother's so-called friend would react to the sheriff's B.S.

Pritchard lit a cigarette and took a deep drag. "Seems as though old George had had a little too much to drink today," he said, exhaling a cloud of fetid smoke. "He was woozy and stumbling when Tony Rossi spotted him in the middle of a downtown street. Tony had rescued George on other occasions when he'd had too much to drink. This time he asked his cousin, Nick, to give the old guy a lift back to the village. Two witnesses saw them drive-off together in Tony's truck."

Lie number one, thought Danny. The government man must have thought so, too. "Sheriff," Matthews said, "I saw George Featherstone acting the same way once. Like you, I thought he'd probably had too much to drink but I've since learned that he's a diabetic and doesn't drink. If he was acting drunk in town, it was because he was disoriented from low blood sugar, not alcohol. He needed insulin."

"If you say so. But he stunk like a brewery and the empty wine bottle we found at the wreck explained why. The point is, George was so out of it he could barely walk and Nick Rossi was kind enough to take him home. His mistake was stopping at Baker Bluff first."

"Why would he do that?" asked Matthews. "Baker Bluff isn't on the way to the village."

Pritchard glared at him. "Are you going to let me tell what happened or keep on interrupting me with a million questions?"

"Sorry. Go on."

"Tony had asked Nick to inspect the property for him. It was for sale and since Nick was assisting him in the real estate business, he wanted the kid to be familiar with what was on the market." Pritchard paused to crush out his cigarette with his boot heel. "Tony is damned upset about losing his cousin, I might add."

"I'm sure he is," said Matthews. "I've met Nick and he seemed like a nice young man."

"You got that right," agreed Pritchard. He glanced at Danny and smirked, "Not like some of the punks I deal with on a regular basis."

Matthews caught the look on Danny's face and quickly said, "That kind of talk isn't necessary, sheriff. Finish your story."

Story is right. Danny didn't believe one word of the tale Pritchard was spinning.

"Okay, where was I?"

"Nick stopped at Baker Bluff."

"Yeah, right," Pritchard said. "That turned out to be a fatal mistake. For some reason, George got it into his head that he wanted to steal the truck. They fought about it and George shot Nick."

Danny couldn't listen to the sheriff's lies any longer. His story about George was so far-fetched that only a fool would believe it. "Steal the truck!" he blurted. "That's just plain crazy. Everyone knows George never learned to drive. And just how was he supposed to

145

shoot this guy? George didn't even carry a fishing knife, let alone a gun."

"And what about the body?" chimed Matthews. "You and I were both at the wreck. There wasn't any sign of Nick or a weapon."

The sheriff raised both hands in the air. "Hold on, will ya? I'm trying to tell you the facts." He ignored Danny's argument and addressed Matthews. "The tow truck driver I took up there to haul back Rossi's truck, Clyde Williams? He was the one who found Nick's body. After George shot the kid, he must've dragged him to the cliff and tossed him over. Only he didn't fall all the way down to the rocks below like George intended. After I'd helped Clyde hitch up the truck to his rig, he took a smoke break at the edge of the cliff and that's when he saw the body. We found the pistol in the brush about halfway down the bank."

Matthews stared at the sheriff with what could only be described as a dumbfounded look. Danny figured Matthews had to be asking himself the same question that he had: *how could someone supposedly too drunk to walk still manage to drag a body to the cliff and toss it over?* But Matthews asked about the weapon instead. "How did you know the gun belonged to George?"

"It didn't. Tony said the pistol was his. He kept it in his truck for shooting rattlers and such when he was scouting out possible listings for acreage in the country."

Matthews rubbed his chin. "So, let me get this straight," he said. "Your belief is that George found this weapon and decided to shoot Nick and steal the truck."

Sheriff Pritchard nodded. "That's exactly what happened. He thought he'd gotten rid of the body and the gun by throwing them over the cliff. Then he gets back in the truck to make his getaway. But he drank too much booze first and wound up plowing into a tree instead. He's lucky we got there when we did or he'd be dead, too."

"Which reminds me," Matthews said. "You got a phone call about the incident while I was at your office. Who called it in?"

"Anonymous."

Danny studied Matthews' face. He didn't look like he bought the sheriff's line of bull and his next question confirmed it. "Have you considered the possibility that this whole episode was a set-up?"

The sheriff shook his head and said, "There is no evidence to suggest anything of the sort." He tapped his holster for emphasis and added, "Now, where are you hiding George? I've wasted enough time yakking about this. He's our prime suspect in the murder of Nick Rossi and I'm hauling his ass off to jail where he belongs."

"No one is hiding George," said Matthews. "He was hurt in the accident, as you well know. He's still recovering from his injuries so I left him in Reba Longstreet's care. If you'll wait here a moment, I'll go inside the Long House and talk to her about George's arrest."

By this time, several villagers had congregated outside the Long House when word of the sheriff's arrival had become known. Pritchard watched the growing crowd warily and said, "Just make it snappy. And don't try any funny business."

Danny didn't think the government man was inclined to turn George over to the sheriff. He'd asked too many probing questions, especially the last one. Danny had to respect the guy somewhat. He wasn't taking whatever the sheriff dished out at face value. Not many whites would stand up to the law for an Indian that way. Danny fought the urge to follow Matthews into the Long House. As much as he wanted to hear what he told his mother, Danny was more interested in what might happen outside the Long House. By now, the entire village was aware that the sheriff planned to arrest George. The number of onlookers had grown to a sizable number and their grumbling rippled through the gathering like water over sharp rocks. They were an agitated and dangerous bunch. If a fight broke out, Danny wanted to be front and center for all the action. He *needed* to fight.

What he didn't need was to talk to Ellie again. He couldn't believe how stupid he'd acted earlier. The wisecrack about her name was one thing, but spouting off about the dam to her father was worse. She probably thought he was a jerk even if what he said was the truth. Danny liked the way she stood up for her father, though. Ellie didn't let on that they'd already met and he wondered why. Indian or white, girls were a mystery. Bella, his sometime girlfriend, could be a real spitfire when crossed, which was another problem altogether. If she even suspected that he might be interested in another girl, she'd dump him faster than a rattler's strike. Not that he was interested in

Ellie. She was so beautiful that she seemed more like a fantasy than a real live girl.

Danny hadn't told anyone about seeing her at the Pioneer Cemetery but Walter knew him too well. He'd guessed something had happened there that affected Danny deeply. Walter said only a woman could be the source of so much emotion. But it wasn't until Walter saw Ellie at the feast that he knew for sure. "Aw, man, you've gone and flipped for a white girl, haven't you?" Danny had denied it, which just made Walter more convinced. "Remember, we have an important meet tonight." Walter had seen Danny with Ellie and her father after the ceremony and his warning still rung in his ears, "Don't waste time with that chick. She's never going to fall for an Indian. Besides, her father wouldn't let her."

Sheriff Pritchard ignored the disgruntled rumblings from the crowd and lit another cigarette. A coughing fit followed his first drag. After he'd settled down, Danny said, "I don't think the government man believes your wild tale any more than I do."

"I don't give a plug nickel about what you believe. Or Sam Matthews, either. You're lucky I don't run you in along with George."

Here it comes. Danny knew the sheriff couldn't resist drawing him into this story somehow. "On what trumped up charge?"

"You can drop the innocent act. You know very well that you've destroyed private property at Baker Bluff. Your signature was all over the place."

"I'd never even heard of the place until a few minutes ago."

The sheriff took another long drag on his cigarette. "So you say, but I have proof." He pointed the cigarette at Danny. "Stay out of trouble or else."

"Or else what?"

Pritchard glanced at the Long House. "Or else you and your buddies will find yourselves in worse shape than old George."

Danny wasn't afraid of the sheriff's threats. The man had no idea what trouble was but he'd find out soon enough. Everyone would. But for now, he'd leave the fight over George to his village brothers. It was past time for him to go.

CHAPTER EIGHTEEN

If Mr. Matthews thought banishing Dessa and Ellie to the Long House would save them from the turmoil surrounding Nick's murder, he was mistaken. Granted, Ellie was upset but her father's dismissal hadn't helped the situation. She complained that he was treating her like a little baby again. "He thinks I'm too fragile to hear what the big brave men have to say."

Dessa voiced a similar complaint but stopped short of expressing her true grievance. Mr. Matthews' annoying assumption that the girls needed to be protected because of their delicate female sensitivities wasn't the problem. A white boy murdered by a Celilo Indian was the scoop of a lifetime for any reporter and Dessa happened to be in the right place at the right time. Except that she wasn't. She was stuck inside the Long House where she couldn't hear a thing. And that was the *real* problem. If there was some way she could sneak outside, she could beat the actual reporters from *The Dalles Chronicle* to the story before they even knew what had happened. She'd already reimagined the headline for her newsletter: *Celilo Indian Arrested for Murder.*

"You and I know you're strong girls," Reba said, in a comforting voice. "But men, especially fathers, can't always accept that. They see their role as protectors." She guided the girls to the same bench they'd shared earlier. "Sit here and I'll be right back with some water."

While she was gone, Dessa scrutinized the layout of the vast hall for an escape route. It was not encouraging. The only way outside was through the door they'd just entered. Even if she could somehow slip away without Reba noticing, she'd have no cover once she'd made it outside, especially if Mr. Matthews and the sheriff were still standing nearby. It was possible that there was another, less exposed exit in the food prep area, but that's where Reba had gone for their water. Another possibility would be a restroom with a handy window — preferably large enough for her to squeeze through.

When Reba returned, she carried two metal cups. "Our water comes straight from the falls," she said, handing the cups to the girls. "We have a pump in the yard but always keep several jugs in a cooler when we have feasts."

"Thank you," Ellie said. "Mmm. Cold and refreshing."

Dessa wasn't as easily pacified as Ellie. It would take more than a cold drink to distract her from pursuing a great story. Unwilling to risk offending Reba by refusing the water, she thanked her and took a quick sip. "Is there a restroom here I could use?" she asked.

Reba shook her head. "Our Long House is built the way our ancestors' built theirs. We use an outside facility."

Perfect. "That's okay," she said, trying not to sound too eager. "Just tell me where to find it."

"I'm sorry, but I must ask you to wait," Reba said. "As soon as Ellie's father comes to fetch us, I will show you. I'm sure we won't be here long."

Drats. Reba might not have known the real reason behind Dessa's need for a potty break, but Ellie wasn't fooled for a minute. She gave Dessa the old "I know what you're up to" eye roll. They had worked together on the newsletter long enough for Ellie to know how much Dessa liked being in on things. The sheriff's account of Nick's murder was just too exciting for her to miss. Dessa should've anticipated that Ellie would see through her ploy. Even though she'd fallen for Tony Rossi's lying eyes and every whopper he'd ever uttered, Ellie had Dessa's number and called her bluff. "You just want to listen to what the sheriff has to say."

Dessa figured Ellie wanted to do the exact same thing, but was too chicken to act on it. She elected to change the subject rather than deny the accusation. "I had a wonderful time tonight," she told Reba. "Too bad the sheriff had to come along and spoil things."

"We're used to it," Reba said with her eyes lowered. "He doesn't like us."

"Why's that?" asked Ellie.

"It's just one of those things." Reba sighed and added, "He's not the only white person who feels that way."

Ever the cheerleader, Ellie said, "If they'd been at the feast tonight they'd change their minds for sure."

Reba sighed again. "You're both sweet girls, but you have much to learn. Some people's attitudes are changing, but it is a slow process. When I first came to Celilo we weren't even allowed to eat in the restaurants in town. They put signs in the windows that said, '*No dogs or Indians Allowed.*'

"What? But . . . but that's just not right!" Ellie blurted.

Ellie's indignant reaction was typical of her. She knew that prejudice existed in the world, but still found it hard to believe the blatant and disgusting examples of it.

Dessa had no doubts. What's more, she knew that the movie theater in town wouldn't let Indians sit anywhere near their white patrons. Indians were restricted to the balcony seats only. If her mother's rants about the "dirty drunken Injuns from Celilo" were any indication, it was no wonder they had trouble in town. "I'm so sorry," Dessa said. Reba assured her that it wasn't her fault but Dessa still felt guilty on behalf of her mother. Maureen was Catholic (considered questionable in some circles) *and* she was married to a Jew, which made social acceptance a doubly difficult struggle. Did she think that her position on the social ladder would somehow rise a notch or two higher if she denigrated those she believed to be even less socially acceptable? If so, that was as disgusting to Dessa as any sign or theater policy in town.

"A lot of things happen that aren't right," said Reba. "Including the sheriff accusing George Featherstone of murder."

"My dad won't let him go to jail if he's innocent," Ellie said confidently.

"From what I've seen, your father is a good man," Reba said with a slight smile. "But the law is not on our side."

"You don't trust the sheriff, do you?" said Dessa.

"Not for a minute. George had no reason whatsoever to kill anyone. Especially not a white man. Such a thing could only bring us more trouble than we already have."

"We knew Nick Rossi," said Ellie. "He was only seventeen and Mr. Rossi's cousin. They worked together at the real estate office and helped us find the house we bought."

151

"His sudden death must be very upsetting for you."

"It is," Ellie said. "But I really only knew Nick slightly. Mr. Rossi, he's the one who'll be upset and sad."

Tony didn't strike Dessa as the type to mourn the loss of his cousin for long—probably no longer than it took to find another gofer. It wasn't easy, but she managed to keep that assessment to herself. If she continued to bite her tongue every time Tony's name came up, her smart-ass reputation was going to take a hit. And her tongue wouldn't fare too well either.

The Long House door opened and Mr. Matthews entered. "How're you girls doing?" he asked.

"They're both doing very well," Reba said. She touched Ellie's shoulder as she rose from the bench. "You have a strong daughter, Sam Matthews. There's no need to worry about her."

Ellie smiled as she brought the water cup to her lips. Whether she knew it or not, Reba had just made a friend for life.

"Thank you," he said, looking fondly at Ellie. "I'm very proud of her." Dessa guessed that was about as far as he would go. No matter what Reba said, Mr. Matthews was the kind of parent who'd never stop worrying about his daughter.

"What did the sheriff say?" Reba asked.

Dessa held her breath while she waited for Mr. Matthews to respond. She knew he wouldn't get into anything gory, but she hoped he would at least cover the where, why, and how of the case. If her article were to be halfway interesting, she'd have to report more than just the name of the victim and his accused killer. Unfortunately for her journalistic aspirations, Mr. Matthews' explanation was short on details.

"Sheriff Pritchard's story has more holes than a leaky rowboat, but we have no choice," he said. "We have to turn George over to him."

"I know, but . . . jail, it will not be a good place for him," Reba protested. "He's too old, too sick."

"It'll be all right," Mr. Matthews said. "I won't let anything bad happen to him."

Dessa knew Mr. Matthews was a nice man, even a good man as Reba had said. But his ardent support of an Indian he didn't know made no sense. What was she missing?

Reba's eyes searched his face for reassurance. From what she'd said earlier, trusting a white man's promises had to be difficult.

Mr. Matthews acknowledged her fears. "Given Sheriff Pritchard's attitude toward your people, George's arrest is a very troubling development. He will need a tribal lawyer as soon as possible. In the meantime, I will do whatever I can for him. You have my word."

Every bone in Dessa's body said there was something going on here besides simple kindness. And she needed to find out what. Any good reporter would do the same.

With Mr. Matthew's pledge still hanging in the air, they went outside. The sheriff stood next to the bird pole smoking a cigarette while a large group of villagers congregated nearby. He'd assumed a casual, relaxed stance, but it was just for show. Hard gray eyes scanned the villagers' movements. His right hand fidgeted with the holster strap. The day had cooled off, but steady drops of sweat ran down the side of his grim face. Nervous sweat. Trembling gun hand. Mr. Matthews read the signs and took the girls aside. "I want you to stay close to me," he said. "This could get dangerous."

Dessa's heart beat faster. It was probably foolish, but she hoped that things *did* get dangerous. A little danger would do nicely for her purposes.

"Where's Danny?" Reba asked, eying the crowd anxiously.

Sheriff Pritchard tossed his cigarette on the ground and crushed it out with his boot. "He took off. Probably up to no good, but I'll deal with him later. Right now, I want George Featherstone." His thin lips twisted in a haughty smirk. "Quit stalling, Matthews. You've hid behind the squaw's skirts long enough. Turn him over. Now!"

If the sheriff's intention had been to arrest George without incident, he'd made a royal mess of it. Furious shouting erupted following his rude and hostility-provoking demand. Reba had been right about this man. He hated her and her people. Her face was impossible to read, but Mr. Matthews' outrage was unmistakable. His whole body bristled. He took the girls' hands in his and stepped forward so that they were positioned between the villagers and the sheriff. Mr. Matthews spoke in a strong, no-nonsense voice that could be heard above the clamor behind them. "Re-phrase your request, sheriff. Respectfully this time."

Dessa looked over her shoulder at the villagers. Mr. Matthews' forceful response to Sheriff Pritchard had grabbed their full attention. It seemed to her that they were taken aback by how he had admonished the sheriff. They'd quieted down but the tension in the air was still raw.

Sheriff Pritchard glared at Mr. Matthews, a muscle tensing in his jaw. There was total silence now, as if everyone were holding their breath to see what the sheriff would do. His eyes shifted from Mr. Matthews to the crowd. Any fool could see that he was seriously outnumbered. The question was whether the sheriff believed his authority as armed lawman gave him the upper hand. It was clear that he didn't like being challenged by Mr. Matthews but he shrugged his bony shoulders as if unconcerned. "Oh, what the hell," he said. "Whatever makes you feel better. How's this? I'd like you to turn over George Featherstone now."

"Not quite there yet."

"I'd like you to turn over George Featherstone, *please.*"

"Please what?"

He gave Mr. Matthews a "damn you" look as he said, "Please, *sir.* As far as the sheriff was concerned, making nice was over. "I'm done playing word games. Time to get me George."

"Not so fast." Mr. Matthews said. He nodded towards Reba. "I believe you owe the lady an apology."

The sheriff's leathery face reddened in an ugly mix of hatred and revulsion. He cleared his throat and spat on the ground. "You're pushing it, Matthews," he said.

"The sooner you apologize, the sooner you'll get your man."

Sheriff Pritchard mumbled something under his breath. Dessa wasn't sure but she thought it sounded a lot like, "*I'll get you for this.*" Then, through clenched teeth, he said, "I'm sorry."

Mr. Matthews still wasn't satisfied. "You can do better, sheriff."

The sheriff's discomfort caused a few laughs to ripple through the crowd. The veins in his temples throbbed as he stared menacingly at them. Just when Dessa thought he'd refuse, he uttered the magic words: "I'm sorry, *ma'am.*"

Mr. Matthews had won the showdown with Sheriff Pritchard, but at what cost? A humiliated man is an unhappy man. A humiliated man with a gun is an unpredictable man. But a humiliated man with a badge and a gun is an unmerciful man.

Reba's face was one big grin. "Follow me," she said, waving everyone on.

As Reba led them through the village, Dessa noted that the houses weren't as dilapidated as her mother had claimed. While some of the weathered gray clapboard dwellings could be called shacks by Hillcrest standards, most looked reasonably sturdy and functional. Celilo didn't have Hillcrest's green lawns, cement sidewalks, and garages but it seemed to serve the villagers well. George's house, on the other hand, was a shocking exception. It was just a small structure that looked as if it would come crashing down in a light breeze.

Several children, trailed by yapping dogs, had run ahead of the group, stirring up dust and yelling, "Sheriff's coming! Sheriff's coming!" By the time they'd reached George's house, the crowd had grown larger and more agitated. The sheriff's demeanor was subdued but his face was still flushed. The situation was no less volatile than before and could have exploded—if Chief Tommy Thompson hadn't been there. He stood in front of the opening to George's house and calmly greeted everyone as if nothing was amiss. He'd changed his ceremonial garb for jeans and a long-sleeved white shirt but still had his walking stick at his side.

"Stay close," Mr. Matthews reminded the girls before addressing the chief. "Sir, we've come for George Featherstone. He's—"

"Under arrest for murder," finished Sheriff Pritchard.

That's all it took for the frenzied shouting to flare up again. Chief Thompson raised his hand to silence the crowd and, in a testament to the respect they had for their leader, they quickly obeyed. Chief Thompson then motioned for Reba to enter the house. In short order, she emerged from the tiny dwelling with an old man who looked on the verge of collapse. Dessa and Ellie exchanged perplexed looks. It seemed impossible that someone so feeble could be an accused murderer. Nick wasn't a he-man but youth was on his side. He should've been able to defend himself quite easily against George Featherstone.

As the sheriff slapped handcuffs on George, a couple of barrel-

155

chested men broke from the crowd and rushed toward the sheriff. Sheriff Pritchard immediately drew his pistol and yelled, "Back off!"

Dessa's heart felt as if it would leap out of her chest at any moment. Here was the danger she'd hoped for writ large. Mr. Matthews released his grip on the girls' hands and quickly shielded them with his body. Dessa poked her head around him in time to see Chief Thompson raise his walking stick above his head with both hands. "Enough!" he said, addressing the crowd as well as the two men. "Do as Sheriff Pritchard demands. There will be no trouble here."

"Sam Mitchell is our friend," said Reba, taking a cue from her chief. "He has promised to protect George." She paused for effect. "And I believe him." As a respected healer, her words had the ring of authenticity.

Mr. Matthews faced the crowd. "George Featherstone's safety will be my responsibility," he said. "I will not fail him. I will not fail any of you."

The sheriff smirked as he holstered his weapon. "There you go folks, a warm and fuzzy deal if I ever heard one." He grabbed George by the elbow. "And now that we've got that settled, I'm taking my prisoner to jail."

Chief Thompson gave his consent with a brief nod. The villagers stepped aside without further protest as Sheriff Pritchard left with his prisoner in tow.

It wasn't the story Dessa had hoped for, but the drama surrounding George Featherstone's arrest for murder was something she could work with. New headline: *Hostile Showdown Disrupts Celilo Arrest.*

CHAPTER NINETEEN

It was obvious from the way Walter stormed over to Danny's truck that he was angry. "You're late!" he snapped. Punctuality had never been a priority for Walter until recently. For as long as Danny had known him, he'd been a relaxed, easy-going guy with a mile-wide smile and care-free attitude. It took a lot to get him riled enough to fight, let alone growl at his best friend for making him wait a few extra minutes. Ever since Walter got hooked up with this so-called benefactor of his, he'd been a changed man. He'd always opposed the dam, but now he was intensely focused on destroying it. He dismissed all the efforts they'd made so far as mere pranks. He claimed they now had a real chance to save Celilo Falls. If true, Danny was all for it. But he didn't need Walter getting on his case over every little thing.

"Don't be such a tight ass, man. So, I got to the Pit Stop a bit late. We can still make the meeting on time." He brushed past Walter and headed for the tavern's door.

Walter shouted, "Stop! He's not meeting us here."

Danny spun around and faced Walter. "Where, then?"

Walter gestured to the 1947 Oldsmobile that belonged to his uncle. "Just get in the car, Danny. I'm driving."

Neither man spoke as Walter tore out of the parking lot and drove east on the highway. After a few miles, they crossed over a bridge to the Washington side of the Columbia River. Danny couldn't take the icy silence any longer. "You gonna tell me where're we headed?"

"Maryhill."

"The museum? Why there?"

"Think about it," Walter said. "Closing time was hours ago. No one will be around to see us. Besides, who the hell goes there anyway?"

He was right. For a secret meeting place, it was ideal. The huge structure was visible from the Oregon side of the river but was quite remote for a museum. It was originally supposed to be a house (more accurately, a mansion or castle) for the daughter of some rich guy named Samuel Hill. For unknown reasons, neither his daughter Mary, nor anyone else, ever moved into the home after it was completed in 1940. It later became the Maryhill Museum of Art. Danny had never been there and doubted Walter had, either. The museum was a white folk kind of place. Danny checked his wristwatch and grimaced. Now he knew why Walter had been upset with him. He had no idea that their meeting place would be twenty-five miles away. Even though Walter had put pedal to metal, it would be touch and go whether they would make the meeting on time.

"Sorry I was late."

"This is serious business, Danny. Try focusing on our plans instead of making goo-goo eyes at some white chick."

Danny glared at Walter. "She had nothing to do with it, man. Blame Sheriff Pritchard. He showed up at the village with a warrant for George's arrest."

"A warrant for what? I thought he was in some kind of accident."

"More like a trumped-up charge . . . for murder."

Walter snorted. "Yeah, right. And just who the hell was old George supposed to have murdered?

"Can't remember the name but it's a white kid who worked with a realtor in town."

"Tell me the chief didn't let the sheriff take George in."

Danny explained what had happened, including Sam Matthews' role in the release. "Never thought I'd see the day a government man would go to bat for one of us. He seemed to think George had been framed. Said he'd watch out for George while he's in custody."

"You believe him?"

"I just wonder why he's taking an interest. Maybe he has some agenda that we don't know about."

Walter grinned. "You're such a trusting soul."

"My dad always said, 'Trust a shuyapu at your peril.'"

"Things change, Danny. Everyone's not against us."

"Then tell me who we're meeting with tonight. I don't like going in blind."

"You don't know him."

"How come *you* do?" It wasn't like either one of them spent a lot of time rubbing elbows with people outside of the village.

"I met him on a job." Walter was a carpenter and worked construction when he wasn't fishing. Although self-taught, he was a highly skilled craftsman, which outweighed the fact that he was just an Indian when it came to hiring. Talent pays. He could've had a full-time job if he'd wanted, but Walter preferred fishing over swinging a hammer. "Remember when I worked on that big housing development in town called Hillcrest?"

"Sort of."

"The guy we're meeting tonight oversaw the entire project. He owns a lot of property in town besides Hillcrest."

"Are you serious? A bigwig from The Dalles wants to help us destroy the dam?" The notion was so preposterous that it would have been laughable if it weren't so dangerous. The influx of workers who'd streamed into The Dalles to build the dam was a boon to the town's commerce — from saloons to churches, all had cashed in. Especially property owners. Why would someone profiting from the golden egg-laying goose want to kill it? The answer was obvious: no one. Danny was skeptical when Walter first suggested that there were powerful people outside of Celilo who wanted to help their cause. He suspected it was a trap of some sort. Now he was convinced of it. Tonight's meeting would be a fatal mistake. Heart pumping and palms sweating, he yelled at Walter. "Turn the car around! We're being set up! Just like George."

"No, we're not," Walter said harshly. He tightened his grip on the steering wheel as if he thought Danny would wrench it away from him.

"You're crazy, man." When Danny grabbed the passenger-side door handle, Walter pressed down harder on the gas pedal. Unlike Danny's beater, the Olds was in tip-top condition and hit seventy-five miles an hour with ease. The dry and barren hills lining the winding roadway were just a blur as the car flew past. Unable to escape, Danny braced himself for the wild ride but could not control the anxiety broiling in his gut. Overhead, a full moon silently witnessed their race toward certain ambush. As they approached the entrance to the museum's parking lot, Danny made a last-ditch effort to stop the meeting. "Dammit, Walter!" he blurted. "This is a bad idea. We need to get out of here. NOW!"

Walter sighed wearily. "Come on, Danny, you need to cool it, okay? Tonight's meet isn't some kind of frame, trap, or set-up." A lone pickup a few yards away flashed its headlights at their car. "That's him," Walter said. "Just listen to what the man has to say and then decide if he's legit or not. Listening ain't gonna hurt us." Walter stared at Danny with a fierce intensity that matched his tone. "This is war, man! We're warriors, aren't we?" He didn't pause for an answer before taunting, "Or, are you nothing but a little chicken shit?"

Stunned, Danny looked his friend in the eye for a tense moment. The urge to lash out spread through his body like a deadly fever. If it had been anyone besides Walter, he wouldn't have attempted to rein in his growing fury. He would've relished a bloody fight. "I may be many things," Danny said in a steely voice, "but I will never be a chicken shit." He opened the car door and climbed out. "I'm a warrior just like you." He gestured toward the idling pickup with its passenger waiting inside. "Let's go do this."

CHAPTER TWENTY

With Walter's "chicken-shit" taunt still ringing in his ears, Danny charged across the parking lot to confront whatever unknown plight awaited them. According to Walter, Stanley Feldman was the richest and most powerful man in The Dalles. But he sure didn't look the part. Judging by the clothes he wore—dirty overalls, scuffed boots, and a sweat-stained hat—he could've passed for a farmer who'd just finished plowing forty acres. The truck he stood alongside was as beat up as Danny's 100,000-mile bucket of bolts. He was short—maybe five-foot-six, if you counted the extra height his boots gave him—and girlishly thin. Danny didn't know what he'd expected a rich and powerful man to look like but this lightweight wasn't it. "I have just one question for you," he snapped. "Why?"

Walter seemed embarrassed by Danny's brash outburst. "Danny, calm down. Let me introduce—."

Feldman dismissed Walter's attempt at civility with a raised hand. "It's okay. I like a man who gets right to the point." For a little guy, Feldman had a deep voice, confident and strong. He met Danny's steely-eyed stare and said, "I assume you are referring to the dam and why I'm opposed to it."

"Walter said you want to destroy it. The question remains, why?"

Feldman fished a pack of Camels from his pocket and took his time lighting a cigarette. "It's a legitimate question," he said, exhaling deeply. "But the premise is flawed."

Danny and Walter looked at each other. "Huh?" they both said at once.

"I represent a group which, like the two of you, is passionate about our cause. But realistically, you have to admit that it isn't possible to destroy the dam at this stage of the game."

Danny's patience was reliably short-lived. "Then what the hell are we doing here?" he demanded.

Feldman picked a flake of tobacco off his lower lip. "Because the U.S. government has failed you."

"You'll get no argument from us on that point," Danny admitted. "But what exactly are you proposing?"

"You can't stop the dam from being built but you can disrupt the process and make it so difficult and expensive that lengthy delays are inevitable. We're talking delays of several months or more. I believe you will agree that expressing your outrage at the government with what we have in mind will be much more effective than the tactics you've used so far."

Destroying the dam had never been a real possibility and Danny had reluctantly come to that conclusion himself only recently. He'd never expressed that opinion, however, and didn't plan to do so. It felt like failure. Walter and the others would have to make up their own minds about the end game. Their pranks hadn't satisfied their need for revenge but would costly delays be any different? And just what did Feldman's group get out of it? He reined in his growing frustration and said, "I've asked it several times now and I still don't know why. Why would this group of yours want to help us *express our outrage* as you put it?"

Feldman crushed out his cigarette and lit another. "It's an attention-getting device. The first of many we have planned. Yours isn't the only cause we're backing. You see, our group isn't just opposed to the government that is building the dam. We are opposed to the capitalist way of life." He paused to take a drag on his cigarette. "But it's more than that; we want to destroy the capitalist system itself."

The man talked in riddles. "If what I've heard about you is true, it seems to me that capitalism *is* your way of life. Danny eyed his truck and shabby clothing. "All outward appearances aside, I imagine it's a pretty good life."

Feldman smiled for the first time. "Yes, I've profited from the capitalist system. Some would even say I've achieved the American dream. My wife would beg to differ. She doesn't think I spend enough on her or our lifestyle. But I am making money."

"Then what's the problem?"

He crushed out his half-smoked cigarette. "There is no problem with milking the system for the greater good."

"The greater good?"

"A system that rewards everyone for their hard work and not just the privileged few."

Walter had let Danny and Feldman carry the conversation ball until now. "I don't get it," he said. "What are you talking about?"

"Communism," said Feldman. "I won't bore you with a discussion of Marxist or Lenin economic theories, but the main thing to know is that we believe in ownership of all property by the community as a whole. Basically, a classless and stateless society and the equal distribution of goods through revolutionary means."

Danny was still skeptical of Feldman's motives but the term revolutionary appealed to him. A revolution was exactly what it would take to keep the government from destroying Celilo. "And just how do we figure into this revolution of yours?" asked Danny.

Feldman walked over to the bed of his truck and pulled back a blue tarp to reveal what it had covered. "Take a looksee," he said.

***

Two days later, Danny was still unsure about the merits of joining Feldman's so-called revolution. Maybe it wasn't a trap; maybe it was something worse. He wasn't especially keen on aligning themselves with the Communist Party. Walter pooh-poohed Danny's concerns. "All that Commie talk is just a bunch of mumbo jumbo," he said. Who the hell cares? He's got his reasons and we've got ours. The goal is the same: destroy the dam. Feldman and his group offer the best chance we have of doing just that."

"He said it couldn't be destroyed at this stage. Only delayed."

"Yeah, yeah. Whatever. I still plan to destroy the dam."

Danny thought Walter was overconfident but he didn't object further. He was tired of playing the Doubting Thomas role. He craved action. Danny felt like a boxer who'd been sidelined with an injury and was afraid if he didn't get back in the ring soon he'd lose his edge. They decided it was time to meet with the other guys at the Pit

Stop to go over the plan. Once they'd settled in at their usual table with beers all around, Danny led the discussion. Ernie's reaction was just what Danny had expected. Always the eager beaver, he was on board even before he'd heard the plan's details. Henry was more measured in his response.

"Who is this guy you met with? What's his beef with the dam?"

"We can't tell you that," said Walter. "You just have to trust us that the man has a legitimate gripe and wants to help us with our cause."

Danny was relieved that Walter hadn't mentioned anything about a communist revolution but he could tell by Henry's sour expression that he didn't think much of what he had heard. Danny understood exactly how he felt. When Feldman had insisted that they couldn't tell anyone his name or how he was involved, Danny was as put off as Henry seemed to be now. "That's not right," Danny had told Feldman. "If this plan goes haywire, we'll be the ones to take the heat, not you or your group. We already have the sheriff breathing down our necks as it is."

"Don't worry," Feldman had assured him. "If anything goes wrong, show them this."

He'd handed Danny an envelope which he said contained their *Get Out of Jail Free* card. Inside was a handwritten letter on official government stationery explaining that Danny Longstreet, Walter Potts and two of their associates were on a special assignment for the Federal Bureau of Investigation. The letter authorized them unlimited access to The Dalles Dam for the specific purpose of preventing sabotage. It further stated that this was a top-secret mission authorized by the Bureau Chief of the FBI headquartered in Portland, Oregon. It was signed and dated by the special agent assigned to oversee the operation.

The letter looked official but it didn't make sense to Danny. "Wait a minute," he'd told Feldman. "Why would anyone believe that the FBI would entrust us to prevent sabotage? Everybody knows we're opposed to construction of the dam and would sabotage the dam ourselves if we could."

Feldman chuckled. "That's the beauty of this deal. The agent in charge isn't a communist but he wants what you want—to disrupt completion of the dam. He's set this whole operation up and is my inside man at the dam."

Walter thought that was just about the coolest thing he'd ever heard. "The fox is minding the hen house," he joked.

"I'm back to square one," Danny said. "Why? Why would an FBI agent want to sabotage the dam?"

Feldman smiled but it was without warmth. "Revenge, my friend. Revenge."

His answer hadn't fully satisfied Danny but he'd accepted the envelope anyway.

"Put the letter somewhere safe and don't tell anyone about it," Feldman cautioned. "You can show it to the authorities if you think we've betrayed you (which we won't) or if you get caught at the dam and are arrested (which you won't). Whatever happens, you will be covered. When this is all over, I expect you to give the letter back to me and we will go our separate ways."

Danny realized that Henry had just asked him a question but he'd been thinking about Feldman and missed it. "What did you say?"

"I asked if you're okay with this guy and his plan?"

Walter had been bugging Danny ever since their meeting to make a firm commitment but he'd been putting him off. It still felt like they would be the losers in the end despite the letter that would supposedly exonerate them. Danny glanced at Walter and shrugged. "It's a risk . . . but one I'm willing to take."

Danny's confirmation earned him a broad smile from Walter. "Me, too," Walter said. "If you and Ernie are with us, then I'll explain how this is all going to work." He paused to give them time to decide but Danny knew they'd agree. Once Danny was behind the plan, he knew the others would follow his lead. And they did.

Henry still seemed troubled. "You said when we first got together that we were going to destroy the dam."

Danny frowned, remembering how he'd let anger overshadow reasonable expectations. Oscar and the other elders had realized the futility of their cause from the outset. "You're right, Henry. Destroying the dam was what we all wanted. Unfortunately, the truth is we really can't stop the government from doing whatever the hell they decide to do. But what we can do is severely limit the progress—

by several months if we're successful. So far, we haven't delayed the project by even one day, let alone months."

"It's not ideal," Walter added, "but a little dynamite can cause one hell of a problem to fix. Our new partner had a starter box of dynamite in his truck for us."

Ernie hadn't paid much attention until Walter mentioned the magic word dynamite. "Wow," he said excitedly, "that's so cool."

Henry rolled his eyes. "How are we supposed to get onto the dam? Four Indians carrying sticks of dynamite onto government property might be a tad bit suspicious, don't you think?"

"Our guy has a man on the inside who is going to get us government passes, an authorized vehicle, hard hats, and everything else we might need," Walter said. He waved a key in front of them. "This here is a key to a warehouse the guy owns. I've already been there to look inside. It has all the dynamite and more that this job will take."

Ernie shot off his chair like it was spring loaded. "Like crazy, man!" he exclaimed. "When do we start?"

CHAPTER TWENTY-ONE

Mildred settled onto the bar stool next to Tony. "I thought I might find you here," she said. "The office is locked and I left my keys at home."

Annoyed, Tony reached into his pocket and tossed her a loaded key ring. He was used to depending on Mildred, not the other way around and it bugged the hell out of him. "I don't give a damn what you do, but I don't plan on working today, maybe even for a couple days."

"Yeah, I didn't think so." She checked out his bruised and cut-up face. "You look like you've been in a fight or something." When he let the comment pass, she patted his shoulder and said, "I'm awfully sorry about Nick. He was a good kid."

Tony slurped the last of his beer. Signaling Dizzy's bartender for another round, he asked, "You want one? It's on me."

"No, thanks, I'm laying off the sauce for a while. It's too hard on my ulcer."

That was the first he'd ever heard anything about an ulcer, but what did he care? A woman her age probably had lots of ailments. Thankfully, she wasn't a complainer. "Suit yourself," he shrugged. Tony felt her eyes boring into him. Judging him. Nothing worse than having a reformed drinker around to let you know how depraved you are. "What are you staring at?" he growled.

"Nothing, boss." She paused while the bartender set Tony's refill on the counter and then ordered. "I'll take a cup of coffee, Freddie."

"You got it Miss Millie. Sugar and cream?"

"No, just black." She waited until Tony had downed some of his beer and then asked, "You want to tell me about Nick?"

"Not much to tell," Tony said. "I asked the kid to give old George a ride back to the village and the damn redskin takes it into his head to steal my truck. Shot Nick and then plowed into a tree. My truck is totaled." Clarice had cooked up a more complicated version, but Tony believed simple was best. Too much detail can trip a fellow up.

Freddie brought Mildred her coffee. She blew on the hot drink and said, "I don't get it. Why in the world would you want Nick to take George home?"

"Huh?"

Mildred eyed him over the cup's rim as she drank. "Never mind," she said. How did Uncle Sol take the news?"

"I haven't called him, if that's what you mean. Let the old coot read about it in the paper like everyone else."

"You think that's wise? What about Nick's parents? Don't you think they should hear about it from you?"

"I'm two beers past caring," he said.

Freddie brought another beer and coffee without asking and gestured to a couple of new arrivals at the bar. "Your gang's all here now."

"Oh, no," Tony said, "spare me." His elusive salesmen, Hoffman and Jensen, were the last people he wanted pestering him with questions about Nick. Mildred was bad enough, but those two clowns would never stop yammering. "We'll take our drinks to the corner booth, Freddie. And do me a favor, will ya?" he said, throwing a wad of bills onto the counter.

"What's that, Tony?"

"Don't let Abbot and Costello run out of beer. I see them anywhere near our table and the party's over."

Freddie scooped up the money and grinned. "You got it, man."

As soon as they were settled in the booth, Mildred pulled a newspaper from the giant bag she called a purse. She unfolded it on top of the table and pointed to the headline: '*Celilo Indian Arrested for Murder.*' This is the Portland newspaper, Tony. When your family sees this they're going to wonder why they haven't heard from you. They've already been trying to reach you at the office. I'm guessing they'll want you to accompany Nick's body back to Portland for burial."

Tony hadn't even thought about a funeral. All he wanted to do was get drunk and forget the whole mess. Why'd Clarice have to kill the kid? All it had done was make Tony's life miserable. Facing a bunch of grieving relatives would be worse than miserable.

"Do you want me to call Uncle Sol or Nick's parents for you?" asked Mildred.

"Hell no!" Tony gulped his beer, hoping a buzz would kick in soon. He felt like a one-hundred-pound-weight was strapped on his back and the alcohol hadn't done a thing to lift it. Just the mention of Uncle Sol was enough to add another ten pounds. "Do you know why that bastard sent Nick to The Dalles? He was Uncle Sol's little spy. The kid wasn't here to learn anything about real estate. He was here to get the goods on us."

"What?"

"You heard me. That little punk ransacked your desk after you split and he found the ledgers—both of them." He knew he was saying too much, but he was just so damn angry he couldn't put the brakes on. "We caught him red-handed."

"We?"

"Me and Clarice. We were heading into the office just as Nick was leaving with the ledgers. He would've made a clean getaway if Clarice hadn't gotten suspicious and asked for the newspaper that he'd used to hide the theft." He took another swig of beer. "The kid even confessed."

"That explains a lot," Mildred said. "I thought your cousin was getting awfully chummy with me." She chuckled, "I didn't think it was because of my good looks. But I never dreamed he was spying on us. So, tell me, Tony, what'd you do when he 'fessed up?"

Tony rubbed his bruised jaw. "What do you think? Pounded him to a pulp."

Mildred was quiet, as if mentally assessing his injuries against his story. "And then what? You sent him off in your truck with George Featherstone?"

"Yeah, that's right."

"Hmm," she said. "I wonder why he didn't hightail it straight back to Portland and Uncle Sol instead."

Now he'd done just what he'd hoped to avoid. Blabbing too much had opened a minefield. He shrugged off the question. "Too dumb to think of it, I guess." Whether Mildred was satisfied with that explanation or not, didn't matter. He was through talking.

"Interesting," she said, downing the last of her coffee and tossing a quarter on the table. "Well, Tony, if there's anything you want me to do, just let me know. You can reach me at home."

He watched her fat behind as she jiggled her way across the room, glad to be finally left alone. It didn't last. As soon as the noon hour approached, Dizzy's began to get crowded and people kept stopping by his table to express their sympathy — and outrage. Sentiment against the Celilo tribe wasn't good before the murder and it had only gotten worse now. The killing of a white kid by an Injun had set everyone on edge. Blaming George had been a brilliant idea; Clarice was right when she'd predicted the uproar that would follow. Except for receiving condolences, the focus was off him. Tony hated putting on the Sad Sack act, but at least Freddie had kept the two bozos, Hoffman and Jensen, away from him. Slipping unnoticed out the bar's rear door, he hopped into the convertible he'd left parked in the alley.

He had no destination in mind as he drove through town. The beer hadn't gotten him buzzed enough so he stopped at a liquor store and bought a fifth of Jack Daniels. He would've gone straight to Monty's Motel and called Clarice, but she'd made it clear that they should cool their relationship until things settled down. He thought about heading out to the Carlton and hooking up with that sexy new hatcheck gal, but a better idea suddenly popped into his head.

He slowed the Caddy as he turned onto Cherry Blossom Lane. The Matthews' house was just around the corner. Seeing that sexy little vixen would boost his spirits. She was virgin territory in serious need of exploration and he was more than ready to get started. He glanced in the rearview mirror and smoothed back his hair. He noted with dismay how dark the circles were under his bloodshot eyes. His scruffy unshaven face looked tired, which wasn't surprising given that he'd been unable to get a decent night's sleep since his meeting with Feldman at the Carlton. But, man, were those gray hairs in his sideburns? This whole sorry mess was aging him fast. He opened the liquor bottle and took a swig. On second thought, what was he worried about? He may be beaten down a bit, but he still looked good enough to turn a few heads. Ellie's included.

Tony was confident that Sam Matthews would still be at work this early in the afternoon. Nevertheless, he checked to make sure his truck wasn't parked in the driveway before bringing the convertible to a stop. Except for the swhish-swhish of lawn sprinklers here and there, the neighborhood was unusually quiet. Tony didn't care about anyone spotting his car in front of the Matthews' house. His job had taken him to Hillcrest so many times that the bright red Caddy was a common sight. No one would question why it would be parked anywhere in the neighborhood. He took another drink and wiped his mouth with the back of his hand. As he was searching through the glove compartment for some breath mints, he heard someone call his name. "Yoo-hoo, Mr. Rossi!"

He straightened up and found the red-haired Feldman girl standing next to his car. "What are you doing here?" she asked with a metallic grin. "Slumming?"

"Not until you showed up," Tony shot back. He unrolled a mint, popped it into his mouth and handed her the pack. "Take it," he said. "Your attitude could use a little sweetening."

She grinned again and peeled off one of the mints. Pocketing the rest of the package in her shorts, she said, "I'm really sorry about your cousin. I liked him." She paused a moment as if expecting a thank you or some other response. "But," she said, "you never answered my question. Are you looking for Mr. Matthews or . . ." she fluttered her eyelids, ". . . maybe it's Ellie you're after."

"What's it to you?" She didn't look much older than twelve, but she was a real wise-ass. It pissed him off and sort of amused him at the same time.

"You haven't forgotten me, have you?" she asked, fluffing up her curly hair and striking what she must have thought was a sexy, pinup-like pose. "I hate to think I'm forgettable. The name's Odessa. But you can call me Dessa."

Tony snorted. That isn't what he'd call her. "I know who you are, Dessa, but you're not my type." He opened the car door and stepped out. "So, why don't you go find someone else to seduce?"

"I thought you liked them young. I'm the same age as Ellie."

If she was trying to get his goat, she had succeeded. "Get lost," he said, giving her a slight push as he passed her. He was almost to the Matthews' front porch when she called out, "By the way, Ellie's not home." Tony turned and stared at the girl. He wasn't sure if he believed her or not. "Where is she?"

"That's for me to know and you to not find out."

Lying little snot nose. He hoofed it straight to the porch and rang the doorbell. He shifted from one foot to the other as he waited. And waited.

"Told ya," Dessa taunted.

Muttering a few choice curses, he marched back to the car. It took all his will power to ignore the mouthy brat. Her father was too crucial to his plans to deal with her like he wanted. As soon as he'd hopped in the car, he grabbed the Jack Daniels and downed a hefty snort.

Dessa put her hands on her hips like a scolding fishwife and said, "You shouldn't drink and drive, you know."

Tony fired up the convertible and pulled away from the curb. *Women! Young or old, they're always telling you what to do. To hell with 'em. Antonio Rossi was going to do whatever he damn well pleased. And when he was through, they'd beg for more.*

CHAPTER TWENTY-TWO

Sam left home early so he could stop at the jail on his way to work. It was the second visit he'd made since George's arrest and he wasn't looking forward to it. He had yet to get George to talk to him. Worse, the last time he'd visited he'd encountered several townsfolk milling around the courthouse steps with no apparent business other than voicing their outrage about the Chambers and Rossi murders. The consensus was that George Featherstone was responsible for both. It was just this type of community problem that Sam had hoped to avoid. He'd warned the sheriff that they could expect more trouble, but Pritchard hadn't even pretended to listen. Still smarting from their run-in at Celilo, the sheriff had made it clear that Sam was on his turf at the jail and he made the rules. Since Sam had no respect for the man and even less for how he represented himself as an officer of the law, he didn't care what rules the sheriff made.

What he cared about was defusing any potential trouble. When Sam complained to Jess Harmon about the sheriff, he didn't get any sympathy. "You know the drill—cooperate with the local officials. Your role is to squelch trouble, not incite it. If this Pritchard fellow gets in the way, you'll just have to figure out how to work around him." Sam hadn't needed the reminder about his role, but he'd accomplished his intent: his complaint had been officially noted for the record. If things got dicey later—a real possibility—then any challenges as to how Sam handled the situation would be minimized. Harmon hadn't dealt with the sheriff yet. When he did, maybe he'd understand Sam 's concerns.

In the meantime, he'd do whatever he had to do. A good stiff drink would certainly make his meeting with the sheriff a little more palatable. But it wasn't doable. He'd avoided any alcohol since arriving in town and he wasn't about to let a man like Leonard Pritchard be the reason he failed again.

As he climbed the courthouse steps, the crowd that had assembled was larger and more vocal than the last time he'd visited. Some of the protesters carried signs and tried to engage Sam with their taunts. When he told the sheriff about what he'd experienced, his worries were once again brushed aside. "People have a right to free speech." He seemed more interested in the bag Sam carried than anything going on outside. "What's that you've got there?" he asked.

"Nothing to get excited about, sheriff. It's just a little treat for George. I thought it might help cheer him up."

Pritchard demanded that he hand over the bag for inspection. When he looked inside, he snickered. "Humph. It's gonna take a lot more than oranges to help that old man."

George was doing well the last time Sam had seen him. His diabetes seemed to be under control now, but his health would always be a worry when confined in Pritchard's care. Alarmed, Sam asked, "What do you mean? Is he having problems?"

"Don't get your panties in a wad, Matthews. George is fine. I just meant that he's in big trouble. And your little visits ain't gonna change that. The murder charge is sticking."

"I'm not trying to change anything. He's got a tribal lawyer coming in from Yakima to represent him. Until that happens, I told the Wy-ams that I'd check in on him and make sure he's okay." He reached for the bag that Pritchard still held. "Oranges are good for him."

Pritchard tossed him the bag. "Why do you care?" It was the same question Sam had asked himself ever since they'd rescued George at Baker Bluff. He liked to think he'd do the same for anyone in similar circumstances. What tugged at his conscience was not knowing whether he was just playing the role his bureau chief had given him or acting out of genuine compassion. He'd dealt with Indians in the past, but he'd never gone out of his way to make any promises to them. His involvement had already raised the ire of the sheriff and complicated future dealings with the man. What had ever possessed him to risk jeopardizing the success of his mission by personally guaranteeing George's safety? The short answer was so obvious it embarrassed him: Reba. The woman was an unexpected development that had him questioning every action he undertook. He dismissed the sheriff's question with a shoulder shrug. "What can I say? I'm just a good-hearted fella."

Pritchard wouldn't let it go. "Injun lover, huh?"

Sam bit his lower lip to keep from taking the bait.

"Well, you're new in town so I guess you don't know any better. You made a point of warning me, so let me give *you* a word of caution: messing around with that Celilo crowd is asking for trouble."

"I get the message, sheriff. Now, how 'bout escorting me to George's cell?" The jail had three cells, but George Stonefeather was the only prisoner behind bars. The accommodations were sparse with just a double bunk, toilet, and washbasin in each of the small quarters. George was stretched out on the bottom bunk, but sat upright when Sam and Pritchard arrived. The sheriff unlocked the cell door and Sam stepped inside. "I gotta lock you in," he said, clanging the door shut and turning the key. "Just holler when you're through gabbin'. . . or when the stink gets too much for ya." He walked down the hall with a cocky stride punctuated by laughter and boots clicking against the cement floor.

Sam greeted George who struggled to stand. He wore the same sweat-stained and rumpled garments he had on when he was arrested. Sam made a mental note to pick up a change of clothes for him when he went to the village again. "Don't get up, George. I'll sit right here alongside you, if that's okay." When George scooted over to make room, Sam gave him the bag. "I brought some oranges for you. Reba said they were your favorite treat." George mumbled a brief thank-you and stuffed the bag under his thin pillow without looking inside. Besides checking on him, Sam had hoped the visits would help him to understand what had really happened at Baker Bluff since Pritchard's story made no sense at all. Engaging George in a meaningful way, however, had so far proved unrewarding. Trust-building took time.

"How's the sheriff treating you, George?"

"He don't bother me none."

"That's good. What about your meals? Are you getting enough to eat?"

George nodded.

"I'm told the café across the street delivers three times a day. I've eaten there myself. Not bad."

George nodded again. "Yeah, they's got a pretty gal working there. She's Umatilla. Brings me fry bread ever once in a while."

"She must like you."

Another nod.

"George, a lot of people like you. And they're concerned about you. That's why I keep coming here. I want to help."

A skeptical look crossed the old man's face. Never mind that Sam had probably saved his life. The reaction was automatic when dealing with whites, especially government types. "A tribal lawyer will be here soon to handle your legal case. In the meantime, Chief Thompson and Reba asked me to check on you. They believe I'm a friend. A friend who can help you."

"Okay."

It was progress of sorts. Now if he could just get him to open up. "George, the only way that I can help is to have you talk to me about the accident."

"I don't remember much."

"That's all right. Just tell me what you can."

"What do you want to know?"

"Let's start with how you happened to be driving that truck?"

"I wasn't driving. I don't know how to."

"Right. You were just a passenger. Who picked you up?"

"Some guy saw me in town and asked if I wanted a ride back to the village."

"Do you know his name?"

George shook his head.

"Had he ever given you a ride before?"

"No white gives Indians a ride anywheres."

"So, this was a first. You didn't wonder about that?"

"Naw. I was tired and not feeling so good. I just wanted to get on home."

"Was there anyone else in the truck besides the driver?"

"Nope. Just me and the white guy."

"Are you sure? No one was riding in back, in the truck bed?"

"Nope."

That made sense. If there'd been anyone else aboard, George would've been told to hop in the back of the truck. Given the way Indians were usually treated it was surprising that he was permitted to ride shotgun even without another passenger. "Would you be able to identify the driver if you saw him again?"

George chuckled and shook his head. "You whites all look alike to us."

Sam smiled. "Yeah, I've heard that before. You know what I've heard about Indians?"

"Nothin' much good, I 'spect."

"I've heard that Indians like to drink. That it's a real problem for some of them."

"Not me. I don't drink."

"I've heard that, too. Alcohol and diabetes don't mix. Sam paused a moment before pressing ahead. "The sheriff thinks you were drunk at the time of the accident."

"He's crazy."

"I won't argue with you about that. To be clear, you're saying you absolutely didn't have anything to drink that day?"

He nodded.

"What about the guy driving? Did he have anything to drink?"

"He had a bottle of something. I don't know what it was, maybe whiskey or wine. He offered me the bottle and when I refused, he drank some. He kept spilling it. Got it all over the seat and me, too." George sniffed his shirt. "Sheriff was right about the stink."

"How'd the guy happen to spill so much of the liquor?"

George shrugged, "Clumsy, I guess."

"Did you ever see a gun? Maybe the driver had one and showed it to you?"

He shook his head. "No gun. I'd remember that for sure."

"Do you know if the driver got out of the truck at any point?"

"We stopped once. Don't know where. I think he had to take a leak or something."

"Do you remember crashing into the tree?"

He patted his still-bandaged head. "All I remember is waking up at the village and seeing Reba."

Sam looked at his wristwatch. He'd stayed longer than he'd planned. "Okay, George. I have to go to work now, but I'll be back to see you again. In the meantime, if you remember anything, anything at all, be sure to tell your lawyer or me." Sam stood. "And enjoy the oranges."

It took several shouts to get Pritchard's attention. His ambling gait and the inordinate time it took to unlock the cell got his message across loud and clear: the sheriff was in control. "Thanks, Sheriff Pritchard," Sam said. "Appreciate your cooperation."

***

Back at the dam, Sam took out a pen and pad to jot some notes for a meeting he had to attend. The pilot of the helicopter company contracted to transport the Indians' remains to the new cemetery wanted to discuss the logistics involved. Now that the Baker Bluff property had been dismissed as unworkable due to Nick's murder, he had to prepare for the newly selected site. Transferring the bones of 2,500 or so Indians from Memaloose Island and some 700 of the ancient and mostly unidentifiable bones from Graves Island would take some planning. Sam poured a cup of coffee and thought about the task. Although he'd willingly accepted the job, transporting the dead wasn't something he was comfortable with. He figured he had no choice in the matter since there was so much potential for trouble involved.

He regretted now that he'd let the sheriff know that he was in charge of the project. That was a mistake he hoped wouldn't come back to haunt him. His relationship with the "Celilo crowd," as the sheriff called them, was as tenuous as gossamer. He walked a fine line between friend and foe when on assignment and he couldn't afford to stumble. "Hell," he muttered, "I've already stumbled. Over a woman, no less." His attraction to Reba had taken him by surprise. Pursuing a relationship with her was not the wisest course of action under the circumstances but she was the only woman in a long time that even came close to capturing his heart. But if Reba or her hot-headed son ever got wind of his real job, it wouldn't be a mere stumble. It would be a total collapse.

178

CHAPTER TWENTY-THREE

Sam didn't like leaving Ellie home alone at night but he didn't have a choice. Jess Harmon wanted to discuss the status of the Chambers' murder investigation with him and they couldn't do it at the dam. The shocking murder of the well-liked foreman was a constant source of rumors and speculation, which dogged Harmon's every move. The FBI agent had commandeered a temporary on-site office but complained that it might as well have been set up in Grand Central Station. Harmon was bombarded with a steady stream of workers-turned-amateur-detectives popping into his office to offer theories and advice. "I'm as popular as a two-bit whore in a mining camp," Harmon said. As a result, he told Sam to meet him at his motel where they'd be able to discuss the case without interruption. Sam waited until Ellie was asleep, then left her an ambiguous note about an errand, and made sure the house was locked and secured before he left for his ten o'clock meeting.

Monty's Motel was a curious choice for Harmon's lodging. His ex-partner had always been fussy about where he laid his head down at night. He had a tidy, well-appointed apartment in Portland and, when on the road, insisted on the best accommodations possible. If their per diem allowance wasn't sufficient to cover the extra cost, he willingly made up the difference. Monty's was a shocking departure from Harmon's usual standards. The L-shaped, ten-unit structure was strictly a low-rent dive. Even in marginal lighting, it was hard to miss the peeling paint, sagging roof, and general rundown appearance of the one-story facility. There were just a couple of vehicles in the, weed-filled gravel parking lot, but a cardboard *No Vacancy* sign was attached to the motel's office door. Sam approached the only unit that had a light on and knocked.

Harmon opened the door wearing jeans and a tee-shirt instead of his usual suit and tie. As he ushered Sam inside, he pre-empted any derogatory comments about his living quarters. "I know what you're going to say, Matthews. This place is a dump."

"I can see that," said Sam. The sparsely furnished room with its thread-bare carpeting, grimy walls, and stained window coverings confirmed that Monty's Motel qualified for flop-house status. But it wasn't the lack of quality décor and furnishings that bothered Sam. Despair born of too much booze, cigarettes, and filth permeated the small room with gag-worthy intensity. Nevertheless, he made light of the situation. "What'd they do?" he cracked. "Cut your per diem rate to the bone?"

Harmon grimaced and lit a cigarette. Exhaling deeply, he gestured to the crime scene photos and investigative notes tacked to the walls. "Think I could put those up in a decent hotel with regular maid service? Hell, I can't even put them up at the office. My so-called point man, Beckstrom, would piss his pants."

"Is he helping you much?"

Harmon sniggered, "You know the answer to that. The guy is a royal pain in the ass."

"Welcome to the club," said Sam, suppressing a grin. He took a moment to study the black and white images of Pete Chambers' body *in situ* while Harmon lit a cigarette. Chambers was sprawled face down on his living room floor, drenched in blood from multiple stab wounds. No stranger to gruesome murder scenes, Sam was still unnerved by the sight of his co-worker's mutilated body. The bloody scene and fetidness of the motel room caused a metallic-tasting bile to rise in his throat. He swallowed quickly and muttered, "Grisly business. Did you find a knife?"

"Forensic boys have been all over the place and found no sign of a weapon. Despite the extensive damage, the coroner thinks it was a small blade, possibly a fishing knife, or even a jackknife. But that isn't what killed him."

Harmon handed Sam a spent shell casing in a protective wrapper. "He was shot with a Colt .45. The local coroner missed it, but we sent his body to Portland for an additional autopsy. The cause of death was verified as homicide by gunshot. The bullet was still in the guy."

"So, the stabbing was overkill or someone's attempt to throw us off what really happened."

"Had to be someone pretty stupid if they thought the FBI couldn't figure out the cause of death."

"Maybe they didn't realize the FBI would be called in on the case and the local sheriff would handle the investigation. From what I've seen, Sheriff Pritchard couldn't solve a crossword puzzle if the answers were right in front of him. What about fingerprints? Get anything useable?"

"Place was wiped clean. Couldn't even find Chambers' prints."

"Have you ruled out robbery?"

"Not conclusively, but there was no sign of forced entry and his girlfriend said she didn't think anything was missing."

"His girlfriend?"

"Guess you didn't know the old codger as well as you thought," Harmon said, crushing out his cigarette.

"Maybe you better fill me in from the beginning."

Harmon gestured for Sam to take a seat on one of the chairs alongside a rickety-looking table. Reaching into a shopping bag stashed next to the unmade bed, he pulled out a six-pack of beer. He took a bottle for himself and offered one to Sam. "We better drink it now while it's still cold from the market," he said.

Sam eyed the bottle. A beer would wash away the traces of bile that lingered on his tongue. And he was thirsty. "Naw," he said, sighing. "I'll pass."

Harmon raised a brow. "First time I've ever seen you refuse a brewski."

"Won't be the last time, either. "No more booze of any kind for me."

"Don't tell me you're on the wagon again?" Harmon's amused tone matched the skeptical look he gave Sam. Sobriety was an elusive goal that Harmon knew Sam had never been able to achieve. "Going to give A.A. another try again, too?"

Sam hadn't always had a drinking problem. Growing up, he was too busy helping his father run the family farm to spend time hanging out with his beer-guzzling pals. In fact, he never drank a drop of alcohol until after he returned from the war. His father had always been the drinking man in the family, although they never referred to him as an alcoholic. The term back then was "hard drinker." But Sam's absence during the war and Mary's illness had made things worse. By the time the peace treaty with Japan was signed, his father had lost the farm, Mary was dying from cancer and Sam's life was forever changed. Drinking became his way to cope. Despite his growing dependence on alcohol, he'd secured a decent job with the FBI through an officer he'd served with in the Seabees. He liked the work and his partnership with Jess Harmon. He even had a reputation as one of the rising stars in the Portland Bureau. All that had come undone in one night of careless drunken stupidity. Harmon's jagged facial scar was a constant reminder of how much pain his drinking had caused others.

"Look," Sam said, "I might as well get this off my chest. I deeply regret my role in the injuries you suffered. If I hadn't been drunk as a skunk that night . . . well, let's just say, the incident was a wakeup call. The Feds gave me a second chance and I don't plan to blow it. Besides, I promised Ellie that things would be different in The Dalles."

"Suit yourself," Harmon said, dropping into the other chair. "I just want us to work together like we did before. If we solve this case, I'm guaranteed a promotion to Bureau Chief and I'll take you with me."

It would never be like it was before but Sam owed it to his friend to at least try. "Okay," he said with a shrug.

"Now that we've got that settled, here's where we are with the case: The killer was probably someone he knew and let into his house. And that's the problem. Chambers was practically a saint. All the good things you said about him were confirmed by his crew, poker buddies, and neighbors. He had no enemies or even a single person I could find who disliked the guy. No crazy relatives or sordid past deeds on record, either. Everyone said he had an amiable relationship with his ex-wife who died several years ago of natural causes."

"Where does the girlfriend come in?"

"I was getting to that. Her name's Lucy Williams and she lives across the street. Supposedly she's known Chambers for over thirty years. I got the impression that their relationship was a little one-sided on her part. Unrequited love and all that. Anyway, she's a nice old lady who spends her day baking cookies and brownies. A real grandma type. She liked to cook for Chambers, too. She usually made breakfast for him when he got off work at seven o'clock. Then he'd go home and sleep most of the day until his next shift. When he didn't show up at her place as expected, she called him. He told her that he'd be over shortly but he never arrived. That was the last she heard from him."

"She didn't go check on him?"

"I asked the same thing. She claimed that he was often exhausted when he got off his shift. As you know, he had a lot of physical ailments which she says wore him out, too. He hadn't made it over for breakfast as promised on other occasions, because he'd fallen asleep. She just thought it had happened again and she didn't want to disturb him. It wasn't until a couple of guys from his crew came looking for him later that night and the cops were called that she realized something was wrong. She didn't have much else to say except to confirm something you'd said about Chambers."

"What was that?"

"That Chambers hadn't been himself lately. He was smoking one cigarette after another and had started drinking more than usual. Said he couldn't sleep. Missed several poker games in a row and had lost interest in fishing. She knew he was obviously worried about something but he wouldn't tell her what it was."

"Did she think it was work-related or personal?"

"No idea. Whatever it was, it might've been what got him killed."

"Have you checked his finances yet? He didn't have an extravagant lifestyle, but he was due to retire soon. Maybe he was concerned about whether he had enough savings or if he could make it on a fixed income."

"I went to his bank today. Got nothing but a run-around. These small-town bureaucrats can be stubborn as hell to deal with. I plan to go back tomorrow with a search warrant and meet with the bank's manager. I can play the stubborn game, too."

"What do you want me to do?"

"Continue looking into the Indian situation. There may be a connection to our case. This town doesn't have much experience with murder and now there're two violent deaths within days of each other. I don't believe in coincidences."

"I don't, either. What I do believe is that George Featherstone didn't kill the Rossi kid."

"What about that young Indian you were telling me about, Danny something?"

"Danny Longstreet. He's been causing a lot of trouble but it has been mostly annoying pranks up to now. Whether he's escalated his game is another question. I have confirmed from a reliable source that the rumor the bureau chief heard is true—they've joined up with another group in town that supposedly has money and means to cause us real problems at the dam."

"You used to get most of your sources from your network of talkative bartenders. I'd think your no-booze policy would make it kind of difficult to do that anymore. Bartenders don't generally trust a man who just drinks soda."

It was true. Sam had found bartenders to be valuable sources in the past, supplying late-breaking stories, tips, gossip, rumors, local color and important background information. "No bars," he said. "I met someone at A.A. who likes to chat."

Harmon snorted as he opened another beer. "You're calling a drunk a reliable source?"

"I'm a drunk. You're taking a chance on me."

"That's different. We have a history together."

Sam glanced at Harmon's scar and grimaced. "A history that didn't end so well. In any event, the tip may not prove useful but I think it's worth pursuing."

Harmon raised both hands in surrender. "Okay, okay. Do what you need to do. Just keep me informed."

***

A red Cadillac pulled into the driveway next to the motel office. The driver turned to his passenger and said, "I'll just pop into the office and grab the room key from Floyd."

"Wait, Tony," said Clarice, tugging on his arm. "There's a light on in room six."

184

"Damn that idiot Floyd. I told him not to rent our room out. It's not like this shithole is short on available rooms."

"Well, well. Would you look at that," Clarice said, pointing to two men who'd come outside the door to room six. "That's the FBI guy who came nosing around the bank today."

Tony squinted in the dim light to see who she was pointing at. "I'll be damned. Looks like Sam Matthews is with him. Wonder what that's all about?"

"Hmm, a lover's tryst perhaps?"

Tony laughed. "You would think of that."

"You know Sam Matthews. Why don't you find out why he's talking to a G-man?"

"Now?"

Clarice gave an exasperated sigh. "Of course not. You're his realtor. I'm sure you can make up some excuse to talk with him. You can then steer the conversation to Monty's."

"Why the hell would I do that?"

"Isn't it obvious? Matthews is mixed up with the debacle at Baker Bluff."

"Good God, do you think he's bringing the FBI into the Baker mess?"

"I don't know but their midnight rendezvous is worrisome and we better make it our business to find out what they are up to."

CHAPTER TWENTY-FOUR

It was a warm moonlit night; a romance-is-in-the-air kind of night. The white kids making out in the Pioneer Cemetery certainly thought so. For Danny, it was a night that proved what he'd thought all along: whites had no respect for their own ancestors. The kids' clumsy attempts at lovemaking on sacred grounds was proof. It made the raid on the cemetery more justifiable in his mind. Staking out the place was a drag, but sooner or later the last of these kids would leave and Danny and his friends could get down to business.

While he waited, he drank a beer and thought about the last time he was there. Ellie's unlikely appearance in the middle of a graveyard had thrown him off balance, but Danny believed he'd recovered quickly and held his own during their brief exchange. Their meeting was a curious episode, but he'd put it out of his mind soon after she'd left the cemetery with her silly friend. Then she showed up at the village. Once again, he was caught off guard. There had to be a reason that she kept popping up in his life; he didn't believe in coincidences.

Her father seemed like an all-right guy for a white man. Danny liked the way he'd stood up to the sheriff. Of course, that could just be an act to get on the villagers' good side before he ruined them. After all, he was a foreman at the dam. That his mother had so quickly accepted Matthews' promises and believed him to be their friend bothered him. Trusting a white man had never proved wise in the past. Sam Matthews had been back to the village several times since the Memory Feast, supposedly to report on how George was faring in jail. He'd heard from more than one villager that Reba and Sam had been seen taking long walks together down by the river. Matthews even brought her flowers the last time he was there. Danny had never seen his mother so . . . he didn't know what. In love? With a white man? That was too wild to even consider.

This whole business with Matthews and his daughter confused him, made him doubt himself and his own motives. Walter had picked up on his uncertainty and challenged him at the Pit Stop. "Man," he'd complained. "What's the matter with you?" Going soft on me again?" Walter hadn't quite accepted that Danny was as committed to their new alliance with the Communists as he'd claimed. "You need to stop over-thinking everything. It's clouding your judgment."

According to Walter, destroying the pioneer cemetery like they'd already decided to do, was the right thing. Just like it was the right thing to do when he'd leveled the car dealership by setting it afire. It was not only right, but inevitable. Graves and Memaloose Islands would be gone for good, covered with a ton of water when the government got through with them. Walter claimed the pioneers didn't deserve any better treatment than their ancestors were getting.

"I know," Danny said. "But why destroy their cemetery? We could just swipe some of the tombstones and make a statement that way."

Walter and the others hooted. "A statement?"

"Yeah, it would be a symbolic thing. They take our ancestors' bones, we take their ancestors' markers."

"That's what we've been doing, man," Walter declared. "Symbolism is a load of unproductive shit, which you've said yourself. I think you're losing your fighting spirit over a little white dolly." That's when Danny charged like a bull and got them thrown out of the bar by a bat-wielding Fitz. Once outside, they'd danced around each other with their fists raised for a minute. It took about that long for Danny to realize that Walter had a point. He'd allowed Ellie and her father to mess with his head. It was a big mistake and he wouldn't let it happen again. The original game plan was back on.

Danny didn't know how much longer Walter and the others would wait before chasing the kids away. He'd like to run them off himself. It was after midnight now and they'd been waiting at the edge of the cemetery for over half an hour. More important, the beer was almost gone. As he reached for the last bottle in the sack, Danny heard an eerie cry pierce the night air. "Who-o-o. Who-o-o." A second cry answered. "Yee-ee-ee." And then a third. He hadn't seen Walter and the others sneak off, but they'd obviously started things without him.

He tossed the sack of beer aside and headed for the entrance to the graveyard. Creeping along the perimeter, he crouch-walked as low to the ground as possible. Another piercing cry.

"Yikes, what was that?" a nearby girl asked.

Danny inched his way toward the direction of the cry. A dark form looking suspiciously like Ernie knelt behind the large tombstone where Danny had first spotted Ellie. Danny crept up behind Ernie and tapped his bony shoulder. Ernie shot upright and spun around to face his would-be attacker with fists raised. He dropped his fists when he saw it was only Danny and not one of the kids or a wayward ghost. "Jeez, Danny," he said. "You scared the shit out of me!"

"Sorry, I couldn't resist. Where're Walter and Henry?"

Ernie shrugged, "I don't know exactly. We split up so we could answer each other's cries. It's working, too," he said, grinning. "You should've seen those kids scatter. They high-tailed it out of here like the devil was after them."

"Good," said Danny. He poked his head around the tree and, using the moonlight to good advantage, noted a few stragglers. "We need to ratchet up the program."

"What're you gonna do?" asked Ernie.

Danny slipped off his white tee-shirt and tied it around his head so that just his eyes were showing. When Ernie saw what Danny was doing, he followed suit. "On the count of three," Danny said. The two masked boys took off hollering and waving their arms. Trying hard not to laugh, the boys pranced about as if possessed by evil demons. A couple lying on a blanket was the first to panic. Their bloodcurdling screams so frightened the other kids that they ran off shrieking. Walter and Henry quickly joined the melee and a few confusing, noisy moments later, a half dozen terrified kids had dashed to the safety of their hotrods.

"Hey, look," said Ernie, holding up a wine bottle. "They beat feet so fast they left their booze behind." All the boys laughed as he took a swig and then swung the bottle against one of the tombstones, shattering the glass into tiny pieces.

"Wow," exclaimed Walter watching the hotrods tear off in a trail of dust. "I didn't know you could burn rubber on a dirt road."

"Holy cow," said Henry, still laughing. "That was fun."

Pulling off his shirt-mask, Walter said, "Now the real fun begins." He told the group to stay put while he went back to his truck.

Danny joked with the others as they untied their masks. Then Henry and Ernie started swatting each other with their shirts and imitating the teenagers terrified screams. Danny watched their antics with growing annoyance and rebuffed their attempts to draw him into their childish play. It was one thing to have a little fun running off the teens, but despite what Walter had said, the idea wasn't to have fun. They were here on serious business. That should've been obvious, but they were still clowning around when Walter rejoined the group. "Here you go," he said, handing one of the sledgehammers he carried to each of them. "Let's do it!"

That's all it took for the rampage to begin. Walter swung first, toppling an already crumbling tombstone. "Hee-haw!" he cried. Ernie and Henry followed his example, whooping it up as the smashed stone markers fell to the ground. It didn't take much force to destroy the old stone crosses and other small markers, but they swung the sledgehammers with a wild, ruinous abandon anyway. Pausing to survey the damage, Walter declared the effort too easy. He pointed to the center of the graveyard where the larger, more ornate monuments were. "That's where we should go," he said. Ernie and Henry agreed and headed out. When Walter noticed that Danny wasn't following his lead, he asked, "You coming, man?"

"Yeah, sure," Danny said, but he was unable to stop staring at the first and only gravestone he'd toppled. The sledgehammers were overkill. All he'd had to use was his boot heel to kick over the small marker. The effort hadn't given him a thrill or sense of triumph like his friends had experienced. All he felt was a chilling numbness. The etching of a baby lamb on the downed tablet caught his eye and he knelt to read the engraved inscription. 'In memory of our beloved daughter,' it began, 'thou hath left us and we are lost. Serena Jackson B. 21 April 1885 D. 22 April 1885.' *A baby. A day-old baby.* Danny had seen baby graves at Memaloose Island, too. He felt bad every time he saw them, but there was one that never failed to get to him. It was a simple wooden cross with a pair of tiny weathered moccasins tied to it. Whenever the wind blew, Danny imagined the shoes were dancing to the sacred beat of little drums.

Danny stared at the inscription for several minutes. In the distance, he could hear Walter and the others hollering and smashing their way through the graveyard. He brushed the dirt off the marker, lifted it upright, and returned it to its original place in the ground. Looking at the restored grave did little to shake the melancholy that had wrapped his heart in a fierce embrace. A prayer his mother had taught him years ago suddenly came to mind. *Grandmother Earth, from your womb all spirits have come. When they return to you, cradle them gently in your arms and allow them to join their friends in the skies. May the Great Spirit watch over you, and may you be at peace.*

When he caught up with others, they were struggling to topple the base of a large gray monument. The statue of an angel that had once rested atop was on the ground, smashed almost beyond recognition. Danny carefully stepped over one of the angel's broken wings and approached his friends who were grunting and swearing as they pushed on what was left of the heavy marker. Seeing Danny, they stopped to catch their breath. Walter wiped the sweat from his brow with the back of his hand. "Hey, man, where've you been? We could use some help here. This is one heavy son of a bitch."

"No," Danny said.

"What?"

"I said no."

"What's gotten into you?" asked Henry, plainly irritated.

Danny surveyed the destruction around him. They'd been busy. The ground was littered with the damage they'd inflicted. "It's wrong," he said.

Ernie scratched his head. "Huh? What is?"

"All of this," Danny said, spreading his arms to indicate the downed tombstones.

Walter snorted. "This was your fucking idea, brother. It's too late to back out now." He nodded to Ernie and Henry and they resumed their struggle with the monument. "Come on, Danny, we need you."

Danny stood his ground, attempting to block their efforts with his body.

VALERIE WILCOX

"Get outta the way or you're gonna get hurt."

A siren's piercing wail interrupted the impasse.

"It's the sheriff!" yelled Henry.

They all stared at Ernie. "You spill the beans about our plans again?" asked Walter.

At first, Ernie denied talking to anyone, but quickly backtracked when confronted with their skeptical looks. "Okay, okay. Maybe I said something to someone I shouldn't oughta," he admitted. The siren's loud cries made him jump. "But it doesn't matter now. We gotta get out of here!"

"No one's going anywhere." ordered Walter. "Keep pushing." As the ground finally gave way, the base teetered and then fell, pinning Danny beneath it. Walter stood over him. "You stubborn fool! I told you to get outta the way." The siren screamed closer.

"Take off," Danny said. "I'll deal with the sheriff."

"We're not leaving you behind, no matter what," Walter assured him. With Ernie and Henry's muscle adding to Walter's effort, they lifted the stone off Danny's leg. Together, they propped him upright, and with his arms wrapped around Walter and Henry's shoulders, helped him hobble to his truck. The siren's warning cry was deafening now. "Get going, man!" Walter urged as they heaved Danny inside his cab. "We'll meet you back at the village."

Danny nodded, but the pain shooting from his ankle to his hip was severe. Feeling suddenly woozy, he closed his eyes and leaned his head against the seat back. His friends jumped in their trucks and took off in a billowing cloud of dust as the lawman's siren drew ever closer. Seconds later, Danny opened his eyes to flashing red lights in his rear-view mirror. He groaned and closed his eyes again.

"Well, well, well. What do we have here?" Sheriff Pritchard leaned inside the open cab window and shined a heavy-duty flashlight at Danny. Getting no response, he hit Danny's shoulder with the butt of the light. "Wake up and get out of the truck! You're under arrest, punk."

CHAPTER TWENTY-FIVE

Reba smiled as she unbraided her hair. She knew she was the subject of much talk around the village, but she didn't care. She was happy. The feeling was like a long-forgotten song that had suddenly come to mind, filling her soul to over-flowing with its sweet melody. Losing Jimmy was a lonesome ache that was as constant as the seasons and, over the years, had become a jealous guardian of her heart. She'd had many opportunities for romance since Jimmy's death, but no one had ever been able to undo the restraints that tied her heart to the past. All that changed when Sam Matthews came to the village. He'd brought such an unexpected joy to her life that she refused to let old memories, no matter how good, ruin her new-found happiness. She had no idea where their relationship might lead, but she was willing to let the melody ring on.

Oscar and Danny had both voiced their disapproval of how friendly she'd become with "that government man" and none of the villagers were going out of their way to include her in any of their gatherings or every day interactions. Since it was customary, she went berry picking with the rest of the women today. The lively conversation she was used to during the outing was subdued. At least she hadn't become an outcast. Her role as village healer saved her from such a fate, but the chattering ravens still caused her difficulties. Reba understood the reasons they were distancing themselves from her. The last time someone from the village had become involved with a white person had caused a lot of grief. The ensuing scandal still caused the villagers problems from time to time. They had to look no further than Sheriff Pritchard when pointing fingers.

She couldn't blame the villagers for being wary of her relationship with Sam. Despite the happiness he'd brought into her life, she was wary, too. It was hard for her to trust a shuyapu, but he seemed so different from the tourists who came to the village to buy salmon or attend their powpows. Standing up to Sheriff Pritchard couldn't have been an easy thing to do. If nothing else, Sam had protected her honor when the sheriff called her a squaw. For that she would be forever grateful. Anything more would be a blessing.

When she was through brushing her hair, Reba finished cleaning up. She was tired after the long day of berry picking, but it was a good tired. Despite the strained relations with the other women, she'd enjoyed herself. Berry picking was one of her favorite activities and there were plenty of opportunities available. From the early summer elderberries to the fall blackberries, there was always some kind of berry growing in abundance in the nearby low hills. Huckleberry time was a major social event, but not as much as it was in days gone by. Oscar said that when he was a youngster his family and others would load up horses and wagons and move to the mountains.

Everyone picked, and as baskets were filled, the men would build a fire for drying the berries. Screens were laid across logs near the fire's edge and the berries were poured out onto the screen. The berries were turned with a long wooden spoon made especially for this purpose. When the berries were sufficiently dried, they were transferred to another screen, cooled and finally stored in baskets. The huckleberry leaves were also collected and dried for tea. This berry-picking event would last several weeks.

Nowadays, it was just the women who gathered the berries and brought them back to the village for processing while the men stayed behind to fish. The times had changed, but Oscar's stories kept the past alive. Reba wondered if some day Danny would tell his grandchildren how he'd fished when Celilo Falls was still a raging torrent overflowing with sacred, life-giving salmon. Would he recall the past with fondness, as Oscar did or would his bitterness overshadow all the good they'd known? She knew the answer and it made her sad every time she thought about it. The good mood she'd had earlier was close to slipping away when a knock at the door diverted her musings.

When she opened the door, Walter greeted her without the usual smile he was known for. This was not a good sign. "Danny's not here," she said. It wasn't unusual for her son to be out all night, and sometimes she didn't see him for days at a time. She was used to his absences even though she still worried about his safety. His fight with the government had attracted a lot of dangerous attention.

"I know," he said. "I'd have come sooner, but Danny said you'd be berry picking all day."

"What happened?" she asked. Walter's grim-faced explanation didn't do anything to reassure her. *Oh, Danny. I knew your anger would bring trouble.* Reba had a lot of confidence in her healing skills, but she knew she'd never be able to calm the fury that raged within her son's heart. Hearing that he'd been arrested was bad enough, but to think he was in pain was almost more than she could bear. "How is he hurt?" she asked. At least she could mend his bones, if necessary.

"He might have broken his leg when the marker fell on him."

Reba hadn't ventured into town for many years, not since Jimmy was killed on the street by two drunks. She'd gone in search of Danny's dog, Tito, that time and vowed that she'd never return. The Dalles held nothing for her. Sam had tried to coax her into going to a movie or to dinner with him, but she'd always refused. She knew he didn't understand her reluctance since she couldn't bring herself to talk about Jimmy's murder. She couldn't even explain why she'd never set foot in the Granada Theatre. Her cousin had been in full-dress army uniform when he went to the movies after serving in the war. He'd just settled into his seat when the usher ordered him to get up. "No Injuns can sit here," he barked. "Balcony only for your kind."

Reba bit her lip as she pondered what to do. Meeting up with Sheriff Pritchard at the jail would be difficult. Without Sam to protect her, she would be at the sheriff's mercy. The thought was disturbing, but her son's plight was even more disturbing. "Take me to Danny," she said.

The closer they got to The Dalles, the more nervous Reba became. She knew she'd made the right decision to come to town, but she questioned whether the sheriff would let her help Danny. She'd brought her medicine bag and the necessary supplies to set his leg if it was truly broken. As worried as she was about Danny, she couldn't help but notice how much the town had changed since she'd last been there. Driving down Front Street toward the courthouse, she counted a string of new businesses that had sprung up during the recent boom years. She noted with some satisfaction that none of the windows carried signs prohibiting Indians. Her satisfaction was short-lived when they arrived at the courthouse. A crowd had gathered on the steps carrying signs of some sort. Walter told her they were protestors. This did not sound good for Danny. "What are they protesting?"

Walter shrugged, "Same ol', same ol': us." He told her he'd find a parking spot in the alley behind the courthouse. There was a back entrance they could use that would be safer, given the circumstances. Once inside, he led her downstairs to the jail. She was grateful that Walter knew his way around the white man's territory, but it wasn't a comforting thought. They didn't fit in and never would. Sheriff Pritchard proved her point when they entered his office. "What the hell are you doing here?" he asked.

Walter said, "We've come to see Danny."

"Visiting hours are over."

"Sheriff, please," said Reba. "We're not here for a visit." She held up her medicine bag. "I've been told he's injured. I'd like to take care of him."

"The kid's okay. He don't need no tender loving care from his mama."

"Five minutes," Walter said. Give us five minutes to check him over. If he's okay as you say, we'll leave."

Pritchard lit a cigarette as he considered the request. "Five minutes," he said, exhaling smoke. "But I'll have to inspect that so-called medicine bag first."

Reba handed it over.

After making an elaborate show of ensuring that she wasn't sneaking any contraband into Danny's cell, the sheriff said, "All right." He took a deep drag on his cigarette and narrowed his eyes. "Just so you understand, I'm not obligated to let you anywhere near my prisoners. So, don't try any funny stuff while you're back there. I won't be able to guarantee your safety if that crowd outside thinks you're up to no good."

Walter and Reba followed him to Danny's cell before he could change his mind. The hallway was dirty and dark, the floor stained with something sticky, while the odor of urine and sweat permeated the confined space. A crushing despair gripped Reba as she passed George's cell. She'd steeled herself to cope with whatever situation she found at the jail, but seeing George and then Danny lying so still on his bunk scared her. He looked up as they entered the cell. His young face seemed older; perhaps it was due to his injury, but the anger he usually wore like a badge of honor was gone; in its place was a weary sadness.

As soon as the sheriff had locked them inside, he said, "Remember, only five minutes." Turning to leave, he looked at Walter and issued a final warning, "And don't give me no trouble or —"

"We get it," Walter said. "Or you can't be responsible for what happens to us."

Sheriff Pritchard shot him a cold look, "You've been warned."

As soon as he left, Reba rushed to Danny's side. He sat upright when she touched his shoulder. As mother and son embraced, he said, "I'm sorry." He didn't have to say more. Reba knew his heart. Her son was ashamed that he'd caused her worry, but grateful that she'd had the strength to come for him. It occurred to her then that they were both warriors. No matter how impossible the battle, they would never give up. She embraced him again and whispered in his ear, "I'm proud of you, Danny. Always."

"Hey, brother," Walter said, as Reba examined Danny's injuries, "How're you doing?"

"A little tired is all."

To Reba, "How's his leg look?"

"Some bad bruising and a sprained ankle, but no broken bones."

"That's good."

"Good for now," Danny said, "But I can't be responsible for later." He glanced at his mother and then winked at Walter.

Reba sighed, but said nothing. Hadn't her son learned anything from his arrest? She had no doubt that his comment meant he was thinking of another dangerous plan. And, as usual, Walter was more than willing to follow his lead.

"Are we clear about that, Walter?"

His friend laughed. "Crystal!"

CHAPTER TWENTY-SIX

Sam checked his wristwatch for the third time in five minutes. His meeting with the California contractor selected for the reburial project was scheduled to begin half an hour ago. Frustrated and sweltering in the afternoon sun, Sam got out of his over-heated pickup to seek some shade while he waited. It was a fruitless search. The site of the new cemetery, to be called Wish-Ham, didn't have one tree or even a tall shrub to offer. The grounds were located alongside Highway 14, a barren, desolate patch of nothingness that had been deemed appropriate for the mission by the powers that be.

The hubris of the U.S. government embarrassed Sam, but there wasn't a dang thing he could do about it. When the Indian tribes objected to Baker Bluff because of the blood that had been spilled there, Sam had pushed his superiors to select his second choice for the gravesite. It wasn't as good as the Baker property, but it was a lot better than this dried-up wasteland. The only thing going for the highway site was the dirt-cheap price, which had settled matters. Sam, like the Indians, would have to accept it whether he liked it or not.

Leaning against the side of his pickup, Sam checked his watch once again. He'd hoped that the meeting would be almost over by now. If the contractor didn't show up soon, Sam wouldn't have time to go out to Celilo Village. He always had some excuse for his frequent visits to the village, but there was only one reason that mattered: Reba. He couldn't count the number of times he and Ellie had been invited to a Hillcrest neighbor's house for dinner. There was always an extra lady at the table who just happened to be single. It embarrassed Ellie and irritated Sam. It was Reba he wanted to have dinner with. He'd asked her several times to accompany him to town for dinner and a movie, but she'd always refused. She didn't have to explain why; he understood her reluctance — bridging the cultural gap between her world and his wasn't easy. He couldn't speak for her, but he was willing to keep trying.

Sam looked up each time a car approached, in hopes that it was driven by William Gross. He checked his watch again as another car barreled past. It was too hot to be waiting out here much longer. If the contractor didn't show up soon, he'd pack it in. A loud buzzing like a million bees on a murderous rampage caused Sam to look skyward. Within moments, the source of the frenzied, whirring noise was apparent. The California contractor had arrived.

"Damn," muttered Sam, grabbing hold of his hat. He didn't realize Gross would come to their meeting in the helicopter. The unusual sight was bound to attract unwanted attention. Several cars had already stopped alongside the highway to watch it land. Although he'd talked with Gross by telephone, this was the first-time Sam had seen him or the yellow-tailed craft that would transfer the Indians' remains from Memaloose and Graves Islands. Dubbed "Operation Whirlybird," Sam and Gross had estimated that the process of transporting the Indians' bones would take two days, possibly three, followed by a ceremony the Indians had planned on the last day. After Gross shut down the engine and hopped out, the men shook hands, and exchanged a brief word about the weather. "Hotter than the hinges of Hell," complained Gross. For a California man, Sam guessed he wasn't much of a sun worshipper. He had a pale, round face that, while sweaty, was as smooth as a baby's butt. He was younger than Sam had expected, maybe twenty-five or so with an easy smile and firm handshake. He pulled a handkerchief from his pocket and wiped his face while Sam eyed the crowd. They'd exited their vehicles now and were gawking at the impressive machine from the edge of the road. Sam suggested they get down to business before the gawkers became too much of a bother.

The agreed upon logistics were straightforward: beginning at nine o'clock Friday morning next, the first two of the 170 newly constructed pine boxes containing the remains would be strapped to the landing skids of the flying rig for transport. "I figure I can make four to five trips an hour carrying two boxes on each trip," said Gross.

Sam advised him that the first half of the project would start at Graves Island. "The most ancient graves are located there," he explained.

One of the kids lining the roadway scampered away from his parents and made a beeline for the helicopter. "Hey, son, not so close!" Gross yelled. He intercepted the boy and waited by the copter until the boy's father caught up with him. "This bird's a damn nuisance," he said when he rejoined Sam, "but it gets me where I want to go faster than the rental car they foisted on me."

Sam looked at the growing crowd with concern. Several of the folks had their Brownies out and were snapping pictures. The whirlybird was too fascinating not to be captured on film. Sam turned away from the picture-happy throng to talk to Gross. The longer he could keep his face from being associated with the project, the better.

"How many graves are we talking about?" asked Gross.

"About 700." They would be interred at Wish-Ham in a common concrete tomb along with the other unidentifiable remains. Memaloose Island was a more recent burial site, but it had its own unknown bodies. Only 124 graves out of 2,500 had been identified and would be given a marker. Reba's parents and husband were among them.

"How many bodies to a box?" asked Gross.

The question struck Sam as callous, but the man had a legitimate right to ask. The pilot needed to know how much weight he'd be carrying. Truth be told, the whole operation bothered Sam. Although he'd anticipated some objection by the Indians, he hadn't really understood what moving the bones meant until Reba brought it up. She was adamantly opposed to the reburial. He'd listened to her talk about Memaloose and Graves Island without comment, but not without guilt. His involvement was just one more secret to keep.

Reba told him that there were three large graves on Memaloose which served as a common burial ground. "In centuries past," she explained, "our practice was to leave the bodies of our loved ones out in the open." Among the ancient bones were the bones of a few horses. Reba said that when a chief died back then, it was customary to send his favorite steed with him to the life hereafter. She went on to explain that over the years storms and winds and occasional grave robbers disturbed their peace so the mass graves were the result. Some of the more recent burials continued to be above ground, but generally the dead were wrapped and put under shed-like shelters.

"It's only an estimate," Sam said when Gross prompted him again, "but I think you can figure on fifteen to twenty remains per box." There'd be another mass grave for the unidentified bones. This time it would be a concrete tomb. That's what angered Reba the most. "We've had to use mass graves ourselves," she admitted. "But concrete? It's not nature's way."

"Fellas!" Gross and Sam turned in the direction of the shout. A portly man had pushed through the crowd and lumbered their way. He wore a professional-looking camera on a leather strap around the thick folds of his neck.

"Well, well," said Gross. "I wondered how long it would take for the press to show up."

"The press?"

"His name is Hiram Potter. Works for *The Dalles Chronicle*." Gross chuckled and shook his head. "I've met his hairy eyeball before. He's like an old sow rooting for corn. Won't give up until he's found the story." Gross whacked the dust off his pants. "We'd better grant him a quick interview and photo or he'll never give us a moment's peace on this job."

Sam pulled his hat lower on his forehead. "No!" He turned toward his pickup. "I've got to go."

"Oh, come on, Matthews. Give the guy a break. It won't hurt none and a front-page story is good for business."

"Not for my business," Sam said, noting that Potter had almost made his way across the field. "Do me a favor, Gross. Keep my name out of this." Sam scrambled into his pickup, gunned the engine and took off.

***

Dodging the local press was a losing strategy. *The Chronicle's* star reporter had been hounding Sam's every move for days and it had become obvious that he would not rest until he got the interview he wanted. The man had somehow learned that Sam was in charge of the reburial project and had been on his trail ever since; it wasn't surprising that he showed up at the Wish-Ham site. Although Sam had preferred to keep his name out of the public record for as long as possible, he knew that it was only a matter of time before he would be identified as the government official overseeing the project. Given the reporter's dogged pursuit, it was something of a miracle that he hadn't uncovered Sam's FBI role also. Nevertheless, the photos of the helicopter and the pilot's willingness to talk had all the makings of a front-page story.

Now that his involvement in the project was likely to be exposed sooner than he'd hoped, Sam knew he had to tell Reba. It was not a conversation he was eager to initiate. It would have to be handled with a lot more skill than he believed he possessed. The relationship that had developed between them, while good, was fragile. As a white man and a government employee, his motives were already suspect. He was reluctant to do anything to cause her to doubt him — and the reburial project was bound to do just that. He had plenty of doubts about himself for both of them. Motives that had been so clear upon his arrival in The Dalles had become as murky as day-old coffee.

As he left Wish-Ham and drove toward town, he mulled over his situation and how he would broach the subject with Reba. The truth wasn't always easy to admit, especially for someone like himself whose life's mission was built on subterfuge and lies. Ever since he'd rescued George and gotten to know Reba, he'd begun to question everything he thought he knew. Was the dam necessary? Were the Indians really the problem? Was his mission in The Dalles a help or a hindrance? How could the government justify destroying a centuries-old way of life? How could he justify his role in that destruction? Most important, how could he ever explain who he was to Reba without losing her in the process?

Since he hadn't been there in a while, Sam decided to make a quick stop at the jail before heading to Celilo Village. His talk with Reba was overdue but he needed some time to get his thoughts together before what would surely be an awkward, unpleasant conversation. He told himself he wasn't procrastinating; he was just preparing. As soon as he saw the unruly crowd that had gathered on the courthouse steps, he knew visiting George and Reba would have to wait. The ugly anti-Indian demonstration was close to escalating out of control. Preventing this type of situation was a primary reason he'd been sent to The Dalles in the first place.

So far, he hadn't been able to do much to quell the mounting public outcry that the murder of Nick Rossi had generated. There'd been plenty of attacks against the "Celilo bunch" in the local media when George was arrested and almost daily demonstrations outside of the jail calling for justice. The crowds were growing in numbers as George's trial date approached. Today's crowd was more agitated than he'd ever seen them. Knowing that the sheriff couldn't be counted upon to do anything to defuse the situation, Sam realized that he'd have to take control. He could kick himself for not interceding more forcefully before now.

Pushing his way into the fray, he cornered one of the sign-waving demonstrators near the entrance. "What's going on?" he asked.

Impeccably dressed in a crisp summer suit and tie, the protester looked like a successful businessman, maybe even a lawyer on his way to court. He didn't appear dangerous with his glasses and slight build, but the crudely written placard he carried and the hateful taunts he spewed, told a different story. "Damn redskin! Murderous savages, the lot of 'em," he shouted.

Sam had a sinking feeling that George's safety was at serious risk now. "Who are you talking about? What redskin?"

"Danny Longstreet, that's who!"

Sam cursed. He should've expected this. The boy was determined to stir up trouble. "What'd he do?"

A woman standing nearby grabbed Sam by the arm. "Haven't you heard? It was bad enough they murdered that young man, but now they've added insult to injury. They destroyed our Pioneer Cemetery last night."

"That's not the worst of it. They want to do the same thing to the dam," finished the man. "Already killed a foreman who worked there. They'll destroy us all if they get the chance. Murder us in our very own beds!"

Another protester chimed in, "But we're not about to let that happen, so help us, God!"

A burly guard stood behind the glass doors blocking the entrance, but he was hopelessly outnumbered. All it would take was for one of the agitators to throw a large rock through the glass and the guard would have a stampede on his hands. Sam figured he had no choice but to identify himself. Removing his wallet from his back pocket, he held his credentials against the door's glass pane. "Let me in," he demanded. "FBI."

The guard skimmed the ID quickly and then opened the door wide enough for Sam to squeeze through. "Man, you're a sight for sore eyes," he said. "I need all the help I can get."

"Where's the Sheriff?" asked Sam.

The guard shrugged. "Haven't seen him yet. He called me late last night, more like closer to dawn. Said I was needed for guard detail today, but he never said nothin' about dealing with these rabble rousers."

Sam gestured to the guard's pistol which was still secured in his holster. "Make sure they can see your weapon," he said. "And don't be afraid to fire if necessary."

"I never shot nobody before."

"A warning shot will get your message across," Sam said as he headed for the stairs. "They need to know you mean business."

"Hey, where're you goin'?" the guard asked. "I thought you were here to help."

"I'll be right back!" Sam flew down the stairs and burst into Sheriff Pritchard's office.

The sheriff sat with both feet propped on his desk as he flipped through the pages of a girly magazine. He tossed it aside and stood as Sam made his hasty entrance. "Hey! You have no right to barge in here like you own the joint! What do you think you're doing?"

"Saving your butt. The protesters outside are about to storm the place. Your guard upstairs needs some reinforcements."

Sam wasn't sure whether the man was unconvinced or simply unconcerned as he settled into his chair again and picked up the discarded magazine. "Ralph can handle it," he said.

"No, he can't."

Pritchard let loose with a string of profanity. "You're not going to tell me how to run my business."

Sam had to restrain himself from pulling the man out of his chair. "Somebody has to."

Pritchard slammed the magazine on the desk. "Just who the hell do you think you are?"

"The Fed, that's who," Sam said, brandishing his FBI credentials in Pritchard's face. His shocked expression was satisfying, but Sam didn't have time to savor the moment. "I have jurisdiction. That means it's my responsibility to act when the situation warrants. And the situation you have outside warrants. I'm ordering you to get upstairs and help your man maintain control."

Pritchard glared at Sam and then stomped out of the office. Sam hustled after him, but instead of proceeding to the stairs the sheriff turned toward the holding cells. "I've got visitors in here," he snapped when Sam protested the detour. "Their safety is *my* responsibility."

Despite the sheriff's sarcastic attitude, he had a point. Jail visitors couldn't be left unattended, especially with trouble brewing. Sam figured Pritchard was more interested in reasserting his authority than any concerns for visitor safety. It was a convenient way to defy Sam's jurisdiction claim. Nevertheless, whoever the visitors were, they had to leave.

Sam expected to see George's tribal lawyer, Thomas Youngblood, when they reached the cells. He'd recently arrived from Yakima and was the only visitor George had ever had besides Sam. When the sheriff by-passed George's cell and stopped at Danny's instead, Sam was brought up short. He and Reba exchanged startled looks as Pritchard unlocked the cell. "Visitors out!" he ordered.

"What's going on?" Danny asked.

The sheriff pointed at Sam. "Ask the FBI," he said, smirking. "And while you're at it, ask him what he's planning to do with your ancestors' bones."

CHAPTER TWENTY-SEVEN

As soon as Sam left the jail, he stopped at the liquor store and bought the first bottle of whiskey he saw on the shelf. The look on Reba's face when the sheriff revealed Sam's treachery was more than he could take. If Danny hadn't been locked up, he'd have attacked Sam with the righteous wrath of the wronged. Sam wanted to forget the whole ugly episode and the only way he knew how was to drink — go on a bender so bad that he blacked out, unable to remember who Reba and the Indians were or why he'd ever cared about them. But first, he called his A.A. sponsor.

"I need your help, Mike."

"What's going on?"

"I'm sitting at my kitchen table staring at a fifth of whiskey. I want to drink the whole damn bottle as fast as I can."

"Whoa, you don't want to do that."

"I sure as hell do."

"No, you don't. You wouldn't have called me if you did. Like you said, you need my help. Give me your address and I'll be right over."

Sam gazed at the bottle for several moments without speaking. "Okay," he said with a resigned sigh. "But you won't be able to talk me out of this."

"Maybe so, but promise me you won't do anything until I get there."

Sam and Mike were an unlikely pair. The lawman and admitted criminal had nothing in common except their addiction, but somehow their relationship worked. They'd met at the first A.A. meeting Sam had attended in The Dalles and, shortly thereafter, Mike had volunteered to be his sponsor. He'd been sober for over five years and his commitment to the 12 Step Program was unequivocal. Sam was impressed with how much the man seemed to be *enjoying* his sobriety. For a role model, Mike was just what Sam had been looking for. As an A.A. saying suggested, "Stick with the Winners." Most of all, he was one person who understood Sam's situation fully and truly cared. Sam could turn to him without embarrassment when doubts, questions, or problems linked to alcoholism arose. They had quickly developed an easy, open relationship in which they could talk freely and honestly with one another.

Mike knew that Sam was charged with the responsibility for the Indian's reburial project, but not his FBI role. Now that Sheriff Pritchard had outed him to Reba, Sam believed he wouldn't stop there. Soon the whole town would know and his mission in The Dalles would be over. Sam's world was crashing down around him and nothing Mike could say would change that. But he would listen to him. Mike's one condition upon sponsoring him was that he'd *always* call him if he was ever tempted to take a drink. And he was tempted all right. More than tempted. So, he'd made the call.

"Knock, knock," Mike said as he barreled through the front door and plopped in a chair facing Sam. If there was a typical Irishman, Mike fit the bill. He had thick red hair, a round ruddy face, an impish grin, and a great repertoire of Irish songs and jokes. He wore an eyepatch, which he said came courtesy of a deadly drunken brawl that caused him to finally turn his life around. "That and the bloody cops," he'd joked. He was supposedly still running from the law when he landed in The Dalles and opened a tavern. It seemed incongruent for a recovering alcoholic to tend bar, but Mike said it kept him focused. Being around booze all day, every day was a constant struggle but one that strengthened his resolve to maintain his sobriety.

"Thanks for waiting," Mike said, registering the unopened bottle in front of Sam. "Now that I'm here, tell me why you're so eager to throw away all the progress you've made."

"I really wanted The Dalles to be different," Sam said. "I promised myself and my daughter that we'd have a fresh start here. But I've already failed."

Mike eyed the bottle again and said, "I see that you haven't taken a drink yet. That's not failure in my book."

"But I will drink. No doubt on that score."

"Okay, I get it. Something has happened to upset you greatly. Something that makes you think you're a loser. Something so bad that you're willing to go back to the one thing that caused your problems in the first place—demon alcohol. I've been there, me lad. Felt the same way you do when life gets unbearable. Then I remember the First Step—we are powerless over alcohol and our lives have become unmanageable. But together we can do what you or I could not do alone—stay with the program; stay away from the first drink. That's why I'm here, Sam. Together we can work through whatever has happened without making it worse by drinking. I'm going to shut up now and listen. Tell me what has happened."

And Sam told him. Told him about saving George and his subsequent arrest on a trumped-up murder charge. Told him about the promise he'd made to Chief Thompson and the Wy-ams to keep George safe. Told him about how he'd fallen for Reba. Told him how his relationship with her had made him question his role in building the dam and the reburial project. Told him about his undercover job with the FBI and how it had caused the end of his budding romance with Reba. Told him about his partnership with Jess Harmon and how he'd been offered a chance to redeem himself by helping solve the Chambers' murder. "But all that doesn't matter now. My cover's been blown, the Indians don't trust me anymore, Reba can't stand me, and I'm unable to fulfill my mission as assigned. Worst of all, I've failed my daughter. She thought I left the Bureau and all the subterfuge behind when we moved here."

Mike was silent as if needing a few moments to absorb all that Sam had said. Then he shook his head. "A G-man, huh? You sure know how to pick a sponsor."

"Your criminal past doesn't mean anything to me. That's why I liked A.A. It's anonymous. I'm used to keeping secrets."

"And now that yours has been exposed you want to give up?"

Sam unscrewed the cap on the whiskey bottle. "Yeah, I do. Sobriety is just one more failure to add to the list."

"Here, let me help you," Mike said, reaching for the bottle. "You need a glass." He got up from the table, opened a cupboard and returned to the table with a small juice glass. "Don't worry about the glass size," he said. "I'll pour you a healthy swig."

Sam's hands trembled as he held the glass and breathed in the enticing aroma of liquor. "I can't believe you did that," he said, carefully setting the glass on the table without drinking it.

"I'm a bartender. I never let my customers drink whiskey straight from the bottle, and especially not my friends."

"No, I mean you're my sponsor. Aren't you supposed to stop me from drinking?"

"It's not up to me to stop you. That's your job. I'm here to remind you that there is a Power greater than both of us who can restore you to sanity. I'm not a religious man but I am a spiritual man. Each A.A. member must determine for themselves what the Step Two phrase about Power means. I find spiritual power in work and helping others. You still have a daughter to raise and a meaningful job. Yes, your cover is blown but you can still work. It will do more to quiet the sorrow and regret you carry than whiskey ever could." He paused and then grinned. "Thus Endeth Today's Sermon."

"I hear what you're saying but . . ."

"But what?"

"My main job here was to prevent trouble with the Indians and the community, determine if the Indians were behind the sabotage attacks at the dam or if there was a Communist connection. The Bureau thought that the best way for me to do that was to go undercover. But I've managed to make a total mess of everything. The town folks are as stirred up as the Indians, I haven't a clue as to who is behind the sabotage attacks or if there is a Communist within a thousand miles of here. So, you see, I can't exactly embrace my work as a way to deal with what has happened."

"There's an old Irish saying: *A handful of skill is worth more than a bagful of gold.* For guys like us the version is: *A handful of skill is worth more than a case full of whiskey.* Nothing you've said convinces me that you don't have the skill to do your job with or without people knowing you're an FBI agent working as a foreman at the dam."

"The job requires more than skill; it requires a certain amount of trust and strategic relationships."

"Well, my friend. That's where I come in."

"What do you mean?"

"I trust you and I'm able to help you strategically."

"I don't understand what you're getting at."

"You know that my bar caters to the Indians and I've come to know Danny Longstreet and the other boys quite well. Didn't I tell you that they've got themselves hooked up with another group that is apparently loaded with dough?"

"Yeah, but I haven't been able to figure out who that might be."

"I'm no investigator, but if I were you, I'd pursue the money angle."

"And why is that?"

"Let me tell you what I know about Danny and his friends first. Danny has a reputation as a hard-headed, ready to fight-at-the-drop-of-a-hat type guy. It's widely known that he's opposed to the dam but the pranks he's organized have been more of a nuisance than a hindrance to construction."

"I'm with you there."

"What isn't so well known is that Danny has a thoughtful side to him. He's smart and can think problems through once he's got his anger under control. He could be your best ally."

Sam shook his head. "Not now. He wants to kill me."

"Let's set that aside for a moment. His friend Walter presents himself as an easy going, good natured guy with a winning smile that endears him to everyone, especially the girls. But don't be misled by his low-key appearance. Walter is far more dangerous than any of them. Henry isn't as smart as Danny and Walter but he does think for himself and isn't afraid to ask questions. The main thing is that he always goes along with whatever plan is made. Then there is Ernie. He's the youngest and most unpredictable. He's a loose cannon that often misfires. Any trouble the boys have gotten into can usually be attributed to Ernie spilling the beans about what they are up to."

"And what does all this background on their personalities have to do with money?"

"A bartender is a good listener and I've overheard plenty. Oh, they try to keep their plans quiet but Ernie can't help flapping his jaws when the rest of them aren't around. He's told me that he can't wait to get going on their next plan because it involves dynamite. A lot of dynamite. Now where would those boys get their hands on dynamite? They have barely enough money to buy beer."

"They could steal it."

"Maybe. Or maybe this group they're aligned with gave it to them."

Sam rubbed his chin thoughtfully, which he hoped would make Mike think he was considering what he'd said. What Mike said did make sense. Harmon was pursuing the money angle with the Pete Chambers' murder investigation. He should do the same—if he didn't have other plans. Mike had overstayed his welcome. It was time to move this chat along and start on the road to oblivion. "Follow the money, huh?"

"Exactly. My grandpop was a rum runner in the old days. He was always two steps ahead of the Feds—no offense to you—and he claimed that the reason he never got caught was because he never left a trail of cash behind. He said if you ever want to catch a thief, follow the money."

"Tell me something," Sam said. "Why are you so willing to rat on your Indian customers?"

Mike shook his head sadly. "Is that what you think I'm doing?"

"Isn't it?"

"Not at all. I said earlier that I believe spiritual power comes from helping others. I believe by helping you that I'm helping them."

"I don't follow," Sam said with a puzzled frown.

"Danny and the others are basically good kids who're reacting to the unjust way the government has treated them in the only way they know how. It's up to us to advocate for them. Think about it." Mike stood upright and pointed to the glass of whiskey. "And think about the power you have over that drink." He pushed back his chair and walked out of the house.

Sam sat at the table long after Mike had gone, his eyes never straying from the glass in front of him.

CHAPTER TWENTY-EIGHT

The protesters were still making life miserable for any Indian who dared come to town these days, but it was Danny who bore the brunt of their rage. The idea that he was eligible for bail on the property destruction charge was resented almost as much as the crime itself. Whoever had paid his bail was the source of much speculation at Celilo. Walter said Stan Feldman had put up the cash, along with a rebuke for their "foolhardy" actions. He made it clear that they were to keep their noses clean until things were in place for their dynamite project. That was job number one.

Danny felt bad that George was still locked up in that hell hole—charged with a crime he didn't commit and denied any hope of release. No bail for an accused murderer. The old guy's spirits had taken a downturn even before learning about Sam Matthews' lies. The Umatilla girl who brought over George's meals from the café told Danny that he'd basically stopped eating. Reba said that was a very bad sign.

Sam Matthews had hurt George and his people big time, but the worst part of all was how he'd wounded Reba. She'd been so courageous to come to town when Danny needed her and had even been relieved when Sam showed up at the jail—until the sheriff turned tattle-tale. Danny had been right all along to suspect the government man's so-called good intentions, but it didn't give him any satisfaction. Not when his mother was so distressed by Matthews' deceit. Despite his protestations to the contrary, it was obvious even to Reba that Sam Matthews had been playing her and the rest of the village from the day he first showed up at Celilo. The look on his mother's face when she realized how he'd destroyed her trust would haunt Danny forever. He would never forgive the man, the *white* man, and he deserved everything that would happen later.

When Danny was released from jail he'd taken the alley exit and had avoided direct contact with the mob out front. Today would be a different story. He had to buy some engine oil or he'd never have ventured into The Dalles so soon after he'd been released from jail. The Shell station was located smack dab in the middle of Front Street and just one block from the courthouse. With any luck, no one would recognize his pickup. He'd make his purchase and zip out of town before anyone at the courthouse caught sight of him. Not that he was worried. He was willing to take on all comers if it became necessary. It's just that Walter and the others were counting on him. The reburial ceremony at the new cemetery was scheduled for Sunday and they had to be ready. Getting into any more trouble before then would mess up all their plans.

When he pulled into the station, the attendant was busy pumping gas for a lady in a wood-paneled station wagon. As soon as he saw Danny hop out of his cab, he gave him a dirty look. It didn't bother Danny. He'd gotten his share of hostile staring, spitting, and name calling, even before his popularity had hit an all-time low. Danny made a point to return the hate-filled reception with a smile and neighborly wave before limping to the service bay. Except for some lingering pain from a sprained ankle and a lot of nasty bruising, he was okay. He just didn't move as fast these days.

The grease monkey on duty was stretched out on a creeper underneath a Chevy. His lanky legs were much too long for the platform and stuck out at an awkward angle. There was a familiar-looking hole in one of his work boots. Danny had built a friendly relationship with the head mechanic over the years. LeRoy Johnson knew more about fixing anything on four wheels than anyone in the whole county. He was also the only Negro in town which made him a kindred spirit as far as Danny was concerned. LeRoy was the man to see if you needed used parts, a rebuilt engine, or retreads. "Hey, LeRoy," called Danny. "Is that you under there?"

"None other," the mechanic said, "Be right with you." When he rolled out from underneath the car, he took one look at Danny and frowned. "Aw, man, whatcha doin' round here?"

"Kendall Motor Oil. I'll take two quarts."

"Didn't you see the new sign?" He pointed to a hand-painted poster tacked to the service bay entrance. *No Indians allowed.*

"I saw it."

LeRoy stood upright and wiped a grease smear from his wrinkled brow with a stained rag. "You're gonna get me in a heap of trouble if you don't skedaddle."

"Just sell me the oil, LeRoy." He took a five-dollar bill out of his wallet. "My money's the right color, even if I'm not."

LeRoy stole a nervous glance at the attendant at the pump. He'd finished filling up the station wagon and was washing off the windshield while keeping an eye on the service bay. LeRoy shook his head and said, "Can't do it, man. You know I'd like to, but I'll get myself fired."

"Tell you what," said Danny, slipping the bill into the front pocket of LeRoy's overalls. "This should cover the charge, plus a little extra for your trouble. Meet me at the Pit Stop after work and no one has to know I bought a dang thing from you." Danny grinned. "Now, shoo me out of here like you mean it."

LeRoy gave him a job-saving send-off which Danny played along with by making a hasty, if gimpy, retreat to his pickup. He intended to go to the Pit Stop, maybe shoot some pool and kick back with a few beers while waiting for LeRoy to show up with the motor oil. Then he saw Ellie. She was the last person he'd ever expected to run into again, but there she was, right across the street. She was by herself, looking at a display in a dress shop window. Despite how Danny felt about Sam Matthews and his lies, there was still a special place in his heart for his daughter.

Danny watched Ellie a moment. She must know about her father's betrayal by now. Maybe she'd been lying to Danny and Reba, too. That's what white people seemed to do best. She'd probably been laughing at him behind his back all along, making fun of him and his friends, their beliefs and traditions. She looked so innocent, standing there in her sundress and sandals, but looks, as he knew full well, could be deceiving. He decided the Pit Stop and beer could wait; he might not get another chance to confront Ellie any time soon. He'd deal with her right now and finally be done with it. He climbed out of the truck, ignored the station attendant's demand to "Get that damn junker off the lot," and headed across the street.

Ellie's attention was still on the window display, so she hadn't seen him approach until he called her name. She turned around and greeted him with a deep dimpled grin. "Hi, Danny."

His resolve melted as soon as she faced him. What was it about this girl that affected him so? He'd been teased unmercifully about falling hard for a white chick, but Danny figured the guys were just jealous. Walter, though, wasn't teasing when he offered a stern warning: "Stay away from her, Danny. She's a pretty little kitten who'll claw the life out of you if you're not careful." She was pretty all right, but there was more to Ellie than just looks. She was smart, funny, and best of all, she was confident without being bossy like most girls he'd known. That she'd just been putting on an act was hard to believe, but maybe Walter was right, "Like father, like daughter."

Now that she seemed so pleased to see Danny, he couldn't think of what to say. It wasn't like him to struggle for words and he felt off-balance. As if by magic, the summer's hot sun had turned her fair skin to bronze, her blonde locks to gold. A slight breeze blew a few strands loose from her ponytail and brushed against her cheek. He felt foolish gazing at her like a lovesick schoolboy, but she'd captivated him like nothing he'd ever experienced. Ellie simply took his breath away.

She tucked the stray hair behind her ears and waited for him to say something. When he didn't respond, her cheerful attitude gave way to concern. "Are you okay?" she asked.

"No."

"What's wrong?"

"What's right?"

"You're not in jail anymore."

"You know about that?"

"It's been all over the news."

"Yeah, but I haven't heard anything about your father in the news."

Ellie frowned. "Why would there be?"

If her innocent look was just an act, he had to admit she was good at it. But it was wearing thin. He shrugged off the tender feelings he still carried for her and lashed out at her duplicity. "Don't tell me you don't know about him." he said.

She flinched at his harsh tone. "What *are* you talking about?"

"Come on, Ellie, you don't have to pretend any longer. Your father is working for the FBI. He's been lying to us from the get-go, calling himself our friend."

"He *is* your friend!"

"A friend doesn't destroy our way of life or dig up our ancestors."

"I don't understand a thing you're saying."

"Yeah, right. Your father came to the jail when I was there and the sheriff set us straight about him. He was sent here by the FBI to make sure we — meaning my people, the Indians at Celilo — didn't get out of control. His mission was to make sure the dam got built no matter what happened to us. Everything your father has said and done has been an act. He was good at it, too. He used his so-called concern about George's safety to make the villagers think he was our friend. But he's nothing but a liar who only pretended to care about us, especially my mother. He's worse than Sheriff Pritchard. At least with the sheriff we know who we're dealing with."

"But he *does* care. He's a construction foreman at the dam and doesn't have anything to do with the FBI."

Danny shrugged, "You can deny it all you want, but his double-crossing days are over. We know who he is and what he is now." He gave her a hard, cold stare. "You can stop acting like you weren't in on the whole thing."

She covered her ears and screamed. "Stop it! You're talking crazy!"

Their exchange hadn't attracted any attention until Ellie screamed. A couple of ladies with shopping bags hurried past, apparently deciding it was best not to stop. As Danny checked on the crowd milling about the courthouse, a woman rushed out of the dress shop with Ellie's silly red-haired friend scrambling behind her. After a quick glance at Danny, she put a protective arm around Ellie's shoulders. "What's going on here?" she asked.

Ellie's friend tugged at the woman's dress, "Mom, that's Danny Longstreet."

Already alarmed by Ellie's screams, the woman seemed terrified now. Danny stifled a laugh. Did he look like a monster to white people? Or was it just his reputation? He leaned in close to the woman's face and whispered, "Boo!"

"Get away from us!" she screeched.

"Don't worry," Danny said, looking at Ellie, "the crazy Indian is outta here." As he turned to leave, he noticed that the ribbon in Ellie's ponytail had slipped off and fallen onto the ground. He picked it up and offered it to her. "Here," he said.

Ellie shook her head. "Just go, Danny."

He jammed the ribbon in his pocket and sprinted across the street.

CHAPTER TWENTY-NINE

Dessa didn't want to go shopping for school clothes since the summer wasn't even half over yet and it was too dang hot to be trying on heavy sweaters and scratchy wool dresses. Dessa wanted to go swimming at the Nat instead, but once Maureen had her mind made up, there was no sense in arguing with her. Dessa should have known that Maureen would invite Ellie to go along with them. She'd use any excuse to encourage the friendship between the two girls. Not that Dessa minded if Ellie came with them. They were becoming fast friends even without her mother's intervention. But Maureen seemed unwilling to accept that her daughter could finally sustain a friendship on her own. As if needing to justify the invite, Maureen said, "Ellie has good taste in clothes. You could learn a lot about style from her." Her mother failed to note — or purposely avoided — the fact that Dessa would need a complete body makeover if she were to look as stylish as Ellie.

Dessa's father was usually tight with his wallet but Maureen had somehow convinced him to come up with a tidy sum for the shopping trip. Mrs. Peabody's dress shop was overpriced but Dessa figured that if she were careful there might be enough left over to buy some typing paper. She needed supplies for her newsletter a heck of a lot more than a new dress or two. Surprisingly, the girls had an enjoyable time shopping. Maureen even promised to take them to lunch after they were done. But that never happened, thanks to Danny Longstreet.

Ellie had gone outside the store to get a better look at a dress in the window display when Danny apparently popped up out of nowhere. Dessa didn't know what he said to her but it must have been bad because Ellie's screams could be heard even inside the dressing room at the back of the store. Dessa was midway through trying on an ugly corduroy jumper her mother had picked out when she heard Ellie's screams. Her mother rushed out of the dressing room while Dessa hurried to get her own clothes back on. When she made it outside, she realized that her mother had no idea who Danny was. The distaste on her face just meant she'd registered the fact that a dirty Indian stood next to Ellie. When she learned that she'd come upon the infamous Danny Longstreet, Dessa was certain her mother was going to wet her pants. Danny seemed angry, then amused by her panicked reaction. He got right up in her face and said "Boo!" which just about did her mother in.

The ride home in the car was strange. Maureen kept pestering Ellie with questions but got nowhere fast. Ellie clammed up and wouldn't say a word about what Danny had said or done to cause her so much distress. Dessa was curious, too, but figured she'd be able to find out when Maureen wasn't around. Luckily, her mother planned to go back to work at the bank as soon as she dropped the girls off. As they turned onto Cherry Blossom Lane, Maureen spotted Mr. Matthews' truck in his driveway. "Is your father home sick?" she asked. "This heat wave, flu, or whatever is going around is hitting everyone hard. We had to cancel our garden club meeting this month because so many were ill." Dessa knew her mother wasn't concerned about her friends' illnesses. She just hated to wait another whole month to tell them about today's terrifying run-in with Danny Longstreet. Dessa had to admit the encounter — especially her mother's over-the-top reaction — would make for an interesting item in her newsletter. But she couldn't and wouldn't do that to Ellie.

Ellie gathered up her shopping bags, offered Maureen a half-hearted thank you for the outing and quickly ran into her house. Fifteen minutes later, she pounded on Dessa's front door. If she'd been upset earlier, she looked unhinged now. She sobbed hysterically and practically flung herself at Dessa, crying again and again, "He lied, he lied. Everything's a lie!" Dessa thought she meant Danny had lied but before she could ask, Ellie said, "Danny was right. My father is nothing but a rotten liar."

She ushered Dessa into the kitchen, sat her down at the table and poured her a large glass of cherry Kool-Aid. It took a while for her to cry herself out and calm down long enough to talk coherently. Even then, Dessa had a tough time following her rambling, disjointed narration. She was obviously angry with her father but it wasn't immediately clear why she thought he'd lied. Dessa gave her a napkin to wipe her tear-stained face but refrained from trying to clarify anything. Given Ellie's distraught state, it was best not to interrupt her so she could explain things in her own way. Hopefully, what she said would make more sense than it had so far.

"I should've known it when I saw that empty liquor bottle in the trash. His promises mean nothing. He's just a drunk and always will be."

Holy Cow! That was news. Mr. Matthews a drunk? Never.

"There's no foreman job at the dam. He's still with the FBI. The Dalles wasn't a fresh start for us. It's just the same old, same old. Lies, all lies!"

Did she say FBI? Who in the world is her father?

Ellie dabbed at her red-rimmed eyes with the now-soggy napkin. "How could he do it to Reba and Danny? That's what I don't get. I'm used to his secrets, but they trusted him. They thought he was their friend. He was supposed to be helping them. But he was just pretending like he always does. Digging up their ancestors is no way to help them." She shuddered. "I can't believe what an unfeeling monster he is." The rest of Ellie's rants were in much the same vein. How Mr. Matthews was mixed up with the FBI still wasn't clear to Dessa, but one thing was certain—Ellie felt betrayed by her father.

Ellie swallowed the last of the Kool-Aid and stood. "I have to go," she said.

"Where to?"

"Celilo Village. I need to talk to Danny and Reba. I have to let them know that my father lied to me, too. That I didn't betray them like Danny accused me of doing. That I'm really their friend, even if my father isn't."

"How are you going to get there? The village is miles from here."

"I have two good legs."

"But it's over a hundred degrees outside! You'll never walk more than a mile before you're dead from heat stroke."

"Honestly, Dessa, don't be stupid. I won't have to walk the whole way. I'll just hitch a ride."

"Like that's a safer thing to do. You better sit back down and think this through."

Ellie straightened her shoulders and held her head up, a determined gesture if there ever was one. "I'm leaving and you can't stop me," she said. "And don't even think about telling my father or I'll never speak to you again. Ever!"

Dessa watched her huff out the door, wondering what she should do. Tell her father? Follow her? Do nothing? Whatever happened, Dessa was afraid it wasn't going to turn out well for Ellie — or her.

CHAPTER THIRTY

The last thing Tony wanted to do was host an open house on a blistering hot afternoon. The Ramseys had been hounding him for weeks, complaining that he hadn't been actively marketing their bungalow. They weren't far off the mark. He hadn't wanted to take the listing, but felt obligated since he'd sold them the place—his first sale upon arriving in The Dalles. The two-bedroom dump had nothing going for it, but it was cheap and that was all the Ramseys, with their three kids, could afford at the time. Now, with kid number four on the way, they wanted to sell the home for twice what they paid for it without sprucing up the overgrown yard or doing anything else to enhance the salability of the property. Nothing Tony said could convince them to lower the sales price to a reasonable amount.

Despite feeling like a pushover, he'd finally given in and run the open house ad in the newspaper. That was before everything had gone to hell. He'd scheduled the event with the intention of sticking Nick with the duty. When his cousin got himself killed, he'd considered canceling, but then decided it was the perfect place to hide out for a little while. He didn't think the house would attract many visitors and it would give him some needed time alone.

Nick's homicide case was front page news and a slew of reporters were dogging his every step, hoping for an exclusive on the "poor suffering family." The media had played up the Indians' problems with the dam—supposedly a contributing factor to George's hatred of whites—and now relations with Celilo Village and the town were at an all-time low. Most of the town believed that George or Danny Longstreet had something to do with Pete Chambers' murder, too. Not that Tony cared. The problem was Clarice. She had insisted that they cool their relationship until things settled down. Then she stopped seeing him altogether when the sheriff dropped the bomb that Sam Matthews was a Fed. Hard to fathom that news but at least it explained why he'd been at Monty's with the other G-man in town. Just when he needed Clarice the most she was unavailable.

Then there was the situation with Uncle Sol. Tony didn't even want to think about the man and what he might do next. The fact that his own uncle had sent Nick to spy on him was bad enough, but making him escort the body back to Portland was almost more than Tony could take. At the funeral, Uncle Sol had threatened to shut down the business altogether. His excuse was that things in The Dalles were getting too dangerous and he didn't want to take a chance on losing Tony, too. What a load of crap. All Uncle Sol cared about was losing money. Not that Tony wouldn't be more than happy to quit slaving for his uncle, but he still lacked enough bread to buy Baker Bluff.

For their part, the Indians were unhappy with the Baker Bluff site and the government bent over backwards to appease them by choosing another, more acceptable location. The town folk didn't care one way or the other about where the Indians were buried, but they were outraged over the unprovoked murder of an innocent young man. The fact that Nick had just been trying to do a good deed by giving the old Indian a lift home only made his murder worse in people's eyes. Clarice had told Tony that she knew the right way to frame the kid's murder to their advantage and she had. Now that the property appeared within their reach again, she told him not to worry. They just had to be patient and it would all come together soon.

So here he was, stuck in a stifling hot cracker box at the end of Dry Hollow Road, pondering why his life had taken such a turn. He'd sat in the tiny living room for two hours already and not even one lookee-loo had crossed the threshold. At this rate, the pint of Southern Comfort he'd been nipping on would be long gone by the time the Ramseys returned home. They hadn't even bothered to wash their breakfast dishes or pick up the toys scattered across the threadbare carpet before they'd left with a cheery, "Good luck." He was a great salesman with or without luck, but selling this over-priced shack would take a miracle.

At the sound of a car pulling into the driveway, Tony parted the frayed lace curtains at the front window to see who'd been foolish enough to stop. He hoped it wasn't some eager-beaver reporter who'd tracked him down. He groaned at the sight of Sheriff Pritchard hustling out of his official vehicle. Tony would've preferred a reporter. The man's leathery face was as white as the proverbial ghost. Whatever had the sheriff scurrying out here couldn't be good news. Tony took a quick nip to fortify himself. He'd barely gotten the pint stashed in his briefcase when Pritchard came rushing into the room gasping for breath.

"Hey," Tony said. "No need to hurry. You're first in line to buy this mansion."

The sheriff shivered despite the summer heat. "We've got a problem. A big problem."

Just what I need. Another problem. Tony sighed, wishing he'd taken a bigger swig from the bottle. "What now?" he asked.

"George Stonefeather is in the hospital," Pritchard said, slumping onto a tattered couch by the door."

Why Pritchard seemed to think that was Tony's problem was beyond him. Tony shrugged. "So?"

"Good God, man. Don't you realize what this means?"

"Why don't you enlighten me," Tony said, sighing wearily.

"He's under Federal jurisdiction now!" Pritchard shouted. "They've even got a guard at his hospital room door. The Feds, thanks to your friend Matthews, think he's at risk from the protestors. When he interfered at the jail, I thought I could handle him, but he's—"

"The Feds?" Pritchard had Tony's full attention now.

"That's what I said. The fuckin' Federal Bureau of Investigation." Pritchard leaned forward with his forearms on his knees. "Matthews will be all over this cockamamie case now—including a formal investigation into Nick's death. Thanks to your murdering girlfriend and my part in the lousy cover-up, I'm facing serious jail time—and, in case you still don't get it, you are, too." He let that message sink in and then added, "Tell me something. Was the pussy worth it?"

Tony whipped out the pint he'd stashed earlier and gulped the liquid with a fierce urgency.

"I could use some of that," Pritchard said, reaching for the bottle.

The mind-numbing alcohol did nothing to alleviate the full-blown panic that this startling development had caused Tony. There was only one way to deal with it. He had to see Clarice. She'd know what to do. She always knew what to do. He tossed the nearly empty bottle to Pritchard, grabbed his briefcase and hustled to the door.

"Wait," the sheriff called after him. "Where're you going?"

Not to jail. Not now, not ever.

***

Where the hell was she? When Tony couldn't reach Clarice by telephone, he checked out all her usual haunts—Dizzy's, Goldman's Jewelry, the country club, their favorite room at Monty's Motel, even Lila's Dress Shoppe—but no one had seen her around for several days. His last stop was Pacific Savings & Loan. It wasn't likely that she would be there, but he was running out of options. Maybe she'd gone to the bank to talk to Warren. God only knows why, unless it was to apply more pressure on him to loan them the rest of what they needed to buy Baker Bluff. If the old cocksucker were being stubborn, she'd pull out all the stops whenever and wherever she could. He *had* to find her even if it meant chatting up her lousy husband.

Tony marched through the bank's glistening glass doors and then paused to survey the interior of the spacious lobby. Clarice was nowhere in sight so he headed straight for Warren's king-size desk. The pompous ass had the handcrafted mahogany wonder imported from Thailand when he made bank manager. Clarice said he liked the feeling of power that the desk represented. Only the truly powerless needed such trappings, as far as Tony was concerned. Warren wasn't sitting in his high-priced executive chair and his desk top had none of the usual clutter. It didn't look like the powerful man had been around for a while; even his fancy gold nameplate was missing. Tony ran his finger over the thin layer of dust atop the bare desk.

A pear-shaped woman carrying a manila folder stuffed with paperwork approached him. "May I help you?" she asked.

"Yeah, you can. Where's Warren?"

"Mr. Warren Nestor?" she asked.

Her prissy attitude annoyed him. "That's right, sweetheart. You can tell him Mr. Antonio Rossi is here to see him,"

The woman shook her head. "I'm sorry, but Mr. Nestor is no longer with us."

She made it sound like he'd died. Tony had no time to figure out whether her brains were scrambled or what. He shot her a no-nonsense look. "What do you mean, no longer with you?"

The woman clutched the folder protectively against her flat chest. "Mr. Nestor resigned," she said. "Rather suddenly, I might add."

The prune-faced broad wasn't making a lick of sense but she didn't seem like the type to kid around. She had to be mistaken. Warren loved his job. Loved it more than Clarice, or so she claimed. "Resigned?" Tony asked. "Was there a problem or something?"

"Certainly not," she huffed. "Mr. Nestor is going into business for himself."

Too stunned to make nice, Tony demanded, "What the hell are you talking about?"

The woman bristled and pursed her thin lips together. "Perhaps you should speak with Mr. Prosser. He's filling in as acting manager until Mr. Nestor's replacement is hired."

"Just forget it," Tony said. Once outside the bank, he hurried to his car and hopped inside. He'd never been to the Nestor's home, but he knew exactly where it was in Fremont Heights. Panic had turned to anger as he sped across town to the shady, tree-lined development. All the bigwigs in The Dalles—lawyers, doctors, bankers, and such—lived in Fremont Heights. Not that there was a glut of professionals calling The Dalles home, but those who did lived in stately, large brick structures that exuded an air of moneyed privilege. It wasn't uncommon to see a parade of housekeepers, Chinese gardeners, delivery boys, and other help coming and going throughout the day. Heaven forbid that the wives should stoop to physical labor of any sort. They were much too busy drinking cocktails at the country club or shopping in Portland.

When he first came to town, Tony had courted the country club set until he finally got the message that his services would never be welcome in Fremont Heights. The owners had made it clear that any number of realtors from Portland would understand their needs better. It was snobby hogwash, but it didn't matter in the long run. He'd done all right without them. The government workers had been more than willing to give him a fistful of business.

As he pulled up to the Nestor's red brick Tudor, he noticed a For Sale sign posted in the middle of the neatly trimmed lawn. A *Sold* banner was tacked diagonally across the front of the sign. *What the hell?* Tony hopped out of the convertible and strode up the sidewalk to the covered porch. Before he could knock on the door or ring the bell, he heard someone call out, "The Nestors aren't home!" The speaker was a smartly dressed old lady in pearls and sensible shoes. Two bright spots of rouge highlighted her thin, sunken cheeks. She stood on the sidewalk holding onto a leash attached to a rag mop posing as a dog. The mutt was busy piddling on a fire hydrant.

Tony flashed his best smile. "Do you happen to know where I might find them?" Thinking fast, he added, "I have some important papers for them to sign."

The dog spotted a squirrel almost as big as it was and cut short his business in mid-stream. Straining hard against its leash, the little beast yapped and yipped itself into a frenzy. "Hush now, Buffy," its owner scolded, scooping him into her arms. "He thinks he's a big game hunter."

"Cute, though," Tony said. He left the porch and pretended to admire the pooch. The old lady seemed pleased with the attention but Buffy didn't appreciate his efforts and snarled at him. "About the Nestors," Tony said, stepping back a bit. "I really need to get in touch with them."

"Oh, dear, that may be a tad difficult."

Tony's patience was non-existent, but he conjured up another engaging smile. "How's that?"

"Well, they're in Portland, you see."

He didn't see. Tony's smile vanished. "Portland?"

"Yes, but don't worry. It's only temporary. Mr. and Mrs. Nestor will be back soon. I understand they're going to open a new business here."

"So I've heard," muttered Tony. He'd had a nagging suspicion that something was wrong ever since Clarice had cut off all contact between them. It had sounded reasonable when she suggested it, but he should've realized that nothing involving Clarice was simple. When he thought about it, she was always doing what he least expected. Murdering Nick was a prime example. Worse, he was starting to believe that she'd been taking him for a ride all along. It scared him shitless, but he had to know for sure. He needed to talk to Stan Feldman.

Feldman's office was located in a small, non-descript industrial complex on the outskirts of town not far from Monty's Motel. His office building resembled a poorly built Quonset hut and was hotter than a sweat lodge, not that Tony had ever been in one. The wily Feldman never seemed to mind the heat. He could be found sitting at his battered second-hand desk seven days a week, unless a good prospect insisted on meeting somewhere more comfortable. Otherwise, Feldman was content to hang out at the office with a telephone receiver growing out of his ear, wheeling and dealing his way to a fortune. The guy was too cheap to hire a secretary so Tony was confident that the busy signal he got when he called ahead of his visit meant Feldman was on the job.

Sure enough, when Tony walked into the office Feldman was on the phone. "That's the price, take it or leave it, Sidney," he said. Looking up as Tony entered, he waved him into a folding chair alongside his desk. He held up an index finger to indicate that he'd be just a moment longer. "Call me if you change your mind," he told the Sidney person. "You know the number," he concluded. "So, what brings Tony Rossi to my cozy hole-in-the-wall?"

Tony hesitated. It was now or never time. "Baker Bluff," he said.

When Feldman burst out laughing, Tony had the sucker punch answer he'd been dreading. "You're a day late and a dollar short, my friend."

Tony couldn't move, couldn't catch his breath. He had to force himself to speak. "Meaning?"

"I told you when we met at the Carlton that Baker Bluff was a hot commodity. You've been outbid."

Tony's gut reeled. Swallowing hard, he fought off the bile rising to his mouth and slumped against the chair's metal backrest. "Clarice," he sighed.

Feldman laughed again. "Let me give you some advice, Tony, my man. Never ever trust a broad, especially a sexy broad in bed with a rich banker."

The jab cut Tony deeper than a knife. Bleeding fury, he lunged across the desk. "How 'bout I give *you* some advice."

Feldman reached inside his desk drawer and pulled out a nasty looking silver pistol. "Don't tempt me," he warned, aiming at Tony's chest.

Tony raised his hands and backed up to the door. Turning, he bolted outside. Halfway to the Caddy he stopped, clutched his gut and doubled over. The retching was violent, a burst of short explosions that ripped at his insides and splattered vomit onto his shoes as it hit the pavement. Uncontrollable tears ran down his face, but it was rage, not despair that had overtaken his body.

Between heaves, he caught sight of Feldman standing in the office doorway. His smirk brought a sudden halt to Tony's spasms. Without bothering to wipe the slimy discharge dribbling from his lips, Tony stumbled to the car and plopped behind the wheel. He would've liked to have taken a moment to get his breathing under control, but he didn't want to give Feldman something else to mock. He gunned the engine and spit gravel as he sped out of the parking lot. *He'd kill her! And Warren, too! Nobody steals Tony's dream and gets away with it. They'd pay. Oh, how they'd pay.* But first things first. He needed to wash away the taste of deceit and betrayal. Luckily, the state liquor store was just down the street.

Fortified with a fifth of Jim Beam, Tony drove east on Interstate 84. He hadn't given thought to a destination except to find someplace where he could get rip-snorting drunk. He hadn't been on a good bender since he'd been exiled to this godforsaken town. He deserved a little mind-numbing pleasure, now more than ever. Tony had driven just a few miles when he spotted her. Ellie . . . the precious gift he'd been trying to unwrap from the first day he'd seen her.

He didn't know why she was walking alone on the shoulder of the road, but he wasn't about to question his good fortune. For once there was no father or pesky girlfriend tagging along to spoil things. Ellie had never looked better. The long summer in the sun had given her skin a sexy glow. Her silky blond hair was a rich golden color hanging loosely about her slim shoulders. She wore short-shorts and a flimsy sleeveless blouse that showed off her budding figure. His loins ached as he pulled the convertible alongside her.

"Need a ride?" he asked. When she looked at him, her eyes were rimmed in red, her face tear-streaked. "Ellie? Are you okay?"

She shook her head and began to cry. Tony hopped out of the car. "Hey, nothing can be that bad." *Except losing your dream to a lying bitch.* He put his arm around her waist and felt her tremble. Despite her misery, she smelled like a sweet garden of flowers; a delicate and fragrant bouquet waiting to be picked. The image made him tremble, too. This girl-woman had stirred him, teased him, and tempted him on far too many occasions to let her get away this time. "You look like you could use a friend, Ellie."

CHAPTER THIRTY-ONE

Danny's truck was acting up again. He'd replaced the spark plugs, changed the oil, and tuned the engine, but the old beater had racked up too many miles over the years to be reliable. Wheeling down I-84 was touch and go at best, but he had no other way to get around. Walter and the others were already at the Pit Stop waiting for him. Leroy had probably already dropped off the oil Danny had bought earlier.

After his encounter with Ellie in town, he'd gone fishing with Oscar. He'd only planned to stay for a short while but the salmon were running like crazy and their haul had been a good one. Oscar said it was like the old days when the fish literally jumped into their nets as soon as they'd dipped them in the water. The day had been a rich blessing for the old man. The plentiful catch had invigorated him, his arthritis temporarily forgotten as he lifted the heavy fish-laden nets out of the water many times over. He'd joked with the other fishermen as they counted and weighed their catch, besting even the famous Wauna Joe for the day. Oscar would sleep well that night.

For Danny, the day had been bittersweet. He liked seeing his grandfather happy, but all the joy and excitement he usually felt when fishing at Celilo Falls was long gone. It had been so different in the beginning. He remembered the day that he caught his first salmon as the most thrilling event in his young life. No other tradition — even dancing — had ever come close to making his heart beat with the pride he had felt that day. According to Oscar, the ancient rite of passage from boy to man was more than tradition, it was a sacred experience. He'd made a speech about salmon at the ceremony for Danny's initiation. "The resource does not belong to us," he'd said. "We belong to the resource." This was their practice and always had been for more than ten thousand years.

It irked Danny that Oscar and the other elders had no more fight left in them. They were resigned to their fate. Maybe it *was* inevitable that the dam would be completed. That didn't mean they had to just roll over and let it happen without any kind of resistance. Their lack of fighting spirit had caused many harsh arguments between Danny and his grandfather. Now more than ever, Danny would have to lead the battle. No matter the cost.

This time he wouldn't wimp out like he'd done at the Pioneer Cemetery. He'd let Ellie and her father mess with his head once too often. He'd been wrong to trust them. Sam Matthews was a liar and his daughter was too stubborn to admit it. The two of them had deceived his mother and almost succeeded in sidetracking him. He would never let that happen again. The plans were set and the dynamite ready. All Danny had to do now was to go to the Pit Stop for their final preparations. He stepped on the gas pedal as hard as he dared. The truck rattled and shimmied as it struggled to pick up speed.

He was halfway to the Pit Stop when he saw a girl walking alongside the highway in the opposite direction. *Ellie.* He'd just been thinking about her and suddenly she appears. Danny slowed the truck to get a better look. She was as stunning as ever, but it was her golden, sun-streaked hair hanging loosely about her tanned shoulders that reminded him of how angry she'd been with him. Her ponytail had come undone and the pink ribbon that had held it together fell to the dusty sidewalk. When he'd scooped it up, she'd refused to take it from him. The warm summer wind blew the newly freed silky strands across her face like soft caresses. He'd never seen anything quite so beautiful and he guessed that was why he'd saved the ribbon. He glanced at it now, tied to the truck's rearview mirror — a symbol of how far he'd wandered off track. His usual reserve and caution vanished every time he was around her. Getting mixed up with a white girl was just plain stupid. No more! He snatched the ribbon from the mirror and tossed it out the open window.

With a determined set to his jaw, Danny fixed his eyes on the road ahead. A shiny red Cadillac speeding down the highway served as a fine distraction from thoughts about Ellie. He'd seen the Caddy in town and had admired it from afar. The ragtop belonged to some rich guy, which always seemed to be the way the world worked. He'd heard rumors that the car was owned by a smooth-talking salesman. Danny wasn't surprised since conning people and lying like a coyote trickster was what white people did best. Sam Matthews had proved that.

When he took a last look at the car in his rearview mirror, he saw that the driver had stopped alongside Ellie. Curious, Danny eased off the gas and pulled to the side of the road. As he watched Ellie chatting with the guy, he felt a nervous twitch in his gut. *What line of bull was he feeding her?* His anxious feeling revved up a notch when the driver suddenly hopped out of his car. Danny strained to get a better look. Despite the distance, he could tell the fellow was good-looking. He had a cocky "look at me" swagger designed to impress the ladies. He wore sharp threads, too. A scheming coyote in disguise. Apparently, Ellie didn't see him that way. She didn't back off, even when he wrapped his arm around her waist. In fact, she let him guide her to the convertible and help her inside. They looked very chummy. Danny shook his head. *White makes right every time.* He quickly shifted gears and entered the highway again as the convertible did the same in the opposite direction.

Danny slapped the steering wheel. *Damn.* He couldn't shake loose his feelings for Ellie, no matter how hard he tried. Seeing her ride off with that con man worried him. Ellie was a smart girl, but she was young and innocent in so many ways. It would be easy for someone to take advantage of her. Despite his earlier vow, he couldn't just drive away. He had to know that she was safe. If he acted quickly, he could follow them and make sure. That's all. Just make sure she was okay. Walter and the others could nurse their beers a while longer. After making a sharp U-turn in the middle of the highway, Danny goosed the truck to catch up with the Caddy. The truck coughed and sputtered, but he coaxed it into gaining enough speed to keep the convertible in sight from a discreet distance. They'd traveled about two miles on I-84 when it made a left turn onto a dirt road.

Danny recognized the turnoff as the quickest way to get to Baker Bluff. He'd only been there one time when he'd checked out George's story—and that was enough. He'd arrived just as the sun was

232

setting—much like it was now—and the view overlooking the river had been spectacular. But as far as he was concerned, Baker Bluff was an evil place that reeked of death. He'd found a sign discarded by the side of the road with a crudely drawn imitation of his signature symbol. Someone had tried to make it look like Danny had been to the bluff before, perhaps even to prove he was responsible for what had happened there. He wouldn't be surprised if the sheriff had planned to accuse him of that white guy's death instead of blaming poor old George. Why he hadn't, remained a mystery. Danny had stayed at the bluff just long enough to look around and then got out of there. If Baker Bluff was where the guy was taking Ellie, then Danny had been right to follow them. He couldn't see anything good happening there.

His major concern now was all the dust the Caddy was stirring up. He didn't have enough money to replace the air filter when he'd overhauled the truck and if they didn't get to the bluff soon, he might not make it at all. Hoping to cut down on the damage, Danny eased back on the throttle to put more distance between the car and the truck. It was too late. The death throes had already begun. A lurch, shake, and window-rattling shudder ended the old pickup's misery.

Glazed with nervous sweat and cursing his bad luck, Danny swung out of the cab and propped up the hood with a determined urgency. There was nothing to do now but fix the problem and fix it fast. He hoped that it was only the filter that had stopped the truck. That he could deal with on the fly. Anything more serious and he'd have to hike the rest of the way to Baker Bluff. The thought made him shiver despite the heat. How far was it? Six miles, seven at the most. His bum ankle would never get him there. He *had* to get the truck going again.

CHAPTER THIRTY-TWO

Ellie turned her tear-streaked face toward Tony. "Oh, good, it's you. I . . . my dad . . . I need to . . ."

Although she was sweaty and her hair had tumbled out of its pony tail, she still looked gorgeous. But it was her troubled expression and confused stammering that aroused Tony more than her youthful beauty. *A distressed woman is a vulnerable woman.* He placed his finger lightly on her quivering lips. "Hush now," he said. "It doesn't matter. I'm here for you. We'll go for a little ride in the Caddy and you'll feel much better."

Ellie smiled tentatively. "Thank you, but . . . but you don't understand. I'm . . . I'm going to Celilo Village. I need to talk to them . . . to Reba and Danny. It's really important," she said in a voice trembling with urgency.

"Of course, I understand," he said. "I can take you wherever you want to go. When she didn't respond, he smiled and added, "You trust me, don't you, Ellie?"

She gave him a half-hearted nod.

"All righty, then. Hop in here beside me," he said, patting the passenger's seat. "Now close those beautiful eyes of yours, lean back, and enjoy the ride." *And what a ride it will be.*

Fifteen minutes later, Tony brought the car to a stop and turned off the ignition.

Ellie opened her eyes and looked around. "Where are we?" she asked.

"Baker Bluff," Tony said. "My favorite spot."

"But you said you'd take me to Celilo. You see, my dad isn't who I thought he was. It's a little hard to explain, but I just found out that he . . ."

Tony half-listened to her ramblings while he gazed at the river below, a grim set to his jaw. He didn't care about her father or whatever the hell she was prattling on about. That Sam Matthews was an FBI agent did give him some pause, though. Tony was already on the man's radar, if the sheriff 's hysterics could be believed. Messing around with a G-man's daughter probably wasn't the smartest thing for him to do right now. But he'd been betrayed big time. When Clarice thought he couldn't get her what she wanted soon enough, she dumped him and got her rich husband to buy Baker Bluff. His dream of a better life out from under Uncle Sol's thumb was dead the moment Clarice killed Nick. And, if all that wasn't bad enough, he could be going to jail for the cover-up, not to mention the fraudulent real estate transactions Clarice had conned him into doing. He looked at Ellie and shrugged. *Might as well get something out of the deal while he could.*

"Uh," said Ellie with a puzzled frown. "I'm not sure why you stopped here but it is a beautiful place."

Tony leaned in close, his lips brushing against her ear as he whispered, "Not as beautiful as you." His voice sounded husky and his breath smelled sour even to him.

Ellie twisted her head away from him. "Oh, no," she cried. "You've been drinking."

Tony grabbed her by the shoulders and pulled her roughly to his chest.

"Don't, she said, squirming out of his embrace.

Angered by her refusal, he grabbed her again. "Hey, now," he said. "You know you want this."

"No, please. I don't."

He glared at her. "Why, you little cock-tease." Pulling her toward him again, he wrapped his arms around her in a tight embrace and kissed her. The more she resisted, the rougher the smashing of lips.

She doubled her fists and pounded on his chest, which was so pitifully ineffective that he had to stop kissing her and laugh. "You're a sexy babe, but a spitfire you're not."

Ellie squirmed out of his embrace and lunged for the door.

"Shit!" he sputtered, grabbing her arm. "You're not going anywhere, missy! We're just getting started."

She whimpered softly as she stared at his fingers digging into her arm. "Please," she said. "Don't hurt me." When she began to cry, Tony shouted, "That's enough!" A stinging slap followed. The surprise attack stopped her tears, but the blow had bloodied her nose. "Fight it all you want, baby. I know you want me just as much as I want you."

While Ellie pinched her nose to stop the bleeding, Tony reached under the seat for the bottle he'd stashed there. "Get yourself together," he ordered. After he'd had several noisy gulps, he offered her the whiskey. "You look like you could use a drink, he said.

She pushed the bottle away. "Your loss, my gain," he slurred. When he'd downed a couple more swigs, he capped the bottle and tossed it aside. "Now, where were we?" he asked, leering down her blouse. "Oh yeah," he said, squeezing her nipples through the thin fabric. "Warm-up act." He ripped her blouse apart and when he'd torn off her bra, he held the lacy garment to his nose. Inhaling deeply, he said, "Mmm, nice. Really nice." Ellie shivered and covered her exposed breasts with crossed arms.

"No, you don't," Tony said, tossing the bra aside and pushing her backwards onto the seat. This time he punched her in the face and gut to stop her crying. "Now, that I have your attention," he sneered, "let's get to it." He pinned her down with his body and ignored her screams as he nuzzled her nipples. After a few moments, he paused long enough to unzip his pants and announce, "So much for the warm-up act." With one swift maneuver, he had her shorts and panties pulled to her ankles. Roughly pawing at her exposed privates, he wrenched her legs apart. Between short gasps of breath, he said, "Time for the main event, baby" and thrust himself inside her.

CHAPTER THIRTY-THREE

Danny unscrewed the wing nut atop the round, frying pan-like apparatus holding the truck filter and removed its lid. Then, lifting the fitting out of the engine and placing it on a dented fender, he removed the filter inside. Just as he'd suspected, the filter was caked with thick dust from the roadway. Most of the dust flew off after he'd whacked the filter against the side of the truck a couple of times. Just to make sure, he blew on it as hard as he could. Once he had the hastily cleaned filter back inside its receptacle and reinserted in the truck, he dropped the hood and jumped in the cab. Danny held his breath, praying the ignition switch would turn the engine over. With a comforting roar, the truck came to life. *Success!* Breathing again, he popped the clutch and headed for the bluff.

He heard Ellie's screams as soon as he'd pulled into the meadow. Her terror was Danny's terror. If he'd ever wanted to kill someone, it was now. Whoever was hurting Ellie would not live to tell about it. He jammed the gas pedal to the floorboard and the old truck took on new life as it flat-out flew across the meadow. But it seemed to take centuries before he braked to a halt behind the Caddy and hopped out of the cab.

Ellie's attacker was too intent on subduing Ellie to register Danny's arrival. The poor girl was nearly naked and struggling to fight him off, but the man atop her had pinned her arms back and spread her legs apart for the brutal assault. Danny grabbed the creep by his shoulders and pulled him off Ellie.

Once he got him out of the car and onto the ground, the guy tried to push Danny away. It was a clumsy, futile effort. With his pants tangled around his ankles, he couldn't get enough traction to stand upright without stumbling. Judging by the stench, the alcohol he'd consumed didn't help his cause. He was an easy take-down. Danny didn't give him a chance to assume an even half-way defensive posture. He kicked and pummeled the man without mercy. Within minutes, Ellie's attacker had passed out. But Danny kept punching and kicking him.

Ellie somehow managed to get her ripped clothing back on during Danny's one-sided fight and scrambled out of the car. "No, Danny!" she cried. "Don't kill him!" But the SOB needed killing and Danny's rage was far from spent.

"Danny, please," she begged. "Stop!"

The fear in her voice broke through the fury that had gripped him. Danny lowered his fist and looked at the wounded deer stumbling toward him. Her bloodied face looked swollen and bruised from the guy's attack. The agony on her face crushed whatever fight Danny still had left. With aching heart, he opened his arms to her. Collapsing against his chest, she whimpered, "Help me, help me."

He gently cradled her trembling body in his arms and hushed her plaintive cries. "It's going to be all right, Ellie. I'm here now. You'll be okay." He would hold her like this forever if need be.

After a few moments, she stopped crying. "Take me home."

He'd do whatever she wished, but he wavered. "Ellie," he said, "I don't know where you live."

"Not there. Take me to your home, Danny. Take me to Celilo."

CHAPTER THIRTY-FOUR

As despondent as Sam had been over his failures, his sponsor Mike's talk had gotten through to him. All that stuff about following the money got him thinking like an investigator again. That and Mike's take on the curative power of work. He'd poured the whiskey down the sink, thrown the empty bottle away and gone back to the dam, after a quick stop at the court house to check on who'd paid Danny's bail. Now it was time to make some amends.

Sam had stayed home this morning specifically so he could talk to Ellie. News that an FBI agent had been posing as a construction foreman at the dam was bound to get around town fast. Ellie deserved to hear it from him first. He hadn't been able to explain his situation to Reba in time and the result had been a disaster. He wanted to spare Ellie and, frankly, himself, from similar pain. He wanted to tell her that he'd been trying to help the Indians, not hurt them. He wanted her to know how much he cared for Reba and the hopes he'd had for their future together. He wanted to apologize to Ellie for the mistakes he'd made in the past and ask for her forgiveness. Yes, he had a lot to discuss with his daughter. But it didn't quite work out the way he'd planned.

He'd let her go shopping with Dessa and her mother because he'd forgotten that he'd already promised her that she could. He'd spent the time that she was gone doing some chores around the house and thinking about the best way to explain things to her. He thought he was prepared, but the way that she stormed into the house with her face flushed and scowling, worried him. A déjà vu feeling overtook him. *Was he too late again?* Hoping he'd misjudged the reason for her distress, he opted for a lighthearted tone. "Hey, kiddo," he said, "What's with the frowny face?"

Her scowl deepened as she stomped her foot. "Da-a-ad! You've got to stop treating me like a baby. Kiddo? Frowny face? Really?"

That went well. He smiled sheepishly. "I know, Ellie. You're not a baby or even a little child anymore. I need to treat you like the young lady you've become. So, let's start right now. There's something I've been meaning to talk to you about."

Ellie looked at him skeptically. "What?"

"Let's sit down in the living room and I'll explain."

Ellie shrugged, which Sam knew could mean just about anything, but she followed him into the living room. After they'd settled comfortably, Sam began. "First, I'd like to know what happened on the shopping trip. You seemed upset when you got here."

"I ran into Danny Longstreet in town."

Oops. Too late. Sam sighed, "I suppose he told you that I'm an FBI agent?"

"How . . . how'd you guess?"

"It wasn't a guess. I *am* an FBI agent. And Danny knows it."

"But . . . I don't understand. You told me you'd quit. That you couldn't do it anymore."

"I didn't think I could. Not after my partner and another agent were seriously hurt because—"

"Because you were drinking on the job."

"Yes, because of me, two men who were my friends, almost lost their lives. But I was given another chance to start over in The Dalles."

"Working undercover again?"

Sam nodded. "As a construction foreman. My boss was afraid there'd be trouble at the dam and he wanted me to be there to stop it."

"So, you lied to me and everyone else."

"Ellie, I had to keep my role at the dam a secret to be effective. You can understand that, can't you?"

She shook her head. "NO! I don't understand. I don't understand how you could make promises and then turn right around and break them. I don't understand how you could look Reba and Danny in the face and pretend to be their friend."

"I *am* their friend."

"No, you're not. Danny told me you just said you were so you could spy on them. You never intended to help George Featherstone.

240

He was just a convenient way to get on the good side of the Indians. Danny said you're even going to dig up their ancestors' graves."

"It's true I'm in charge of the reburial project but—"

"I thought Danny was lying about you. But you're the liar."

"No, Ellie, I—"

She put her hands over her ears. "STOP! I don't want to hear any more of this. You lie about everything. You haven't even quit drinking like you promised." She noted Sam's head shake. "Don't try to deny it, Dad. I saw the empty liquor bottle in the trash. "You're still a drunk and always will be." With tears streaming down her face, she bolted out of the chair. "I HATE YOU!! I HATE YOU!!" she cried before running out of the room.

Stunned by her emotional outburst, Sam wasn't sure if he should go after her. When he heard the front door slam, he got up and looked out the window. Ellie had raced across the street to Dessa's house and was on her way inside. He told himself that that was probably for the best right now. She was in no mood to listen to anything he had to say. Maybe talking to a friend would help somehow. Sam had no idea how to deal with a teenage girl like Ellie. He could use a parent sponsor like he had for A.A. The whole exchange had worn him out. He decided to sit in his recliner and rest a bit until Ellie came back home.

Two hours later, he woke up and realized that Ellie still hadn't returned. He walked across the street and rang the Feldman's doorbell. "Is Ellie here?" he asked, when Odessa opened the door.

"No," she said.

"Have you seen her today?"

"Yes."

"Do you know where she is?"

"Yes."

If she were purposely acting obtuse to frustrate him, she was doing an excellent job. "Odessa, I need to know where Ellie is. Please tell me. It's important."

For a moment, he didn't think she was going to say anything. "She said she'd never speak to me again if I told you," Dessa finally said. "I'd hate to lose her as a friend, but I'm more afraid of what might happen to her."

241

"Because?" he asked, heart racing.

"Because Ellie told me she was going to hitch a ride to Celilo Village."

Not what he wanted to hear. Sam had warned both girls about the dangers of getting into a stranger's vehicle. Ellie said the kids did it all the time and he was just being overly protective. The baby thing again. Sam had seen too many hitchhiking incidents turned deadly to allow Ellie to do it. As far as he knew, she never had. Was this her way of showing that she didn't believe anything he said anymore? The thought made him shudder.

"Thank you," Sam said, turning to leave.

"She was very upset with you."

"I know."

What he didn't know was why Ellie would want to go to Celilo. The more he considered it, the more it made sense. Reba would understand what Ellie was going through since she had suffered from Sam's duplicity as well. His biggest regret all these years was that Ellie didn't have her mother. As hard as he'd tried, Sam was no substitute for the comfort that only a mother could give her daughter. He winced as he remembered the awkward way he'd explained what the blood spots on Ellie's underpants meant. She'd thought she was dying of some dreadful disease. Menstruation was something a mother should discuss with her daughter.

Sam didn't feel comfortable going to Celilo, but if Ellie were there, he had no choice. He needed to bring his daughter home.

CHAPTER THIRTY-FIVE

As soon as Sam drove into the village, he noticed that the usual tourist crowds were absent. The faded yellow flag atop the Long House flapped noisily in a strong breeze. No fishing would take place this day, which accounted for the lack of tourists. Another fisherman had probably fallen into the falls. It was a dangerous business, but everyone accepted the risks, just as Sam had accepted the risks his job entailed. He wondered if the inevitable deaths at the falls caused the villagers to question their jobs as Sam did his. He didn't think so. His job was just a career choice. Theirs was a way of life.

Sam's relationship with Reba had caused him to look at everything with new eyes. Despite his doubts about the morality of the dam's existence, he still admired the skill of the workers charged with its construction. The structure was unquestionably a magnificent engineering feat. The electricity generated by the dam would benefit thousands. Maybe he was wrong, but he chose to believe that it was his deceit and not his work at the dam that had tarnished, and eventually ruined things with Reba.

Fortunately, his pickup hadn't attracted any attention from the few villagers who were outside. The last thing he needed was another confrontation. He parked outside Reba's house and knocked on the door, hoping that Danny wasn't home. Sam's efforts to build a relationship with him hadn't succeeded and most likely never would now.

Reba opened the door and stepped outside. When she'd closed the door behind her, she said, "I thought you'd come." Her voice carried none of the hurt and disappointment that had marred their last meeting.

Seeing her again made his heart beat faster. He loved this woman and nothing could change that. He would've given anything to tell her how he felt, but his priority now was his daughter and only his daughter. "Is Ellie here?" he asked.

She nodded. "But she doesn't want to see you."

"I kind of figured that," he said, running a hand over his crew cut. "*I* want to see *her*, though."

Reba shook her head. "I'm sorry, Sam. Ellie is hurt."

"I know. That's why I need to talk to her. I've got to make things right, if I can."

"You don't understand." She looked at him with a tenderness he hadn't expected. "Ellie was raped."

He couldn't comprehend what he heard. *Raped?* "No, that's not possible . . . I can't . . . what did you say?"

"She was attacked. She wouldn't say who did it, but Danny told me. His name is Tony Rossi."

My God. He knew the man was bad news from the moment he met him. His mind raced as he tried to come to terms with what had occurred. With righteous anger tempered by profound regret, he asked, "When did this happen? Where?"

"Danny was the one who found her. He told me that Tony picked her up in his car along Highway 84. He took her to Baker Bluff, supposedly to comfort her, since she seemed so distraught."

Sam bowed his head. "This is my all fault." When he looked up he said, "I need to see her. Please."

"I'm taking care of her. You shouldn't come back here again, Sam," she said. "It's not safe for you." The breeze that whipped the flag atop the Long House had picked up strength. The fierce gusts were tearing the faded symbol to shreds. Reba pointed to the flag. "It flies today for George. He's dead."

"What?" Sam had visited George at the hospital yesterday and was happy to learn that he'd come out of the coma earlier that morning. The protestors were milling around outside the building but the extra security he'd arranged seemed to be keeping things under control. George should've been safe. "Did Sheriff Pritchard—"

"The sheriff had nothing to do with it. George recovered from the coma only to die of cardiac arrest. The doctor said the strain of the ordeal he'd been through was just too much for him. You broke your promise, Sam. You told us—and George—that you'd protect him. And you didn't. You betrayed us all."

****

His failures were piling up like overdue bills. He'd failed George. He'd failed Reba. He'd failed her people. But the worst failure of all was that he hadn't protected his daughter. The only greater sin was what Tony Rossi had done to her. Sam's shock had quickly turned to anger, then overwhelming rage. Nothing—not the FBI, the dam, Celilo, or even his own life—mattered more than destroying the man who'd destroyed his only child. It was a father's mandate.

Traffic on Highway 84 heading into town was traveling at glacial speed. Cursing the dawdling Sunday-like drivers, Sam dodged in and out of the passing lane until he figured he could make better time by driving on the narrow shoulder. Unfettered by the speed limit, he floored the Chevy all the way to Front Street. He braked the truck to a screeching halt in front of Rossi's Real Estate and grabbed his service weapon.

Except for target practice and routine cleaning, it was the first time since he'd come to The Dalles that he'd taken the Smith and Wesson out of the glove box. If he'd been following FBI protocol, Sam would've approached the office with caution; he was thinking as a father, not an agent. A furious surge of adrenaline and deadly intent propelled him through the office door, but he stopped abruptly when he got a good look at the interior. The trashing was thorough: chairs upended, contents of desks emptied and tossed onto the floor, file cabinet drawers opened and hanging askew.

His first thought was that vandals—maybe even Danny and his gang—had ransacked the place. Whoever they were, they were long gone. The only person in the room was a silver-haired man in a rumpled suit standing next to one of the file cabinets. He was short and stocky with a belly gone soft around the middle. Chomping on an unlit cigar at the corner of his mouth, he eyed the gun Sam pointed at him, more irritated than alarmed.

"Where's Tony?" Sam demanded.

"Who wants to know?"

"The man who's going to kill the S.O.B."

The old man broke into a yellow-toothed grin, dropped the papers clutched in his liver-spotted fist onto a nearby desk and shuffled toward Sam. "Pleased to meet you, mister. But you'll have to stand in line. I plan on taking down Tony myself." He pointed to Sam's weapon. "Why don't you put that thing away and let's discuss the matter."

Sam didn't know what to make of the guy. "Who are you?" he asked.

"Solomon Rossi," he said, "the S.O.B.'s uncle."

Sam hesitated a moment before stuffing the gun in his belt. "Where is he?"

Rossi shrugged. "Damned if I know," he said, dropping his fleshy frame into the only chair that was still upright. "No one's been here all day, near as I can tell. Not even the secretary or the two jokers who call themselves salesmen that Tony has on my payroll. "Take a load off, yourself," he said, motioning to a nearby chair, "and I'll tell you what I do know."

Sam's outrage over what Tony had done to Ellie hadn't dissipated. He was determined to put him in the ground. He had enough adrenaline pumping through his body to keep him up all night searching if he had to. He decided to listen to what Rossi had to say. Maybe the man was full of hot air, but if nothing else, he might give Sam an idea where to look for the bastard.

Sam found a chair, righted it, and sat down. Rossi continued, "My double-dealing nephew is a cheat. And he's cheated me for the last time." He shook his head in disgust. "What's your beef with him?"

"It doesn't concern you," Sam said as he surveyed the mess around him. "What happened to the office?"

Rossi chuckled. "That was my doing. I've been hunting for evidence."

"What do you mean, 'evidence'?"

If Solomon Rossi had any qualms about sharing his findings with a total stranger, a stranger with a gun no less, he didn't show it. He seemed more than eager to tell what he meant, starting with how he owned the real estate business and why he'd sent Nick to spy on his cousin. "I suspected that Tony was cheating me from day one, but I wanted proof to show my brother what an ass he'd raised. More important, I wanted to get my money back. Nick didn't find out squat and then he got killed. I figured I owed it to him to come out here and finish his job. I probably should've done it myself in the first place."

He got up and went to the file cabinet where he'd been standing earlier. He brought back a couple of bound ledger books and a stack of papers. He laid them on a nearby desk and tapped the ledgers with a stubby finger. "It's all right there. I saw right away how he'd been cheating me. Simple skimming the top off my commissions. It looks like Tony has something else going on, too—something that pulled in a lot more dough. I just haven't figured out what yet."

Rossi caught Sam studying the dried blood on the ledgers. "You think that's something, you should see the mop in the storage room. Looks like it cleaned up a bloodbath. That or a very bad nosebleed."

The news that Tony had been cheating his uncle wasn't surprising and Sam didn't much care. The blood was another matter. Reba said Ellie had been attacked at Baker Bluff. If the blood wasn't hers, whose was it? Standing, Sam said, "Show me."

"But, that isn't . . ." Sam's determined look made Rossi close his mouth. He led the way to the storeroom at the back of the office. The mop hung on the wall by a small safe that had been jimmied. As Sam examined the mop, Rossi explained the safe. "It took me awhile, but I managed to pry the stubborn thing open. I thought I'd find the money Tony stole in it, but all it had was a bunch of paperwork."

Sam rubbed his chin. He could think of only one reason why there would be enough blood in the office to require a mop and it wasn't due to anything as innocent as a nosebleed. In the corner was a waste can stuffed with wadded rags caked with dried blood. He had a hunch that Solomon Rossi's "evidence" was linked to the blood. And Tony was right in the middle of the whole thing. To Rossi, he said, "I'd like to take another look at those ledgers and the paperwork, also, if you don't mind. Maybe I can help you figure it out."

Rossi appraised Sam, cocking an eyebrow at his work clothes. "I consider myself a savvy businessman and I haven't been able to put the pieces together. No offense, but you look like you belong on a construction crew somewhere. What makes you think you can . . ."

Sam pulled out his wallet and flashed his FBI identification and badge.

"You're a G-man?

"Not for much longer."

"I guess offing Tony *would* sort of end your career."

An hour and several phone calls to a financial analyst at FBI headquarters later, Sam had the answers Rossi was looking for. As Sam explained, "It looks like your nephew used his knowledge of the real estate market to identify houses in the area that suited his purposes."

"What purposes?"

Sam pointed to an entry in the ledger. "See how some of the houses listed as sold have the initials 'DG' alongside them?"

"Yeah, I noticed that."

"The paperwork you discovered in the safe identified DG as the initials of a company called the Destiny Group. It's supposedly run by a woman named Mildred Simmons."

"That's the name of Tony's secretary. How would she know anything about running a company?"

"She didn't have to. It's just a shell business. A way of purchasing the houses Tony identified without his name being involved."

Rossi ran a finger down the list of houses the Destiny Group bought. "Looks like she bought them for a song."

"That was the deal. Find the houses they could snap up with very little capital and then turn around and sell them at an inflated price."

"Tony always was hell on wheels when it came to selling."

"He didn't have to do much selling."

"What do you mean?"

"He used straw buyers." A confused look flickered across Rossi's face so Sam explained further. "He recruited a couple of guys named Jensen and Hoffman to enter into purchase agreements to buy the houses at the higher price."

"Ha! He didn't have to do much recruiting, either. Hoffman and Jensen are the part-time salesmen here. I never understood why Tony hired them. They weren't even licensed. The idiots couldn't possibly have made enough money to buy a pup tent, let alone a house at an inflated price."

"That's the beauty of straw buyers. They don't have to have any money. The paperwork is phony, made to appear that they are qualified for the mortgage loans and planned to occupy the houses."

"How did it get by the bank? They have some sharp cookies working there."

"I suspect a bank employee, probably the loan officer and an insider at the escrow office were involved in the scheme. It would be easy for them to falsify the documents needed—like appraisals, verification of deposits, employment records, and closing documents."

"I get it now," Rossi said, nodding. "The major players split the proceeds from the fraudulent mortgages and the straw buyers pocketed a fee for their role."

"Exactly. The homes eventually wound up in foreclosure and the bank sucked up the losses."

"You'd think the bank's auditors would eventually catch on."

"It's just a matter of time. If Tony and his accomplices are as smart as they seem to be, they're probably making other plans for just that eventuality right now."

Solomon Rossi said he was impressed. "I can't believe Tony came up with this scheme all on his own. Petty thievery, sure. But a scam like this is way beyond anything he could pull off."

Sam shrugged. "Maybe not, but I know for a fact that he's capable of something a whole lot worse."

"Must be personal, the way you came storming in here. Otherwise, you'd have identified yourself right off as a Fed."

Sam didn't take the bait, preferring to deal with the question that still nagged at him. He pointed to the storeroom. "Why do you think there's so much blood in there?"

"Somebody got to Tony before you?"

"No, I think Tony got to Nick before he wound up at Baker Bluff."

"I was told he was shot by a drunken Indian who tried to steal Tony's truck."

Sam shook his head. "The Indian in question was a diabetic and didn't drink. He didn't know how to drive, either. He was supposedly too drunk to walk which is why Nick gave him a ride out to his home in Celilo. Yet, he was sober enough to find Tony's gun in the glove box, shoot him, and then drag his body out of the truck, and toss him over a cliff."

Rossi scratched his silver mane. "That doesn't make any sense.

Why was he arrested?"

"The sheriff has a hang-up about Indians and George was convenient. Either that or Sheriff Pritchard was in on the cover-up."

"And you suspect that the cover-up involved my cheating nephew?"

Sam pointed to the blood-stained ledgers. "What if Nick found these ledgers and Tony caught him. Tony would realize then that Nick was about to expose him and —"

"Killed him first." Rossi was quiet for a moment. "If that's true, then you'd better catch up with Tony before I do."

CHAPTER THIRTY-SIX

Tony spent the night crumpled in a fetal position on the ground, fading in and out of consciousness. He was still disoriented by morning, but aware that someone had shaken his aching shoulder. His head hurt like the wrong end of a battering ram and his gut felt even worse. Whoever was manhandling him could take a hike. And he'd tell them so if he could just get his parched cotton mouth to work.

"Hey, Buddy, what's the matter? You hurt?"

"Naw, he's just hung over," said another voice. "Seven o'clock in the morning is too early to sober up."

With great difficulty, Tony turned his head toward the speakers. His eyes were swollen slits, but he could make out two pairs of dirty work boots standing next to him. When one of the boots prodded his shoulder again, pain shot through him like a bolt of electricity and wrenched his bruised face into a grotesque grimace. *Jesus! Have mercy!*

"Must've been quite a night. His pants are still down and he looks too wasted to know it."

Tony had no idea why he was on the ground and the subject of these clowns' abuse. He just wanted them to go away.

They apparently had no intention of doing so. "Party's over, pal," one of them said. The boots sprouted hands and rolled him onto his back. "You can sleep it off at home."

Tony propped himself up on wobbly elbows to eyeball his tormentors. Despite his limited blurry vision, he saw what looked like construction workers; maybe government types in overalls, long-sleeved work shirts, and hard hats. He sat up and rubbed his aching shoulder. "Who the hell are you?" he asked.

The bigger of the two men said, "None of your business, smart-ass."

His partner frowned. "Aw, Frank, cool it. The guy's in a bad way." Reaching for Tony's hand, he said, "Here, let me help you."

Once on his feet, Tony pulled up his pants and leaned against the Caddy for support. Cold from lying on the dew-covered ground, he warmed himself by folding his arms on his chest. He shook his head in a wasted effort to clear it. His body ached all over, but aside from a wrinkled, bloody shirt and some grass-stained trousers ripped at the knees, he didn't seem to be damaged too much. He had a vague notion of a fight, but he couldn't remember who'd decked him or why. The only thing he knew for sure was that he was at Baker Bluff. He stared back at the two guys staring at him. A truck was parked next to his convertible with *Cascade Survey Company* printed on its side panel. "That your truck?" Tony asked.

The fellow who'd helped Tony to his feet said, "Yep. Got a job here today." He seemed friendly enough, but his partner wasn't so inclined.

"You're trespassing on private property," he said. He gestured to the convertible. "Time to shove off before the owners arrive."

The owners? Anger surged through Tony's cold, wet body as the grim reality of the situation triggered his memory. He remembered full well now what had happened yesterday. Clarice's betrayal had ruined his miserable life. She'd screwed him over royally. "I know the owners," he said.

The friendly guy seemed doubtful. "Warren Nestor?"

"And his lovely wife, Clarice," Tony sneered.

Frank spit on the ground, just missing Tony's shoes. "I'm duly impressed, but you still have to hit the road. We've got work to do before our meeting."

"Clarice and Warren are coming to Baker Bluff?" asked Tony.

"Today at noon," said Frank.

***

Tony's thoughts turned to Ellie as he drove through town. There was bound to be trouble with her father. He'd have to deal with him sooner or later, but maybe he could blame everything on the Indian

252

kid. It would serve him right for butting in where he didn't belong, not to mention the beating Tony had taken from him. Shifting blame on a redskin had worked for Clarice; maybe it would work for Tony, too. Mildred had warned him about Clarice, but he'd always assumed that she was just jealous. He should've paid attention to her nagging. If he'd kept his eyes open around her like Mildred had advised, he might not be in this stinking mess. He wouldn't relish hearing her say that she'd told him so, but Mildred was the only person in town he trusted right now. Since it was too early for even Mildred to be at the office, he drove straight to her house.

"What in the world happened to you?" Mildred asked upon answering his knock. "You look like death warmed over."

She didn't look so hot herself in a ratty bathrobe and pink hair rollers. Under normal circumstances, Tony would've countered her cutting remark with one of his own. But these were not normal circumstances. If they were, he wouldn't be standing on her front porch at seven-thirty in the morning. "Let me in, Mildred. I need to talk to you."

She stepped aside so he could pass by and said, "Come into the kitchen. I've got a fresh pot of coffee on. You look like you could use a cup."

He'd never been to her place before, but it looked just like her – frumpy and old-fashioned. As he passed through the living room to the kitchen, he noted with some amusement that she must have gotten a good deal on lace doilies. The place looked like an explosion in a doily factory. The lacey doo-dads were everywhere—on table tops and the arms and backs of every chair and sofa in the place.

In the kitchen, Tony sat down at a chrome dinette table while Mildred fussed with the coffee. The kitchen was painted a pale yellow with frilly curtains on the window over the sink. A collection of tiny ceramic cats sat next to a green leafy plant on the window ledge. The décor was much too girly-girl for Tony's tastes, but it was a good fit with the doily theme Mildred had going.

"You want some breakfast?" she asked as she set their mugs on the table. "I can scramble up some eggs real fast."

"No," he said blowing on the coffee. "But if you could add a little nip to the java, I'd appreciate it."

253

"I'm on the wagon, Tony. Don't you remember?"

"Come on, Millie, you've gotta have a little something stashed away. Have mercy on a wounded man."

She laughed and said, "Well, since you put it that way." Standing on tiptoes, she retrieved a nearly empty whiskey bottle from a top shelf in the cupboard.

"Hah! I knew you wouldn't keep a completely dry house."

"For medicinal purposes only, boss," she said, filling a shot glass for him. As soon as he'd added the whiskey to his coffee and downed a couple of quick sips, she asked. "Now, are you going tell me why you're here so early in the morning looking like you got hit by a truck?"

Tony rubbed his aching shoulder. "I'm in big trouble."

"I can see that. What happened?"

"Some damn Injun picked a fight with me," he admitted. No sense telling her any more. He didn't think she'd understand about Ellie. Not that he had a clear understanding himself. He shook his head at how stupid he'd been. "The beating isn't the problem." He paused and looked down at his coffee mug. "You were right about Clarice all along. She's a two-timing bitch."

"What'd she do?" asked Mildred.

"She stole Baker Bluff from me, that's what! I guess she got tired of waiting for me to scrape together the rest of the dough we needed. She sweet-talked Warren into springing for the purchase."

Mildred was quiet a moment. "I knew she wasn't trustworthy, boss. But it could've been a lot worse."

"It is. Old Injun George died at the hospital yesterday. The Feds were already on the case because of Sam Matthews' interference. You heard that he's a G-man, right? He claimed jurisdiction over Sheriff Pritchard and had George put under guard at the hospital."

"What for? He wasn't a flight risk in his condition."

"Who knows or cares? The problem is that it's only a matter of time before the Feds come after me. Asking a bunch of questions I don't want to answer."

"I'm confused. Why would they do that?"

Tony hesitated and then asked, "Can I trust you, Millie?"

She leaned forward and patted Tony's hand. "Boss, you should know by now that I will never let you down. Never."

"That's what I wanted to hear because what I'm going to tell you now can't leave this room."

"Go ahead," she said, settling back in her chair. "I'm listening."

"Clarice killed Nick."

If Mildred was surprised by this revelation she didn't show it. "I thought something was a little off about the story," she said, "especially the part about you asking Nick to take the Indian back to Celilo."

"That was all Clarice's doing. She said if Nick's body was found at Baker Bluff, the property would be off-limits for a burial ground."

"Smart. The Indians wouldn't want their ancestors laid to rest on a site where a murder had taken place. Spilled blood and all that."

"Exactly," Tony said. "The government would be forced to locate the graves somewhere else and the property would be ours for the taking."

"She was right about that. According to this morning's newspaper, a new site has been chosen out by Highway 14. There's even a photo of the helicopter that they're going to use to move the bones."

"Here's the thing. The original plan didn't even involve Nick. Clarice's plan was to drive Injun George up to Baker Bluff and fill him with enough booze so that he would drive the truck right off the bluff himself. It was supposed to look like a drunken accident, not murder."

"What changed?"

"Old George passed out before he could even get the truck in gear."

Mildred got up to replenish her mug. "Want a refill?" she asked.

The whiskey bottle she'd left on the table was calling. "As long as you jack it up a notch."

"Okay," she said, pouring him another shot. "You deserve it."

"And I haven't even told you everything. Pritchard is convinced that we'll all be going to jail when the Feds get through with us."

"How is Pritchard involved?"

"Clarice had him over a barrel." He explained how Clarice threatened to make his job go away by spreading the dirt about his wife and the Indian from Celilo if he didn't help to frame Nick's murder on George Featherstone.

Mildred chuckled. "That explains why he's always been such a hard-ass about anything to do with Indians or Celilo. If he had his druthers, the falls wouldn't be the only thing destroyed by the dam. Maybe he thought an Indian responsible for killing an innocent kid like Nick would lead to the destruction of the entire village. The town folk have sure been riled up about the murder."

"Yeah, tell me about it."

"Tony, there *is* something I should tell you."

"Hold it right there," he said, raising his mug in the air. "If it's something I'm not going to like, then I'll need another refill." He meant more booze, but Mildred brought the coffee pot and poured him a warm-up.

Mildred said, "You know how I've never trusted Clarice. I thought she was dangerous."

Tony groaned. "You needn't remind me."

"I was worried about you, that's all. Anyway, I've done some digging into her background. You'd be amazed at what you can find in the library these days. The librarian keeps all the back issues of various newspapers, including *The Oregonian.*

"So?"

"We know Clarice was living in Portland before coming to The Dalles. It never made sense to me that she would willingly leave the excitement of the big city to live here. I had a hunch that she was running away from her past. And I was right." Mildred stood up. "Wait here, I have something to show you."

Tony watched her waddle out of the kitchen and then grabbed the nearly empty whiskey bottle. "Might as well top off the coffee with the last of the good stuff," he muttered.

When Mildred returned, she handed him a newspaper. "I swiped this from the library. Clarice was front page news in Portland several years ago." She pointed to a faded photo. "This here is our Clarice. Only she was calling herself Colleen back then."

Tony rubbed his eyes. "My peepers aren't focusing too well right now. What's the article say about her?"

"Just that your sweetie pie has murdered before. Seems her hubby in Portland was rich like Warren. Somehow, he wound up dead, stabbed to death in his own home. Clarice was the main suspect, but eluded arrest by claiming self-defense. Supposedly, he was outraged because she was leaving him and attacked her first."

"That's possible."

"Yeah, that's what I thought, too. Then I kept reading the back issues. Turns out, Clarice was the sole beneficiary of a healthy life insurance policy. An investigation was launched, but she was never charged. There was talk that she bribed the police with the insurance money she got. In any event, she left town quickly."

"Talk about a black widow," Tony cracked. "I should let Warren know that his days may be numbered."

"Oh, I think you should do more than that. Wouldn't you like to keep your Baker Bluff dream alive?"

"What do you think?"

Mildred smiled. "Then I have an idea that just may solve all your problems."

Tony snapped to attention. His instincts had been correct—Mildred was the right person to go to for help. For the first time in two days, he had a glimmer of hope. "Spill it, woman," he said.

CHAPTER THIRTY-SEVEN

Danny opened one of the boxes containing the dynamite and took out a stick. Walter had transferred the boxes from the warehouse so that they could assemble and test the dynamite. Since none of them had any experience with explosives, Feldman wanted them to have a trial run before what he referred to as "Operation Red" was carried out. With 41 acres of village land to choose from, it wasn't hard to find a remote spot where prying eyes wouldn't find them. Danny set the stick on the duct tape he'd laid out in front of him and rolled it up part way. Then he added a second stick and kept rolling, adding more sticks as he went along. The process was much like the way he'd seen Fitz add cinnamon and sugar as he rolled out dough for cinnamon rolls at The Pit Stop. When Danny had assembled seven or eight sticks, he secured the entire bundle together with more duct tape.

"It don't need to be so perfect," Walter complained. "You're taking way too long." Walter and Ernie had finished wrapping their bundles while Danny had only two bundles to show for his efforts.

Ernie pretended to throw one of the sticks at Danny. "Hurry up," he said, or we'll use you for target practice."

Believing dynamite wasn't something to fool around with, Danny took his time. Henry should've been here. Danny could always count on him to take things seriously. "Why didn't Henry come along?" he asked.

"He had stuff to do for Chief Thompson," Walter said. "Besides, the real fun will take place at the dam."

True to his word, Feldman had introduced them to his inside guy who said he'd provide everything they needed for the operation. He also advised them on how to get onto the spillway from the Washington side of the river without being noticed. But, in case they were, he'd promised to give them hard hats, work boots, and false name badges so that they'd look legitimate. The plan was to destroy the sluice gates which were located on top of the spillway. They'd use the rope they'd been given to lower the dynamite to the gates. Walter wanted each of them to lower a bundle. "Four big holes in those gates would set the project way back," he said.

"With seven or eight sticks to a bundle, you're talking about a huge explosion," countered Danny. "It's a major risk." He was okay with blowing up the sluice gates, but he didn't like the idea of an explosion so intense that it would take out any workers who happened to get in the way. When Danny thought about it — as he had a lot lately — the government employees were just doing a job to feed their families. Even as despicable as Sam Matthew's betrayal was, he'd only been trying to provide for Ellie in the best way he knew how. The only person Danny wouldn't regret seeing dead today was Tony Rossi. By dynamite or other means, it didn't matter.

Walter downplayed the risk. "Don't be such a spoilsport."

Danny shook his head at how aggressive Walter had become since they'd joined forces with Feldman's group. He seemed to actively court danger whenever he could.

Danny sighed and shook his head. He'd heard Oscar tell about an incident with dynamite that had scared the bejeesus out of him. His grandfather said he was picking cherries for the Seufert company when, unbeknownst to him, another crew at the orchard had been tasked with blowing up some stumps. Oscar was 150 feet away from the target stumps, but he almost got killed when the blast went off. Boulder-sized rocks, a sea of dirt and splintered wood flew past his head like it had all been shot out of a cannon. Oscar said the guy had overestimated the strength needed. He'd used three sticks when just one would've done the job.

The remote site they'd chosen for testing was the site of several abandoned shacks. No one could remember what their purpose had been originally, but they would be put to good use now. With three outbuildings, they'd each get the opportunity to blow one up. When Walter started things off by selecting an entire bundle of eight sticks to throw, Danny intervened. "Hey, man, why the overkill? That timber palace is practically falling down as it is. One stick or two at the most should do the trick."

"I know what I'm doing."

"Yeah," chimed Ernie. "Let the good times roll."

"You're gonna get us killed before we even get started," Danny said. He pulled a stick from one of his bundles. "I'll show you exactly what one stick will do, but you two better take cover first."

"Oh, I'm so scared," Walter mocked in a high-pitched voice. "Danny's going to make boom-boom. We gotta run and hide, Ernie."

Ernie laughed and imitated Walter's skittish dash to their truck.

When he knew they were a safe distance away, Danny lit the fuse and threw the single stick at the sturdiest of the shacks. And ran like hell.

The blast was nothing like the firecrackers they sometimes set off. The shack blew apart with a fierce ear-splitting thunder. The energy from the blast shook the other buildings so hard that they, too, collapsed. The debris field reached all the way to Danny's truck where the boys had taken shelter. A jagged hole in the ground had replaced the dilapidated structure.

Walter and Ernie were duly impressed. "Holy smokes," cried Ernie. "That was really something."

"Just one stick," Danny reminded them when they inspected the site. "This is nothing compared to what a bundle of seven or eight sticks will do. The concrete at the dam is gonna come flying apart like giant buckshot." Whether that would satisfy Walter's growing need for violence remained to be seen. It struck Danny that Walter had more rage burning inside him than all the Wy-ams and other tribes combined.

With the shacks destroyed by Danny's single test, they loaded the rest of the dynamite into his truck. "I can't wait until we do this for real," Walter said.

"Yeah," Ernie agreed. "It'll be a blast!"

CHAPTER THIRTY-EIGHT

Mildred's first time riding in the Cadillac didn't prove to be a pleasant experience. She fidgeted with her bra strap, tugged at her sagging stockings, and squirmed each time Tony goosed the gas pedal. She had a death grip on the door handle as if she were responsible for keeping it attached to the car. The frozen look on her face suggested that rigor mortis had already set in. "I don't have a good feeling about this, boss."

Her discomfort made him laugh. "You ain't seen nothin' yet," he teased. "Wait till we hit the highway. This baby's gonna flat-out fly."

Mildred let go of the door handle long enough to don a headscarf. Her frizzy bob was plastered down with so much hair spray that it'd take a hurricane to mess it up. A bit of fresh air running through those gray roots might do her some good. "Aw, Millie," he said, "Don't be such a fuss-budget. I'm a damn good driver. Ditch the scarf and just relax already."

She turned on him. "Riding in this flashy babe-mobile isn't what's bothering me. Go ahead, put pedal to the metal all you want. I'm ready, willing and able to do whatever makes you happy. I think I've proven that repeatedly. Give me a little credit, for God's sake. I've always had your back."

Mildred's sudden outburst was not like her. If she weren't so old, he'd swear that she was on the rag. The switch in her attitude was annoying. "What's your problem then?" he snapped.

"Clarice."

"What's that supposed to mean?"

"She's too clever by far. I'm afraid she won't buy the plan."

"Hell, yes, she's clever. That's what I'm counting on."

"Hmm."

"Don't hmm me," Tony said. "Just stick to the script we worked out. You got hold of Pritchard, right?"

"Yes, he'll be there."

"With backup?"

"It's all arranged."

"Then relax." He repeated what Clarice had once said to him: "Just follow my lead and do exactly what we planned and everything will be fine."

"Whatever you say, boss."

The rest of the ride to Baker Bluff was fast and silent. Mildred still fidgeted and squirmed in her seat but Tony ignored her. He concentrated instead on Clarice. She'd made a big mistake by double-crossing him and he couldn't wait to give her a little pay-back. He had nothing to lose at this point and everything to gain. And, by God, he would succeed. He hadn't slaved for Uncle Sol all these years to have his dream stolen by a so-called clever broad. No, Antonio Rossi would have the last laugh despite her conniving ways.

When he pulled up at the bluff, Clarice and Warren were already there. They huddled with the two surveyors that Tony had met earlier. The group was so busy discussing the location of the newly planted survey stakes on the property that they failed to notice the arrival of the Caddy. Tony and Mildred got out of the car and watched them for a moment. "Look at 'em," Tony sneered. "Warren and Clarice are holding hands like a pair of lovebirds. What a crock."

Mildred shrugged. "They sure look happy."

"Ha! Not for long." Tony gave up waiting for the group to notice them. "Come on," he said, nudging Mildred. "Grab that folder of yours and let's go give the happy couple something to think about."

Tony was a man on a mission, striding across the meadow with confidence oozing from every pore. Mildred trailed behind him reluctantly. "Are you sure about this?" she asked when Clarice spotted them. "She looks ready to shoot us both."

"This was your idea, for cryin' out loud. How many times do I have to tell you that it's brilliant?" He flicked his wrist at her. "Get a move on, will ya? It's party time."

The remnants of his run-in with the Indian kid—cuts, bruises, and a wicked black eye—were still visible. As Mildred had noted, Clarice was not pleased to see him, battered or not. If looks could kill, he was a dead man walking. Her hostile manner delighted Tony. He greeted her intense glare with a peppy, "Hey, doll. Sorry we're a little late." He nodded to the survey crew and Warren. If the men remembered him, they didn't let on and Tony didn't give them a chance to think about it. He quickly said, "Don't stop the meeting on our account. Clarice can fill us in on what we've missed."

Warren's Adam's apple protruded like a deformed goiter. Whenever he was confused (which was often, according to Clarice), he'd swallow so hard that the goiter bobbed up and down like it was trying to escape. After a couple of rapid swallows, he stammered, "I . . . I uh . . . I don't understand. What are you . . ."

Clarice came to his rescue. Patting his shoulder, she said, "Honey, it's nothing. I can handle this. Why don't you and the guys go check out the soil test. It's the next thing on our agenda anyway."

Tony was amused that Warren seemed put off by his roughed-up face. The putz no doubt thought Tony might take a swing at him. With a derisive laugh, Tony said, "Yeah, shove off, Warren. We have a different agenda to take care of."

Clarice squeezed Warren's hand. "It'll be all right, dear."

When Warren didn't get going, Tony laughed again. He had a putdown ready, but Mildred cut him off. She held up the folder that she'd been clutching to her ample bosom. "It's just another appraisal," she said. "We need Clarice to look it over." By now the two surveyors had walked off. Warren had no choice but to follow them or look sillier than he already did.

As soon as they were out of earshot, Clarice assumed a tough girl stance. "Okay, Tony, what's going on? And don't give me any shit about another appraisal."

With a broad sweep of his arm, Tony said, "According to Feldman, this is all yours now."

A sly smile played at her lips. "You know how it goes. The early bird gets the worm."

"And what do I get? A swift kick in the pants?"

"Don't be so dramatic. I did what I had to do. Things were spiraling out of control. Warren wasn't going to approve your loan, no matter what. The bank auditors—not to mention the Feds—were getting a little too curious about some of his other loans and the investments he managed. It was time for a change. And, as you well know, your favorite uncle was breathing down our neck by sending Nick to spy on us. To cap it all off, George's accident was a total screw-up." She gave him a cold stare. "Thanks to you and our dim-witted sheriff."

"But killing Nick was brilliant."

Clarice glanced at Mildred.

"Don't worry, she knows everything now."

"Then you both understand that I had no choice concerning Nick."

"Let me get this straight," said Tony. "You tell me to cool my heels while things settle down after you murdered him. Then you go behind my back and buy Baker Bluff all by your lonesome."

"I couldn't take any more chances that the property would slip out of our hands."

"*Your* hands, you mean."

She shrugged. "Warren had the dough; you didn't." She looked toward her husband and the surveyors. It appeared they were about to wrap up their test. "I don't have anything more to say to you." She turned to go. "Now, if you'll excuse me, I have some test results to review."

Tony held up both hands. "Not so fast. We weren't jawing when we said we had some papers for you." He turned to Mildred. "Show her what you've got there, Millie."

Mildred opened the folder and handed it to Clarice, who scanned the faded newspapers tucked inside. "If you're thinking of blackmailing me with these, you can forget it," she said. "Warren knows all about my past." She thrust the folder back into Mildred's hands. Looking squarely at Tony, she said, "I have no secrets from my husband."

"Just from me, huh?"

"Look, Tony. What we had was fun while it lasted, but in the end, money talks. You should know that by now."

"What I know is that you cleaned out the Destiny Group bank account. I had a stake in those funds, too, as *you* well know."

She smiled without warmth. "It was my name and my name alone on the bank account."

"And it's your name alone that will have to answer to the Feds when they come calling."

"The Feds? What do they have to do with anything?"

Tony grinned. "Seems your little scheme has hit another snag. Old George has died."

"How is that my concern?"

Tony turned to Mildred. "Give her the news."

"George was in Federal custody at the hospital, thanks to Sam Matthews' intervention. Now that he's died, you can bet Matthews' will have lots more questions about Nick's murder. From what Sheriff Pritchard says, Matthews already had doubts about the story you concocted. It's the sheriff's duty to be as forthcoming as he can."

"Fine. He can be forthcoming all he wants. But, don't forget, you're all involved, too. I think they call it accessories to a crime."

"Think again, sweetheart," said Tony. "The sheriff has the pistol you used to kill Nick. It hasn't been processed yet, but whose fingerprints do you think they'll find when it is?"

A horn's shrill blare cut short whatever comeback she had in mind. She flinched and said, "Now what?"

Tony waved as Leonard Pritchard and another man climbed out of the sheriff's vehicle. "Well, well, well," Tony said. "Looks like we have some company." He nudged Mildred. "Time for you to meet and greet. And don't forget to take that folder with you."

As Mildred trudged off to meet the sheriff, Clarice glared at Tony. "What are you up to now?"

"I know you recognize the sheriff. What about the bald guy with him?"

Clarice stepped closer to Tony until she was inches from his face. Her familiar lavender scented perfume made him feel slightly dizzy. Overcome by a sudden longing, Tony wondered if he'd misjudged her. Could they still salvage their relationship? Then she spoke and stomped on whatever feelings he had left for her. "Listen, I don't give a flying fuck who Leonard dragged out here. And, if you think it makes any difference to me whether Mildred sticks those newspapers in their faces, think again, jackass."

"Jackass? Oh, babe, where has all the love gone?"

"Straight to hell. Which is where you're headed if you even think of blackmailing me. Forget my fingerprints. As I said before, if I go down, you and Leonard are going down with me."

How could he have thought there might still be a chance for them? She was a heartless bitch and they'd never have a life together. "I'm sure that would be the case," he told her. "So, no, I don't intend to blackmail anyone. Let alone you."

Clarice studied him for a moment. "Then what do you intend?"

"It's been my experience that the public is rather quirky. Especially those who patronize high-class hotels and resorts. I think you'll find that rich snobs tend to be a little put off by murder and such things as you've been involved in. Not here, of course. In Portland. Now, here's the deal," he said, pointing at the bald man. "That guy is a reporter for the local newspaper. We invited him out here to give you some advance publicity about the super new development you're planning. He's anxious to get an exclusive interview and hear all about the exciting things you and Warren have in mind for this place. You can't beat free publicity."

"But?"

"All I have to do is give Mildred the high sign and the publicity gets a slightly different slant. Including a hot tip on Nick's murder case. That should make the Feds salivate. Don't worry about the rest of us, though. Pritchard, Mildred and I have agreed on an air-tight alibi. Too bad you don't have anyone in your corner anymore."

"You bastard! What do you want?"

"What I've always wanted, Clarice. Ownership of Baker Bluff."

She shook her head. "Not possible."

"Oh?" Tony caught Mildred's eye and started to raise his hand.

"Okay, okay. We can put your name on the deed. Satisfied?"

"Nope. I want a split of the action. Fifty-fifty like we planned."

"No way. Warren and I have put up all the money for this deal."

"Yeah, I know. Must have been a little short, though. Is that why you raided the Destiny Group account?" When she didn't respond, Tony shrugged and said, "But a girl's gotta do what a girl's gotta do, right?"

"Don't be glib. If I hadn't made those appraisals work, there wouldn't have been any funds for the account in the first place."

"That's beside the point now, isn't it?"

"Tell you what, Tony: I don't have a problem with you. Warren doesn't, either. So, let's settle this here and now. I know that you've got 25 Gs stashed in the office safe that you swindled out of Uncle Sol's share of your sales commissions. You ante up that dough and we'll call it a deal."

"What about Leonard and Mildred?"

"I couldn't care less. Just as long as he loses my pistol, Leonard can head up security or something if he still wants to stick around. It's always useful to have a crooked lawman on your team. Mildred can still be your buddy-buddy secretary. But they both need to keep their traps shut."

Tony grinned. Mildred shouldn't have worried. He still knew how to work the ladies. "I've always liked the way you think, babe."

"No more bullshitting, Tony. You or Leonard pull any more funny stuff and—"

"And what? You'll whack us?"

"Get that reporter over here. I'm done talking to you. Just get us the money or I'm calling the whole thing off, publicity or no publicity. Let the chips fall where they may. I've taken care of myself before and I can do it again."

"Where're you gonna be? I heard you've moved out of your house already."

"Warren and I are attending the Indians' Reburial Ceremony on Sunday. You can meet us at the new cemetery."

Just when Tony thought he had Clarice's number, she came up with something new. "Since when have you been interested in what the Injuns do?"

"Think about it, Tony. They're going to be out of work as soon as the dam is completed and the fishing goes bye-bye. We'll need cheap labor to get this project off the ground."

Tony snorted. "God help us! You're gonna hire a bunch of savages? What makes you think those lazy good-for-nothing redskins will have anything to do with you? Last time I checked they weren't so keen on whites, especially since they believe old George was falsely accused of murder."

Clarice shrugged. "Hunger is a strong motivator."

***

Tony whistled as he drove back to town. He'd pulled another disaster out of the fire and all was right with the world again. Well, almost. He still had Ellie's father to deal with, but Tony could cook up some plausible story to appease him. Hadn't he handled clever Clarice with ease? Handing over the twenty-five thousand to her and Warren was irksome, but a small price to pay for freedom. He'd planned to spend it on the purchase anyway. He was just a day away from the clutches of Uncle Sol, after all.

Mildred said, "I take it Clarice agreed to our demands."

"Yeah, no sweat. I told you I could handle that woman."

"You sure did, boss. We ought to celebrate."

Tony shook his head. "Not today. I've got some business at the office to finish up. Listen: why don't you take the rest of the day off? You deserve it."

"I didn't do much but stand there." She tactfully avoided mentioning that the plan was her idea.

"Standing next to the reporter with the folder in your hot little hands was enough to make Clarice see the error of her ways."

Mildred laughed as he pulled the convertible alongside the curb next to the office. "Glad to oblige," she said, exiting the car. "If you need me again, I'll be at home."

He waved her off and entered the office. The shades were drawn and it took a moment for his eyes to adjust to the dim light after the sun's bright glare.

He blinked twice and then gasped. As he stared at the extent of the destruction, it hit him. *The safe. Oh, my God. The safe!*

"Don't worry, son. You ain't been robbed," said Uncle Sol. "I have!"

CHAPTER THIRTY-NINE

Tony didn't know what stunned him more—Solomon Rossi showing up at the office or the fat old man exerting himself enough to search the place. It didn't matter; he had the ledgers. Tony's gut wrenched as if he'd been sucker punched. He knew he looked as bad as he felt. Suddenly light headed, he reached for the nearest desk to steady himself.

"Sit down before you fall down, why don't ya?" Uncle Sol's tone was controlled, but Tony had no doubt that he was in for it. His uncle did not suffer fools or cheaters lightly and Tony was guilty of both sins. He had to think fast if he was going to wrangle his way out of this one. Tony slumped into a chair and, stalling for time, pulled a handkerchief out of his pocket and wiped the sweat off his forehead. The office was stifling hot, but his skin was cold and clammy. He wracked his brain for something he could say, something that would sound believable. "Uncle Sol," he began. "I can explain."

"No, let me explain, Antonio," he said. The controlled tone had given way to fierce anger. "You've been cheating me since day one!" He slammed the ledgers onto Mildred's desk.

Tony swallowed the bile rising in his throat and stammered, "But I—"

"Shut up!" Uncle Sol shouted. "It's all right there," he said pointing a stubby finger at the ledgers. "You've been keeping two sets of books—one for the real figures and one for cheating me with."

All Tony could think of was to play dumb. "Two sets of books? I don't know what you're talking about. Mildred handles the records, not me."

"Are you saying that your secretary has been fiddling with the numbers behind your back?"

Now that he mentioned it, why not blame it on Millie? She was the perfect patsy. Tony scratched his head as if considering the possibility that he'd been duped. "Who else could it be?" he asked. "No one in the office besides her has access to those books, not even me. Millie guards them with her life, but I just thought she was being extra careful. I never thought she was covering her backside by keeping them off limits." He shook his head, feigning disgust. "I trusted that woman completely. Damn!"

Uncle Sol didn't say anything for a moment and his expression was hard to read. There was no mistaking that he was angry. The ruddy jowls and bushy eyebrows scrunched together like a brutal gash were a dead give-away. But whether he'd bought the yarn Tony had made up on the fly was not clear. He'd never expected his uncle to come snooping around the office—the man practically lived in his recliner—or he'd have had a story all prepared. Tony cursed himself for not staying on top of things. Murder or not, it wasn't like Uncle Sol to just forget about why he'd sent Nick to spy on him. It was all Clarice's fault. Killing Nick and then double-crossing him had thrown Tony off his game.

The old geezer hadn't seemed to notice the bloodstains that were still visible on the cover of the ledgers. Tony had no idea how he would ever explain that. Thankfully, Uncle Sol was only interested in what was inside the ledgers—and his missing twenty-five large. He rolled his buggy eyes at Tony. "You stupid idiot! Don't you know any better than to trust a broad? Especially with money. *My* money."

If Uncle Sol only knew . . . Tony had been betrayed all right, but the broad pulling the fast one wasn't dear old Millie. He shrugged his shoulders to acknowledge his misplaced trust. "You're right, Uncle Sol. I should never have trusted Mildred. I thought she was loyal, but I guess it was only to herself."

"Where is she?" he asked.

"Who?"

"Who do you think? The swindler you call a secretary, that's who."

"I guess she's at home. I gave her the day off."

That answer wasn't what Uncle Sol wanted to hear. He berated Tony for several minutes, the gist of which was that his nephew was a stupid fool. He'd not only hired a cheater but had allowed her and his two salesmen to take the day off. "It's summer, not Christmas!" Uncle Sol shouted, spittle flying. "This office ought to be hopping with business. No one should be wasting time at home when there's money to be made." He pushed Mildred's desk phone toward Tony and said, "Call her up, Antonio. Tell her to hot-foot it over here right now."

"Aw, Uncle Sol, don't worry. Go on back to Portland. I can fire the bitch myself."

"Don't you get it, boy? I want my dough. And I'm not leaving until I get it."

Tony had no problem convincing Mildred to come back to the office after he'd given her the day off. She was probably glad he'd called her. What worried him was what her reaction would be when Uncle Sol confronted her. Tony hoped to God she'd play along and take the fall. She should know he'd make it up to her somehow.

Mildred had never seen Uncle Sol in person, but she was no dummy. She didn't say a word when she hustled through the door and saw the trashed office—or who was sitting at her desk. There was only one man alive who could make her boss look so miserable and that's exactly how Tony appeared when she glanced his way. She still hadn't spoken, but her eyes told Tony that she knew the jig was up. Uncle Sol glared at her with such menace that it was a wonder she didn't turn around and high-tail it back home. Instead, she greeted him as if she'd been invited for a pleasant visit. "You must be Uncle Sol," she said. "I'm pleased to meet you at last."

Uncle Sol snorted, "I wouldn't be so sure about that." He flipped open one of the ledgers. "Not after what I've seen in this here little book of yours."

Tony met Mildred's questioning look with a non-committal shrug. *Here it comes.*

"My nephew says you've cheated me out of 25 big ones," Uncle Sol said. "It's time for you to pay up."

Mildred didn't flinch at the accusation or try to deny it. Just as Tony had hoped, she came through for him. Even with her back to the wall, her first instinct was to protect him. "I'm so sorry," she said. "I don't know what I was thinking." She mustered a contrite look and laid it on thick. "You've always been good to me, boss. I never meant to do you or your uncle harm."

Tony breathed easier, but she'd said nothing to satisfy Uncle Sol. "Spare us the sappy act, lady," he said. "I don't give a tinker's damn how sorry you are." He held out a beefy hand palm-side up. "Just fork over the dough. All of it."

Mildred's eyes darted to the store room where they kept the safe. No, Tony thought, alarmed again. *Not the safe, woman. Not the safe.* Everything depended on keeping the money stashed there. He had to turn it over to Clarice on Sunday or he was out of the game for good. Surely Mildred realized that. Tony warned her with a slight shake of his head. Don't, his eyes pleaded as he held his breath again.

Mildred said, "What makes you think I still have any of the money?"

Tony exhaled slowly and suppressed a nervous grin. *That's the way, old girl.* Millie got what the situation called for and delivered.

Uncle Sol stood up faster than Tony thought possible for such a bulky ox. "Listen, sister," he growled, "maybe I didn't make my meaning clear. I want my money. And I want it NOW."

Mildred tried again. "But I don't have it, sir. I spent every last dime."

Tony couldn't have been more pleased with her performance. She was quite the little actress. Uncle Sol was so angry his jowls began to shake like Jell-O. "Don't give me any of that malarkey," he said. "Lover boy over there blamed the theft on you, but I know the two of you are in this scheme together." He grabbed some papers off her desk and continued his tirade. "Before Nick got himself killed, he told me Tony was itching to buy some hot property. I figure that so-called missing twenty-five thousand would be enough to buy something mighty fine." He waved the papers he clutched in Tony's face. "And these here papers prove you've got a nice little shell game going." With a bitter laugh he said, "Destiny Group, my ass!"

Tony was speechless, astounded that his uncle knew anything about Destiny. He was no dummy when it came to business and even had a few shady deals going himself, but Tony had never thought he'd be able to uncover the Destiny Group's activities. The paper work he waved around wasn't exactly easy to follow. Clarice had seen to that.

"I know you don't run a scam like this without help," Uncle Sol continued. "I figure there's gotta be more cheaters in on this than just you and your secretary."

Tony and Mildred exchanged looks but said nothing.

Uncle Sol sneered. "Don't worry, that part don't concern me none. So, let's cut to the chase. The only thing we need to discuss now is my share."

"Uh," Tony stammered, "your share?"

"Time to divvy up the proceeds, boy. The scam is over. You used my business to put yourself in business and now I aim to collect what's owed me. We can start with the money you cheated me out of. Think of that as a business loan that you're repaying."

Tony glanced toward the store room. The money inside the safe was all he had left. That had to go to Clarice, no matter what. Once again, his dream was slipping out of his grasp. He could imagine all too well what would happen when Uncle Sol forced him to open the safe. He would push Tony and Mildred aside and stick both greedy fists inside and scoop up the stacks of twenty dollar bills as fast as he could. He'd yell for Tony to get him a big bag to carry it all.

Uncle Sol caught him looking at the store room. "Don't bother with the safe. I already checked. It's empty."

The safe is empty? He whirled to face Mildred. She was supposed to be play-acting. Had she betrayed him for real? "What . . . what have you done?"

Mildred seemed quite pleased with herself. "Given her past, I knew Clarice would eventually double-cross you, Tony." She sighed. "And double-crossing you meant I'd be left flat broke. I'm not a young woman who can start all over again. I had to take some precautions to protect my interests. I invested the twenty-five thousand in my own little dream. I'm set for life now."

Tony had to believe that Mildred was still play-acting. She must have moved the money when she learned about Clarice from those old Portland newspapers. She probably figured it would be safer stuffed under her mattress. There was no way she'd ever betray him like Clarice had. Not after she'd come up with the plan to use the money in the safe to pay off Clarice. Tony decided to play along and make the act look more convincing. Tony took a step toward her, outrage plastered on his face. "Why, you two-timing hussy. I trusted you!"

Uncle Sol grabbed Tony's arm. "Don't feel so good does it, boy?"

Tony shook himself loose from his uncle's grasp. He was buying both their acts. "I'll kill you!" he shouted at Mildred.

Uncle Sol scowled. "Like you killed Nick?"

Tony stared at him open-mouthed. "What?"

"Don't think I haven't noticed the blood on the ledgers or the mop in the store room. No old Injun murdered Nick." He pointed a finger at Tony. "You did!"

Tony squeaked out a denial. "You're wrong."

"Maybe so, but I'm not the only one who thinks you're guilty of murder—and apparently, a sin he thinks is a whole lot worse."

"I have no idea what you're talking about." It was the first truthful thing Tony had said yet.

Uncle Sol shrugged. "Well, you better figure it out soon, boy. I'm gonna let you off the hook for sharing any of your other ill-gotten gains with me. All I want is the money you stole from me." He paused to light his cigar. "But hear this: you got a lot more to worry about than me." Using his fingers to form an imaginary pistol, he aimed it at Tony and grinned. "There's one hell of a ticked off FBI man out there gunning for you."

CHAPTER FORTY

Jess Harmon looked up from the paperwork on the bank's conference table that he'd been studying and frowned at Sam. "What are you doing here?" he snarled. Sam's bureau chief had taken the news that his undercover role had been compromised without censure but Harmon hadn't been so understanding. He'd claimed that Sam's ability to help him with the Chambers murder investigation had been irreparably damaged. He'd told Sam to stick to dealing with the Indians and he'd solve the case without his assistance. It was a radical turnaround from the amiable but insistent way he'd encouraged Sam's participation early on. The tension between the two men had become so strained that Sam found himself avoiding his former partner unless necessary. Today was necessary.

"I'm here to follow the money," Sam answered.

Harmon gestured to the stacks of files in front of him. "What do you think I've been doing?" he asked. It was a rhetorical question sarcastically delivered. "I thought I made it clear the last time we talked. I'll handle the Chambers case. You have plenty to do without interrupting my work." He adjusted his glasses, opened a file and began to read.

Sam was in no mood to be dismissed. "Listen, Jess, you can drop the aggrieved partner act. You know I never wanted to work on the Chambers case but I agreed to team up partly because of a guilty conscience and partly because I wanted to prove myself worthy of your respect. I was relieved that you didn't seem to harbor any ill feelings toward me, despite what my mistakes have caused you. Aside from all that, Pete Chambers was a decent and honorable man who didn't deserve to die the way he did. It's because of Pete that I'm at the bank now. I've just learned some information that may be related to the financials you're examining."

Harmon peered at Sam over the top of his glasses. He sounded as skeptical as he looked. "Yeah? And what's that?"

"Tony Rossi is a realtor in town who is involved in a complex real estate scam known as the Destiny Group." Sam decided not to reveal that Rossi was also a rapist and more than likely involved in the murder of his own cousin. As far as Sam was concerned, Tony Rossi's fate was sealed. He would see to that himself.

"Rossi's a top-notch salesman," Sam continued, "but not smart enough to put a complex scam together without some help. And I believe he got the help he needed right here at the bank."

"Okay, you have my attention," said Harmon. "But I don't see how a real estate scam is related to Pete Chambers' murder."

"I have a hunch it's connected.

Harmon tossed his glasses on top of the file. "Jesus, you barged in here based on a hunch? I need evidence, not hunches."

Sam raised his hand palm side out. "Just hear me out a minute. When I got my bank loan to buy our house, the appraisal was handled by a woman named Clarice Nestor who is supposedly Tony's mistress. Unlike Tony, she has some smarts — enough to put together a profitable plan like the Destiny Group. The appraisal went through without a hitch, but afterward she contacted me about an investment opportunity that her husband managed.

"Her husband being Warren Nestor, the bank's manager?"

Sam nodded. "I never had any extra funds to invest after buying the house so I never spoke to the man."

"And you won't — at least about any investment to make. He has resigned his position and I'm told he's starting his own business."

"Very interesting," Sam said. I never paid much attention to the name of the investment his wife pitched at the time, but — "

"Let me guess," Harmon said. "The Destiny Group?"

"Exactly."

"I think I know where you're going with this. I've been reviewing Chambers' financial records and I've discovered something odd. He'd been making some significant money in an investment portfolio managed by Warren Nestor for the past two years. Then about two weeks before his murder, the account balance had inexplicibly dropped to practically nothing—with no record of any withdrawals by Chambers or any other documentation to explain the loss. That may be the source of the change in his behavior that you and everyone else had noticed."

"Makes sense," agreed Sam. "When he found out that the investment he'd been relying on to fund his retirement was suddenly no longer available, he would've been undeniably upset."

"So, he confronts Nestor and demands his money back or threatens to expose the fraudulent investment and—"

"Gets killed for his trouble," Sam finished.

"That might explain Warren Nestor's sudden departure from the bank, but it doesn't prove he killed Chambers."

"It's just speculation at this point, but if Chambers had accused him of theft or fraud, Nestor would've had motive to shut him up."

"I guess I have some more digging to do," said Harmon. With a forced smile he added, "Want to stick around and give me a hand with the shovel?"

Sam supposed Harmon meant the offer as an apology of sorts but he was too late. "Sorry," Sam said, "I have some urgent digging of my own to do."

CHAPTER FORTY-ONE

Mildred plopped down on the barstool next to Tony's and said, "We gotta stop meeting like this, boss."

Tony shifted on the stool so that his back was toward her. He'd been laying low ever since he'd learned that Sam Matthews was looking for him. Although Uncle Sol hadn't mentioned him by name, it only made sense that Matthews was who he meant. Tony didn't want to see anyone right now, least of all a ticked off FBI agent with a gun. But he was tired of playing hide and seek and took a chance on getting a couple of beers at Dizzy's. Running into Mildred was almost as bad as facing Matthews. "Get lost," he growled.

"You still mad at me?"

"What gave you that idea?" How the woman could even think he'd forgive her for selling him out was beyond him. "You're no better than Clarice."

"I take it you're referring to the cash in the safe."

He didn't want to see her, let alone talk to her, but she'd egged him on. He whirled around to face her. "You mean the cash *not* in the safe."

"Oh, that."

What he'd thought was only an act turned out to be true. Mildred had helped herself to his money. But she hadn't spent it all like she claimed. She finally came clean and coughed up the twenty-five thousand when Uncle Sol refused to leave without it. Now she had nothing to show for her cheating ways, just like Tony. He signaled for another round and drained the glass dry as soon as Freddie had placed it in front of him. "Hit me again," he said when Mildred ordered coffee.

After Freddie left to fetch their drinks, Mildred asked, "Have you

278

heard the latest news?"

Tony gave her a disgusted look. "How could I hear anything? Been living underground like a goddamn mole for two days now."

"You really think the FBI is after you? I thought Uncle Sol was just trying to scare you."

Mildred had no idea about his little fling with Ellie—and he wasn't about to enlighten her. "Yeah, you're probably right," he said. "Uncle Sol would say anything to get his money but I'm not taking any chances when it comes to the FBI."

"I bet Uncle Sol just got the name wrong. The FBI was really after Warren Nestor."

"What the hell are you talking about?"

"That's the news I've been trying to tell you. The FBI has arrested Warren."

"Ha! What'd the wimp do? Jaywalk across Front Street?"

Freddie arrived with their drinks and Mildred waited until he'd left to continue.

"Turns out Warren wasn't as clueless as we thought. He and Clarice have been running another scam right under our noses. Only it wasn't so little. I've heard they made off with a bundle in some phony investment program that Warren ran. The word on the street is that Warren killed that foreman who worked out at the dam. Apparently, he was one of the investors who got taken to the cleaners. When he threatened to expose the scam, Warren got rid of him."

"Jesus," Tony said, shaking his head. "I didn't think Warren had enough guts to kill a spider. What about Clarice? How come she didn't get arrested? She's the killer in that family."

"As far as I know, she's still walking around a free woman. You know how clever she is. I can't imagine she'd leave anything behind to incriminate her."

Another more horrifying thought suddenly occurred to Tony. "Can the Feds link Warren's scam to the Destiny Group?"

"Don't worry about that, boss. After Uncle Sol's little visit, I got rid of everything to do with the Destiny Group that could be traced back to us."

"But . . . but the ledgers . . ."

"Uncle Sol didn't care about them after he got his money. They're nothing but ashes now."

Tony breathed a sigh of relief and gulped down his drink.

"Aren't you going to thank me?" she asked.

He ignored her and concentrated on downing his beer.

Finally, she asked, "What are you planning to do, drink yourself into oblivion?"

"Might as well, I don't have nowhere else to go, thanks to you."

"Aw, boss, that's just not true."

"How could you do it, Mildred? How could you turn on me after all I've done for you?"

"I got Uncle Sol off your back. That ought to count for something."

"Oh, sure. He's fat, dumb and happy, now that you paid him off." He slammed his empty glass on the counter. "With the goddamn money that was supposed to go to Clarice!"

Freddie was in front of Tony in a flash and picked up the glass he'd slammed. "Hey, man, ease up. You want a refill; all you have to do is ask."

Tony waved him away and leaned in close to Mildred. "You knew I was counting on that dough to keep the deal alive."

"The deal *is* still alive."

Tony stared at her. He had no idea what she'd been drinking but it wasn't coffee. "Are you out of your mind? Warren's arrest doesn't change the fact that Clarice is still in the game and expecting twenty-five thousand in cold hard cash. And, as you well know, I ain't got jack shit now."

Mildred opened her purse and took out a small account booklet. "Not exactly true." She placed it on the counter in front of Tony. "Take a look at this."

"What is it?" Tony asked, without picking it up.

"A record of my saving account deposits. Note the balance. It's more than enough to pay off Clarice and then some."

Curiosity got the better of Tony and he picked up the booklet. He studied the account a moment and then blurted, "Jesus H. Christ! There's a fortune here. How in the hell did you pull this off?"

Mildred shifted on the barstool. "Well, it's like I told Uncle Sol: I had to protect my interests since I didn't trust Clarice any more than

I'd trust a junkyard dog not to bite. I've been siphoning off the top of every Destiny Group sale since the very beginning."

Tony shook his head. What a fool he'd been. He'd be outraged if he didn't feel so stupid. Two of the slickest con women around and he had to hook up with both of them. "And now you're set for life, is that it?" He tossed the booklet at her. "What're you trying to do, make me feel even worse?"

"No," Mildred said, "I'm trying to make you feel better." She signaled for Freddie and told him to refill her coffee. "Bring a cup for Tony, too. And keep the java coming, Freddie. Tony and I have some plans to discuss." She hoisted herself off the barstool and motioned for Tony to follow her to one of the corner tables. "You're going to like what I propose to do with the dough."

Curiosity got the best of Tony. He'd even drink coffee if that's what it took to discover what Mildred had in that scheming mind of hers now. He couldn't trust her any more than he could trust Clarice, but at least he could listen. He might even pick up a tactic or two. "Okay," he said after Freddie had brought the coffee to their table. "What's the latest con you've got hatched up?"

"It's not a con. It's an offer. I propose that we use the money in my account to not only pay off the twenty-five thousand promised to Clarice, but offer to buy her out completely."

"We? You're including me in this?"

Mildred grinned. "Of course. You didn't think I'd taken the Destiny Group funds just for myself, did you?"

Tony slurped his coffee. Eying her over the rim, he asked, "Tell me the truth, Millie. This isn't another one of your clever switcheroos that I'll regret later, is it?"

"The only thing you'll regret is if you don't buy out Clarice and open the resort yourself."

"What makes you think she'll take the money and run?" Despite his earlier misgivings, he liked what Mildred had said. If what she proposed was on the up and up, then everything might work out after all. "Why not just pay her the money she wants and go forward as partners like we'd already agreed?"

"Listen, I know you have a thing for Clarice, but it's time you woke up and faced facts. Your sweetie pie is a schemer, not a lover. I don't think she'll stick around even for you as soon as we start waving the greenbacks in front of her. She must be a little worried, now that Warren got caught. I wouldn't be surprised if she killed that foreman instead of him. Maybe she'd rather not take a chance that her hubby turns on her. I think she'll take the money in a flash.

"Well," Tony said, "I guess there's only one way to find out."

After she left the bar he wondered if he should've told her about his other problem. She was so good at coming up with plans, maybe she could figure out how he was supposed to deal with Sam Matthews. If Tony had only known Matthews was a Fed from the get-go, he'd never have come within six feet of his daughter. What was done was done. He could still blame the Longstreet kid. Everyone in town believed he was single-handedly trying to shut down the dam. That he'd attacked an innocent white girl was certainly possible, too. Besides, Tony reasoned, who'd take an Injun's word over his, a respected member of the community? A traumatized girl's account wouldn't hold any weight, either.

He smiled as he sauntered back to the barstool. Mildred and Clarice weren't the only clever ones around. "Forget the coffee, Freddie," he told the barkeep, "and bring me some whiskey."

"Are you celebrating or commiserating?" Freddie asked.

"Neither," Tony answered. "Just getting ready."

"Ready?"

"Haven't you heard? The Reburial Ceremony for the Injuns is this Sunday. I plan to be there with bells on."

Freddie shrugged, a puzzled look etched on his usually placid face. "Whatever you say, man. Whatever you say."

CHAPTER FORTY-TWO

There was a commotion at the village when Danny arrived home. Oscar stood outside their house talking to several villagers who'd gathered around a familiar looking government vehicle. Reba had warned Sam Matthews not to return to the village, but Danny figured the warning would have no effect. What father could stay away from his daughter, a daughter who'd suffered as much as Ellie? It was only a matter of time before Matthews showed up.

Now that he was on their turf again, the overriding sentiment at Celilo was "to hell with him and his government." Danny felt the same way, but he had an additional score to settle because of Ellie. He'd fight Matthews himself if she didn't want to see him. She'd been adamant about not wanting anything to do with her father and Danny was only too happy to oblige.

He nodded at Oscar as he exited his truck. His grandfather nodded back. The message was clear: "We've got a problem here." To make matters worse, more than a few of the men had been drinking; the stench of liquor and sweat was overpowering. Danny noticed that Sam's truck tires had already been slashed. The tires would be the least of Mitchell's worries. The guys were itching to give Ellie's father a nasty beating. Danny knew every one of the men who were standing around the truck acting more and more agitated. He'd even gotten into a scrape with one or two of them himself and knew what they were capable of. They would turn on him or Oscar faster than a woman changes her mind if Danny didn't do something to diffuse the situation.

With a reassuring nod to his grandfather, Danny quickly made his way through the crowd to seek out Clarence Thunder Clouds. "Hey, brother, what's going on?" Danny asked. Clarence was the best drummer in the village and was well respected by everyone. Danny had danced to his beat many times at the Long House and knew him to be an even-tempered guy. Not today. He was as worked up as the rest of the men milling about.

Clarence glanced toward the house and scowled. "You got uninvited company inside there."

"Is that right? Who?"

"That no-good liar, Sam Matthews. He didn't do nothin' to protect George like he said he would."

Danny nodded. "Since when has a white guy ever done what he said he would? Especially if it involves us."

Clarence hooted. "You got that right, man!"

Danny gestured to the crowd. "So, you guys plan on teaching him a lesson, or what?"

"Yep," he said, patting the knife sheath he had strapped to his leg. "You joining us?" He pointed to Oscar standing guard duty at the front door. "Or are you gonna play peacemaker like your grandfather over there?"

"Hell, no," Danny said. After getting out of jail, he'd made no bones about wanting to beat the living daylights out of Matthews. "I'm going inside right now and drag the S.O.B. out here. Tell the others to give me a few minutes and he'll be all yours."

Oscar took Danny aside at the door and said, "You in with these boys?"

Danny shrugged. "I know what I'm doing."

His grandfather raised a doubtful eyebrow. "He's FBI, Danny. Taking him on won't be good for any of us."

"I get that." Danny looked out at the growing crowd and frowned. "But I'm not so sure they care." After a short pause he asked, "Does Reba still have that medical stretcher?"

Oscar nodded, but the question threw him. "What are you —"

"Don't worry, Grandpa. I've got this covered."

CHAPTER FORTY-THREE

Reba knew Sam wouldn't stay away from the village while his daughter was here but she hadn't expected him today. She'd warned him that his presence at Celilo would enrage the villagers, but he'd come anyway. He lied just like all the other shuyapus but he wasn't a coward. The only thing he feared was losing Ellie. Reba had refused to let him see her the first time he came by because it was too soon. Ellie had insisted that she wanted nothing to do with her father and Reba had honored her tearful demand.

Reba didn't want to see him, either, but she felt he had a right to know what had happened to his daughter and George. He needed to understand what his betrayal had cost them. Reba could tell he'd been crushed by the news, but she'd felt no satisfaction in seeing his pain. She'd seen enough suffering and she was tired of it. She might never forgive him for using her—and Celilo—to further his career, but she didn't seek the revenge that Danny and the others clamored for. Reba was a healer and healing was what she wanted.

Caring for Sam's daughter was a responsibility she'd willingly taken on, but it would take time to repair the loss Ellie had suffered. The damage to her body was temporary, but the damage to her heart and soul was permanent. The best Reba could do was to be there for her. She could keep her safe and secure and even loved, but what she really needed was her father so Reba wasn't inclined to refuse Sam's entry a second time. Although Ellie didn't realize it, sending him away again would have just prolonged her recovery. She was a strong girl but the ordeal she'd been through had nearly broken her. She'd hardly spoken in the few days she'd been at Celilo and preferred to be by herself. She slept a lot but it was a fitful, unrestful sleep. She said she had no appetite and it was a struggle to get her to eat at all. Ellie had basically shut down and Reba was very concerned about her long-term health. How she'd react to seeing her father again was problematic but Reba had to believe it was for the best.

Oscar was more concerned with the trouble that Sam would cause them, than with Ellie's health. He was right to insist that Sam hurry inside the house. By tacit agreement, Oscar would try to defuse any hostile actions by the villagers and Reba would try to unite father and daughter. Neither task would be easy.

Reba set a pitcher of water and glasses on the table. "Water is my blessing on both of you," she said. "Drink."

After they'd taken a few sips, Ellie addressed her father in a soft but firm voice. "I can't believe you came here again. You knew I didn't want to see you."

"I understand that you don't want me here. No one at Celilo does. But no matter how much you hate me right now, no matter how much I deserve your hatred, you are my daughter." His voice broke as he looked at his daughter's bruised and swollen face. "You're all I have, Ellie. I promised your mother before she died that I'd always protect you. But when you needed me the most, I failed you. And for that I will never forgive myself. I don't expect you to forgive me, either. The best I can hope for is that you will let me into your life again."

"What life is that? The real one or the one you made up?"

Sam faced Reba. "It's a question that you deserve answered as well." He pulled his wallet out of his back pocket and withdrew his FBI badge. Tossing it on the table, he said, "I'm not an agent anymore."

Ellie shrugged. "I don't believe you. You'll just say whatever you think we want to hear."

"You've really quit?" asked Reba.

"Not yet. First, I have to—"

"I knew it. Ellie said. "You're not quitting."

Reba took hold of her hand. "Let's hear him out."

Danny opened the front door and stomped into the room. "Yeah, let the man spin us another tall tale."

"Sit down, Danny," ordered Reba. She poured him a glass of water from the pitcher. "Drink and then you can join the conversation."

Danny glanced at Ellie, who'd folded her arms and pointedly glared at her father. He downed the water in one long gulp. "Matthews can have his say," he said. "But we've got a big problem outside." He held his hand palm-side up to reassure his mother. "Don't worry, I'm on it." He turned to Matthews. "Whatever story you have in mind, you better spit it out fast."

Sam nodded. "I realize full well that I don't deserve the trust of anyone here, but what I'm going to tell you now is the absolute truth." Sam ignored Danny's derisive snort and continued. "When Reba told me what had happened to Ellie, I was determined to kill Tony Rossi. I didn't care about my job or anything else. I wanted revenge and I wanted it now."

Danny didn't say anything, but the hard edge in his eyes and jaw softened a bit. Reba's son knew about revenge.

"As soon as I left Celilo, I headed straight to Rossi's office, but he wasn't there. The place had been ransacked—chairs upended, files scattered across the floor, and desks raided. It was a thorough trashing." Sam looked at Danny. "My first thought was that you'd beat me to the punch."

"Naturally I'd be the first one to blame. The savage Indian strikes again."

"The blame actually belongs to Tony's uncle, a man named Solomon Rossi. He admitted that he'd torn the place apart."

"What for?" asked Danny.

"Turns out he owns the business and had long suspected that his nephew was cheating him out of money that was rightfully his. He tore the office apart looking for the proof."

Danny looked at Ellie. She had begun to shiver at the mention of Tony Rossi. "So, what? We all know Rossi is a no-good bum."

"I'm getting there. Solomon Rossi claimed he sent Nick to work in the office so that he could learn the business from his cousin. But Nick was really sent to spy on Tony. He was supposed to get evidence that proved Tony was cheating his uncle. Unfortunately, Nick was killed before he could do so."

Ellie sighed. "So, Nick was just like you—claiming to be someone he wasn't."

Sam winced and continued. "I think Nick found the ledgers, which was the proof his uncle wanted, and Tony caught up with him before he could act on it."

"You think he murdered his own cousin?" asked Reba.

"Maybe," Sam said. "I definitely think George Featherstone was at the wrong place at the wrong time and got picked as the scapegoat. Nick was killed at Tony's office, not Baker Bluff. Someone had cleaned up a bloody mess but the leftovers were still in the storeroom. Whether the murder was by Tony's hand or someone else's, remains unclear. There was blood all over the incriminating ledgers."

"Poor Nick," said Ellie, shuddering. "Even if he was a liar, he didn't deserve to die."

"But Tony does," said Danny.

"I felt the same way when I found out what he'd done to Ellie," Sam said.

Reba noted that when Sam reached for her hand, Ellie didn't pull away. A good sign.

"I'm so sorry all this has happened, Ellie. I meant it when I said I was quitting the bureau. I hope with all my heart that we can start our lives over. I have just a couple of things to do first."

"Like what?" asked Ellie.

"Like overseeing the Reburial Ceremony on Sunday."

"Ha!" Danny said. "Never mind Tony Rossi. Getting those old bones into the concrete pit is a bigger priority."

"No," said Sam. "The reburial is my responsibility and I plan to make sure that it's conducted with the respect your ancestors deserve. My priority is to arrest Tony Rossi. He's going to jail for rape and suspicion of murder."

Danny exploded. "That's chicken shit! I thought you were going to put him in the ground. What happened to your so-called need for blood revenge?"

Sam glanced at Ellie. "Oh, I still feel the need. I could act on it just like I could act on the need I still have for whiskey. I almost gave myself permission to do both. As an FBI agent, I could even make killing Tony look justified under the law. My assignment gives me vast latitude in determining proper action."

"So, why didn't you do it then?" asked Danny. "Don't tell me a trained G-man like you couldn't find the lowlife?"

"No, I stopped looking for him."

Danny threw his hands in the air. "You've got to be kidding!"

"I don't have to look for him. Thanks to a reliable source, I know exactly where he's going to be on Sunday — the Reburial Ceremony."

"Good," said Danny. "Then I know where to find him, too."

"You might want to think about that some."

"Why?"

"Because the more I considered it, the more I realized that killing Tony, like my drinking, was the easy way out." Sam turned to his daughter. "Believe me, Tony will pay for what he did to you. A court of law will guarantee that."

"Not if I find him first," said Danny. "*I* will guarantee that."

Oscar opened the front door and shouted, "You 'bout done? Things are getting ugly out here."

Danny said to Reba, "We'll need your medicine bag and plenty of bandages. And the medical stretcher, too."

Reba wondered what he had in mind, but didn't ask any questions.

"Ellie," Danny said. "Go get a blanket off one of the mattresses and bring it in here."

"What's going on?" asked Sam.

"I'm going to help you leave the village in one piece."

Sam pushed his chair away from the table and stood up. "I'm not afraid to face whoever's outside."

"It doesn't matter. You're going to go along with me on this. Just know that I'm doing it for Ellie and my mother, not you. The truth is, I hadn't decided for sure when I came in here whether I'd help you, even for them."

"What changed your mind?"

"Ellie is still angry and confused, but even I can tell she loves you." Danny caught Reba's eye as she carried the supplies back to the table. "The same goes for my mother. And that's good enough for me."

Reba smiled. *My son is a wise warrior.* Sam wasn't convinced. "I don't need you to protect me, Danny."

Reba laid her hand on Sam's arm. "Let him help you. It will do you both good."

A few minutes later, Danny and Oscar carried Sam out of the house on the stretcher. He was covered in a thin blanket and bandaged from head to toe. "Sorry, guys, Danny said to the waiting crowd. "I got to him first."

CHAPTER FORTY-FOUR

"Okay, let's get this bird in the air," said Gross, swinging his legs into the pilot's seat.

"Be right with you," Sam said.

As soon as his men had loaded and strapped the final pine boxes containing Indian remains onto the loading skids, Sam conducted a last-minute check. They'd already transported 170 of the coffin-like cargo from Memaloose and Graves Islands to the new cemetery at Wish-Ham without incident. This would be their final trip before the ceremony started and Sam was leaving nothing to chance. The Reburial Ceremony was an important spiritual occasion for the Wy-ams and other tribes who had ancestors buried at the former site. Sam was determined that the reburial process would be conducted with the respect and honor their ancestors deserved. That meant double-checking the transport portion of the process to make sure it went as smoothly as possible. When he was satisfied that the straps holding the boxes in place were secure, he inspected the outside of the craft one more time before climbing aboard.

"You ready now?" Gross asked, irritably. No matter what Sam said to the contrary, Gross had interpreted his cautious approach to their task as a reflection on him. His piloting skills were never in question, as far as Sam was concerned. After so many trips, the process had become almost routine, but never unimpressive. The maneuvers during liftoff had to be coordinated just right. First, to get everything centered, Gross moved the stick around and adjusted the rudder pedals. Next, he rotated the throttle and pulled up on the collective. Once the craft rose into the air, he eased the stick forward and headed for the new cemetery. As the big bird flew, it was only two miles from the rocky crest of Memaloose Island to Wish-Ham.

Their route took them over the turbulent waters of Celilo Falls and the Wy-am fishermen perched along its banks. Not for the first time, Sam regretted his role in the destruction of the falls and all that the Indians held sacred.

Leaving Celilo Village on a stretcher in the back of Danny's truck was not his finest moment. The government truck he'd driven that day was still sitting out at Celilo with four slashed tires. At least Sam had accomplished what he'd set out to do—he'd seen his daughter again. Ellie hadn't been as receptive as he'd have liked, but it was a first step. After what she'd experienced, he was more than willing to let her work through her feelings toward him for as long as it took. He just wanted to have her back with him where she belonged. Quitting the bureau and remaining sober would go a long way toward restoring her faith in him.

Reba's response to his visit was more positive. Despite his failure to protect George as he'd promised, and the animosity his undercover role had caused, she seemed willing to give him another chance to redeem himself. The villagers at Celilo were another matter. He'd be hard pressed to do anything that would regain their trust. The best he could do was to ensure that the Reburial Ceremony came off without a hitch.

Midway through the shuttle from Memaloose to Wish-Ham, they flew over the dam. Sam had been tipped off by Mike that "something big" was in the works by Danny and his gang. The details were sketchy, but Sam figured that whatever they had planned wouldn't be good, especially since Ernie had been heard bragging about all the dynamite they had on hand. "They're aiming to take out the dam," warned Mike. Sam knew that wasn't possible, but they could do enough damage to crack the structure and set the project back by months, not to mention endangering a few lives in the process.

With Mike's warning in mind, he gazed down at the dam through the helicopter's Plexiglas front. Although it was a Sunday, construction did not stop. The crews were on site 24/7 and, as the dam neared completion, the schedule would undoubtedly involve overtime. The activity Sam observed at the various work sites seemed normal, but the crew assembled on the spillway gave him pause. Hard hats were de rigueur for Corps employees and none of these men was wearing one. Although it was a flagrant safety violation, it wasn't an unusual occurrence. What caught Sam's eye wasn't what they *weren't* wearing, but what they *were*—jeans, tee shirts, and sneakers instead of standard work clothes and boots.

"Gross, can you drop a few feet closer to the dam?"

"What the hell for? We're within minutes of landing."

"It won't take long. Something doesn't look right down there."

"Nothing looks right to you lately."

"Just do it." Sam ordered.

Gross shot him an exasperated look, but he backed off on the throttle and eased the collective downward. "Where do you want me to go?" he asked.

Sam pointed to three men standing in front of one of the sluice gates. "Over there." As they descended, the noise from the 'copter's whirling blades caused the men to look up. "Oh, shit," Sam said when he got a look at their faces. "I need you to set this thing down. Now."

Gross objected to landing atop the dam's spillway. "Not with these boxes on board. There's not enough room." He was right. The roadway running the length of the spillway was only one lane wide and framed by four-foot high safety walls on each side. It would be a tight fit for the helicopter, but adequate for its intended purpose of providing construction access. Later, when the dam was completed, the road would be used for maintenance.

Sam searched the surrounding area for a better landing site. "Okay," he said. "Put her down near where those two trucks are parked." He'd spotted an open space, mostly gravel and dirt, at the north end of the spillway on the Washington side of the river. Gross would have plenty of room to maneuver without hitting the trucks. Sam couldn't tell for sure, but he thought he recognized both vehicles. He checked his service revolver while Gross maneuvered for position. Sam had been wearing the Smith and Wesson in a shoulder holster ever since Ellie's rape.

"I'm giving you fair warning," Gross said as he prepared to land. "Side trips aren't part of the contract I signed. I've got a schedule to keep." He dipped his head toward the darkening sky. The clouds rolling in looked like dirty sweat socks spilling out of a laundry basket. "There's a storm heading our way and the bird and I aren't sticking around for it. We're flying to Sacramento as soon as we dump this load at the cemetery."

"I hear ya. Now get me on the ground."

Sam hopped out, ducked the still-spinning blades, and ran to the trucks. Just as he'd suspected from the air, Danny's truck was parked alongside the vehicle he'd left at Celilo. The damaged tires had been replaced with bald retreads. The boys must have figured the government vehicle—with its official Army Corps of Engineers decal in the front window—would bolster their chances of gaining entrance to the dam undetected and had "borrowed" it. Sam quickly checked out the truck beds. Danny's was empty, but when he peeled back the tarp partially covering the bed of his "borrowed" truck, there were half a dozen empty boxes inside. Although the boxes weren't labeled, Sam knew right away what he was dealing with. He just hoped to God he could make it to the spillway in time.

Good thing he'd given up smoking or he'd never have covered the 150 yards without having to stop and catch his breath. Sam figured the sluice gates were the boys' intended target. The gates were open now, but when the dam was completed they'd be closed and used to regulate the amount of water behind the dam. It was an important function, and damage to any one of the twenty-three gates would jeopardize the completion schedule. What Sam couldn't get his head around was why the boys hadn't already lit the fuses and high-tailed it out of there. They'd seen the helicopter and must have known when it landed that he, or someone like him, would be coming to stop them.

As he covered more ground to the site, Sam had his answer. Two workers in hard hats had already confronted the boys. They had to have been working on one of the sluice gates and were hidden from his earlier view. All construction work on the gates was accomplished from scaffolding lowered over the safety wall. Sam figured they heard the helicopter the same time the boys did and emerged from their perch to check out the source of the noise. He could only imagine their reaction when they saw three Indian kids standing on the spillway with a load of dynamite. As near as Sam could tell, the boys had been in the process of positioning the bundled sticks in front of the gates when the workers discovered them.

As Sam approached, Danny shouted, "Back off, Matthews."

"You know that's not going to happen," Sam said, advancing closer.

Sam didn't recognize the two workers standing next to Walter, but the name on their hard hats identified them as Palmer and Lynden. "Hey, bud," Palmer called, eying Sam's shoulder holster. "They've got a shitload of dynamite with them."

"Show him the letter, Danny," Walter shouted. "We're authorized to be here."

Danny pulled the letter from his back pocket and handed it to Sam. "He's right. We're doing a job," Danny said. "Undercover, just like you."

Sam quickly scanned the letter Danny gave him. The signature at the bottom had to be fake. "I've never heard of this agent," he said. "The Portland Bureau wouldn't authorize such an operation."

Walter snorted. "It's top secret, G-man. Only those with a need to know would be aware of it. Obviously, they didn't think you had a need to know. Now get the hell out of the way. We have our orders and they don't include you." Walter brandished a bundle of dynamite at Palmer and Lynden. "You can take off, too, or suffer the consequences." He pulled a lighter from his pocket.

Sam drew his weapon and assumed a shooting stance. "All of you: put the dynamite down. And your lighters, too."

Danny hesitated a moment, then set his lighter and dynamite carefully on the ground. He raised his hands and said, "It's over, Walter. Do as he says. You too, Ernie."

"No way," Walter said. I finish what I start."

"You red bastard!" shouted Palmer, lunging at him. Caught off balance, Walter stumbled slightly. It was enough. Lynden pounced next, swatting the bundle out of his hand. It landed at Ernie's feet as Walter twisted out of Lynden's grasp.

"Kick it away," Sam ordered.

Ernie looked at Danny for guidance.

"Do it," Danny told him.

Walter backtracked a few paces from them. With a triumphant grin, he pulled a single dynamite stick from his jeans' pocket and held it aloft. "Like I said, I finish what I start." Flicking open his lighter, he brought it toward the fuse. "I'd start running if I were you."

Sam couldn't get a good bead on Walter with the others in the way. "Get going!" he shouted.

Ernie and the workers darted to safety, but Danny stayed put. "Don't do it, Walter," he pleaded. "Nothing's worth losing your life over."

"That's where you're wrong, my brother," Walter said, bringing the lighter closer to the fuse. "Now, beat it. I'll take you with me if I have to."

Danny gave him one last look then broke into a run. As he dashed past Sam, the flame from Walter's lighter touched the fuse.

Chapter Forty-Five

The noise generated by the explosion was louder than a violent thunder storm, but the deafening rumble was nothing compared to the bloody mess left in its wake. Walter's death shook Danny to the core. He choked back the bile rising in his throat, too stunned by the grisly scene to do anything but lean against his truck for support. Gratitude for escaping an almost certain death was tempered by overwhelming sorrow for Walter—and anger. He'd committed a foolish act of defiance that could've killed everyone present. Luckily, the energy wave generated by the explosion hadn't reached the rest of the dynamite. If it had, the bundles would've been detonated and the blast would've been ten times worse than any thunder storm. The carnage left behind on the spillway would've been a gory splattering of blood, bone, and flesh. Just like Walter.

Ernie started puking as soon as he caught sight of what was left of their friend. "Oh, man, that was fucked up," he said, wiping the spittle from his mouth. "We gotta cut out now! Henry's waiting."

Ernie was right. The cavalry would be charging to the rescue at any moment. If the two workers they'd stumbled across hadn't already alerted the authorities, the blast would surely do it for them. The letter he'd given Matthews was worthless now, thanks to Walter's deadly stunt. But what alarmed Danny more than certain arrest was the reference to Henry. "What do you mean, Henry's waiting?"

Ernie risked another glance at the bloodbath on the spillway. Shuddering, he said, "I wasn't supposed to tell you, but I guess it don't matter now. Walter told Henry to wait at Wish-Ham for the chopper. He gave him half a dozen of them bundles. Henry's gonna blow that whirlybird to smithereens as soon as the coffins are unloaded." Ernie gestured to the spillway where Sam Matthews lay face down. "He ain't gonna stop nobody now."

Danny took off running.

"Hey, where're you goin'?"

When Danny reached Sam, he'd begun to stir. Slowly rousing himself, he sat up and shook his head a couple of times. "My ears are ringing," he hollered.

Danny helped him to his feet. "Are you hurt?"

Sam cupped a hand to his ear. "What?"

Danny shouted, "Are you hurt?"

Sam took a quick pat-down inventory. "Don't think so." He eyed the bloody aftermath of the explosion and cursed. "If I'd been much closer, it would've been a hell of a different story." He cast a suspicious look at Danny. "What are you still doing here?"

"Listen, we don't have much time."

Sam rubbed his ears. "Huh?"

Danny shouted louder. "Henry's waiting at Wish-Ham for the 'copter! He's going to blow it up!"

Sam's eyes widened in panic. "I've got to warn Gross," he said.

"Too late. Your pilot hauled ass when the blast hit."

"My God."

"It gets worse," Danny said. "Henry has no idea how much power there is in those bundles of dynamite. He's got six of 'em. If he sets them all off, everybody within a hundred yards will wind up like Walter. Including Reba and Ellie."

"They're at the ceremony?" Matthews asked. His face turned a sickly ashen color when Danny nodded.

Although older, Matthews beat Danny running to the trucks. "You got my keys?" he asked, gasping for breath as Danny caught up with him. Danny pulled a key ring from his pocket and tossed it over the hood.

Ernie had already climbed inside Danny's truck. "Hurry up!" he urged as Danny jerked open the driver's side door.

When Sam's truck roared to life, he called over to Danny, "That piece of junk won't get you there in time. Hop in with me."

For a split second, Danny debated what to do. There was no doubt that Matthews needed his help. Too many lives depended on it. The unreliability of his truck, though, wasn't the issue. By joining forces with Sam Matthews—even to save lives—was the same as admitting that his betrayal of the Wy-ams didn't matter anymore. Walter had betrayed them, too, in the worst conceivable way. And no matter how he looked at it, Danny was just as culpable. It was time to pay for what he'd done before anyone else got hurt or killed. As unlikely as it seemed just a few minutes ago, Danny and Sam Matthews needed each other. Danny slapped the cab roof. "Head on out, Ernie. I'm riding with Matthews."

Sam had his truck in gear and was about to take off when Danny scrambled aboard.

Speeding down the highway, Sam asked, "How're you doin'?"

"Scared shitless."

"Whatever possessed you guys to pull something this stupid?"

"The dam was destroying us. We had to fight back somehow."

"And you thought dynamiting the hell out of everything and everybody was the answer?"

Danny stared out the cab window. Sam drove fast, but with an expert hand as they zigzagged in and out of the traffic. Drivers in the cars they passed honked and cursed at them. No matter how fast they barreled down the highway, it seemed to be taking an eternity to get to Wish-Ham. "Look," Danny said. "Walter wasn't himself lately. He'd become fixated on the dynamite to solve all our problems. Ernie and Henry just got carried away with the excitement of it, like it was a game. I knew it was a fool's game."

"Yet you did nothing to stop it."

Sam was right. It didn't matter that Walter hadn't trusted Danny enough to tell him about Henry and the helicopter. He must've figured something might go wrong at the dam and hedged his bets. Uprooting and transporting their ancestors' bones from their final resting place was as obscene as the dam. And if Walter couldn't destroy the dam, the helicopter was the next best thing. Danny had let things get so far out of control that Ellie and Reba and a hundred others were minutes away from a horrific death.

"Who gave you that phony letter? Did you really think the FBI would recruit you for something like this?"

Danny had suspected the letter was fake but had brushed his

doubts aside. He'd gotten carried away with the plan just like the others. He hadn't wanted to appear weak in his friends' eyes by voicing any more concerns than he already had.

"I know Stanley Feldman bailed you out of jail," Sam said when Danny didn't answer. "Is he mixed up in this somehow?"

Danny nodded. "Yeah, he gave us the dynamite and introduced us to his inside man at the dam who made all the arrangements. He got us a government truck and promised to furnish the other gear we'd need but he never delivered."

"That should've been a big red flag."

Danny nodded. "Yeah, but we were too committed at that point to care."

"Why'd you take my truck when you already had a government vehicle?"

"Ernie got drunk and went joy riding. He isn't a good driver even when sober so he crashed straightaway. He was okay but the truck was totaled. Your truck was handy; you'd even left the keys inside, so all we had to do was find some retreads that fit and we were good to go."

"Who was your contact man at the dam?"

"Never got his name, but we assumed he was the same guy who signed the letter. He said his signature would get us off the hook if we were caught."

"You can forget the letter. If I didn't need your help at Wish-Ham, you'd be in handcuffs right now."

"I figured as much."

"What I can't figure out is why someone as prominent in the community as Feldman would want to sabotage the dam."

"He's a Commie," Danny said. "He said he wanted to destroy the capitalistic way of life. Damaging the spillway was supposed to get everyone's attention."

"Hell's bells. He certainly accomplished that goal."

"Feldman manipulated us, but I won't make excuses for what we've done. Just get us to Wish-Ham and I'll do whatever you want me to."

"That's what I wanted to hear," Matthews said. "You find Henry and I'll deal with Gross and the chopper." He floored the gas pedal.

When the speedometer hit 100, he said, "Whatever happens when we get there, I have your back."

Sam only glanced at Danny but it was long enough to see the wary look etched on his face. "You had my back at Celilo because of Reba and Ellie," Sam said. "It's because of them that I'll do the same for you today."

Minutes later, they skidded to a halt at Wish-Ham, horn blaring. The helicopter had landed and men were unloading the attached boxes. "There he is!" cried Danny.

"Henry?"

"No," Danny said, pointing to two men standing near the landing area. "It's our contact man. The one who signed the letter I gave you."

Sam quickly eyed the men Danny indicated. "Can't be," Sam said. "That's my partner and the lead engineer at the dam." Sam swung his long legs out of the cab. "Go look for Henry. I'll get Harmon and Beckstrom to help me with the chopper."

CHAPTER FORTY-SIX

When Ellie hadn't come back home with her father, Dessa was worried. Did Ellie even make it to Celilo or was she somewhere else altogether? There were tons of rumors floating around Hillcrest about what had happened to her. Word had gotten out that Mr. Matthews was an undercover FBI agent, which only caused the stories to become more far-fetched. *Ellie had run away from home; Ellie had done something very bad and her father kicked her out; Ellie had some mysterious illness and was dying; Ellie had run off with an older lover.* Since Dessa had earned a reputation for always being in the know, she'd been peppered with questions about her friend. Some even expected Dessa to print what had happened to Ellie in the Hillcrest newsletter and, when she didn't, accused her of covering up the truth.

Dessa wanted to talk to Mr. Matthews but he'd hardly been home since Ellie had left. She figured he'd be at the Reburial Ceremony on Sunday since he was leader of the project. Dessa could catch up with him there—if she could persuade her mother to let her go. Her father was in Washington D.C. attending a public session of what he called a "blatant witch hunt" by Senator Joseph McCarthy. Why he was so interested in the House Un-American Activities Committee made no sense to Dessa and even less to Maureen. All her mother could talk about was how her father willingly spent money on himself for an unnecessary trip to Washington D. C. but wouldn't even consider the trip to Palm Springs that Maureen wanted. Her mother's bad mood worked in Dessa's favor. "I don't care where you go," she said when Dessa asked about attending the ceremony. "You and your dad always do what you want anyway. I'll just sit here at home all by myself like I usually do."

If her mother's martyr act was intended to goad Dessa into

staying home, it didn't work. Dessa skipped out of the house with a clear conscience and found a ride to the ceremony with a family next door. She was lucky to get a ride. Most of their Hillcrest neighbors had declined to attend the ceremony, supposedly because they feared there'd be trouble. Despite George Featherstone's death, the protestors hadn't stopped demonstrating against the Indians and were likely to show up uninvited and unannounced. Under normal circumstances, Dessa would've welcomed the possibility of trouble. She was always in search of a story but not this time. She just wanted to talk to Mr. Matthews and find out if Ellie was all right.

The heat wave had eased off to a sultry seventy-five degrees. The clouds that had been building for several days darkened the afternoon sky. There'd been a slight drizzle when she first arrived at Wish-Ham but it'd quickly died out before the opening prayer service began. Dessa wished she'd thought to bring her plastic rain scarf in case it started to rain in earnest later. A good soaking would be a welcome treat even though it might squelch potential news-worthy violence if the protestors did come to spoil the party.

Dessa found a seat in the bleachers that had been erected for the viewing public. The ceremony had attracted a big crowd. Most were Indians, of course, but quite a few white people had turned out, too. Given the anti-Indian sentiment in town, Dessa thought they had to be tourists hoping to catch a good photo of the history-making event. The drummers and dancers had just entered the area near the gravesite that had been cleared for their performance when Dessa spotted Ellie. She hadn't expected to see her at the ceremony but the fact that Ellie was present, standing alongside Reba Longstreet, was a relief.

As far as Dessa could tell from a distance, Ellie seemed okay. She didn't have any obvious injuries like an arm or leg in a cast, but there was something different about her. She still looked beautiful dressed in a gorgeous blue frock that matched Reba's outfit. No, the difference was the subdued, almost resigned attitude that she projected. Her shoulders slumped forward as if she were carrying an immense weight on her back. Her head was bowed, not in prayer but in defeat. The last time Dessa had seen Ellie she'd been furious with her father, sobbing and ranting about how he'd lied to her. She'd been angry but just as resolute in her need to right some wrong that her father had supposedly committed. Ellie was so strong-willed that a suffocating heat wave hadn't stopped her from setting out on the long walk to Celilo. That girl wasn't here today.

"Hi, Ellie." When she didn't respond, Dessa couldn't decide whether she just hadn't heard her greeting or had purposefully ignored it. Dessa drew a little closer and addressed Reba. "It's good to see you again."

Reba was as welcoming as ever. "Dessa, what a pleasant surprise. Thank you for coming today."

The drummers and dancers were about to start their performance. "Is Danny dancing today?" Dessa asked. She hadn't seen him with the others.

Ellie faced Dessa at the mention of Danny. "What?"

"I asked about Danny, but I'm more concerned about you," she said, studying Ellie closely. Although she kept her head down so that her long hair covered most of her face, it was still possible to see that Ellie was recovering from some nasty bruises and facial swelling. "Are you all right? Everyone has been worried about you."

A tense silence followed until Reba intervened. "Ellie, why don't you invite your friend to sit with us in the bleachers. The dancing is about to start."

Ellie shrugged, which Dessa took as the best she was going to get for an invite.

Although the colorful dancers were entertaining, Dessa's mind wandered. She hadn't learned a thing yet about Ellie's ordeal, or even if whatever had happened to her *was* an ordeal. If the bruising on her face was any indication, it was something bad. Ellie might not be able or willing to talk about it, but that was okay for now. Dessa's reporter instincts were aroused and she wouldn't be deterred from discovering what had happened. Not for a news story but simply because Ellie was her friend. It was a friendship she'd never sought when they first met, but which had come to mean everything to Dessa now.

A sudden droning sound in the sky caught her attention. As she looked up, a huge mechanical bird whirled toward the open field. As she watched the craft descend, she noticed two big boxes strapped to either side and concluded that they contained the cargo of bones to be reburied. Several men had assembled at a safe distance to wait for the helicopter to land. She assumed that they were government employees since they wore the same type of hard hats and work clothes Mr. Matthews favored. Ellie's father was supposed to oversee the whole shebang, but he didn't seem to be anywhere around. Dessa asked Reba, "Where's Mr. Matthews?"

"He's on the helicopter," she said.

The dancing and drumming ended just as the bird set down. As the blades slowly stopped rotating, the men in hard hats got ready to remove the boxes. Meanwhile, the dancers and other Indians began to form two parallel lines stretching from the landing area to the gravesite. "What's going on?" Dessa asked.

"Our ancestors have arrived," Reba said. "We're lining up now to welcome them to their new resting place." She tapped Ellie's shoulder as she stood. "Come, child. It's time to go."

Ellie didn't seem eager to join the welcoming committee. She stared at the helicopter and said, "Do I have to go?"

When Reba hesitated, Dessa said, "She can stay with me." Half-turning in her seat, she waved in the direction of her neighbors. "It's okay, I'm here with family friends." Calling them family friends was overstating the relationship, but it was close enough.

Reba looked at the helicopter. The pilot had climbed out and the men had begun to unstrap the boxes. No sign of Mr. Matthews yet. Turning to Ellie, Reba said, "I guess it's all right if you stay here. If you see Danny, let me know."

As they watched Reba join the welcoming line, Dessa asked, "What's up with Danny? I thought he'd be here front and center? You said he danced at all the pow-wows."

Ellie's look was derisive and her tone dismissive. "This isn't a pow-wow." She might as well have added, "you fool."

A truck traveling at breakneck speed with its horn blaring flew past the bleachers toward the landing area. "Hey!" someone shouted behind the girls. "What's that maniac think he's doing?" The Indians in the welcoming line stood unfazed as the truck tore past them. The men carrying the boxes, though, were so startled by the commotion that they stumbled and nearly dropped their cargo.

When the truck reached the landing area, the driver slammed on the brakes and fishtailed to a stop in front of the helicopter. Mr. Matthews bounded out of the driver's door as Danny exited the passenger's side.

"I thought your father was supposed to be riding in the helicopter," Dessa said. "And why's Danny with him?"

"Something's wrong," Ellie said, springing to her feet.

By now, most of the spectators in the bleachers were on their feet as well, craning their necks to see what was happening. A woman next to Dessa asked, "Is this part of the program?"

While Mr. Matthews talked to a couple of men who'd been standing near the helicopter, Danny ran over to where the Indians had formed the greeting lines. Ellie was anything but listless as she scrambled out of the bleachers and raced to join him. Dessa caught up with her just as Danny grabbed Ellie by the shoulders. His eyes were wide with fear. "Have you seen Henry?" he cried.

Reba broke through the crowd. "What's the matter, Danny?"

"We've got to find Henry quick!"

"Why wasn't Sam on the helicopter?" Reba asked.

"There's a big problem." He gestured to the Indians who'd begun to break from the line and mill about. "I need you and Ellie to get everyone moving as far away from the helicopter as possible while I look for Henry."

Reba seemed to understand the urgency, if not the source of Danny's panic, and began at once to herd the welcoming party toward the safety of the bleachers. Ellie chased after Danny but Dessa was torn. Should she help Reba or follow Danny and Ellie? The decision was made for her when she heard the unmistakable sound of the helicopter's whirling blades. Whatever Danny feared would happen wasn't going to involve the helicopter. It was in the sky. The pilot maneuvered the craft so that it skimmed beneath the mean-looking cloud cover that ominously announced an impending storm. Within seconds of the 'copter's departure, raindrops began to splash onto Wish-Ham's rocky soil.

Danny looked up briefly as the bird disappeared out of sight, but he didn't stop his frantic search for Henry. "Have you seen Henry?" he asked repeatedly as he darted through the crowd. He asked the drummers, the dancers, and every other Indian he encountered, but no one had seen the elusive Henry.

CHAPTER FORTY-SEVEN

Sam's heart banged against his chest as he flung himself out of the truck to reach the helicopter in time. It seemed a little odd that Jess Harmon and Phillip Beckstrom were at the landing site. Even odder that they were standing side-by-side, as if they were old buddies. Harmon had made a point of ducking his designated point man whenever he could and Beckstrom had no interest in anything that involved the Indians. Since warning Gross was uppermost in Sam's panic-stricken mind, he didn't bother to question their presence. He was just grateful that they were on hand. He would need all the help he could get to find the dynamite that Henry had planted somewhere nearby.

Thank God you're here!" gasped Sam.

Harmon nudged Beckstrom in the ribs. "Did you see the way he handled that truck? You've missed your calling, man. You should be on the race car circuit. The gibe at Sam's expense got a chortle out of Beckstrom but Harmon's jovial mood was short-lived. He glared at Sam and growled, "What's the big fucking rush?"

His partner's attitude was exasperating but Sam didn't have time to deal with it. "I need your help!" he blurted. He glanced toward the helicopter. "Gross and his craft are in extreme danger."

Beckstrom smirked as Harmon said, "Hold on, partner. There's no need for hysterics. Everything's under control here—even if you're not."

That Harmon and Beckstrom had so casually discounted the seriousness of the situation angered Sam. "Listen, guys, I'm not joking around!" He quickly told them what had happened at the spillway. "And they've targeted the chopper with an even more powerful blast. We've already got one person dead and everyone here is at risk, too.

We've got to warn Gross and find out where the dynamite is stashed."

"No," Harmon said. "I'm warning you. It's time for you to come clean."

"What . . . what are you talking about."

"Gross told us how you made him drop you at the spillway so you could meet up with your Injun buddies. He bailed when the blast went off and he's not sticking around here, either." He gestured to the pilot who'd climbed back into his craft as soon as the boxes were unloaded. "Sorry to disappoint you but whoever you were expecting to rescue us from, never showed up with the dynamite. Gross is more worried about the storm that's coming." The whirring noise from the helicopter's rotating blades made his last point unnecessary. "He's leaving now." Steady rain drops began to fall as Gross maneuvered the craft into the air.

Sam was at a loss for words.

"Didn't think we'd catch you, did you?" Beckstrom said with a triumphant sneer. "I knew you weren't on the up and up from the moment you arrived at the dam." He pulled a piece of paper from his shirt pocket. "And this is the evidence that proves I was right about you all along. You're nothing but a Commie sympathizer posing as some kind of patriotic government man." He spit at Sam's shoes. "You disgust me."

"No, I . . ."

Harmon put his hand up to stop Sam. "Don't try to deny it. The letter Beckstrom found in your office desk is what you used to trick the Indians into helping you with your sabotage plan. They stupidly believed that you had approval from the Portland Bureau to recruit them for some cockamamie project. Your investigation of Danny Longstreet and the others at Celilo was just a big ruse to throw us off." His accusatory diatribe was cut short when something behind Sam caught Harmon's eye. "What the hell?"

As Sam turned around, a dozen protestors carrying homemade cardboard signs marched onto the rain-splattered grounds, chanting and waving their fists in the air.

"Shit!" roared Harmon. "Beckstrom, take a couple of your men and head off those loonies. I've got enough to deal with here."

Philip Beckstrom's disappointed expression wasn't hard to read. He'd much rather watch Harmon destroy Sam than chase down protestors. After he'd trudged off, Sam said, "What's going on, Jess? You know damn well I'm no Commie saboteur."

Harmon's lips twisted in a bitter smile. "No, but you are a drunk who ruined my life."

"Is that what this is all about? Revenge? Getting back at me for your suffering?"

"Ha! You don't know the half of what I've suffered. I almost died because of you. I had two major surgeries in as many months, spent thirty days in a coma, and underwent weeks of physical therapy just so I could walk again without looking like some goddamn pitiful gimp."

"You know how bad I feel, and if I could — "

"I don't give a rat's ass about how you feel. My fiancé took one look at my scarred face and left, I missed the filing deadline for promotion to Bureau Chief while I was hospitalized, and every day is a constant struggle to get back even half the life I used to have. They assigned me to the Chambers' homicide investigation because I pleaded on bended knee that I could handle more than the desk duty they stuck me with after my so-called recovery."

"I see," Sam said. "You planted the phony letter in my desk for Beckstrom to find and encouraged his doubts about me to fuel the flames of your revenge. I'm sure you've manufactured additional evidence proving my guilt. What's next? You plan to arrest me?"

"Your detective skills are fucking amazing."

"There is one minor matter we need to clear up first."

"What's that?"

"According to Danny Longstreet, you were Stan Feldman's contact man at the dam, not me. When I found out that Feldman had paid Danny's bail, I had the Bureau run a background check on him. Turns out they confirmed that he *is* a Communist. I realize now that you already knew it and purposely withheld the information from me. You exploited Feldman's Communist ties to frame me for the sabotage. Longstreet and Feldman will confirm everything I've said."

"You think anyone is going to take a lying redskin's word against mine? Or the word of a treasonous, card-carrying Communist like Feldman?" He paused a moment to let the truth of his words sink in. A malicious grin spread across his disfigured face. "You're all going to prison for a long, long time."

CHAPTER FORTY-EIGHT

There was a lot of confusion at the burial site but it wasn't until the protestors showed up that things got truly chaotic. Some of the government men tried to restrain the protestors but they hadn't been able to keep them from parading in front of the bleachers. The Indians who'd formed the welcoming line for their ancestors had closed ranks to give the intruders a far different welcome. Most of the tourists and other non-Indians in attendance fled the scene when it looked like violence could erupt at any moment. Dessa watched as her neighbors, too, scrambled out of the bleachers and ran to the safety of their car. In their haste to escape they'd forgotten all about her, which suited Dessa just fine.

No one in charge seemed to know what to do. Would the ceremony be cancelled? The dead still needed to be buried with or without the planned fanfare. To add to the confusion, the intermittent drizzle had become a steady downpour. The few tourists who'd stuck around put their cameras away and took out umbrellas, apparently more curious than fearful of what might happen next.

Dessa expected Danny to join his brethren as they faced off with the protestors but his attention was focused elsewhere. A heated argument had arisen between Mr. Matthews and another man which seemed to bother Danny greatly. "Stay with Reba," he told Ellie. "I'll be back in a few minutes."

"Where're you going?" she asked.

He gestured towards her father. "I think I know what's going on over there and it doesn't look good—for him or any of us."

As he left, Dessa said, "I don't know about you but I'm not staying here. I have to find out what's happening."

"Me too," Ellie said.

They caught up with Danny just as a scar-faced man told Mr. Matthews something about no one believing his word against "a lying redskin and a card-carrying Communist." His rant didn't make sense to Dessa but Danny was all over it. "Maybe they won't believe us," he told him. "But pictures don't lie."

The man he'd confronted started to object but Mr. Matthews intervened. "No, Harmon, we're on Indian land. Let him speak."

"As the saying goes," Danny continued, "a picture is worth a thousand words." He pulled a stack of photographs from his pocket. "The guys all thought I was paranoid when I decided to record our meetings." He handed the photos to Mr. Matthews. "As you know, we've been burned by the white man's promises before. I wanted more than a questionable letter to cover our butts." Danny addressed scar-face. "These photos prove that it was *you*, not Sam Matthews, who used us to do your dirty work."

Mr. Matthews shielded the photos from the rain as he shuffled through the stack. Dessa sidled closer to him so that she could see also. Two photos were of special interest to Mr. Matthews. He waved them in front of the man. "Danny's right. Pictures don't lie. He caught you in the act, Jess." The first photo showed him handing one of Danny's friends a key to a government pickup. "And here you are with Henry and Walter as they loaded the same vehicle with several boxes of dynamite." Mr. Matthews grinned. "*Incriminating*, as we say at the Bureau."

Harmon shook his head. "Those photos don't prove a damn thing. I can think of several reasons to explain what—"

"NO-O-O-O-O!!" Ellie's loud cry pierced through the pelting rain with a startling intensity. Her ashen face was streaked with a mixture of tears and rain as she pointed a trembling finger at a couple near the bleachers.

It was clear that the couple was the source of her anguish but Dessa didn't understand her emotional reaction. "Oh, that's just Tony Rossi," she said dismissively. "The woman is his secretary, Mildred." She wasn't slutty enough in her frumpy, old lady dress and shoes for anyone to mistake her for a new girlfriend. Dessa scooped up the photos that Mr. Matthews had dropped when Ellie screamed. "Here," she said, holding them in her outstretched hand. "They're a little wet but I don't think they're too damaged."

Mr. Matthews never registered Dessa. He was too focused on comforting his daughter who'd begun to whimper like a wounded pup. At first, Danny looked shaken by Ellie's distress but his concern for her quickly turned to rage. "I'm going to kill him this time!" he shouted over his shoulder as he took off running.

Mr. Matthews wasn't the cussing type but he muttered a few choice expletives, including the F-word when Danny bolted. "Stay right here, girls," he ordered before he, too, made a hasty exit.

A brisk wind had come up, whipping freezing rain about them from all directions. It ran down their face and into their eyes, drenched their hair and soaked their skin but the effect was strangely refreshing. It was if the storm had washed away the agitated state that had stricken Ellie earlier. She had the appearance now of someone who'd made a tough decision and was fiercely resolved to carry it out. Without a word to Dessa, she began running after her father and Danny.

Was it something I said? wondered Dessa as she, too, joined in the pursuit of Tony Rossi.

Mr. Matthews waved his badge in the air, yelling, "Stop! FBI. Both of you, stop! Stop where you are!"

Mildred put on the brakes as ordered but Tony never altered his course. "Tony, come back," Mildred called. He ignored her and picked up his pace but his get-away attempt was short-lived. Danny easily caught up with Tony and tackled him to the ground. He pummeled him unmercifully with doubled-up fists that drew blood. Mr. Matthews struggled to pull Danny off for several moments until he finally succeeded. "That's enough, Danny!"

Dessa and Ellie arrived just as Mr. Matthews unholstered his gun and aimed it at Tony. "You're under arrest, Rossi. Get your hands up where I can see them."

Tony's secretary—wet hair plastered to her face, soaked dress clinging to her misshapen body—appeared on the scene, gasping for breath. "Do as he says, Tony. We can straighten all this out in no time."

Tony raised his hands in the air. "What's your problem, Matthews? I've done nothing wrong!"

313

The wind and torrential downpour howled so loudly that it required a determined effort to be heard above nature's fury. And only if shouting and yelling were employed. "Rape and murder are about as wrong as it gets," Mr. Matthews countered.

Mildred's frizzy eyebrows almost jumped off her forehead but Tony seemed to take the accusation in stride. "Don't look at me," he said, dipping a shoulder at Danny. "There's your rapist."

If looks could kill, Tony was already a dead man. There was no doubt Danny would've leapt over Mr. Matthews and anyone else to get at Tony if it weren't for Ellie. She had attached herself to Danny's arm like her life depended on it.

"Save your lies for the courtroom," Mr. Matthews said. "I'm arresting you for the rape of my daughter and suspicion of murder in the death of Nick Rossi."

Dessa was as shocked by the news as Tony's secretary seemed to be. Rape? Nick's murder? No wonder Ellie got so upset at the sight of him. No wonder Danny wanted to kill the man.

"Wait," Mildred pleaded. "Tony's not a rapist. And he didn't kill Nick, either. Clarice Nestor did."

"We'll let a court of law decide that," Matthews said, pulling a set of handcuffs from his back pocket.

"Don't need no court of law," Tony said. "I didn't kill anyone. And I didn't rape your precious little daughter, either. She asked for it, man. The slut was always after me when you weren't around. I just did what any man would do; I gave her what she begged me for. Best pussy I ever had, too."

That did it for Danny. He shook loose of Ellie's tight grip and lunged at Tony. Mr. Matthews still had his gun pointed at Tony when Danny charged and blocked his aim. It didn't matter. A sudden, forceful, ear-splitting blast came out of nowhere and slammed them all to the ground.

Aside from a little dizziness and smoke in her eyes and lungs, Dessa wasn't hurt. As she lay on the ground, coughing and spitting to clear her throat, she tried to figure out what had just happened. The entire area, including the ceremony site and bleachers, was engulfed in smoke and falling debris. People screamed and wailed. Many laid where they'd fallen and others who were still on their feet ran in all directions, dazed or unable to process where to go or what to do. The roar of thunder punctuated the already cacophonous melee, followed by lightning that pierced the dark sky like a macabre exclamation point.

Ignoring the hard rain pelting her like rocks, Dessa stood up and took a moment to steady herself. She could hear crying nearby and, as the smoke began to clear, she saw Ellie kneeling beside her father. His gun was in her hand. Nearby, Tony lay sprawled on the ground. Dessa looked for Mildred but didn't see her. Judging by the blood pooled on the ground, the secretary's boss and Ellie's father were both dead.

"All my fault," Ellie wailed. "All my fault."

Danny limped to her side and pried the gun from her hand. "No," he told her. "It was Henry. Not you. He blew up Sam's truck."

"But I killed him," she said.

"It's going to be all right," Danny said. He put an arm around her shoulder as Reba arrived carrying her medical bag. She'd somehow found them in all the confusion. "Reba is here now," he said. "She'll take care of Sam."

Reba knelt alongside Ellie and opened her medical bag. As she checked on Sam Matthews, Ellie asked, "Is he dead?"

"No," Reba said. "He's breathing on his own, but he's lost a lot of blood. It looks like he got hit by some of the debris." After stopping the blood flow and applying bandages, she asked Danny, "Were you in on this debacle?"

He nodded. "Sort of. Henry had planned to blow up the chopper. When it lifted off, I thought we'd avoided disaster. I should have known he wouldn't give up so easily. Henry must have figured Sam's truck was just as good a target." He shook his head. "He's as mixed up as Walter was."

"It could've been worse," Reba said. "If you and Sam hadn't arrived when you did and cleared the area, we'd have had a lot more injuries."

"The storm helped to dampen the blast," Danny said.

"I killed him," Ellie said again, struggling to catch her breath.

Reba felt Ellie's forehead. "I think she's in shock. Her skin is moist and clammy and it's not because of the rain."

315

"What should we do?"

"Let's have her lie down," Reba said. "We need to keep her warm. This rain isn't helping. I wish we had a blanket."

"I have one in my truck." Danny smacked his forehead with an open palm. "Shit, I forgot. Ernie took it back to Celilo."

"I'm okay," Ellie said. "It was an accident."

"We know that," Danny said. "Sam was hurt in the explosion. You had nothing to do with it."

She resisted his attempt to help her lie down. "But his gun. I had his gun. And now he's dead."

"Your father isn't dead. He's badly injured but he will be all right."

"I think she means Tony Rossi," Dessa said.

Reba and Danny both looked at Tony. He laid unmoving in a puddle of rain and blood. "I'll check on him," Reba said. After a brief examination, she nodded. "Ellie's right. This man wasn't killed by debris. He was shot."

"I told you I did it," Ellie mumbled through her tears.

Danny looked at the gun he'd taken from her. "I should've been the one to kill him, not her."

"That's neither here nor there," Reba said. "We've got to protect Ellie now."

CHAPTER FORTY-NINE

Present Day
Interview Room #1 – Odessa Feldman Langston

"And that's the last time I saw Ellie Matthews," I said. Leaning back in the metal chair, I rubbed my aching shoulder. Although I hadn't been aware of it, I must have been holding myself rigid during the entire two-hour interview.

Detective Steve Burroughs turned off the recording devices. "I think we need a break," he said. Noticing my untouched coffee cup, asked, "How 'bout a refill?"

"No, thank you, but some ice water would be wonderful." My throat was parched. "I'm used to writing, not speaking."

"I'll have someone bring you a glass of water right away."

***

Later, after he'd smoked a much-needed cigarette, Detective Burroughs joined Detective Brad Rycoff who stood at the two-way mirror outside of Interview Room #1. "How's it going?" he asked Burroughs.

"Odessa Langston is a real corker. Fragile but hard as nails at the same time." He watched her for a moment through the glass. She'd crossed her legs but otherwise hadn't stirred since he'd left her alone with her memories. "Must have been a hell of a journalist in her day. She has almost perfect recall of events that happened nearly sixty years ago."

"You think she's telling the truth?"

"Maybe. I will have to see how she does with some follow-up

questions. How about you? How's your interview with Ellie Matthews going?"

"She's tired, maybe even a little scared, but determined as hell to get her story out. She's pushing seventy-five and doesn't look a day over fifty. Botox and a few tucks here and there have preserved the old gal nicely."

Burroughs shrugged. "Lots of women go in for that kind of thing nowadays, if they can afford it." He decided Odessa Langston wasn't one of them.

"Ellie can afford it—and anything else she wants. The Sears catalog look she has going for her today isn't her usual style. Google her and you'll see what I mean."

"Why don't you just tell me."

"The lady is richer than God. She's been a regular on the social circuit in New York for years. Believe me, she wouldn't be caught dead in the neighborhoods she frequents wearing the Timex she's got on her delicate wrist. A Rolex is more in keeping with her lifestyle, but it's not just that. She's a class act underneath all that plain Jane, *what you see is what you get* image she's working hard to promote."

"You think she's hiding something?"

"Count on it."

"Odessa claims it was Ellie who shot Tony Rossi."

"Yeah, Ellie has admitted it."

Burroughs looked at his watch. "What do you suggest we do now?" he asked

"Lean on 'em both."

***

Interview Room #1 - Dessa

Detective Burroughs set another glass of water on the table when he returned to the interview room. "Just in case you're still thirsty," he said. He took off his jacket and loosened his tie before turning on the recorder and video camera again. "Now, Mrs. Langston, let's get back to where we left off—the explosion."

"Please, call me Dessa. Everyone does."

318

"Okay, Dessa. You said Ellie killed Tony Rossi with her father's service weapon?"

I took a sip of water and swallowed. "It was awfully confusing when the blast went off and the storm hit full force at the same time. I really don't think Ellie meant to kill him. It was just an accident."

He waited while I took another sip. "Was it just an accident when she killed the woman, too?"

I jerked as if poked in the back. "Woman? What woman?"

"Oh, come off it. You don't have to protect Ellie any longer. You finally decided to come clean after all these years. Why hold back half the story?"

"I have no idea what you're talking about." I bristled that he'd even suggest a thing. "I just spent two hours telling you everything I know about what happened that summer."

"We didn't release all the information we had when the skeletal remains were first examined," he said. "The evidence points to two homicide victims—Tony Rossi *and* an unidentified female. We got lucky and could determine Rossi's identity from old dental records. His dentist had long since died, but his son took over the practice and believed no records should ever be destroyed. But we have nothing on the woman. So, I'll repeat the question, who is she?"

***

Interview Room #2 – Ellie Matthews Conrad

Detective Rycoff asked Ellie Matthews the same question in Interview Room #2.

"If I knew I'd tell you," Ellie said.

"You're sure about that?"

She stiffened. "Of course. I don't lie."

"No? Maybe shading the truth is more accurate. You came in here today pretending to be someone you're not. Someone who wears a Timex instead of a Rolex. Someone who shops at Penney's instead of Neiman Marcus."

She arched an eyebrow.

"Don't look surprised. I may be a small-town cop, but I've heard of Neiman Marcus. And Tiffany's. Even Gucci and Prada. The point is, you've taken pains to hide your upper-class background. It makes me wonder what else you're hiding—like knowing the identity of our second victim."

"Look," she said, resting her hands on the table. I thought if I didn't come off as some wealthy dowager from New York City, whatever I had to say today would be better received. I'm terribly sorry if I misjudged the situation. You have to believe me, I didn't know anyone besides Tony had been killed." She paused as if something else had just occurred to her. "There were people killed that day from the dynamite blast. The remains could've been one of them."

"No, all of the injured and those killed by the blast were accounted for shortly after the incident."

"Well, then, maybe the woman was Tony's secretary, Mildred Simmons. I never saw her after the explosion."

"That's what—" A knock at the interview door interrupted whatever he was about to say. Detective Rycoff turned off the recording devices as a young woman entered the room. She bent over and whispered something in his ear.

"Excuse me," he said. "I'll be right back."

***

Interview Room #1 - Dessa

Detective Burroughs eyed Dessa closely, waiting for her to respond.

"You can repeat the question all day long if you want, but my answer will always be the same. I have no idea who this female victim is that you're talking about."

"Okay, Dessa, let's set that issue aside for a moment. "Tell me more about Danny Longstreet and Sam Matthews. You indicated that they both had reason to kill Rossi for what he'd done to Ellie, but she was the one who actually pulled it off."

I nodded.

"And then she enlisted you to cover up the murder, along with Danny and his mother. That about right?"

320

"Not exactly. Ellie never asked us to do anything. We all decided to protect her. I promised that I'd never tell anyone what really happened and didn't for almost sixty years—until today."

"Why now?" he asked.

"Because when I heard that Danny had been arrested for Tony's murder, I couldn't keep silent any longer. He didn't kill Tony but he will do anything to protect Ellie, including taking the fall for her."

"Danny Longstreet has confessed and is sitting in jail as we speak."

"Like I said, he's still protecting Ellie after all these years."

"But you're no longer protecting her," Burroughs said.

I sighed wearily. "It wasn't just loyalty to a friend that kept me from talking until now. I may have been only fourteen, but I understood that my actions made me an accessory to a crime and I was scared. I don't know what the statute of limitations is, but I'm relieved to finally get the truth out, no matter what the consequences are. The whole thing has been a tremendous burden."

At a knock at the door, Burroughs turned off the video and recorder. A young woman came into the room and whispered something in the detective's ear. "Excuse me," he said, pushing his chair away from the table. "I'll be back shortly."

***

Interview Room #2 - Ellie

Half an hour later, Detective Rycoff entered the interview room where Ellie had been waiting. He carried a file folder and a plastic bag with a pistol inside and set them on the table. He pushed the plastic-encased weapon closer to her. "Recognize it?" he asked.

Her face blanched. "It looks a lot like my father's gun," she said in a shaky voice.

"A Smith & Wesson .38 revolver with a J frame," he said. "A little heavy for a young girl, but it has excellent trigger pull. We found it buried with the victims."

"I don't know anything about what happened to the gun."

Burroughs smile was without warmth. "You just killed the man

321

with it, right?"

She heaved a shoulder-racking sigh. "How many times do I have to say it? Yes, I killed Tony Rossi."

The detective tapped the plastic bag. "With this revolver?"

"Yes."

"Then care to explain why it still has all its bullets intact?"

She looked at the weapon again and then searched Rycoff's face. "What?"

"The ballistics report confirms that the slugs discovered near the gravesite do not match the .38."

"But that means . . ."

"You did not kill Tony Rossi. At least not with this weapon."

"I don't understand."

"Who are you protecting?"

"I'm not protecting anyone."

Rycoff opened the folder he'd placed on the table earlier and flipped through a few pages. Closing the folder, he said, "We know who the female victim is now."

"Mildred?"

He shook his head. "No, Mildred Simmons lived to the ripe old age of ninety-eight. She was well-known around these parts for her generous charitable contributions, primarily to shelters for abused women. She was also quite successful as the owner and proprietor of Baker Bluff Resort and Spa."

Ellie thought a moment about what he'd said. "Hillcrest Development was a hotbed for gossip back then. When Tony disappeared, I heard that everyone thought he left town because he was involved in a major real estate scam involving the purchase of Baker Bluff. We never talked about it and I'm not sure to this day whether my father ever knew what really happened to Tony."

Rycoff said, "The rights to Baker Bluff were signed over to Mildred Simmons by Clarice Nestor on the same day that the reburial incident occurred. Warren had already been arrested for the murder of Nick Rossi but he put the blame on her. A warrant for her arrest had been issued but she was never seen after she sold the property to Mildred. She's the second victim discovered at the river."

"How do you know for sure? DNA?"

"Something a little less sophisticated." Detective Rycoff stood and picked up the folder and bagged weapon. "I think you need to hear something." He took her by the arm and led her down the hallway to a second interview room like the one they'd left. They stopped outside a two-way mirror. "Do you know her?" he asked, gesturing to the woman sitting at a table inside the room.

"No."

"She hasn't aged as well as you, but surely you remember your old friend."

Ellie studied the woman. Although she was sitting down, she appeared short and stubby, especially around the hips. She was wrinkled like a wadded-up newspaper and her short hair was dyed a hideous orange. "It can't be! Is that Dessa? Odessa Feldman? What is she doing here?"

"Same as you. She came in to tell us what she believes happened during the summer of 1956 when Tony Rossi was murdered."

"And?"

"She confirms that you killed Tony Rossi, not Danny Longstreet."

"Good. Now you have to believe me."

When a detective entered the interview room, Rycoff activated the audio system. "That's Detective Burroughs. Let's take a listen to what your old friend tells him."

Interview Room #1 - Dessa

"You've told me a fascinating story today," Detective Burroughs said. "The problem is that there's a huge hole in it."

She set the glass down that she'd been sipping from. "What hole?"

"The weapon found at the gravesite doesn't match the ballistics report."

"What are you implying?"

"I'm not implying anything," said Burroughs. "I'm coming right out and saying it." The detective leaned over the table and stared at her, a steely-eyed, no-nonsense expression etched on his youthful face. "Ellie Matthews didn't shoot Tony Rossi. You did."

She shook her head vigorously. "That's absurd. I had no reason to kill the man. I was only a kid back then."

"So was Ellie."

"But Tony raped her."

"By your own admission, no one liked you much. You were thrilled when Ellie seemed willing to be your friend. If you killed her attacker, then she might think of you as not only a friend, but a best friend. Kids have killed for less."

"You're wrong! I don't know why you're accusing me, but if Sam Matthews' gun wasn't the murder weapon, then perhaps . . ." She ran a hand through her colorful hair. "Yes, that has to be it." She leaned back in the chair with a satisfied grin. "The gun I saw in Ellie's hand must have belonged to Danny. He took it away from her after the shooting."

"What about Clarice Nestor?"

"What about her?"

"She's been identified as the other murder victim but the slug we found embedded in her skull matches the slug in Tony's rib cage. Did Ellie kill her with Danny's gun, too?"

Dessa didn't respond, confusion stamped on her wrinkled face.

"I . . . I don't know what you mean."

Remember my partner, Detective Templeton? He had to skip your interview because of a new development in the case." He slid a folder across the table. "Here's what he found."

"What is it?"

"Read it. I think it will clear up your confusion."

Outside the interview room, Detective Rycoff handed Ellie a similar folder. "Mildred Simmons' attorney has held an envelope in his safe ever since her death ten years ago," Rycoff explained. The attorney said he'd been instructed not to open it unless the Baker Bluff property was ever placed on the market. And since it's just been listed for sale, he opened the envelope and found this letter. When he read what was inside, he contacted Detective Templeton."

"What does it say?"

"Read it for yourself, Ellie."

CHAPTER FIFTY

To Whom It May Concern,

If you're reading this letter, then the Baker Bluff property has been listed for sale. It was my intention that the property should always be used as a retreat for battered women. I've been offered a lot of money over the years to sell the property, which I refused to do, no matter how much it increased in value. I left specific instructions in this regard when I willed the property to Odessa Feldman. She assured me that she believed in my vision and would keep that vision intact after my death.

Since the property has been placed on the market, it's more than likely that the new owners will have some other purpose in mind for Baker Bluff. Therefore, I've instructed my attorney to file suit on behalf of the women's retreat if the sale results in its dissolution. Funds have been set aside for this possibility.

In any case, I always wanted the truth revealed about how I came to own Baker Bluff. I'm aware that some people in town have long suspected that there was something fishy about the deal. If they're still around when this letter is discovered, they will probably nod and say, "I always knew that woman was no good." I leave it to you to judge whether they are right.

The first thing you should know is that I killed Antonio Rossi. It wasn't something that I'd planned to do. In fact, it was the last thing I ever thought would happen. My husband was a mean drunk who abused me for years until his liver finally gave out. I was broke and desperate when Tony gave me a job. It's true that he was a little rough around the edges and didn't always treat me with respect, but there is no denying that he was a super salesman. I could've been happy working for him for the rest of my life. That all changed when he met Clarice Nestor.

Tony had been skimming the top off the commissions he owed his uncle and getting nowhere fast until Clarice came along. She concocted a real estate scheme called the Destiny Group which prospered beyond our wildest expectations. Tony was on the fast track to making his dreams come true. As it turned out, I was the one who wound up living the dream.

I never liked or trusted Clarice and only joined in her real estate schemes because of my loyalty to Tony. It didn't take me long to realize that I had to look out for myself and I did. I think she planned to double-cross Tony from the get-go. She just upped her time table after she murdered his cousin Nick.

We went to the reburial ceremony for the Indians because that is where she said she'd be. Our plan was to present her with an offer to buy Baker Bluff with the funds I'd secretly embezzled from the Destiny Group. We had just arrived at the new cemetery when we were accosted by Sam Matthews. When Uncle Sol claimed that an FBI man was gunning for Tony, I thought he was bluffing. I'd already paid off Sheriff Pritchard for what he knew about Nick Rossi's murder and he'd left for parts unknown. I'd also made sure nothing could be traced back to us regarding the Destiny Group. I was shocked when Matthews pointed his gun at Tony and accused him of raping his fourteen-year-old daughter and murdering Nick Rossi. Tony denied the murder charge and I expected him to deny the rape as well. When Matthews brought out the handcuffs, Tony lost it. He admitted that he had been with Ellie Matthews. He even bragged about it in the most vulgar terms imaginable.

The words he used were the exact same words I'd heard before. Many times before. Everyone knew that my husband was a sleaze ball who treated me like shit, but that wasn't the worst of it. He had two drinking buddies who cornered me whenever they felt like having a little fun. Every time his buddies raped me, they'd claim I'd asked for it. At the time, I was too frightened and too helpless to fight back. When Tony made the same vile boast, all the terror and powerless feelings I'd stuffed deep down inside came roaring to the surface. The difference was that this time I could fight back.

When the truck exploded, I shot Tony with the pistol I always carried in my handbag. As a rape survivor, I like having a measure of self-reliance that only a weapon can provide. I never expected that I would ever use it on Tony. Luckily, the explosion and ensuing confusion allowed me to get away without being seen.

When I found Clarice, I insisted that we drive over to Baker Bluff to avoid all the chaos at the cemetery. Clarice never even questioned why Tony

326

wasn't with me once I started talking cold hard cash. Predictably, she wanted more money than what I was willing to pay. I was in no mood to negotiate the terms. We argued about it for a few minutes until I realized that if I gave her too much grief she'd have no qualms about whacking me. So, I agreed to her terms. Once she'd signed on the dotted line, I shot the bitch right between the eyes.

I knew that a couple of Indian boys had disposed of Tony's body because I saw them carry him off before I made my escape. It took some doing, but I located the same boys and paid them well to dump Clarice's body. It was only later that I learned that they'd buried them both by the river at Baker Bluff.

Money really does solve a lot of problems. My only worry over the years has been that the bodies would be discovered somehow, especially if the property was sold and any renovations involving excavation work were undertaken. They may never be found, but if a sale triggers such a result, I don't want anyone falsely accused of Tony and Clarice's murder. For proof, my attorney has been instructed to open the package that accompanied this letter. It contains the gun I used in the murders and a sketch of where the bodies are.

All things considered, I've lived a good life. Condemn me if you will, but I have no regrets.

Mildred Simmons.

CHAPTER FIFTY-ONE

Ellie took off her glasses and looked at Detective Rycoff with tears running down her aged but attractive face. "All these years," she said, "it was Mildred Simmons' guilty secret I carried, not mine. I've been living in Celilo's shadow most of my life with a burden that wasn't necessary." Searching through her purse, she found a tissue and wiped her eyes. "I'm not sure why I'm crying. I thought I'd shed all the tears I had in me a long time ago." When she handed the letter back, he wanted to know if she believed Mildred's version of events. "Don't you?" she asked.

"At first, we weren't sure," he admitted. "But the forensics match her story. The gun Mildred left with her attorney is a .22. It's the same caliber weapon that was used to kill Tony and Clarice just like she claimed in the letter. Her sketch of their grave site is accurate. She couldn't have known where the bodies would be discovered when she wrote the letter unless she had first-hand knowledge."

"Will you press charges against me?"

"What for?"

"I didn't bury Tony, but I was involved in the cover-up. Isn't that illegal?"

Rycoff shook his head. "The statute of limitations ran out on that aspect of the case years ago."

"Then I'm off the hook as far as you're concerned?"

"Dessa, too. I'm sorry I gave you so much pushback earlier. Keeping quiet for such a long time couldn't have been easy. Then, to have your story questioned when you finally did talk . . . well, let's just say you're one tough lady."

"What about Danny? Will he be released now?"

"It'll take a couple of days to process the legal paperwork, but yes, he'll be free to go, too."

It could've ended much differently and Ellie breathed a grateful sigh of relief. "Ever since that day I've been obsessed with the past, haunted by it, actually. Even though I knew it was cheating the present and betraying the future, I couldn't let go of the memories and the guilt I felt. The longer I kept silent, the worse it became."

"Why did you come forward now?" he asked.

"That's easy. I couldn't let Danny go to prison for something I'd done."

"I'm curious about that," Rycoff said. "Why did he confess to Rossi's murder if he was innocent?"

"I tried to talk him out of it but Danny was convinced that he owed it to me. He'd wanted to kill Tony back then but I got to him first. Danny felt like he'd failed to protect me once and he wasn't going to do it again."

"He must really love you."

Ellie beamed. "And I love him."

"We told Dessa that you're here and she would like to see you. Are you willing to meet with her?"

When Ellie hesitated, he gave her a way out. "You don't have to. She said she'd understand if you'd rather not."

"It's not that. She's lived with the same guilty secret all these years, too. I'm surprised she wants anything to do with me."

"You ladies can sort all that out in the conference room. It's a lot more comfortable than the interview rooms. We've cleared it for your use. Take as much time as you want."

CHAPTER FIFTY-TWO

I've traveled all over the world as a journalist but walking down the hall to the conference room was the scariest trip I'd ever taken. I very much wanted to see Ellie again but I wasn't sure how she'd react to seeing me. We greeted each other with an awkward hug. "My God," I said. "You're as beautiful as ever, Ellie."

She smiled warmly and brushed my compliment aside. "I see you still have a way with words."

She was too polite to comment on the change in my appearance. I laughed and patted my substantial hips. "I'm not the skinny kid you used to know but I have made a good living stringing words together. How about you? Did you stick with your art?"

"I dabble with it now and then but just for my own amusement. I worked for many years as a model."

"Makes sense that you'd choose the glamorous life."

The conversation stalled a moment and then started up again with both of us talking at the same time. Laughing, Ellie said, "You go first."

"Let's sit down then. I've got bad knees and can't stand up for too long." I dropped my bulky frame into a soft leather chair. "Ah," I sighed. Much better. That metal wannabe chair in the interview room just about killed me." I took a deep breath and said, "Look, Ellie, I have to say this: I'm sorry that I had to tell the cops about you."

"No, no. I'm the one who should apologize. You kept a secret— we both did—that wasn't even true. I'm amazed that you never said anything before now. You really have been a loyal friend."

I shrugged. "Don't be so quick to thank me. Truth be told, my silence was self-serving. I ensured that my own role in the cover-up was never discovered."

"Nevertheless . . ."

I held up my hand. "Stop. That's over and done with now, but there are a few questions I'd like to ask you. I gestured to the chair next to me, "Come sit a moment. "I'm sure you have a few things to ask me, too."

Ellie settled in the chair and said, "You're right. I've been wondering why Mildred Simmons willed Baker Bluff to you."

"I guess because she thought of me as the daughter she never had. I started working for Millie when I was still in high school. My parents split up shortly after the cemetery incident. As much as my mother desired to be part of the social set in town, our family was never fully accepted. We were grudgingly tolerated, mostly because of Dad's wealth. When the news broke that he was not only a card-carrying Communist but he'd supplied the Indians with the dynamite to blow up the spillway, we sunk to persona non-grata status.

"My mother freaked out and thought the one saving grace would be the money she'd get in their divorce. Turns out, none of Dad's wealth was in his name. It belonged to the U.S. Communist Party and all the assets were frozen by the Federal government before she could get her hands on any of it. Being broke and a social outcast didn't suit her well. She committed suicide when I was a senior in high school."

"I'm so sorry," Ellie said.

"Don't be. It turned out all right in the end. Millie took me under her wing and offered me a job at her resort. After I graduated from high school she covered all my expenses to attend the University of Oregon. She wanted me to come back to The Dalles afterward and run the resort, but I had my heart set on a career in journalism."

"What do you think about her confession?"

"Millie was fairly easy-going, but you didn't cross her when it came to battered women. Given her background, I think it was a foregone conclusion that she'd react the way she did when Tony admitted to attacking you."

"Why'd she kill Clarice? Do you think she was really afraid that Clarice would "whack" her first?"

"Who knows?" I shrugged. "Maybe she was just in a killing mood. The point is, she's the guilty party, not us. That's the good news. The bad news is that I unknowingly triggered a potential

331

lawsuit when I put Baker Bluff on the market."

"Maybe," Ellie said. "But we'd never have known about Mildred's confession if you hadn't."

"I wish now that I'd done it years ago. There's still something that I have to know." What happened to you after Tony was killed? I never saw you or your father again. It's like you disappeared off the face of the earth." A worried frown creased Ellie's brow. "I hope I'm not dredging up too many bad memories," I said.

"Not at all. We never went back to our home in Hillcrest because we stayed with Reba and Oscar at Celilo until Sam was well enough to travel. Then we flew to Washington D.C., where Dad was honored by the FBI for his courageous action that day. He made good on his promise and quit the Bureau soon afterwards. We didn't even wait for the house to sell before moving to Idaho. Sam took up farming again and never regretted the decision, especially with Reba by his side. Oscar was part of the deal, but he missed the river too much to stay on the farm for very long. He moved to the new village that the government built for the Wy-ams displaced by the dam. Sam and Reba were married for over thirty years. They're gone now, of course."

"What about Danny?" I asked. I know he was sentenced to fifteen years at the state pen in Salem, but I never heard anything more about him or his gang."

"It was a harsh sentence, but it could've been worse. The judge took into consideration the lives he saved along with Sam's testimony on his behalf. Ernie didn't adjust very well to life behind bars, but Danny made the most of his time. He took some classes and when he was released, he attended Oregon State on a full scholarship. He finally learned how to deal with injustice in a productive way and became a tribal lawyer. Danny has won some very significant cases against the federal government that have benefitted his people."

"That's so good to hear," I said, and meant it. "You said Ernie didn't do so well in prison. How did his friend Henry fare?"

"That's the interesting part. We all thought Henry was the one who blew up Sam's truck when he couldn't get at the helicopter. It turns out, he never even made it to the reburial site. He decided that Walter had gone off the rails and wanted no part of the plan. He ditched the dynamite Walter had given him and stayed in Celilo. He was never prosecuted."

"But who blew up the truck if Henry didn't do it?"

"Remember Sam's partner, Jess Harmon?"

"The scar-faced man?"

Ellie nodded. "He blew up the truck."

"What for? I thought he was an FBI agent like your father."

"He was an agent but he was nothing like my father. He blamed Dad for the injuries he suffered on another assignment. Harmon was sent to The Dalles to solve the murder of a foreman. What he really did was try to frame Dad for the sabotage at the dam. He didn't care how many people were killed or injured so long as he got his revenge."

"But wasn't he killed in the explosion, too?"

"He was, indeed. He even received a posthumous award for bravery."

"Your father didn't tell the authorities about what he'd actually done?"

"No, Dad said it was better that Jess Harmon was remembered as a hero than as a rogue agent."

"Wow, I'm surprised by his attitude. The man tried to ruin your father."

"Dad quit the FBI but he still felt a duty to preserve the public image of the Bureau. He said tarnishing Harmon's reputation wouldn't bring back any of those killed and would only foster public mistrust of the FBI. He was instrumental in getting the Federal Government to monetarily compensate the injured and the survivors of those killed."

The way Ellie glowed when she talked about her father was certainly different from the way she'd ranted about him when she was a fourteen-year-old girl. "I always liked and respected your father," I said. "It sounds like you do, too."

"I love and miss him very much."

"Okay," Dessa said. Now to the question I'm dying to ask. Did you and Danny ever get together?"

"Danny was my first love, but the timing was never right for us. I wrote to him while he was in prison and went with Sam and Reba whenever I could, to visit him. He was released before serving his full sentence, but I'd already started my modeling career. By the time he graduated from law school, I was engaged to someone else. We used to joke that it wouldn't have been good form for a brother and sister to date one another, anyway."

"Did he get married?"

"Yes. He married a young woman named Loretta from the Yakama nation. She was a lawyer, too, and together they made a formidable legal duo until they retired a few years ago. Loretta is a remarkable woman. She fully supported Danny's decision to protect me by confessing to Tony's murder."

Keeping a secret for decades was something I could relate to, but confessing to a murder you didn't commit? No way did I get that. I shook my head. "That's beyond support. That's amazing."

"Loretta and Danny are both amazing people."

"Sounds like you've had a good life."

"What about you, Dessa? Did you ever marry?"

"Briefly. My husband was a photojournalist and was killed documenting the Viet Nam War."

"That was such a tragic period in our country's history. Any children?"

"No," I said. "But it's just as well. I've never really had the time or inclination to raise a kid. What about you?"

She smiled but I detected a profound sorrow behind her eyes. "Like you said, I've had a good life in many ways." She paused for a few moments as if she were deciding whether to go on. In the past, I would've jumped right in with another question, but I've learned over the years that you often learn more by keeping quiet.

"I thought that the rape was the worst thing that had ever happened to me," Ellie continued. "But it was nothing compared to losing a baby. Tony's baby. She was stillborn."

"Oh, my God. I'm so sorry, Ellie."

"It was a long time ago and I had plenty of therapy and a loving family to help me through it. I couldn't have any more children, but Danny and Loretta gave me the honor of being their twin daughters' godmother."

It was a downer note to end our reunion and so I asked her about her marriage and life as a model. She'd been widowed for several years but had no money worries due to her husband's success as a hedge fund manager on Wall Street. We were surprised to learn that we'd both been living in New York. "Two small town girls take on the big city and survive," Ellie said.

"No," I said. "Two small town girls take on the big city and thrive." We both laughed but it was true. We'd survived and thrived.

Our talk turned to the changes in The Dalles since we'd both been gone. "Regrettably," Ellie said, "not all the changes have been for the good."

"You must be referring to the dam."

She nodded. "I'm just glad I wasn't here to witness Celilo Falls destroyed."

I remembered it well. "Hundreds of people turned out to witness the dam's huge steel and concrete gates close and the rising waters choke back the downstream surge of the river."

"Danny was there," Ellie said. "It took place shortly before he was arrested. He said the Wy-ams and other Indians stood on the bluffs overlooking the river to watch their way of life disappear forever. They stayed on the bluffs for three days and nights with no sleep, singing sacred funeral songs to mourn their loss. It only took six hours for everything—the rapids, the fishing platforms, the burial islands, and Celilo Village—to drown and wash away. Vanished as if they'd never existed.

"The mighty Columbia River had become just another placid, smooth-flowing body of water. Danny said the most shocking part was the silence. The river gods' thunderous roar—as much a part of his life as breathing—had finally surrendered to man's resolute power. Celilo Falls was but a whisper on the wind."

We parted outside the police station without any pretense that we'd meet again or keep in touch. It is what it is, I thought, as Ellie walked away. She retrieved a ringing cell phone from her purse. "I'm free to go," she said into the receiver. "No, Loretta, it's all good. I'm coming to see you and Danny now. I'll explain everything."

THE END

AFTERWORD

Vice President Richard M. Nixon was the keynote speaker at the dedication of The Dalles Dam in 1959. Today, the Columbia River Basin is the most hydroelectrically developed river system in the world. More than 400 dams and hundreds of other structures on tributaries block river flows and tap a large portion of the estimated Columbia's generating capacity—more than twenty-one million kilowatts. Hardly any major stream of the 260,000 square-mile Columbia River watershed has been left untouched. The 1,214-mile "raging river" has practically become a back-to-back series of reservoirs from the Canadian border to Bonneville Dam near Portland, Oregon. Less than two hundred miles of the United States portion of the Columbia remain free-flowing.

The combined consequences of dams, increased ocean fishing, deterioration of stream and river habitats, and changing river conditions have made the Columbia less and less habitable for native fish. Ever since the early 1970s, the fish catch has dramatically declined, with hatchery-raised species making up more than eighty percent of commercially caught salmon in the river. The situation has become critical for some salmon and steelhead runs and too late for others. Some stocks have disappeared altogether.

The drastic decline in fish runs has brought a great deal of money and attention to the problem through the years. Numerous groups, including Native Americans, commercial interests, and sports enthusiasts, are working to achieve what they consider their fair share of the dwindling resource. Compounding the controversy are advocates who suggest that the salmon runs would benefit the most by removing or breaching and decommissioning the dams.

Source: Bill Lang, Professor of History, Portland State University and former Director, Center for Columbia River History.

OTHER NOVELS BY VALERIE WILCOX:

SINS OF SILENCE

SINS OF BETRAYAL

SINS OF DECEPTION

CONCIERGE CONFESSIONS

View other Black Rose Writing titles at www.blackrosewriting.com/books and use promo code **PRINT** to receive a **20% discount** when purchasing.

BLACK ROSE writing™

CPSIA information can be obtained
at www.ICGtesting.com
Printed in the USA
FSOW02n1725140617
35183FS

9 781612 968803